Barefoot

Arlene Fisher Hann

ISBN: 0692830138
ISBN 13: 9780692830130
Library of Congress Control Number: 2017900185
arlenehann, Glen Ellen, CA

Acknowledgement

Thank you for the help and encouragement Louise Manos and my grand-daughter, Michelle Hann.

CHAPTER 1

On The Road

*B*ang! A loud noise jolted me wide awake. I bounced from my wedged in position in the camper to lying flat of my face, on the camper floorboard.

But wait, to tell this story right I must go back to four A.M. this morning. we were all rushing around packing up and loading all our belongings into the trailer and camper that Daddy has built on top of our 1932 Model A truck. Daddy's really smart that way, he knows how to build things. He was a carpenter before he started working for the government in the reclamation department, delivering water to the farmers that needed water for their crops.

"Zemma honey," Mama called out to me, " can you keep an eye on Jenny while Daddy and I load this big box into the trailer." She rushed past me, carrying a small bundle of something in her hands. On out the front door, she went to join Daddy where he was waiting outside, with a flashlight.

Since I'm twelve, and the oldest girl of four kids, it was always my job to watch Jenny, my two year old sister, who believe me, is the devil incarnate. At the moment her devilish, eager bright blue eyes were looking back over her shoulder at me. She giggles, turns and makes a beeline for the wide open spaces beyond the door. She's on the move, on her way in the dark, outside and on down the dusty road. When I realized what her intentions were, I made a run and barely caught her, just in the nick of time, before she went through the door on her way outside to certainly collide with the busy traffic. As I ran I tripped on a crate filled with packed stuff and almost broke my neck. I caught myself just as I grabbed her by the shirt tail and hung on for dear life. I was so out of breath when I do catch her I can hardly breath.

"You snot nosed little brat, you, nincompoop you-you," I screamed at her.

1

Jenny giggles and wiggles and tries, to escape my grasp and almost got away. I hadn't realized she was so strong.

"She's a handful, huh?" Junior, my cute dimpled, freckle faced little brother was standing there. He was watching me with sympathetic blue eyes. He nodded his white, towhead and gave me a sweet smile that was missing two front teeth.

He was only six, but he was like a wise old soul. What a little sweetheart.

"You were never like this," I assured him, as I looked back at him. That was when I noticed one overall strap was hanging loose. I hung onto Jenny with one hand, she was still wriggling, trying to get loose, and with the other hand I reached over and hooked his overall strap back up.

"What's all the racket about," Sally yelped in a high pitched voice that sounded like sandpaper rubbing against a glass window. She sashayed by me hanging onto her doll by the neck in one hand and a bundle of something in the other hand, which was apparently precious because she had it clutched tightly to her chest. I had to admit I was curious. I leaned in for a closer look. I was surprised. It was a diary. I had no idea.

"I didn't know you were keeping a diary," I gasped, looking at her.

"Aw shut up," she snorted as she glared at me.

About Sally, she's fifteen months younger than I am. I had heard people say, they could tell we were sisters because we both had round faces, freckles, green eyes and dishwater blond hair with bangs. That's where the similarity ends. She was six inches shorter than I was, and fifteen pounds heavier. But our noses were different. She has a pug nose and I have a thin nose with a hump in the middle of it.. Whenever we would get mad at each other, we would always insult each others noses. I'd tell her that her nose looked like a pig snout, and she'd say my nose looked like a witch or an ugly old sea hag. I would worry a lot about the bump on my nose. I didn't want to grow up and look like a witch or a sea hag. How awful. That's not much fun looking forward to.

" The racket, oh yes that's about this one here," I nodded toward Jenny, who I still have a good solid grip on the back of her diaper, "I have to watch her," I said coming back to the present.

"Yeah, she's hard to keep track of," Sally nodded her head, looking at Jenny.

"I could use some help with her," I said hoping Sally would have a weak moment and agree to help me with her. But knowing Sally, that wasn't going to happen, not till hell freezes over, that was.

"Can't right now, I have to make sure my doll gets a safe place in the trailer," and out the door she went. We had a trailer that we could pull behind the truck. We had it pilled high with all our belongings.

"Darn it Jenny! Did you wet your diaper? That's disgusting," I snorted as I looked around for the diapers. I spotted a stack of them in the corner of the almost empty room.

"Junior, could you bring me a diaper for jenny, and a can of baby talcum powder. please?"

"Sure Zemma, coming right up." He looked at me with a grin, "I would have bet she would do that."

"Really how did you know that?" I asked, as he handed me the diaper and powder.

"I don't know, I just did,"

"You must be psychic," I said, grinning as I teased him.

"Can I help you with anything else?" he asked as he watched me stretch Jenny out on the floor. She was kicking, squealing and twisting her body around, making it hard to get the diaper on.

"Stop it, quit it you little rug rat, Do you want to live in these wet pants?" I yelled at her.

Junior leaned over and whispered, "She's just gonna make you wear the wet ones if you're not careful, so you just better be good."

Her blue eyes opened wide and she looked at Junior, startled, and quit kicking immediately.

I was shocked. I looked at Junior as I continued to pull the wet diaper off and wrap the new one around her.

"You did that, how on earth did you do that? That's amazing. She understood what you said and obeyed you. How did you work your magic on her." I picked her up, stood her up on her feet, and looked her over. Her pink top with kittens on was still dry, thank goodness. I looked around, spotted the playpen, walked over and put her in it.

"I'll put this in the garbage," Junior picked up the wet diaper, trotted over and gingerly dropped it in the open garbage can.

I was still astounded and I kept looking at him, "You certainly have hidden talents."

I heard Nonie and Coco barking. They are our two little dogs. Little Nonie's four pounds and Coco's ten pounds but they are frisky, and I am afraid they will work the locks loose on their cages and get out

"Sally," I called out to her, "Make sure Nonie and Coco are locked up tight in their cages. Check the locks."

"Okay," I heard her yell back.

"I think we're ready to leave," I heard Daddy yell. "So let's take one last look through the house to make sure we're not leaving anything behind."

"Listen kids, Daddy's got the flashlight, so all of you follow him through the house and look around. Since it's still dark, it'll be easy to miss something, so keep your eyes open," Mama cautioned us.

"Say good by to our little old, white, stucco house in Fabens, Texas," I yell and follow Daddy, feeling a little sad, thinking about leaving a place I'd known for so long, to go someplace strange and new to me..

"And here we come good, old Sebastopol Mississippi," Daddy laughed and raised his voice so everyone could hear him.

"Yep, here we come," Junior said mimicking Daddy.

We're finally on our way. This is it, the big trip. The one we'd been planning for over a month. This trip had not been one from choice, but one we'd been forced to make because of the depression.

Mama and Daddy both got in the cab of the truck. Mama tucked Jenny in between her and Daddy and we all crawled into the camper and settled in our prearranged spots. I'm scrunched between Sally and Junior. Not too comfortable. We let Nonie and Coco out of their cages to sit in our laps.

"I've got this all figured out," Daddy announced, "It will take us about one thousand and fifty miles. That means we'll be on the road several days driving eight hours a day". Daddy looked back at us, with a confident grin.

After Mama got settled she brought out the newspaper she had tucked under her arm. She opened it up to the front page and started to read the headlines.

"My goodness just listen to this," she raised her voice, and shook her head, "This is all bad news about the depression. People are dying from starvation, actually dropping dead, while they're standing in a soup line waiting to be fed." She stopped for a minute, took a deep breath, then went on to explain to us kids, what they mean by soup lines and soup kitchens. "They call them soup kitchens because different agencies, including government agencies are being set up by President Roosevelt to serve and feed the poor and hungry people, who are actually starving to death because they have no money or jobs."

"My goodness, just listen to this, It says here, a New York man jumped fifteen stories from his office building, because he lost all his money in the stock market," Mama read on, and gasped, "Isn't that terrible?"

"Its certainly scary," Daddy said, then he paused and chuckled, "We don't have to worry about losing our money because we have none to lose, and no jobs to lose either."

We all began to speculate about the depression, as we start our trip from Fabens Texas, which is about a mile from El Paso, Texas, to Sebastopol, Mississippi, which is about fifty miles from Jackson, Mississippi and it's the capital of the state.

When I say we, I mean the six of us, Mama, Daddy, Sally, Junior, Jenny, and me, then there's Coco and Nonie. I must say six is quite a bunch to be all together in one truck.

We all have on our Sunday best clothes. Mama looked pretty in her yellow flowered print dress, that she made herself. She looked great in yellow because of her olive complexion, dark brown hair and blue eyes. This is the only other dress she had, besides the one she had on, and she made both of them herself. People were always surprised when they found out that she was the mother of four kids. She was about five foot eight inches tall, and she would tell you she's a little on the plump side, but Daddy would say no, she's just right, he said he liked a girl with a little meat on her bones. Mama was always on the go, quick moving, especially when she was after one of us kids.

I began to notice that when people complimented Mama, Daddy would always beam from ear to ear.

Daddy was also dressed in his Sunday best, which was brown khaki pants and a blue striped shirt. Mama always described Daddy as a looker. He was tall, a little over six foot, and slender. His hair was black as coal and his eyes were green as grass. Of course, I realized that Mama was prejudiced, but in this case I agreed with her. He had a widows peak in his hairline, and Mama said that a widow's peak was very attractive. I think he looked like the movie star Robert Taylor.

Sally and I had on our new print dresses, Sally's dress had blue flowers in the print design, and mine had red flowers in it. Mama made our dresses special, just for this trip. Junior wore his brand new overalls from Sears Roebuck catalogue and Jenny wore the pretty new pink dress that Mama had just finished making two days ago.

We left early enough to miss most of the desert heat, but by six o'clock in the morning it was already a little warm.

I wriggled around trying to get more comfortable in my awkward position in the camper. I was scrunched between Sally and Junior. Drat! And speaking of Sally, she was something else. She was loud and noisy. She would do almost anything to get attention. She liked to make fun of people. And when she succeeded, in getting the attention she wanted, it always embarrassed the heck out of me, especially when we were out in public. I would even pretend I didn't know her.

I felt my eyes slowly close, and I began to drift off to sleep listening to the comforting sound of Mama's and Daddy's voices as they talked about when and where we would stop to sleep on our first night on the road. It was exciting, just thinking about all the new people we would meet. The back window between the truck's cab and the camper was open, so it felt like I was sitting right up there with them. I could bat I could still hear them above the noisy motor of our 1932 Ford Model A truck, mixed in with the hum of the tires rolling and bumping along the rough worn highway. They have Jenny up front with them. When she was not sleeping, she was crying, hungry or wet. Sally, Junior and I were all entrenched in our sleeping positions, with Nonie and Coco asleep in out laps.

When bang! We that's it. Now, we're up to date with our story.

Sally's screaming her lungs out, Junior's face had turned white and now he was gasping for breath. Jenny was crying, her tears were flowing nonstop down her pink cheeks. Oh my gosh! I thought this is it. Finally, the end of the world. It's all over with, just like the preachers on the radio had been predicting. With both hands I hang on for dear life, as I'm being slung from one side to the other, then I land against the backside of the cab. The truck screeches to a bumpy stop, and my head bounces hard against the backboard. Ow! Oh, my! Does that hurt. Dust is flying up from the camper floorboard and into my nose and lungs. I start snorting and can't stop sneezing dust up my nose. I put up my hand and search blindly for something to grab and hang onto. I finally pulled myself up to a sitting position on the camper floorboard.

At first I can't figure out what's happening. It must be the bump on my head that's causing my thinking to be so muddled. Mama and Daddy are dead silent. I finally figured out what it was. We'd blown a tire. Thank goodness, I hope that's all that it was.

I grabbed Junior and started shaking him, I had to make sure he was still breathing. He coughed and started breathing almost normally. I looked over my shoulder and yelled at Sally because she was still just yelling her head off.

"Aw Shut up Sally, you're alright."

"Hey Spindle Shanks, is everyone o.k. back there?" Daddy asks, his voice sounded anxious..

"Yeah we're all o.k.," I yelled back kind of half way laughing. Spindle Shanks is the nickname my Daddy gave me because I'm so skinny, bless his pointed little head.

We all had nicknames, Sally's nick name was croupie because when the sun went down, her voice would get low and scratchy and she'd sound like she had the croup. Junior was called Junior because he was named after Daddy, Claude Middleton Carter, therefore Junior. So far Ginger hadn't earned a nickname. I can personally think of a few, but they wouldn't let me call her any of those. But soon, I'm sure she'll get a name that will stick.

Although it's new to us, our truck is only a year old. And since we are going on such a long trip, Daddy bought new tires all around. So we should not have had a flat tire.

"They cheated us, they sold us bad tires," I yelled again, reminding them that we had bought new tires. I was hoping to be heard above all the racket the other kids were making, the dogs barking and Jenny screaming.

"No, no, settle down Spindleshanks," Daddy said, shaking his head, and looked down at the flat tire. "It's probably a nail, these things happen."

Already I am beginning to hate this trip. Thank goodness, it's still spring and not summer, or the heat would have been unbearable.

"Heaven help us when the sun comes up," I said, looking up at the sky, it had just now begun to get light pink over the tops of the blue mountain ridge.

"Lordy, lordy, it's hot as Hades," Sally yelped, as she climbed out of the camper.

Junior was the only one that was quiet. Since he was the only boy in the family, he was doing his best to be the tough little man.

"Alright kids, everything's okay. We just had a flat tire, and Daddy's going to fix it," Mama said, the voice of the eternal optimist. "This will be a learning experience. That way, you'll all learn how to fix a flat tire, which everyone should know how to do anyway," Mama said in a calm voice. She always said everything was a learning experience. "Just pay attention and life will teach you all you need to know,"

"I don't need to know this, " I mumble as I looked around.

"What's that you said," Mama asked, turning around and looking at me.

"Nothing," I mumble, and I sniff the air. The sand smelled burnt and hot. There's nothing around us except tumbleweeds, sand, dust and cacti. I'm really surprised, because I didn't know cacti grew this big, they were huge. Some of them were taller than Daddy. I wiped the sweat out of my eyes. We are stuck smack dab in the middle of the desert.

I watched a puff of wind pick up a swirling thread of sand, twist it together into a whirling balloon, then it flew straight up into the sky, upward, and outward and onward across the desert disappearing into the distance.

Poor Daddy starts muttering, talking to himself. He shook his head, walked completely around the truck and looked at it, as if it's his mortal enemy. He slowly takes off his hat, brushes back a lock of black hair that had fallen into his eyes, he shook his head again and puts his hat back on, sideways and crossed his eyes.. That's Daddy the comedian.

We all laughed, including Mama. That was our Daddy, I thought, as he brought a smile to my glum face. He always made us laugh, even when things looked really bad.

"Daddy, you're something else." Mama said laughing and wiping the tears out of her eyes.

"There's just no way around it," Mama looked at him and giggles, she shook her head and continued to look at him, "You're just going to have to change it," she whispers, as she switches Jenny to the other arm, then she went over and sat down on the running board of the truck, looked up at Daddy again and smiled, and continued to watch him.

Daddy looked down at her and asked "Did anyone ever teach you how to change a tire?"

She smiled up at him," Nope," she shook her head. "Now, I'm too old to learn."

"That's too bad," he said, pretending to be sadly disappointed.

He looked up into the sky, as if he's seeking help from the heavens above. He reached up and switched his hat back to the other side of his head. We all started to giggle again. We glanced at Mama and she's still smiling up at Daddy.

We hear the rumble of a vehicle approaching.

"What? God, My prayers answered already?" Daddy said, looking startled, he turned around, still looking up into the sky and dropped his gaze.

Just now a smooth, shiny, white Model A car rolled up. And to our surprise, it stopped and a man got out and came around to where Daddy was standing. Daddy glanced at the man, turned, put his serious face on, and opened up the back end of the camper. He casually started throwing things out on the ground, until he came to the spare tire. He pulled it out and bounced it a couple of times on the pavement. Then he turned and looked at the stranger.

"Afternoon, ladies," the strange man said, and tipped his hat to Mama and me.

Never before had anyone ever tipped their hat at me before, so I was quite taken aback. I just stood there and remained speechless.

"Here, Sir," the stranger said and, placed his hand on the top of the tire, "you look all tuckered out. Looks like you can use some help. Let me fix that tire for you. Then maybe you can help Mother here with the kids. Please let me help you, sir," he continued, his blue eyes watching Daddy. "I can see you got your hands full," he insists, glancing around with his hat in his hand and a big grin on his handsome face. He wasn't very tall. He was blond with kind of a sweet baby face and I thought he was extremely good looking, like a movie star, even more handsome than Robert Taylor. In fact he was so nice I would have liked to take him with us. I smiled thinking about what Aunt Mable, Mama's younger sister, would say.

"I sure would love to tuck him in my pocket and take him home with me." She would say whenever she saw a good looking man and every body would laugh. I thought about saying it, but then I thought better of it. It's a good thing because I don't think I would have gotten a laugh.

The stranger moved closer to Daddy, reached out and quickly took the tire iron from his hands. Daddy had a dumbfounded look on his face, then he looked up at the sky,

I know what Daddy was muttering under his breath, "God, really God, really? " He shook his head and looked back at the stranger.

"Well, sir, never before have I ever run into such kindness," Daddy finally said.

"Your family here reminds me of my own family back in Oklahoma," the stranger said. He took off his white jacket, carefully folded it and laid it down on the empty car seat.

It is so quiet as he looked over the situation, you could hear a pin drop in the sizzling heat.

The stranger took the tools, squatted down and started changing the flat tire. He looked back up, as sweat dripped from his tanned forehead and ran into his eyes. He wiped his eyes, with his white shirt sleeve and grinned at us kids. He stopped for a moment and caught his breath.

"Where you folks headed?" he asked with a slight southern accent.

"Mississippi, Sir, Sebastopol Mississippi, that's my home and it's been quite a while since I've been back there," Daddy said, as he shifts self-consciously from one foot to the other.

The man looked surprised, "Yes I know the place," he said, and he was quiet, for a minute, then he looked at us kids and asked? "Guess what's black and white and red all over?"

We were dumfounded and I asked, "We give up, what?"

"The newspaper," he said, "and I most likely will be on the front page next week."

We all laughed and Daddy said, "I'll have to remember that one."

"Tell us how and why you know you'll soon be on the front page of the newspaper," I insisted, I had to know.

He just shook his head and smiled mysteriously. When he was finished, he quickly stood up, picked up the tools and handed them to Daddy. He looked around, his eyes searching the barren desert. "Heck of a place to have a flat tire isn't it?" he asked, as he reached into his pocket and pulled out a white handkerchief. He closed his eyes and wiped the sweat from his face, and then he wiped the dirt off his hands and put his handkerchief back in his pocket. He casually picked up his jacket with one hand, slung it over his shoulder and held out his other hand to shake Daddy's hand. Daddy quickly shook hands with him.

"I really can't thank you enough sir," Daddy said, the laugh lines around his mouth deepened as he smiled.

The man was definitely a gentleman. He tipped his hat again to Mama and me, and walked back to his car. He waved bye, and then said a very strange thing before he got into his car.

"If I were you I would stay out of town for the next week or so. I heard there might be a bit of trouble at the bank," he smiled, displaying a dimple and a beautiful set of white teeth.

"Wait a minute Sir, I didn't get your name, I need to know who to thank for this kindness," Daddy said.

"Well Sir, right now I'm not at liberty to say who I am," he said as he bent down, and with his bare hand, wiped the dust off his black patent leather shoes. He stood back up, glanced quickly around, smiled mysteriously, leaned forward and said, "But I'm sure you will soon know who I am." He straightened back up, tipped his hat again, got into his car, and drove away in his white Model A Ford, just like the hero in a dime store cowboy novel.

The handsome cowboy hero always rode off into the red sunset on his big, white horse, both of them disappearing in a cloud of grey dust, while the beautiful girl (me of course) sadly watched the man she loved disappear leaving her to wonder if she would ever see him again.

"Zemma Pearl Carter, what's the matter with you, get in the truck, and don't forget it's your turn to sit in the middle," Sally yelled in my ear, which jolts me back into the real world and then some.

"Good grief, Sally you could make me go deaf, and you're crazy. I've been sitting in the middle the whole time."

"He does look familiar," Daddy said scratching his chin as we all watched and wondered about the stranger, who disappeared in a cloud of desert dust.

"I wonder who he really is?" I wondered out loud, and the guessing started. We all took turns guessing why he wouldn't tell us his name.

"Maybe he's a famous movie star," Sally guessed.

"No, I think he could be a famous cowboy," Junior guessed. Junior loved to listen in the evenings when Mama and Daddy would read aloud the western cowboy stories that Zane Grey wrote. We all loved to listen to the stories. In the end, the handsome cowboy always beat up the mean, evil, bad guy, and he would always fall in love with and marry the beautiful, young girl.(Again me of course.)

"He must be famous alright," Mama said, "Maybe a millionaire otherwise he wouldn't have said we would soon know who he was."

"He mentioned the bank, maybe he bought the only bank in town," Mama speculated (speculated, a new word for me, one I had just learned.) "I say that because he must have lots of money to have such an expensive, flashy, new car and expensive looking clothes.

As we bumped along the hot dusty highway, we continued to talk about him and wonder why he was so mysterious.

The reason our ride was so rough was because we had all of our belongings stacked super high on top of our truck. As for the rest of our things, we had them in a little trailer which followed along behind us. I kept looking back because I was worried about my doll Betty, not that I play with dolls any more, but she's still my most prized keepsake. She'd seen me through some tough times. She'd been mine since I was five. She was in the trailer, and I was afraid the trailer would come loose and run away with her.

"The thing I worry the most about are the tornados they have in Mississippi," I complained.

"Not to worry," Daddy said, "We have storm cellars just for that very reason. We always got notice ahead of time, when there's going to be a tornado. When we got a notice, we were supposed to hightail it out to the cellars. In other words head for the cellar. There we'd be completely protected when we're in one of those things, I'm told. The cellars also serve another purpose. We could store food and canned goods in them for the winter."

"Do we have one of those in our house?" Junior asked.

"You bet we do. I'd dig one myself with my bare hands if we didn't have one." Daddy laughed.

"And I'd be right there with you," Junior said.

"Me too," Sally said, giggling.

"You can count me in on that, too." Mama said, with a laugh, her blue eyes twinkling.

"I remember one time, one of Daddy's sister wrote and said that a tornado had torn through, only three miles away from the house we'll be living in," I said.

"Not to worry, remember we have a storm cellar," Daddy assured us.

"Claude, are you sure it's safe?"

"Of course, Leota, you know I would never put my family in danger."

That was good enough for me, I thought.

Driving though the desert wasn't any fun, but the sunsets were like little, jeweled pieces of heaven. I had never seen sunsets, anything like these before. The beautiful reds, oranges and purples along the horizon. The mountains would turn purple with hints of pink and blue. That was when I wished I'd been an artist so I could paint a picture and take it with me wherever I went. I must say I could just sit in the desert and look at the sky and mountains change color all day long, if I weren't afraid I would die of a heat stroke.

The gas stations where we stopped were really bad because they actually charged for drinking water, just like they charged for gas.

Nighttime was a different story. It became freezing cold, so we'd do a lot of our driving at night. Every day was almost the same. We'd spend some of the days in small unpleasant motels. The motels would usually have giant spiders and ugly, scaly lizards living inside the rooms. I made sure my bed was free of all vermin and nasty insects, all except the Daddy long legs, which I don't really mind. But I still don't want them in bed with me. So what I do is catch them and put them outside for the night.

Sally caught me saving the Daddy long leg spiders and screamed, "You're crazy, Mama look at her, she's crazy."

Mama just smiled and winked at me, "Not crazy but maybe a little strange," she said as she continued making the bed.

I grinned back. I felt a hundred percent better. Just one of the reasons I loved my Mama.

I'd pretend we are brave explorers who were successfully making a dangerous trek through a foreign jungle that was filled with giant blue green cacti. When we'd finally reached the lush wooded areas of Louisiana and Mississippi, I was really happy. I had been afraid everything was going to be like the desert.

It got late and Mama and Daddy decided to stop for the night at the first motel we came across in Louisiana. The motel wasn't very pretty. Most of the white paint had peeled off and two of the outside windows are broken.

The man that greeted us was short, thin, old and grizzly looking. His face was wrinkled, with a white, stubbly beard and mustache. His eyes were grey colored and squinty. He looked angry because the frown marks between his eyes were deep and permanent. Two of his front teeth were missing, and the left side of his mouth drooped, and a little stream of spittle dripped down one side of his mouth when he talked. He talked slow and with some kind of accent. I don't know what, but some sort of broken English. His worn blue shirt was dirty and had holes at the elbows and his overalls were also dirty, and had holes at the knees. When we got into the room we were renting, it smells moldy and old, with a hint urine smell.

Mom checked the bed sheets, she pinched her nose and shook her head. "This will never do," and she started pulling the sheets off the bed. "Zemma, please grab the other end of the sheets, and we'll put new ones on."

What I liked about Mama, she always said please and thank you, when she asked you to do something. I had heard other kids mother's and they never said please or thank you. They just yelled at them to do something.

"I don't think these have been washed lately." We'll take a couple of the sheets we have in the truck and spread them out, over the two beds.

It's so cold I don't waste any time, I crawled under the covers and pulled them up around my ears. I drifted off to sleep listening to the coyotes howl outside. They sounded like they were right outside our window.

Early in the morning, we were back on the road. We stopped and made sandwiches for breakfast and dinner. Every so often we would have to stop while Mama changed Jenny's diaper. We also stopped at a grocery store and bought food and water. The food was different because Mama usually cooked our food. She always made biscuits and then we would make sandwiches out of the biscuits. Before, we never bought sliced bread, which we called light bread to make sandwiches. The lady in the grocery store told us how to make peanut butter and banana sandwiches. So we bought peanut butter and bananas and made peanut butter and banana sandwiches out of the sliced light bread. The sandwiches were delicious. The lady talked funny but she was so very nice. We asked Mama if we could have a candy cane, but Mama said no we just couldn't afford it.

The lady smiled, reached into the candy jar and brought out five candy canes, and handed each one of us a candy cane, even one for Mama and Daddy.

I was so shocked I could hardly mumble my thanks.

Mama and Daddy were really surprised, their faces turned bright red.

"Oh no, you shouldn't," Mama stammered, handing the candy back to her. "I can't take this."

"Please take them. You'll hurt my feeling if you don't. Now you go on, move on out of here, like a herd of turtles," the lady insists, laughing.

Daddy stretched out his hand and shook the lady's hand, "You are very gracious, and I hope someday to return the favor. Thank you so much."

We all turn and leave clutching our candy canes as if it was pure gold.

That was all we could talk about for the next few miles, as we lick our candy canes.

It started to drizzle rain, but it wasn't cold, it was nice. The sky became dark and grey and we had to put on our lights. The weather was really different than it had been in Texas. I'm sure it was still hot in Texas.

Back in the truck and on our way, we start to sing, when Mama started singing "Let's have another cup of coffee," Daddy joined in. Then we all sang," Let's put out the lights and go to bed." Then we sang one of my favorites, "I've got the world on a string."

I noticed the banks along the sides of the road were red, like red clay. I also noticed a heavy growth of mostly pine and oak trees, lining the roadside. Thick green bushes with yellow and purple wild flowers grew along the banks, the growth was mixed in with the underbrush between the trees. We continued to sing as we looked at the houses that began to appear between the trees. The houses were really different. More different than any of the houses I had ever seen before. We looked over all the houses, we passed. Some were beautiful three storied mansions, like castles.

"I have never ever seen houses like these before," I gasped, stretching my neck around the corner of the camper window, trying to get a better view.

"Wow, I want to live there, in that one, the one that looks like a three story castle, fit for a king and queen," Sally squeals.

I can't imagine living in one of those houses," I said, shaking my head in disbelief. But they weren't all like that one. We start to go through a few miles of neighborhoods that have nothing but falling down shacks. Some of them looked like they were ready to hit the ground any minute now. This must be where the poor people live. That would be us. I began to worry,

"Daddy what kind of house will we live in? Will they be like the ones we are going through now?" I asked fearfully.

"Oh no honey, it will be much nicer, not as nice as the two and three story mansions, but better than these, thank goodness," Daddy nods his head toward the shacks we just passed.

"Yeah this house looks like its ready to fall down, and heaven forbid, crush the two poor little old, white headed people sitting in the rocking chairs," I nod toward the shack I'm peering toward, through the camper window.

" Zemma, there she goes again, you and your imagination running away with you again, " Sally squawks, shaking her head.

I just ignore her, pretending I didn't even hear her.

It seems like this is their entertainment; to watch the people in the cars, and in our case a truck passing by their houses. Some of the houses had black people in them. Others had white people, some had people that are really old people with snow, white hair sitting in wheel chairs. Some just have regular people sitting and talking.

I was beginning to worry, afraid of what our house was going to be like. We should be getting there pretty soon.

It stopped raining and the sun came out.

CHAPTER 2

Our Arrival

*F*inally we reached our destination. And all my apprehension was swept away.

It was about six o'clock and I was pleasantly surprised. The house wasn't a white two story mansion, but it was nice. It was gigantic, a one story wooden structure, with many rooms that were dissected by a huge hallway that ran right down the middle of the house dividing it into two sections, that was connected with a long front porch. It was constructed of wood and shingles, not like our small adobe house in Texas. So this was my Daddy's old homestead, the one, that held so many stories and secrets of the past, the one he'd talked about so much. Daddy had always loved being close to nature and was happiest when he was a farmer, like his Daddy. I had overheard Mama and Daddy talking about whether he should give up his secure job with the government to become a dirt farmer. He had a job as a water master for the big farmers. He divided and delivered the right amount of water to each farmer. Daddy was always fair with the farmers, and the farmers knew it. He always gave each farmer the right amount of water to each farmer. He couldn't be bribed to give one farmer more water than they deserved. Of course, as he said, the farmers all thought they needed more water than what they got, which made Daddy's job very stressful.

Mama was really uncertain about pulling up roots and moving to Mississippi, but, she knew this was Daddy's dream, and she wanted him to be happy, so she agreed to go.

So here we were, in our new home, this huge, old, house. I looked up and I could see it had a large, spacious attic with windows in it. The house had lots of windows with small panes of glass. It also had two fireplaces.

And, as I looked around I could see a large stack of firewood stacked against a brick fence in the backyard. By that I knew the fireplace wasn't just ornamental, but it was used to keep the place warm. Outside, were a number of wooden lawn chairs, two swings, one on the front porch and one in the yard. There were two long wooden tables with wooden benches, stretched out underneath one of the three large oak trees in the front yard. On the other side of the house was a huge mulberry tree and under the mulberry tree were also two long wooden tables and two wooden benches for each table. There were tons of flowers and green and yellow bushes everywhere. And on the other side of the house under another oak tree, there stood a large, round oak gazebo. I knew it was a gazebo because I had seen pictures of them in catalogues. And inside the Gazebo, it had a table, chairs and planters filled with flowers.

As soon as we got there, we crawled out of the truck, all bent over, so stiff we could hardly move. Junior and I had Coco and Nonie in tow. It seemed like hundreds of people came out of the wood work to greet us. It was really exciting. They were all kinds of people, young, middle aged and old. There were blonds, brunettes, red heads and a lot of white and grey haired men and women. They were all different, tall, short, thin and fat people. Anyway it was more people than I had ever seen before in one place. Some of them were relatives I had heard about; in fact I found out later, that most of the people in Scott County were related to us in one way or another.

It looked to me like they all bought clothes at the same place, most of the men were wearing the same kind of overalls, some were wearing coveralls and long sleeved knit shirts with the sleeves rolled up. A few were wearing blue striped work shirts. A lot of the men had mustaches and beards, but most of them were clean shaven, which I thought made them look much nicer. That way, you could also get a good look at what they really looked like.

The women were all wearing homemade print dresses, with longer than usual hemlines. There was something about their dresses that looked homemade. I guess I knew that, because our dresses were usually homemade.

Everyone brought food and drinks to celebrate our arrival. This really made me feel special. They had a long table set up in the kitchen with all kinds of delicious looking goodies on it.

Several of Daddy's brothers and sisters came up and gave Daddy hugs and kisses.

One of them exclaimed, "Well I'll be diddle-lee- dee-dee, little boy, the last time I saw you, you were just knee high to a grasshopper."

"Say you're still a kid at heart, I see, you brought your dogs with you, now, isn't that something," Aunt Mable was laughing as she walks up.

"Yep their part of the family," Daddy assured them with a grin.

"Well, that's nice," Aunt Mable said,

Aunt Ginger and Aunt Hilda were standing there, and they both nodded their heads at the same time.

"Oh, I also think of my little Danny as part of the family," Aunt Ginger said

"Exactly the way I feel about my dog Jamie," Aunt Hilda agreed.

"And by the way Mable," Daddy interrupted her, "that's not true, it hasn't been that long, since you saw me. I'd say it's been about eight years, when Mama passed away. I came back home when you wrote me Mama was sick," Daddy reminded her.

"All right, you got me on a technicality," she laughed.

Aunt Ginger, grinned, and gave him a little nudge in the ribs. "You got her there little Buddy." It's one of his oldest sisters. Her hair looked like a big, white snow cone, all rolled up in a bun, and piled high on top of her head. The skin on her face was a mass of tiny, little wrinkles. Her thin, bony arms and hands were covered with deep wrinkles crisscrossing, across her fragile skin. Her small, skinny body looked frail and she was as flat and thin as a board. She looked like she was least a hundred years old. Well I could be exaggerating a bit. But her eyes denied it all, they were eager, bright, twinkly and young looking. I heard someone call her Aunt Ginger.

For some reason, I couldn't say why, but she was as cute as a button.

Most of the people around us looked like they were around a hundred. Some of them were about my Daddy's age, but since Daddy's the baby of the family, almost everyone else, except the kids were a little older than he was. Daddy had told us he was from a big family, and he wasn't exaggerating, twelve to be exact, and by golly, he was right.

I heard several people say, "Claude is the spitting image of his Daddy."

I really enjoyed listening to them. I had to stop and listen close to some of the things the relatives were saying, for instance, "He's about as smart as a post," talking about how dumb one of our uncles was, "Bless your pea picking heart," when they were thanking somebody "This aint my first rodeo you know," talking about how they knew how to do something. "You keep that up and I'll skin you alive," that's when they caught one of the kids in the food or doing something they shouldn't be doing." "They just live a hoot and a holler down the road," talking about how far away someone lived.

Junior came up with another little boy, who looked about the same age as Junior.

"Zemma, this is Harry, and we're going to play marbles," he told me, then he turned, reached back and took the bag of marbles from the other little boy's hand and held them up for me to see.

"That's nice," I said. "You found a friend already. But I thought you both had to have marbles to be able to play a game."

"Yes you do, but since I don't have any, Harry, here, gave me ten marbles to start with, wasn't that nice?"

"It certainly was," I turned and looked the little boy over good.

He was a cute little towheaded boy that looked enough like Junior to be his brother. Only, he had more freckles, his hair was straighter and longer and he was taller.

"That's very generous of you," I smiled, reached my hand over and patted Harry on the top of his head.

He jumped back and looked up at me startled.

"I'm so sorry, I am just trying to tell you how nice you were to give Junior the marbles," I apologized.

"Thank you," he mumbled, looked up at me, his little round face turned red, and then he looked down at his feet.

I instantly liked the little boy. I watched them walk away hand in hand.

When I looked around I felt like an alien, where a foreign language was being spoken. There were all kinds of relatives, aunts, uncles and cousins and they all talked funny. I enjoyed the fact they all had a talent for telling stories, which I thought was just wonderful. I loved the stories, when I could understand them.

I heard one of the male relatives say, "When are we gonna eat, I could eat a horse and a half, and a chocolate mule with a peppermint tail."

I started laughing, and Sally, who was standing next to me spoke up, "Whatcha laughing about?"

"Didja hear what that man said?" I asked nudging her, and looking toward him.

"Yeah," she grinned, "that's funny," then she slapped a mosquito. "Got him. These darn mosquitoes are driving me crazy, These things are much bigger than the ones we had in Texas. Watch out, here comes a drove of them," she added and she jerked her head, dodging the mosquitoes.

Junior came up about then, "You're right, I think they're going to eat me alive," he shook his hands, then started scratching his arms, "Good grief! Ouch."

One of the Uncles came up to me, put his forefinger under my chin and tips my head up," Now don't you look prettier than a glob of butter on a stack of wheat cakes."

I started laughing and couldn't stop, "I really hope not, "I giggled.

Sally and Junior joined me, they couldn't stop laughing either.

He started laughing, "Would you jess listen to this young'un now."

I got a complete education in an hour, just by listening to all the relatives joking and laughing.

A man arrived; who I later found out is Uncle Lester, and he's Aunt Mable's husband. He had a newspaper in his hand, and he was waving it all around.

He was all excited about something that had just happened the morning before we got there. The only bank in town had been robbed. No one was hurt, but all the money was taken. About ten thousand dollars, according to the special edition of the newspaper. They really had a good story going.

"The infamous, notorious bank robber Baby faced Nelson has just robbed the only bank in our little town. He had two other bank robbers with him," the newspaper said.

Uncle Lester continued to wave the paper around. It was the latest edition of the Jackson Harold.

"Can you imagine Baby Face Nelson in our little town," he kept yelling.

I heard someone say, "Aw, you're making a mountain out of a molehill."

On the front page was a huge black and white picture of our benefactor, the handsome stranger, who changed our tire. I looked at the photograph and right into the eyes of Baby Face Nelson. I was so thrilled I started shivering and couldn't stop.

About that time Junior came rushing up with his new friend Harry.

"See Harry I told you about the guy that fixed our flat tire on the road, for free, and now he's on the front page of the newspaper for robbing a bank," Junior was out out of breath, he was nodding his head toward the newspaper that Uncle Lester held in his hand.

"Wow! Now isn't that something," Harry said, looking at me, shaking his head.

"That's him. Oh my gosh, I swear that's really him. But he was one of the nicest people I've ever met. That's the man who stopped and fixed our tire. I just can't believe it," I squealed, pointing to the newspaper.

"Yep that's him," Daddy nodded. His face had turned a little pale.

"Are you okay Claude?" Mama looked at Daddy as she put a comforting hand on his shoulder. "He was really a nice man," Mama said, looking defensively at the shocked audience.

There was kind of a hushed mumble among the natives as Daddy would say.

"Where can I get a copy of the paper?" Daddy asked.

Uncle Lester looked surprised,. "Hey I've got lots of copies; here you can have this one," he insisted..

I snuck up next to him and whispered, "Can I take a look at it Daddy?"

"Sure, but bring it back in good shape," he said, and looked down at me, a little smile tugging at the corners of his mouth.

"He really didn't hurt anyone now did he? Just took some money from a rich bank, haven't you ever heard of Robin Hood?" I asked, looking around at the sea of faces that seem to be in shock at what I had said. But I didn't care, I think I would even hide him out if I were given the chance, but I had better sense than to say so. After all he really didn't hurt anyone.

"Well what does she know, she's just a kid," I heard someone say..

"Yeah, well I don't see him giving any of that money to the poor, and I'm sure enough poor," my uncle said, laughing.

By the end of the day, I knew a lot of their names.

But the sad thing was, there didn't seem to be any kids around my age. I kept an eye out, but everyone seems to be either a lot older than I was, or they were all much younger, just not anyone near my age. It looked very dismal for me. Oh well, it seemed my best friend was going to be Aunt Ginger. Which wasn't too bad, because I did like her.

Sally and I were dressed in the newest dresses we had. The dresses were really cute with colorful floral prints all over them. Mama had ordered them from Sears before we started our trip. It was the first time we had ever had bought dresses.. Sally and I were standing in the kitchen doorway trying to listen to all the funny sayings.

I started laughing and couldn't stop.

"What's the matter with you?" Sally demanded.

Did you hear what Aunt Mable just said to her son when he stole a cookie?"

"No, what did she say?"

She said "I'm gonna slap you naked and hide your drawers," just saying it again made me start laughing.

"Oh my God," Sally said, and started laughing.

I heard someone say, I'magoodamy to do it," I finally figured it out. It meant, "I'm a good mind to do it."

I heard my Aunt Hilda tell my Aunt Ginger, "You're just about as much help as a rubber crutch." I caught on to the banter between Aunt Ginger and Aunt Hilda. They went back and forth, and were really funny.

My aunt Ginger answered, "Yeah, and you're crazier than a run over dog," Aunt Ginger gave Aunt Hilda a little nudge in her ribs.

At one point Aunt Hilda brought her family over to meet us. She had her husband Jack, her daughter Margaret, and two sons Richard and Jason. She also brought over her niece Constance. They were all pleasant. Her husband Jack, was short, plump, white headed and old like she was. The two boys were somewhere in their late teens, her daughter and niece were somewhere in their late teens or their early twenties. They were all slender, blond and nice looking.

Aunt Ginger and Aunt Hilda continued joking back and forth, and, they didn't seem to get seriously mad over the insults. I saw my Aunt Mable sneak a slice of lemon pie.

"Oh my goodness, this pie's so good it makes yo wanna slap yo Mama," She said winking at me, because she saw me watching her. I just grinned and winked back.

One of the boy cousins came into the kitchen and sneaked a cookie; Aunt Hilda saw him and yelled,

"Ima gonna skin you alive," and she swatted him with a dishtowel.

I had to go find a bathroom so bad I could hardly stand it. I looked around, but I couldn't see anything that looked like a bath room. So I picked out the friendliest looking aunt which happened to be Aunt Ginger. She was easy to spot; she had on a bright yellow flowered dress, with a yellow bow in the white bun on her head. Darned if she wasn't cute. I quietly sidled up to her, and asked her where the bathroom was.

"Oh my goodness child, I'll show you." She took me by the hand and started walking me through the house, and on through to the back door and outside. As I walked holding her hand, I felt the skin on the back of her hand was rough, dry, and wrinkly. I decided it must be from years and years of hard work in the fields. I don't know why, but I had a certain, friendly feeling toward Aunt Ginger. We walked toward a small brown, funny looking building. I was puzzled, why outside and why a separate building. I looked up at my aunt trying to figure out if she had all her marbles. Maybe I had asked the wrong person.

When we reached the building, Aunt Ginger opened the door to the little building.

"Good grief" I gasped and backed up. "My goodness does this stink."

"Great balls of fire, child, haven't you ever seen an outdoor toilet before?"

"No, if that's what this is, I can't say that I have. In Texas we had an indoor toilet and sinks and faucets and running water."

My aunt started laughing and had a hard time stopping "That means you haven't set up a pee pot for the night time?" Finally my aunt stopped laughing.

"No, I can't say that I have," I mumble.

"I'm sorry child; I didn't mean to laugh at you. I'm just surprised, is all."

I was embarrassed and mortified.

"Well for night time you'll have a bucket with a lid on it, you'll use that so you won't have to come out side when it's cold and dark to do your business. Then in the morning you'll bring it outside and empty it in the toilet here.

"See," she goes into the little house, raises up the round lid then she points to the hole. You sit on that, do your business and use a page or two of this Sears catalogue to wipe and put the paper in the hole and that's all there is to it. I thought of Sally. She would not be able to use that Sears catalogue for that purpose.

I stood in horror, looking at the black hole that stunk so bad with flies buzzing all around it. I really had to go, it was either that, or go in my pants. I had to fight the flies for the space to sit down. Oh my goodness, I thought how am I going to get through this? I shut my eyes, sat down and did my business, as Auntie would say, I wiped with a perfectly good page out of a perfectly good catalogue. I jumped up and got the heck out of there.

Aunt Ginger was waiting for me a few feet away from the building. She had a wide smile on her round wrinkled face.

"Shame to waste that good Sears catalogue," I grinned at her, trying to make a joke of the situation.

"I'm sorry honey, I didn't mean to laugh at you," she repeated.

When we finally got back, the excitement had died down. Everyone had resumed telling stories about Daddy when he was young. I realized he was really popular. They had all gathered around Daddy, talking, patting and hugging him.

"I'll have to introduce you to my kids, I have a girl seventeen, named Nancy and a boy twenty one, named Sam Junior," Aunt Ginger goes on. "Oh there they are," she was pointing to a small group of young people, on the other side of the living room.

"See the girl in the green dress, well that's my Nancy. And see the young man that's sitting down. He's wearing a white shirt, well that's my Sam Jr. Lets go meet them."

"That sounds good," I walked ahead, filled with curiosity.

When Aunt Ginger introduced me, Nancy wasn't impressed at all. "It's nice meeting you," she nodded her head, then she turned back around, dismissed us with a toss of her head and continued talking to her blond girlfriend. Well, well I thought to myself. I don't think she's all that, either. Which she really wasn't. She wasn't pretty and she wasn't ugly. She seemed kind of plain, with light brown hair, a round face with brown eyes, and just a little on the plump side. Aunt Ginger looked a little embarrassed and looked at her son, who was quietly watching. It was sad that Nancy didn't have her mother's personality, too bad I thought.

"Hi," I greeted Sam. I felt, just by looking at him, he was just a little nicer and friendlier than his sister. He was definitely better looking, with dark eyes and dark brown hair. He was tall and slender and had a really nice smile.

"Hi," he returned the greeting and smiled. "Really nice to meet you. Well, how do you like it here so far?"

I grinned, "Well, so far so good," really appreciating the fact he was making an effort to make conversation.

Aunt Ginger, Sam Jr. and I made more small conversation, then Aunt Ginger and I moved on.

As we walked away, I felt like I had to make a comment, "I really like your son, he's very charming," I said, but I said nothing about her daughter.

I felt sorry for Aunt Ginger, for the way her daughter was behaving.

I looked around, everyone was having a good time. Especially Daddy, he was the king for a day.

But where was Mama?

As time went on, I noticed they were sort of ignoring Mama. Poor Mama, I could see, she was not happy. It's really making me madder by the minute, the more I watched. So, when my aunt Ginger started talking to me, I saw my chance to straighten this matter out.

The two of us went out to sit in the porch swing. She started talking about all the southern customs and how they were probably different from where I came from. That's when I decided to confront her with a few questions of my own, especially the one about why were they treating my Mama so bad.

"Aunt Ginger, why are you and your people ignoring my Mother, you're making her feel so unwanted?"

Aunt Ginger's mouth dropped open, and her face suddenly looked a little tired, "Well honey it's like this, it's kind of hard to explain. Your Daddy is, or was a very popular, handsome, young bachelor, and all the single girls around here are, or were pretty upset when he went clear out of the state and married a stranger."

"I see, they think he should have married one of them," I growled angrily.

"Well to tell you the truth, we all think your Mom is pretty dark complexioned. She must be part Indian or part Mexican, which we don't cotton too, so much, around here."

I like Aunt Ginger, but she was so ignorant.

I was absolutely furious, I jumped up and glared at Aunt Ginger, "That's the most shameful thing I've ever heard in my whole life. Shame on you people,"

I stomped off to find my Mother. I found her sitting by herself holding little Jenny. Jenny looked really cute in a frilly, little white dress Mama made for her, just for this occasion. Mama also put pretty little pink ribbons in her hair, and Jenny I saw, kept pulling them out. and Mama patiently kept putting them back in.

When I walked up, Mama was sitting in the kitchen bay window, looking out of the window, at the most beautiful hanging lavender wisteria vine I had ever seen. The lavender scent was intoxicating and the scene was heavenly. It was draped all over a tall, white lattice archway. Anyway, I sat down beside Mama and started talking about the beautiful flowers. I would never tell her about the conversation I had just had with Aunt Ginger. I might tell Daddy, so he would know what rotten, narrow minded, two faced hypocritical relatives he had.

I left Mama and went back into the kitchen and found Sally and Junior sitting at the long kitchen table just munching away. I sat down in a chair next to them.

Sally looked up, her mouth full. "Isn't this food the best, and there's so much of it. It's so good," she mumbles with her mouth full.

"Uh, huh," Junior nods with his mouth full.

I got a plate and proceed to fill it heaping to the top. Some of the stuff I didn't even know what it was, but it was so good.

While we were sitting there, another lady came up and introduced herself.

"Hi kids, I'm your Aunt Jane, and you must be Zemma, Sally and Junior.

She seemed nice. She looked a lot like Aunt Ginger, only she was taller and a little plumper. She had the same round face, white hair up in a bun, and the same small facial features, except her nose is a little crocked in the middle. That must be the Carter nose Daddy's always talking about.

She talked for a little while, and then moved on.

"I guess she's nice," Sally, mumbled with her mouth full, and Junior nodded his head, his mouth still full.

All three of us were so full that Sally and I had to take off our belts. I had never been so full in all my life. We finally stopped and all we wanted to do was find a good spot, lie down and go to sleep. But it was too early to go to bed, so we had to leave in search of Mama and Daddy.

Our first night in our new home was exciting and scary, because we didn't have electricity or running water. What we did have instead, were kerosene lamps with handles on them, so they could be carried around from room to room. No one but Mama and Daddy were allowed to carry the lamps with them. It was disconcerting (a new word I had just learned) and it's scary. The giant shadows played against the green colored plank walls, leaping and jumping from floor to ceiling. It was unnerving to see the shadows we were casting. At first, it was making a wreck out of me, getting used to all this spooky activity, being followed around everywhere by threatening black giants. We had our first supper by kerosene lamp light. It was a good thing we weren't hungry because we had eaten so much before, because now, it was really hard to concentrate on what I was eating, because of the leaping, jumping shadows. The huge, flickering lamp shadows moved up and down, when ever we took a bite. Shadows of our hands and arms were moving from floor to ceiling wherever we reached for something. I wondered if I 'd ever get used to this.

I didn't think I would sleep a wink the first night. Sally, Junior and I found a bed in one of the bedrooms; we crawled up on it and went sound asleep. That's all she wrote until the next morning.

In the morning we found ourselves, with our shoes off, and in different beds, so someone must have moved us around and put us to bed.

When we got up and went into the kitchen, Mama and Daddy were both up and eating breakfast.

"Well here are the three sleepy heads," Mama greeted us with a smile.

After breakfast Daddy changed from his dress clothes, which were the tan shirt and pants that he wore in Texas, and into the farmer's overalls with buckles and straps, and a striped shirt that his brother had given him. That's what everyone seemed to be wearing. It was almost like a uniform. Apparently that is the farmers uniform. He looked totally different.

All kinds of people I didn't know, but were Daddy's friends or relatives wondered in and out all day.

I noticed Aunt Ginger and Aunt Hilda were here all day. They showed Mama where everything was, and how to do different things. Aunt Ginger kept watching me out of the corner of her eye, so apparently our little talk had done some good. She must have mentioned it to Aunt Hilda, because they were both being really nice to Mama. I felt happy and instantly forgave them. They really were good people after all.

Our next night was weird. I just rattled around from room to room. First off, we just weren't used to such a big house. I felt like I could get lost in it. That night Sally and I settled down, in the bedroom, on the far end of the hallway. Ii was a small room which was across the hall and all the way down to the end of the hall. It had two nice big windows in it, but no curtains, but that was alright, we could hang something over the windows, so people couldn't look in.

The full moon was out and everything looks spooky when I looked out the window. Oh goodie, I could see fireflies. It was thrilling to watch them. They were absolutely beautiful. There were so many of them, the sky was filled with them. I had heard about them, but I had never actually seen one. Why were they the only ones with lights? It was a mystery to me.

Since the windows had no curtains, I could clearly see the dark outline of tree tops and bushes that stood like dark shadows silhouetted behind the huge barn that leaned up against the smaller chicken coops, and the fence posts that outlined the pens that the cows, horses and pigs moved about and around in.

The juicy round orange moon and the stars were super bright, shining against the darkest deep, blue gray of the sky.

There were some strange squeals and whistles which I figured must be night birds. I would ask Daddy tomorrow to make sure.

The exotic sounds of frogs croaking, and all the crickets and katydids singing their songs were interrupted by the lonesome wail of a passing train going by in the distance. I just realized there was a train somewhere near us. The sound made me feel lonesome and all alone. I hurried up, got into bed and pulled the covers up over my head.

Sally was halfway on my side. I tried to move her over without waking her up, but that just wasn't going to happen. She growled and squealed and refused to budge. I finally had to wake her up, and oh my, that was a noisy mistake. What a ruckus she made when she did wake up. I would have been better off just sleeping on the floor.

It was Sunday and we didn't go to church. I just had that one new dress that Mama got me for our trip, and I couldn't wear that every Sunday. The rest of my clothes were worn and patched, not the right kind of clothes for church. I didn't care, because I didn't want to go anyway.

CHAPTER 3

Arrival of Uncle Oglee

*A*unt Ginger and Aunt Hilda went together and got Junior, Sally and me a pair of overalls. They were hand me downs, but they looked brand new. We had been here about three weeks and it was a Sunday afternoon.

Sally and I put on our new overalls and went outside to play hide and seek. I started running down the rough red clay road, barefooted of course, being careful not to run into any of the many blackberry bushes and their painful stickers. I looked for a good place to hide, and I decided that behind the giant Hickory Nut tree would be the best place to hide, Sally would never find me there, because at the bottom of the tree there was a bunch of new branches starting to grow. It was just high enough for me to hide in and behind..

I was on my way, when I ran right smack dab into this big tall guy with black hair and black eyes. He had a long stick over his shoulder with a bundle of something wrapped in a red handkerchief that was tied to and hanging from the end of a long stick. He was wearing a red plaid shirt and blue jeans. He looked like a handsome devil may care hobo. Sometimes the hobos would get off the train in the hopes of getting a handout of food from the farmers, in exchange for work. Yesterday, I overheard one of the ladies talking about the depression, and how it had caused an increase in hobos. No actually he looked more like a pirate. All he needed was a bright red handkerchief, wrapped around his head, with a black skull and crossbones painted on it.

"Oh my gosh!" I let out such a loud yelp; you could hear me in the next county.

"Who are you?"

"Hey where're you going young lady?" He stared at me for a full minute "Don't you know me, Zemma?"

He stood there, his black eyes dancing and twinkling. He batted his black eyes, and his dimples played peek a boo on his cheeks.

I stood there for a long minute and looked up at him, trying to figure out who he was. Who in the world was he? He looked really familiar. Then I knew. Only one person in the whole, wide world had black eyes with long black eyelashes like that.

"Uncle Oglee," I screamed, I loved Uncle Oglee. He was my most favorite person in the whole world, except for Mom and Dad, of course. He was my Mama's baby brother. He must be about twenty by now I thought, but I hadn't seen him for about three years. He'd really taken a growing spree. He always kept in touch, by writing us letters.

"You've gotten so big. You look like a man. Put a cowboy hat on you, and call you a cowboy." I stood back, my hands on my hips, looking him up and down, like I had seen grown up people do.

He laughed the laugh I loved. He reached down, scooped me up, threw me over his shoulder and carried me off like a sack of potatoes, as he walked up the incline of the brick pathway, to our house.

I was squealing and laughing and yelling for Mama as she came out on the porch. Sally was close behind us, yelling and screaming to the top of her lungs. When Mama saw us, she dropped the dishcloth she had been holding and started running down the shaky wooden steps toward us.

They were both crying when he sat me down and reached out for Mama.

"Oh my God, you dear boy, how did you ever get here?" she cried out, as she held him tight. "I just can't believe my eyes." She held on to his hand and kept looking up at him as if she was afraid he would disappear in a puff of smoke. Holding onto his hand, she kept pulling him down the brick pathway, toward the house.

"Claude, Claude look who's here, you'll never believe it."

"Oh my God," Daddy hollowed and he jumped down the steps two at a time, to meet Oglee.

"It's good to see you son. Don't tell me you hitchhiked all the way from Texas?"

When Mama had him comfortably seated in a cane bottomed chair, at the old, oak kitchen table. She was still holding onto his hand, she sat down at the table in the chair beside him. She looked at him sternly and said, "Explain your-self, don't you know it's very dangerous hitchhiking all by yourself. There are all kinds of criminals out there, ones they haven't caught yet. You know Pretty Boy Floyd, Dillinger, and all the others; she didn't mention Baby Faced Nelson because I knew she must feel, like I did, a certain loyalty because he did help us. "My goodness what if someone like that picked you up and used you for bait."

Uncle Oglee laughed. "You think they'd bump me off for my belongings," he pointed to all his worldly goods lying on the floor wrapped up in a red handkerchief."

"No, but they might just like to use you for target practice, because they were bored that day," Daddy was laughing.

"We're tickled to death to see you son, but why did you leave home?" Mama asked.

"Well you know how Pa, is?" he answered, looking at Mama, "He had enough of me, he was so mad he chased me right out the front door with a shot-gun, yelling, "Get out you dammed, no good rugrat, and don't you ever cross my doorway again."

"You know how Mama is, just the sweetest person alive, well she was crying and yelling at Pa to stop it. That's why I decided it was time to come see you."

"What happened, I mean how did it all start?" Mama asked.

"As you know Pa's a Communist, and I'm a Democrat. We started discuss-ing politics, that's when he decided to win the argument. First he grabbed a stick of wood and started whacking me with it, and then he decided that wasn't serious enough so he grabbed the shot gun, and that's when I decided to get the hell out of Dodge and never come back. He took a shot at me just as I jumped over the fence but he missed, thank the Lord.

"Wow! Your own Daddy shot at you?" Junior asked. We didn't even notice junior was back inside, and was now kind of hiding behind Mama.

"No honey, not really on purpose. He didn't mean to hit him, he was just trying to scare him. That's not right, of course, but sometimes Grandpa doesn't always do what's right."

Junior just stared at Uncle Oglee, "Did it scare you?"

"You know it did," Uncle Oglee nodded his head and grinned back down at him, "Wouldn't it scare you?"

"Boy I'll say it would," Junior agreed, nodding his head, turning and looking at Daddy. "Daddy would never do anything like that, would you Daddy?"

"No, no never," Daddy said, running his fingers through Junior's hair, ruffling up his hair.

Junior suddenly smiled mischievously, "Daddy's not that good a shot, he might not miss me, but hit me, not on purpose, of course."

Everyone's mouth dropped open; we all turned and looked at Junior.

"What! What! What do we have here, a comedian," Daddy looked down at Junior, his green eyes twinkling.

Junior just grinned up at him, with that crooked, missing two front teeth smile.

"Well I'll be, you got that right," Uncle Oglee kept on laughing.

Mama stopped laughing, turned and looked at Uncle Oglee.

"Now Oglee, you know he missed you on purpose," Mama insisted.

"I know, but I'm not taking any chances, " Oglee was shaking his head, laughing, "And anyway I want to show you something," he reached into his pocket and pulled out a wrinkled piece of paper, "I think while I am here, I will do a little gold hunting."

"Have you lost your mind? Let me see," Mama asked laughing, she reached out to grab the paper.

"No, No it's all here," he pushed the wrinkled piece of paper toward her.

"I got this paper in town, on my way here."

The paper described how two train loads of gold had gone missing while it was being transferred from Georgia back to France. France had lent it to the confederacy when the civil war begun. Jefferson had promised to return it, at the end of the war. No one ever knew what happened to it. It was rumored that it had been taken to the Chennault plantation. It had been brought from Richmond, Virginia, to Anderson, South Carolina and from there to who knows where. The Chennault family had been tortured and interrogated to no avail. Anyway, there were all kinds of rumors as to what happened to it. Ever since then, all kinds of people have taken streaks of hunting for that lost gold. It was said to be buried in graveyards, or under houses that have since been burned to the ground by General Sherman, when he and his troops raged through the south.

I was fascinated when Uncle Oglee read aloud from the paper he had. I was behind Uncle Oglee and could see the date on the newspaper clipping.

"My gosh, Uncle Oglee, that paper is only two weeks old," I gasped, surprised.

"Yeah, I know, this article is creating a new interest in gold hunting. That's why I have to get busy, because there'll be a lot of people interested in the same gold hunt."

"We better get going," he told us. "First, the library, then we can check with everyone who knows the history of the civil war, and you know what, I hear there used to be another house that sat exactly here, where this house sits now. That was before General Sherman burned it down, when he raged through the south burning everything in sight on his way through.

"So, there could be gold right here, buried underneath this very house. Can you believe that?" The more I listen, the more excited I was getting.

"Okay, tomorrow we start" Uncle Oglee is already planning for the next day..

I began jumping up and down. This is really exciting.

Daddy was standing there. He just shook his head, smiled, turned and walked away, not his usual cheerful, upbeat self. Mama looked after Daddy, smiled, looked back at Uncle Oglee and winked.

"He's still mad about the way the war ended, even though it was before his time," Mama grinned.

"I'm going to find that gold, if it's the last thing I do," Uncle Oglee's jaw is stubbornly set. He's adamant (adamant a new word I have just learned from the newspaper).

"It might really be the last thing you do. Do you know how many people have spent their lives looking for that gold?" Mama questioned him, her eyebrows rise with the question.

He grinned that devilish grin.

The unusual thing about Uncle Oglee was that he wanted, in the worst way, to be smart and educated. He only went to the tenth grade, but he desperately wanted to be more educated. In his hip pocket, he carried a small Webster's dictionary with him wherever he went. He was constantly looking up new words. If he heard a word he didn't know, he would reach into his pocket and pull out the dictionary. The funny thing is he always remembered a new word. What a great memory he had. It's like he had a photographic memory.

Mama loved to tell stories about him and his search for a higher education. He really admired anyone that was smart.

"Now who have we got here?" Uncle waved toward little Jenny, when he saw her standing in the playpen, chewing on her favorite rubber duck toy. He walked over, reached down into the playpen and picked her up. "Aren't you just the cutest thing," he said, hugging her.

I think for sure she'll start screaming her lungs out when she sees the black beard, but she doesn't. She smiled, gurgled, reached up and started pulling on his black beard. She was beginning to talk.

"That's Uncle Oglee," I kept telling her.

She kept trying to say it, but all she'd get out was something like in-gle - eee

"I just can't believe this," I exclaimed. She liked him. She usually doesn't take too much to strangers."

"I guess we'll have to start calling you ingleee," Sally laughed uproariously.

"Ah-h-h don't you know I have a way with babies and ladies," he made a statement looking down with that wicked grin.

I really had to laugh; he's such a kick in the pants.

Since today's Sunday, we don't have to do any work; we can play and visit with Uncle Oglee all day. We spent the rest of the day showing Uncle Oglee around the place. Daddy showed him our cotton and corn patches. All the fruit trees and vegetables we're growing.

Uncle Oglee's really impressed. "Good grief you have everything imaginable. There's nothing you don't have. This is like the Garden of Eden.

"Not really'" Daddy said laughing, "we have to work like Hades to keep this all growing."

Of course, after it got dark and after a supper of fried chicken, gravy, potatoes, potato salad and apple pie, we had homemade ice cream.

"My goodness you people live well," Uncle Oglee leaned back and rubs his stomach like a big old brown bear, after finishing his last spoonful of ice cream.

We all go to bed later than usual because Uncle Oglee was here.

But we know we will be back to work as usual in the morning, so off we go to bed and to sleep instantly.

Uncle Oglee was still asleep when we go off to work.

I wanted to visit longer with Uncle Oglee, but duty calls, we had our chores to do. Sally and I find our hoes and go to the cotton patch to chop cotton. One good thing about our work Sally was quiet when we worked, and that was nice.

The ground was getting so hot; it sizzled, burning my bare feet. I had to stop and stand on one foot for a minute and then the other. Not only that, but the flies were pesky I have to stop chopping cotton, long enough to swat the flies, that kept buzzing around my blistered face.

Even though I had on a huge, too big, for me, straw hat, I still had to cup my hand above my eyebrows, and peek up from under the brim, into the clear blue sky. It's so hot the ground sends wavy rays of heat that wiggles like transparent snakes moving continuously up toward the sky. I looked up, I longed to see rain clouds, I wanted to see them so bad I could taste it. Not even one tiny little cloud appeared in the sky. No hope for rain, today. I was so miserable I had actually resorted to praying for rain. If it rained, I could quit and make tracks back to the house. I looked back, longing to be in that large cool, welcoming, wood framed house. It stood in the distance with the open windows that beckoned to me to come home. The house was shaded, by three giant oak trees, and one old mulberry tree, with huge arms that spread protectively out, and over a long wooden table that sat outside the house, underneath the tree. The huge limbs were hanging, heavy with purple berries and leaves that drooped toward the cool shady ground. I turned and looked at Sally. She was standing still, motionless like a statue in the middle of the next row of new baby cotton sprouts.

I remember Daddy saying, "You can't go wrong if you just chop the cotton the width of the hoe, then the plants will be thinned just right."

"Sally," I yelled as loud as I could, darn it, she was leaning on her hoe handle again, looking across the way, at a group of black birds on a barbed wire fence. She wasn't doing a darned thing. And I was just chopping my little butt off, rushing as fast as I could.

Sally jumped straight up, about a foot high off the ground and dropped her hoe, that tickled me so bad I couldn't stop laughing. This made her so mad, when she reached down to pick up her hoe, she also picked up a clod of dirt and threw it at me, hitting me in the leg. It hurt, but it was worth it and I continued to giggle.

She looked at me and growled.

I want to hurry up, because as soon as we can get this patch of cotton rows chopped, we can go back to the house, grab a tall glass of cold sweet ice tea and plunk ourselves down on the rough wooden bench beside the oak table, which Mama has covered with a red checkered table cloth. We could sit and maybe have a visit with Uncle Oglee.

"Hey, that's not fair, you have to work too," I yelled at Sally

"I'm working, I'm working." Sally snorted and started chopping cotton like crazy, making red dirt fly every which way, her short dishwater blond hair was bouncing, flopping up and down as she shook her head furiously.

Suddenly my heart does flip flops because I could see Daddy walking down the narrow, red, dirt road toward us, which means maybe, we can quit now and go home.

When I looked back up, he stoped and motioned for us to come back to the house.

"We can quit," I shouted at Sally, and threw down my hoe. I started running toward Daddy. Halfway there I turn, stop and look back, and Sally ran right into me. She' right behind me.

"Don't you think it's too hot for you girls to be out here working right now?" Daddy hollered at us. He was looking at us with a grin on his sunburned face. He was being funny of course. He knew we would jump at the chance to quit.

I looked up at the sky and nodded solemnly. The sun was straight up in the middle of the sky, high noon they called it. Time for dinner, oh goody, I thought.

Sally and I both were looking up at him, grinning from ear to ear, wanting to know what was up. "I think maybe tonight we might make some homemade vanilla ice cream. What do you think?" Daddy looked at us..

I nodded my head so hard; I felt a muscle pull in the back of my neck. When we got to the house, we were out of breath, because of the long strides; we had to take to keep up with Daddy.

I looked up at Daddy again. Yep, I think by anybody's standards he was a handsome man, even better looking than the movie stars, Clark Gable or Robert Taylor. He was tall and black headed with a widow's peak, which made his face even better looking. A widows peak is when the hair line comes down to a point in the middle of the forehead. He had what he called a Roman nose. All the Carter's had a Roman nose, I had heard the relatives say.

Oh dear, I finally understood what my nose really was. It was fast becoming a Roman nose. A Roman nose has an arch in the middle almost a hump. I hoped my nose wasn't going to turn into a Carter Roman nose when I grew up. A roman nose looks great on a man, but not so great on a woman. Drat!

Daddy's green eyes always danced and sparkled with good humor. Everyone agreed he was the best looking of the six Carter boys. There was twelve kids in the family, six boys and six girls. He was the youngest. The baby they called him. He always made everything fun. Mama called him the comedian, cutting up all the time. I'm really proud everyone loved and admired him.

Mama was waiting for us in the kitchen with Jenny, Jenny was standing up in a playpen that Daddy made for her, out of oak wood. On the playpen floor, was a patchwork quilted blanket, which somebody has made for her as a gift. The playpen was right in the middle of the kitchen floor.

Junior's also curly headed, which left Sally and me with straight as a board, hair. What was God thinking? He gave the only boy pretty, curly hair and the two girls ugly straight dirty blond hair. But he did relent and give Jenny curly hair. Sally and I did agree on that. It just isn't fair at all. Junior's a boy, and didn't need curly hair like we did, being girls and all that.

Junior was bringing in firewood for the kitchen wood stove, and the fireplace. He was closely followed by Coco and Nonie. He was making sure that we could have a fire in case it turned chilly this evening. He considered that his job, it made him feel grown up, he told me. He placed it in a wooden bin beside the old iron wood stove, which was great for heating the drafty old house, as well as for cooking.

Mama and Daddy both loved to sing around the house. They both had good voices, I thought. I could listen to them all day. They didn't usually sing together. Which come to think of it, was surprising? I wondered why.

At the moment Mama was singing, "I've told every little star just how wonderful you really are," Sally and I joined in singing to the top of our lungs. Then we went into" Let's all sing like the birdies sing," then we changed and started singing, "It don't mean a thing if you aint got that swing." Mama did a little dance to that one. We finally got it out of our system, winding down to a low hum and finally shut up.

Junior just stood there and listened with a silly grin on his face. He was only six, but since he was the only boy, he was too embarrassed to sing with the girls. Go figure, where did he get such an idea.

"Guess what everybody?" Mama announced, "I did have time to make sugar cookies, so sit down and have a cookie and a glass of milk now before dinner, the rest is after dinner," Mama stated, pleased with herself.

What a surprise, Mama's always full of surprises. Oh goodie, cookies. I thought I had died and gone to heaven. I remember thinking earlier this morning, I had smelled cookies, but I decided it was just my imagination playing tricks on me. Usually we had biscuits with sugar and butter, which were good too, but not like real cookies. They were still warm, oh yumm. Even the smell was yummy.

Even though Mama has a quick smile and a sense of humor, she didn't put up with any nonsense.

I remember in the old days when we were still young enough to get spankings, that was I'd say up until, I was about six, about six years ago. We don't get spankings anymore; instead we get lectures now, which are much worse than spankings. Now when we do something bad, Mama will say, *I have to tell your Daddy and he will talk to you about it*. That was terrible. I would feel so much worse. I had rather have a spanking and get it over with, than to get a lecture. Nothing is worse than to have Daddy be disappointed in you.

When Sally and I did something we knew we shouldn't, we'd first think about the consequences. We would figure out if it was worth taking a chance of getting caught, and then getting punished as a consequence. We'd think it through and then go ahead and do it anyway. In the old days when we got spankings, Mama didn't hesitate to get the switch, and the leaves did fly. We'd usually have to go outside and pick our own switches. I didn't like that, but I had long since discovered, that the switches with a lot of leaves were the best ones, because they didn't sting, they just made a lot of noise.

Sometimes I got lucky. I would act dimwitted and silly, until Mama had to break down and laugh.

When that happened, we knew we were saved. No switching today only a talking to, and even that wasn't bad because you could tell her heart wasn't into it. When Mama couldn't spank us, she made us promise we would never, ever do it again. I realized Mama was pretty smart when it came to spanking. It didn't take me long to catch on to her tactics. She would always start with Sally, because Sally would scream a blood curdling scream, even before the first swat. Which of course sent shivers of fear through me? It filled me with such a terrible dread just listening to Sally's screeching screams. It was much worse than the spankings.

When the spanking was over, which was about four swats, the floor would be littered with leaves. Mama would clean up the leaves.

Mama spoke up interrupting my thoughts.

"We'll have dinner in an hour or so. I made Oglee take a nape and rest up before he starts helping us with the crops."

"What's for dinner?" Sally wanted to know.

"Black-eyed peas, ham, red beans with pork, candied yams, corn bread and apple pie."

CHAPTER 4

Daddy Needs New Shoes

Aunt Ginger and Aunt Hilda came by earlier than usual. Not only that, but Aunt Hilda had brought members of her family. I had met them the first day we arrived. I think they had heard by the grapevine, about Uncle Oglee, Mama's brother, being here and they were dying to get a good look at him. I was tickled, I was getting a bang out of it, cause I was so proud of him. I really wanted to show him off. Not only was he good looking, but he was charming with a magnetic personality. I saw them walking toward our house, down the brick pathway that's been interrupted with green grass growing in between the bricks in the pathway.

I opened the door to greet them. "Well, hello there, come on in and meet my Uncle." I'm, being friendly but, thinking to myself, *come on in to my parlor said the spider to the fly.*

In they came, all five of them and started looking around, I offer them cane bottomed chairs to sit in. They settled in at the kitchen table. Mama and Daddy both greeted them with a pleasant smile and a hello.

About that time Uncle Oglee blew in, like a fresh breeze from outside. "Oh I didn't know we had company," he greeted everyone, surprised. He looked questioning at the aunts. As I mentioned before Uncle Oglee wasn't a bit shy. He enjoyed talking to people. As a matter of fact he was quite a chatterbox.

"We just thought we'd stop by for a visit," Aunt Ginger explained, as she looked at Daddy, who was standing by Mama at the stove, with the lid of a pan in his hand, getting ready to put the lid back on the pan with the corn in it.

Daddy gathered several more chairs and brought them into the kitchen and sat them down at the table. As he went by Mama, he gave her a playful little pat on the rear.

43

"Are you planning to stay with us for a while or, are you only here for a visit?" Aunt Ginger questioned him. "No, no I plan to stay for a while," Uncle replies with an engaging grin.

"Stop it, you rascal you, people will see you," Mama whispered to Daddy.

"Oh, I don't think so, I'm just too fast for them," Daddy whispered back, chuckling.

"What?" Aunt Ginger heard him, turned and looked at Daddy.

"Nothing, just said something to Leota here."

"So you're from Texas," Aunt Ginger goes back to her conversation, "How do you like it here so far?" she continues with her interrogation, her eager blue eyes digging into him. (a new word I just learned from the radio.)

The two girls were definitely interested in him.

"I think you'll like it here. We have dances on Saturday nights," Connie offers as an enticement for him to stay.

"Yeah, and the guys play baseball and basketball at night time at the high school," Margaret added.

"Wow, that does sounds interesting," Uncle Oglee nods, struggling to look interested.

"Oh yes and we have all kinds of night classes at the high school," Aunt Ginger added.

"Night classes, you say, I really like that idea." he perked up at that and takes the bait, " I'm definitely interested in furthering my education," Uncle Oglee looked up, perking up at this kind of news.

"Are they free, the classes that is?" he continued, looking up more interested by the minute, at Aunt Ginger.

"Why sure they are," Aunt Ginger answered, surprised.

I jump in at that, "Did you know Uncle Oglee has the best vocabulary of any body I know. "He carries a dictionary around with him wherever he goes."

Everyone looked surprised at that.

"Is that right?" Aunt Ginger asked.

"Yep," he agreed, and reached back into his hip pocket and brought out his small worn, tattered, Webster's dictionary, "My best friend," he laughed and patted his dictionary.

"Well, I'll be darned, that's certainly unusual," Connie jumped in. "Seems like we have us a scholar here." she smiled and winked at him, I could see, that took him back a bit.

He sat back in his chair, blinked and batted his long black eyelashes a couple of times, stared at her, and reevaluated the situation.

The eyelashes had a definite effect alright.

Connie looked startled and confused for a second and then just stared at him.

I was so surprised, a giggle escaped me before I could stop it.

He looked at her, smiled and said, "Well listen here little Missy, you might just be right about that." He paused his smile turned into a chuckle, and his black eyes twinkled.

"Uh, huh," she nodded her head, "I really think that's a possibility," she leaned back and grinned back at him as she recovers.

And I think, oh yes, something's going on here.

Margaret turned and stared at Connie like she had lost her mind.

"Well, we best be going," Aunt Hilda stated as she began to pull herself up out of the chair. Up until now; she hadn't managed to get a word in edgewise.

"That's right," Aunt Ginger said, "Unless you girls want to stay,"

Connie opens her mouth to say something, but Margaret jumps in, "No, that's alright," time we left too."

They all shook hands with Uncle Oglee, but Connie lingered a little longer than the others shaking hands, I noticed.

Uncle Oglee looked at them with a definite interest as they left.

After they leave, Sally spoke up with her dimes worth of observations. "Hey Uncle Oglee, I think you've got a girlfriend, and she's the prettiest one too."

"I think he kinda likes her too," Junior, put in his two cents.

Of course I had to say something, "By golly, I think you're both right."

"You're very quiet Oglee, what do you think?" Mama smiled and urges him to say something.

"Well, let me tell you, I think they're both right," he said,

"I think so too," Daddy chimed in.

"Well we have some time before dinner."

"If it's okay, I think I might take a little nap before dinner," Uncle Oglee stretches his arms above his head and yawns, "Dinner's in a couple hours, right?"

"We'll have dinner in two hours, You have time for a nap," Mama assured him.

Daddy looked down at his feet, shook his head sadly, and made an observation,

"God, I hope we make enough money to buy me a new pair of shoes. These have seen their best days and their gone, gone, and gone," Daddy groans, and raised his foot up and looked at what was left of his shoes. "It's really tough trying to plough in these things."

I gasped. "Daddy how can you even plough in those things tied to your feet, they aren't even shoes?"

"How can I plow without them? Its tough plowing bare footed."

"After dinner we will tie strips of gunny sacks around what's left of the boots," Mama told him. "The first money we get from the cotton crop, we'll use to buy you new boots from the Sears and Roebuck catalogue. "

"Daddy your big toe's bleeding," Junior looked at Daddy's toe and moved over closer to him as if to protect him.

I looked at Daddy's foot and I couldn't believe it. His toe was bloody, and dripping blood. "Mama look," I gasped, "We've got to do something."

"My goodness Daddy, that looks terrible. What if your toe fell off," Sally commented, looking closely at his toe.

"My, my honey you're sure a comfort," Daddy leaned over, giving his foot a closer look.

"Hush that, Sally, It'll be alright. We just need to clean, and doctor it up really good, which we will do right now." Mama assured everybody.

"Why don't we just do it now and get it over with," Mama stops and rethinks her plan, she paused for a moment with her finger on her chin, thinking about it.

"Alright, let's do it," Daddy agrees.

"The bleeding looks like it's stopping. I'll get the Iodine, cotton and strips of cloth and we'll fix that up, right now," Mama, jumped up, and put Jenny back on the blanket on the floor.

"Oh no, no, not the Iodine," Daddy yelps, sitting up on the floor, waving his dirty foot up and around in the air, making crying noises like he was in terrible pain.

Sally was holding her sides, she was laughing so hard.

"Oh shoot, stop it Claude, and sit still. You're setting a bad example for the kids," Mama laughed. "Your driving Coco and Nonie crazy, they think I'm killing you "You're such a clown," Mama shushed him, and swatted him with a dishcloth.

"He's just too funny," Sally was sitting on the floor squealing and laughing.

"Look at that," and she points to Coco and Nonie. They're running in circles, barking their heads off. All of us kids were laughing at Daddy except Jenny, she had her thumb in her mouth, sitting on the blanket looking at him; her big blue eyes were wide open with a surprised look on her face.

Mama disappears for a moment and reappears with bandage makings, Iodine, a pan of water and a washcloth. Sally and I can't quit laughing, as we watched Daddy squirm and holler when he got up off the floor and sat in a chair; waiting for what Mama was going to do to him next.

Mama pulled up a chair, sat down and put Daddy's dirty foot in her lap. She playfully slapped his leg as he wiggles and squawks. She carefully washed the red dirt off of his foot. When she applied the Iodine, Daddy fell out of the chair, screamed a blood curdling scream and rolled over on the bare wooden floor, moaning and groaning.

The more Daddy acted up, the more Sally would squeal and laugh.

Little Junior was looking more nervous by the minute. His round face had turned pale and tears started running silently, down the sides of his face. Daddy stopped, looked at Junior, then he suddenly straightened up, reached over and pulled Junior into his lap.

"I 'm so sorry, I'm only playing," he murmured, he hugged him and assured him that everything was all right and he was just playing a game.

Junior just nodded, but he still looked unconvinced.

The rest of us all knew he was playing. So when Mama finished, we helped Daddy up from the floor and back into his chair.

"You should sign up for the next actor's part in a movie," Mama whispered in his ear, as he stood up.

"Does it hurt Daddy?" Junior asked, his small, round face is screwed up as he used his blue stripe shirtsleeves to wipe away the tears he'd been struggling to keep from coming back.

"No son, Daddy's only playing, just trying to get a little sympathy," Daddy winked and grinned at Mama, "but I don't think anything's coming my way."

Daddy got up and reached back down and picked up Junior and hugged him tight. When he put him back down, he ran his rough, work, worn fingers through his towhead.

"You know Daddy's just cutting up. It really didn't hurt."

A look of relief crossed his little tear stained face and he broke into a grin. "I thought so," he said, nodding his head trying to look happy.

"Time to eat," Daddy announced.

Uncle Oglee came into the dining room, his hair standing straight up, all over his head. He looked like something that just popped up from the deep sea..

Everyone started laughing.

He looked surprised, then began to laugh good naturedly, "That bad, huh? he questioned his audience.

We all sat down. The dogs settled down and went to rest on their cushions and wait patiently for someone to bring them their share of food.

I loved this time of the day best, and supper time. Daddy would always tell jokes and we would all share any news we heard that day.

"Tonight after supper, when it gets dark, we'll make ice cream," Daddy let us know.

We were all looking forward to sitting on the front porch and waiting for the best part of the day, waiting to eat ice cream. And the best part, while we were eating our ice cream, was listening to the night sounds of crickets, katy-dids, frogs, owls and all the other night birds, plus the unknown night animals that came creeping out at night and rustled about in the dark. Oh, how I loved the feel of the cool, fresh breeze against my warm skin as I sat on the front porch soaking up all of this atmosphere.

"Again, oh goodie, ice cream! But, it's not Sunday," Uncle Oglee insisted. "Is it a special occasion or something?"

"Sure is," Mama said, "Uncle Jim and Aunt Katrina and his bunch will be over. They'll spend the night, cause it's a long way to drive back at night."

"Good, we can play games," Sally reminded us.

Mama didn't look too happy about the prospect.

I just nod. I know Mama isn't that crazy about Aunt Katrina or Uncle Jim for that matter. Mama thought Uncle Jim was a bad influence on Daddy, because Uncle Jim drank too much, and loved to talk about women. Aunt Katrina thought that was just fine, but Mama did not.

"Good, I like to play with little Jimmie," Junior raised his voice and jumped around, imitating Daddy when he was showing off.

I liked it when they came, and we could play with their girls Janie and Christie, but not Sara. I didn't think much of her. She just thought too much of herself, was the best way I can explain it.

I looked around; there's plenty of room to play games. I loved the way our house was built. Plenty of places to hide when we were playing hide and seek. I especially liked the long, wide hallway that divides our house, into two sections, as I have described before. I loved the long porch in the front of the house. That's where we always made the ice cream. That's also where we would sit in rocking chairs and visit with friends and neighbors, that stopped by. I liked the stories they would tell about the way things used to be. They said there used to be a huge kitchen built separate from the rest of the house, where they would feed the hired hands. But for some reason it was either torn down, or burned down. Someone said that it caught on fire one morning when they were cooking for a large group of hired hands.

"Looks and smells like rain," Daddy said. "No more field work for now."

"Happy days are here again," I raised my voice.

"Hey look, storm clouds," Sally points up to the sky. Sure enough, when I looked outside, I could see the clouds gathering along the horizon, moving swiftly, sweeping upwards toward the center of the sky. The clouds had become black and ominous.

"After we're finished with dinner, we'd better get ready for the rain," Daddy said.

Usually, in the evenings we had gotten into the habit of listening to the radio. After the news we always listened to One Man's family, Fibber Magee and Molly, George and Gracie Allen, Jack Benny and Fred Allen, Amos and Andy and my favorite, The Shadow Knows. We would make sure we always listened to Amos and Andy because Junior liked that one best.

The old wood framed house was several generations old. Oh how I loved to sit and listen to the grownups talk about the old days. Especially, legends about the confederacy and civil war. Two of my great, grand parents had died in the civil war. My grandmother's father and my grandfather's Daddy were both killed in the war and that left them orphans. There were endless stories and legends about the days of the civil war. One story I really like and never get tired of hearing about was at the end of the war.

A couple of confederate soldiers brought back a load of gold bouillon, and hid it in various places. Some said it was buried under a confederate soldier's grave. Others said it was buried under an old house, and I often wondered if it could be buried under our old house. Once, there had been a huge colonial house, that had belonged to our great grandpa. It had been built right here, where our house now stood. It had burned to the ground when General Sherman and his soldiers came through the south and burned down a lot of the colonial homes. There were all kinds of stories of murders and disappearances of people searching for the gold. The gold was never found.

I also like the legend about how my great grandpa Carter built the house we were living in, out of the timber he cut from his own land. Even to this day, the bare oakwood floors have never known a rug. When it's scrubbed, it's with a pail of lye water and homemade soap. The water would run through the cracks in between the wooden oak planks, and was rinsed off with clean water drawn from the well outside in the yard near the kitchen.

What spooked me was how the house creaked at night. I could just imagine strange ghosts, with chains around their ankles, tromping around in the attic, during the night. Oh yes, that's right we had an attic as I mentioned before. That's when I really thought about all those legends and stories the grownups would tell. The stories I didn't like were about the tornadoes. Those scare me to death. Daddy would always reassure me, by telling me that's what the storm cellars were for.

We sat down and ate dinner in a hurry. When we were finished, we pushed our chairs back, get up and rushed outside, and started covering things up..

"This looks like it's gonna be a good one," Daddy said. "Come on kids, let's cover everything up, we don't want things to get wet and cold.

Hurry, get the baby chicks in the coup. We don't want the little guys to catch cold and die. Cover up the chicken feed, too. If it gets wet, it will rot."

"Hey Junior, bring in the pee pot," Mama yelled, as we ran around covering things up." That's it for today girls, no more cotton chopping."

"Hallelujah!" I squealed. "It's fun time."

"Not so fast girls," Mama said. "We have some beans to snap and corn to husk. All of a sudden the sky opened up, and a frenzy of rain poured down in a torrent. It swept onto the porch and down the hallway. I liked it, it was exciting. The trees shivered and shook and the sky got black. Mama grabbed two kerosene lamps, she lit them and sat them on the dinner table.

Daddy came in wet, through and through. He sat in the chair and started pulling off his socks and what was left of his shoes. Mama brought him another shirt, took the wet one and threw it in the laundry basket.

I loved the smell of the fresh, wet dirt when it rains. Especially, when it's the first rain it smelled good enough to eat, but I knew that wasn't a good idea, because I remembered trying that when I was just a little kid. Nothing else smelled like it, I just couldn't explain it.

"Does this mean Aunt Sara and Uncle aren't coming?" I asked, feeling just a little disappointed, but not too much when I thought about Sara?

"Probably not, but they'll call," Mama nodded, looking at the black phone hanging on the kitchen wall.

We're lucky I think, not everyone had a phone, but we had one because we lived so far out in the country and the closest neighbor was several miles away.

"That is if they can get through. There were lots of people on this line and sometimes teenagers get on the line and talk forever, that is if their parents don't catch them," Mama said, shaking her head.

"Will we still have ice cream tonight?" Junior asked sadly.

"Course we'll have ice cream," Daddy assured us.

Junior's face perked up, "I'm so glad, I was really looking forward to ice cream tonight, yum- n -m. he said with a sly smile and looked around to see how many people agreed with him.

After all the commotion, we got everything covered up and also got dry ourselves. The time had really flown by, and it was almost time to eat again.

There was always something unexpected happening, I thought. That's what made it pretty exciting.

"Never a dull moment. That's what I like about it around here," I said. "The rain's still coming down pretty good."

When we all sat down to eat, it was story telling time. I could hardly wait to hear what story Daddy was going to tell today.

"Old White Paint almost made it in-to town today," Daddy laughed as he reached for the corn bread and butter. He started his story about the old Indian man that liked to get drunk and come to town. "He was riding into town in his buckboard, drunker than a skunk. He raised all kinds of cane until finally, when he fell off the buck wagon leaving his wagon and horses to run free down the street, kicking and braying. They finally wound up on the plank sidewalk in front of, and almost in Mr. Baker's General store. That's when the Sheriff arrested him and threw him into the drunk tank to sober up.

Old White Paint screamed all kinds of profanity and put unbelievable curses on the Sheriff's head. Of course old Dan just laughed it off. He'd heard these curses so many times before, according to the curses, he should be burning in hell long before now. The facial expressions Daddy used and the way he told the story had us all holding our sides, we were laughing so hard. It wasn't the story that was so funny, it was the way Daddy would tell it. Mama couldn't stop laughing either, although she had heard it a dozen times before.

Oglee said "I have a joke I heard today, and it's pretty funny.

"Go for it, let's hear it," Mama said.

"A Texas couple was stuck in the airport with a couple from New York after their flight was canceled.

The Texas woman asked the New York woman, "Where ya'll from?

The New York woman just stared at her and replied," Where we are from, we don't end our sentences with a preposition.

To which the Texas woman replies, "Oh well, where are yawl from b.i.t.c.h. Uncle spelled bitch out. We all laughed so hard we had to hold our stomachs. "Get it," I said, explaining it to Junior. He said bitch at the end of the sentence instead of the preposition from.

That reminds me of another joke I heard today Daddy said. "Oh goodie," I yelped, "tell us."

"There's these three fishermen in a boat and they are stuck out in the middle of a lake, for a while. So they decided to kill time, they would tell each other their most private secrets, and they promised they wouldn't tell any one the secrets. The first guy said, "*My secret is I have a terrible gambling problem,* the second guy said, "Well my secret is *I cheat on my taxes and playing cards.* The other guy said, "*Wow,* and they turned to the third guy, because so far, he'd been very reluctant to reveal his secret. "*You have to tell your secret because we told our secrets. Ok, ok my secret is I can't help it, but I gossip.*"

We all laughed, and continued on with any other news we could think of.

CHAPTER 5

The Magic Trick and Ice Cream

After supper Mama mixed up the vanilla ice cream. We all rushed around and crawled into the new pajamas Mama made for us before the trip. The pajamas were made out of some kind of thick flannel material, that had pretty pictures of Unicorns, Mermaids and Horses in all kinds of beautiful colors in the material's design. Junior, Daddy and Uncle Oglee had Horses, Sally and Jenny had beautiful Mermaids, and I had Unicorns. That is until Sally made a fuss. For some reason she always wanted whatever it was I wanted or had. I soon learned to play the game to get what I really wanted. I'd pretend I wanted something that I really didn't want, to get what I really wanted. Confusing, right. For instance in this case I'd pretend I really wanted Unicorns, which I didn't want,. Of course Sally insisted she really wanted Unicorns. Then Mama asked me if it would be alright with me if she gave Sally the Unicorns.

And I'd say, "Well o.k. I'll take the Mermaids, but I'd say that I really wanted the Unicorns," and then I act like I wasn't too happy about it all. Actually I really did want the Mermaids and I got the Mermaids and everybody was happy, and Sally was never the wiser. I think Mama knew what was going on, because when she looked at me, she had a little smile tugging at the corner of her mouth, when she handed me, my little Mermaid pajamas.

Ah yes the wicked web the spider weaves.

I looked up and saw Uncle Oglee standing behind Mama, looking at me with a strange look, an almost smile on his face.

I couldn't resist grinning back at him. As I watched him, I couldn't believe my eyes, he silently mouthed, " You sly little devil."

Oh my God, I thought he knows my secret. Afterwards, he never mentioned it, but I knew he knew my secret plot to get what I really wanted..

Daddy brought out the old, well used, wooden ice cream bucket. He sat the metal bucket, filled with vanilla ice cream mix, into the wooden bucket, and then packed rock salt and ice all around it. Then we all took turns churning the ice cream maker. That's when I started to drool. We could hardly wait until it was ready to scoop out into bowls and eat. We continued to turn the churn and wait.

The rain stopped and the full moon snuck out, and peeked over just above the horizon. It was beautiful, shining through the tops of the trees. I could clearly see all the different trees, pine, English gum, walnut and hickory nut trees. The moon became huge, it looked like a giant glowing orange. I felt like I could reach up and pull it down, right out of the sky. It was just magic. The stars glittered like little jewels, like Christmas ornaments hanging against the deep, blue-grey sky. Everything was beautiful.

"Now ain't this something," Uncle Oglee inhaled and expelled a deep breath, "life is beautiful, just can't be any better than this," he relaxed, leaned back against his chair with his hands and arms stretched out above his head, his fingers clasped together high in the air, behind his head.

The fireflies were glittering, dancing, and flashing about like lightning. That must be why they're called lightening bugs, I decided. A hoot owl started making his presence known. He was settled in the tree next to the house and started hooting making the katydids, crickets and frogs sound less important. I loved it all. We didn't have any of this in Fabens, Texas.

We were all seated in our favorite spots on the front porch. I could feel the left over rain drops slowly dripping, falling from the eve of the house, hitting my toes and wet bare feet. I liked sitting with my bare feet on the end of the front porch with my legs dangling over the edge of the wooden porch, my feet barely touched the damp ground. It made me feel close to the earth.

Daddy took the first turn churning the ice cream maker, he smiled.

"Just wait old John will show up in a few minutes, I'll give him five minutes," Daddy turned, reached into his pocket and pulled out his pocket watch. He laid it on the chair beside him and waited until John showed up.

John was the only black man that came to visit Daddy.

"I knew John when we were little kids. We used to play together and go fishing in the creek when we were little." Daddy told us.

Sure enough, he was right. John suddenly showed up with a big grin on his face. "I heard the ice cream maker going, and I just couldn't stop myself," he was standing in the lantern light, holding his little girl, Lena's hand. He stood tall in his striped shirt and overalls. They hung loose by one buckled strap on his lean frame. He was clean shaven and pleasant looking with a big friendly smile on his black face.

I'm the same age as Lena. I liked her. She was motherless and didn't have any siblings because her mama died in childbirth. I thought she was pretty, with her rich black satin skin, and big brown eyes. She was thin and a little shorter than me. The dress she was wearing was too big for her, and it hung to her ankles.

"Hi Lena. That's a pretty dress," I told her

"Thank you," Lena looked down shyly. "This dress is a hand me down you know." She said as she looked down, and spread her fingers across the front of the skirt, smoothing the wrinkles out. All of my dresses are hand me downs. I don't mind hand me downs, because if I didn't have them I wouldn't have anything to wear." She explained and kind of half giggled.

"Pull up a chair and sit down," Daddy said as he leaned back, reached behind him, snagged a chair with one hand and pulled it forward so John could sit down.

"Here have a seat." He chuckled and patted the damp chair. "I had you timed for how long it would take you to get here," Daddy nodded and pointed to his pocket watch lying on the porch.

"Get out of here," John shook his head in disbelief, turned and looked down at Lena, "Didn't I tell you he knew we were coming."

"Yeah, you did Daddy," she smiled, looking up at her Daddy, with a big smile and two missing front teeth.

"Zemma, can you please bring them a couple of bowls?" Daddy looked at me.

"Coming right up," I answered, and jumped up, ran into the kitchen, and grabbed two bowls with spoons. I gave them each a bowl and spoon and sat back down.

"Come sit by me, Lena," I looked at Lena and patted the wooden porch beside me.

After we all got our ice cream, John settled back in his chair, and he and Daddy started talking about the crops and how they were doing. They discussed all the events of the day.

"Did you read where they finally convicted the woman doctor that killed her doctor husband?" Daddy asked John.

"Shore nuff did. Seemed like she took her time and slowly poisoned him with arsenic, I hear."

"People just never seem to be happy with what they got. I expect she was in love with that other doctor, you know the younger, good looking one.

"I believe she'd be the first woman to hang in Mississippi," Mama spoke up.

"Yeah when they hang somebody, it's usually a black man." John said, he didn't sound angry about it, just matter of fact.

"Is that right? Uncle Oglee asked.

"Yeah, that's the God's truth," Daddy said.

"I think there's quite a large insurance policy involved, too," Daddy said.

John chuckled, "That might have something to do with it, with this depression and all, that must have been mighty tempting."

They both chuckled.

"What was her name Dr. Ruth or something Dean," Mama said.

"Really a slow cruel way to die, arsenic poisoning," John said, doing a make believe shiver.

They switched the subject to the depression, thank goodness, I thought. Enough of the arsenic poisoning.

"Thank God for Roosevelt. If it wasn't for him I don't know what any of us would do," John made a comment.

"We'd all starve to death," Mama said.

"Did you tell John about White Paints antics?" I asked.

"Oh, White Pain he's at again, is he?" John asked.

Daddy relayed the story about the antics of White Paint, and they all laugh.

They talked about the weather some more, and how it would affect their crops. John was a share cropper. He had about forty acres he works. A sharecropper is someone who rents the land to farm and then at harvest time the sharecropper will give the owner a large percent of the harvest money at the end of the season.

John's the only black man I knew, and I liked him. He'd always tease and joke with me and Sally. He called us little Missy and I liked that. Although I'm only twelve and Sally's younger, it made me feel kind of grown up and important.

He always helped Daddy out when he needed an extra hand, and Daddy always helped John out when he needed it. John did sharecropping for a man named Johnson.

"Does anyone want more ice cream," Mama asked.

Everyone said they were full, except Junior.

"I'd like a little more," he said.

"You got it," Daddy said reaching for his bowl and filling it to the top.

"Oh boy! Thanks,"

"He's a bottomless pit," Mama laughed, reaching over and ruffling his hair, Junior smiled his happy smile, and lapped up his ice cream. He was always a kick. I decided to spring a surprise on Lena.

"Did you know my Daddy could do magic?" I was tickled at the expression on Lena's face. Her black eyes opened wide and were shining in the moonlight like two bright shiny marbles.

"No, I don't believe that. Surely you're joking. Only Jesus can perform miracles," Lena exclaimed.

"Oh no I didn't say miracle, I said magic. There's a difference," I said defensively.

"Oh, do tell," Lena had a look of surprise on her face, when one eyebrow lifted and a half-smile with dimples surfaces on her round face.

"Wait I'll show you. Daddy show us you're magic. Lena wants to see."

"What are you talking about?" Daddy looked surprised.

"You know the white light doing what you tell it to do," I told him, I could hardly wait to show off how clever my Daddy was.

"Daddy looked confused for a second, and then his face brightened. He suddenly smiled. "Ah, oh yes that's right, the magic trick."

"Okay, I'll have to put myself into a magic trance, I'll have to leave for a second and have a little chat with my inner self, to see if my inner self is in the mood," he added, with an impish grin on his face. He got up from his rocking chair, turned around in a circle three times, went into the house, came back out, turned around three more times, then he turned around the other way three more times.

He sat back down in his rocking chair, closed his eyes and mumbles, "Abra, ca, draba, ching a ling a link." He opened his eyes. "You must realize this is pretty hard on me emotionally. Okay, just look straight out toward that log, watch closely, don't look away for a second, or you might miss it."

Suddenly a round ball of fire and light appeared on the ground beside a log, and it leapt up from the ground, to land on top of the log.

Lena squealed, everyone gasped.

Uncle Oglee jumped out of his chair and yelled, "Dam."

Even John jumps, "What the hel-," he stopped himself just in time.

"Come a little closer, don't be afraid, come on, come here," Daddy coaxed. He waved his right hand in the air in a circle, then he wiggled his forefinger in a come here, motion, and whispered, " Come here".

The object moved closer.

"Oh my God," Lena gasped, and reached for her Daddy's hand, but he's speechless.

"Now can you do a little dance for me, please?" Daddy whispered.

Everyone held their breath, waiting, afraid to speak and break the spell.

The sparkling, glittering object started dancing and jumping around.

Lena grabbed my arm and hung onto me for dear life," I'm so scared," she whispered.

I can see she's panic stricken. "Don't worry, it won't hurt you," I reassured her.

"Don't be afraid, come a little closer," Daddy urged the object.

It started moving closer and closer at a faster rate, jerking from side to side. Suddenly it jumped right into Daddy's hands.

"That's alright little buddy you're safe with me," Daddy reassured the little object. It was trembling. Daddy held the little object up in the air, as he petted it, and then handed it to John. John instinctively jumped back, opened his hand and dropped it.

"Oh no," Daddy yelled "Did you hurt it?" Oh no, you hurt it," Daddy reached down and picked the little trembling thing up. "Did he hurt you?" Daddy asked looking at John accusingly.

"I'm sorry," John said, backing up, "Didn't mean to hurt it."

I looked at Daddy, he could have been an actor, and I almost split my sides trying not to laugh.

"That's alright, John," Daddy chuckles, "You didn't hurt it, and John, it won't bite you."

"You promise," John gasped, "You sure about that?" he asked and reluctantly took the ball of twinkling light between his two large, black, workworn hands.

Everyone held their breath in horror.

He held it in his hands, quietly studying it, he looked at it thoughtfully as he turned it over and over in his hands.

"I know this is fluorescent, but I don't know how the heck you managed it like you did," he said scrutinizing Daddy's smiling face in the moonlight.

Daddy just grinned, "Maybe someday, I'll let you in on my little secret."

"Tell me, tell me, I have to know," Uncle Oglee begged "I have to know. I won't rest until I find out how you did that."

I grinned. I knew what the secret was, but I would never tell. I had finally figured it out. Daddy had a string tied to the piece of fluorescent wood and he would just let it sit there all the time, until some unsuspecting victim came along, then he would pull off the string when he had it in his hand, before he handed it to the other person.

"I just don't get it," Sally gasped. "And I just don't care if I get it or not. And I don't care that Zemma get's it, so what. Do you get it, Junior?"

"No, but I'm gonna work on it till I figure it out. It's a puzzle of some kind."

"Maybe someday, Oglee, maybe on your twenty first birthday, "Daddy promised,

Daddy reached over and patted Uncle Oglee on the back.

'I just don't think I can wait that long," Uncle Oglee insisted, but Daddy wouldn't give in.

"When someone asked me what we do for entertainment,' Daddy always answered, "I always tell them the kids. We never get tired of teasing them."

"You know that's so true. I never get tired of teasing them," Daddy said looking over at us."

"Yeah, and I'll just bet you do figure it out," Daddy looked over at Junior, who is eagerly nodding his head.

"Amen, and what do you think of all that," I added to the conversation. I looked at Lena, who was sitting with a puzzled look on her face and she nods.

The phone rang and it was Aunt Katrina. She called to let us know they wouldn't be able to make it tonight, but they would be here the night after, next night.

"That's fine," Mama said, and hung up. "Not a word out of you, young lady," she shook her finger and looked at me, with her all knowing smile.

I looked up and smiled, "I know you're tickled to death."

She snapped her dishtowel at me, "Now get."

I ran out of the kitchen giggling.

"Day after tomorrow is wash day, so you better get your rest," she yelled after me.

CHAPTER 6

Wash Day

A ll four of us, Mama, Sally, Lena and I were snapping beans, peeling potatoes, and peeling apples, for apple pie, getting ready for company day after tomorrow. We knew that Jim, Katrina and the kids would stay about a week or so. We were planning what we would cook, when they got here.

"Tomorrow's Saturday and its wash day," Mama reminded us, changing the subject.

In the beginning, when we first began doing our wash on the creek, Aunt Ginger and Aunt Hilda would come over and show us how to do the wash on the creek. Before that we didn't have a clue of what to do. But it didn't take Mama long to get the hang of it.

"Get out all your stuff and put it in a pile so we can wash it." Mama turned to Lena and "Lena honey, if you and your Daddy have any washing to do, bring it over and I'll just add it to our wash."

"Oh thank you, Mrs. Carter, I believe I will. I can help you with the washing, too," Lena offered anxiously hopping around and picking up clothes and putting them in separate piles.

This didn't come as a surprise because Mama had always, offered to include them on wash day.

When Mama realized Lena didn't have a mother or any women for that matter in her house to do their washing, she offered to include them in our wash day.

At first they were self-conscious and didn't accept Mama's offer, but when Mama kept insisting each wash day they finally gave in and said yes. Aunt Ginger and Aunt Hilda arrived with their aprons on, ready to help. They had become our best friends.

I noticed my two aunts dressed different than other grown women I'd seen. They wore long dark patterned dresses that went all the way down to their ankles. They usually had a long sleeved undergarment on under their long dresses. The dress material was usually a pretty floral pattern against a rich dark background. They would also wear thick flesh colored, cotton hose, and high top shoes. I had never seen any women dress like that before. Then to dress up their outfit they would always wear a gold necklace of some kind. To top it all off, they both had their long white hair done up in a large, twisted bun, either at the back of their necks or on top of their heads. Usually wisps of white hair would always escape from their buns and float loose around their faces. This always gave them an innocent childlike look. It was really, cute I thought.

Well, anyway when Mama offered to do Lena's and Jim's wash, I thought for sure Aunt Ginger and Aunt Hilda were going to have a stroke, or throw up or something. The two looked quickly at each other, and then they looked at Mama. They both moved next to Mama, and Aunt Hilda whispered where Lena couldn't hear them.

"You can't do that, we don't do that, wash their clothes with ours."

Mama looked them both straight in the eye and asked, "Why not?"

Aunt Ginger looked nervous, "Well-uh- you see no one ever, ever does that here."

"Well it's about time we changed that," Mama suggested, looking at them unwavering, "don't you think?" and she went about sorting her clothes for tomorrow.

Aunt Ginger turned, walked over to the nearest chair and sat down.

"Well I never," she mumbled, looking at Aunt Hilda.

Aunt Hilda just stared back at her.

I thought they were going to leave, but they didn't. They didn't offer to help with anything, anymore either. They just sat around and watched.

"I can't thank you enough, Mrs. Carter," John smiled, revealing his missing tooth in the top row of teeth. I liked the look. I think it gave him character.

By the time we got everything ready for wash tomorrow, it was close to supper time.

Mama asked my Aunts to stay for supper, but they said no, and decided it was time for them to leave.

"I don't think they will be here to help tomorrow," I said, looking at Mama.

"You just never know," Mama said with that all knowing smile.

The next morning we got up at four a.m., as usual.

And a huge breakfast as usual, pancakes, bacon, ham and eggs, biscuits and white gravy. This kind of breakfast was a southern custom, because we never did have a breakfast, like that in Texas.

I didn't mind wash day, in fact it was fun.

It was still dark in the morning after breakfast when we each grabbed a lantern and took it with us and headed for the barn to do our chores. The three of us would take turns doing the chores feeding the chicken, slopping the pigs and gathering the eggs.

"Uncle Oglee, we decided that milking the cows would be a good job for you. You know you're so big and strong," I said, smiling up at Uncle Oglee.

"Say what? Who died and made you boss, young lady," he yelped. He crossed his eyes and held his nose.

I laughed and offered him the two buckets I was carrying.

"A-h-h-h, all right," he said pretending to be upset. He reached down and grabbed the bucket, and headed for the barn.

"Her name is Molly and the other one's name is Josephine," I called after him as he disappeared through the barn door.

"I'll come help you, if you're not done by the time we're done," I yelled loud making sure he could hear me. Then I went on my way, giggling to myself.

By the time we were done, it was beginning to get daylight, and we were ready to get started doing the wash.

We were so busy, we had to wait on the cotton planting until the next day. Today would be even more fun because Lena was there to talk and play with us. She would also help us with the wash.

I thought Sepsi Creek was a great place to do the washing. I worried about the creek water looking brown and muddy, but when we put the water in the pot it looked clear I couldn't figure that out. It must be because the creek bottom and sides were redbrown mud.

Lena's Daddy brought their clothes in a woven Indian basket, the local Choctaw Indians had made. Lena and her Daddy only lived about a half a mile down the road from us. That's about the same distance we had to walk in the mornings to catch the school bus.

And of all things, mysteries of all mysteries, Aunt Ginger and Aunt Hilda did show up. When I really thought about it, it didn't surprise me. That's like them, they were usually quick to change their minds. I think it was partly out of curiosity, and partly because they really did have good hearts. When it came right down to it, they just couldn't stay away. As soon as they got here, they jumped right in and started helping with taking the clothes down to Sepsi creek and bringing water back up from the creek.

It was truly amazing and I couldn't help but feel a little, tiny bit of love toward them. Bless their hearts and their little pointed heads.

When John got here, he started a fire under the huge cast iron pot, we used to boil our clothes in. Mama thanked him and we all got busy bringing our clothes from the house to the creek. We started our usual routine, which was easy. We did all our washing on the banks of Sepsi Creek which is about two hundred and fifty feet down the hill, or so Daddy told us. John half filled the pot with creek water. Next we would finish filling the pot with lye and white homemade soap. Afterwards we would throw the heaviest clothes, like overalls and coveralls into the pot and let them boil. Oh how I loved the smell of the wood burning under the pot. It smelled like the fireplace smelled in the morning. I really liked it. It smelled fresh and new. I just couldn't explain what I liked about it.

All of us, Sally, Lena and I had to do was keep punching and moving the clothes around in the boiling pot. We used two wooden paddles Daddy had created, made just for the occasion. The steam boiled up, smelling like homemade soap, sweet, clean and fresh. We had to be sure to keep the fire stoked while the water boiled. We used the wash board and another pot of hot water to hand wash the finer stuff. That was easy cause we had very little finer stuff. We took turns washing clothes on the wash board. We ran back and forth to the creek with our clothes, hauling them up and down the slick, muddy banks of the steep hill. It was slick, with red, muddy clay. It was really slippery going up and down the bank.

I watched my Aunts, I didn't realize my they were so quick and athletic. It must have been from working so hard in the cotton fields all their lives. I really had a tough time trying to keep up with them.

Lena was even quicker, and stayed ahead of us most of the time, until finally she stopped and waited for me to catch up with her. She moved closer to me, leaned over and whispered in my ear, as she watched for Mama over her shoulder, making sure she was out of earshot. She didn't want Mama to hear what she had to say.

"Why does your Mama wear her gown, instead of a dress under that long, heavy sweater? Doesn't she get hot?"

I laughed, "I guess that does seem like quite a mystery, but it was really simple. She only has one everyday dress and one good dress, so she had to wear her gown, while she washed her everyday dress.

"Oh that's too bad," Lena"s black eyes opened in surprise, as she backed up.

"We ran out of money last fall. When we bought material for our dresses, and we didn't have enough money for material to make a dress for Mama. But when our cotton crop is harvested, we'll make up for it. We'll have enough money to make Mama two new dresses. She certainly deserves it."

Lena just shook her head sadly.

"That's alright Mama doesn't mind, we just ran out of money, so we can't buy any more material. Before she just barely got enough to make Sally and me a new dress for school. We only need one dress a piece because most of the time we wear overalls like the one I have on now."

Mama came down from the house from time to time to make sure we we're watching the pot, feeding the fire, and not goofing around. She was always carrying Jenny tucked under one arm and a load of clothes under the other one.

Junior and Oglee went to help Daddy plow the bottom field. Junior always followed Daddy behind the plow and picked up the long weeds, putting them in a pile, because Daddy didn't want the weed's seed to grow and reseed the ground with weeds. He really wanted a good crop of cotton, corn or whatever we were planting, not a fine crop of weeds.

In the meantime between our chores, we, Sally, Lena and I would all build stick houses. We would each pick a spot, get a bunch of sticks, rocks and what ever we could get our hands on and start building beautiful homes. Or we'd just sit and talk.

"Hey look what I found," Sally yelled at Lena. She had found a neat pile of little bones. "These will make great windows and doors. Look," she grabbed them and laid them out in a neat row on the ground in the middle of our play houses.

"That's really nice, I would like to have more." Lena says.

"Go look by that old rotten stump, the one that has green moss growing all around it, I think there's more there."

I thought I'd help her, so I ran over to the stump, scratched around but couldn't find any more. What I did find wasn't what I was looking for.

I screamed. "It's a water moccasin."

"Don't move. Stand still," Sally yelled.

"Oh dear God I'm a goner," I moaned. I looked down and the snake was about two inches away from my naked big toe. The snake raised its head looked around, his long pointed tongue darted in and out. I knew his darting tongue was looking for something to put his teeth into. I couldn't breath. I closed my eyes, I couldn't watch, I'm waiting for the sharp pin prick of teeth to stick, and sink in my big toe. He put his head back down and slithered over my bare foot and wiggled on down to the creek's edge, he paused for a second, then slid over the creek bank and down into the muddy, brown water.

I dropped to the ground with my head in my hands and started to cry. I was so scared. I had heard all the terrible stories about what happens to people that have gotten bitten by water moccasins. I had heard that sometimes the limb, leg or arm whatever it was that was bitten, would just swell up, turn purple and then fall off the next day or two.

"That's alright," Sally said patting me on top of my head, which made my short, straight, brown hair bounce up and down with each pat.

"You didn't get bit, now did you, so count your blessing," Sally consoled me, shaking her head from side to side, chastising me for hollering.

That really irritated me, how dare she. I raised my head, tears running down my freckled checks. "Forget about the water moccasins. We gotta watch out for the copper heads too," I yelled, looking around, "And they can get you too," I reminded her.

"Here take some of my bones. I have too many now anyway," Lena is pushing her hand out toward me. She changed the subject, and opened the hand that's filled with bones.

"Okay," I quieted down, quickly recovered and wiped away the tears, "Lordy, you know water moccasins, can kill you?"

"Sure," she nodded her head, looked up for a minute then went back to the business of putting more doors in her house.

We divided up the bones and continued building our houses.

"I think I'll put curtains on mine like it has in the Sears's catalogue, we can use leaves for that," I said.

"Me too," Sally said, jumping into the conversation.

"Here comes Mama. Should we tell her about the moccasins?" Sally asked, looking apprehensive.

"I don't know. Maybe we should because if we don't, it may come up later to bite us in the butt," I said. Saying butt was a no, no, but I felt I had a right, cause I had almost been bitten by a moccasin.

Sally and Lena giggled, because they knew I wasn't supposed to say butt.

Mama came back down and I decided to tell her.

"Mama, a water moccasin almost got me," I said calmly as if it were an everyday happening. *Mama must be thinking what a brave girl.*

"What." Mama said, looking around alarmed, just as I knew she would. "You sure it was a water moccasin?"

"Positive," all the girls exclaimed.

"Well that does it. I'm staying down here with you girls."

"You don't have to do that Mama. He's gone now."

I heard a rustle in the bushes, I jumped, "He's back," I shrieked.

Daddy, Oglee and Junior appeared from behind the bushes.

"What the heck's the matter with you girls?" Daddy asked, looking around, and decided everything was o.k.

"I've been doing some thinking. I'll tell you what I've decided to do," Daddy said.

CHAPTER 7

Our Own Cotton Patch

"Would you like to have a piece of land all your own, you can plant a crop of cotton, that would be all yours?" He asked, looking at me.

"Really! You're not joking, are you?" I gasped. This could just be one of his playful jokes.

"No siree bob, I mean it, all your own, that way you could learn how to be a real down to earth business person. You and Sally could each have a piece of land on just the other side of the house. You can both have the same amount. It's already plowed and ready to be planted. You two can start right now, planting your cotton. I have enough seed to let you each have the same amount."

Sally and I started jumping up and down, while Lena stood by silently listening.

"I wonder if my Daddy would let me do that." She asked, looking sad.

"I'll just bet he would. We'll tell him what Daddy did," I said.

"You think he would?" Lena asked her face lighting up like a Christmas tree, "He might think I'm too young."

We nodded, "Yeah maybe, but maybe not, after all you're his only child, and you've just got to ask him. *You know nothing ventured, nothing gained,* I was quoting Mama, of course."

We were all in great spirits after that, just thinking about our wonderful future. The three of us took turns punching the pot of clothes and boiling water with paddles, with a new vim and vigor.

I suddenly stopped as a thought struck me, and I looked at Lena. "Why don't you go to our school?"

"Oh that's cause I'm black and you're white."

"Really," I said, and went back to punching the paddle and mulled that over. I stopped again, "And why would that matter. What difference would that make?"

Lena stopped and thought for a minute, "Well I really don't know."

"But why's that? That doesn't make any sense at all. It just doesn't seem right now does it?" I asked, thoughtfully mulling it over.

"Cause that's just the way it is. It's a rule," Lena said.

"Oh, but I wonder why."

"Just don' know," Lena said.

We just dropped the subject for now, since there didn't seem to be anyone around to give us any answers.

The promise of a cotton crop of our very own was unbelievable. I knew we could do it. A whole new world of dreams opened up, a world of endless possibilities. It was the most exciting thing we had ever experienced.

"Just think Sally, we could buy anything we wanted," I said shaking with excitement.

"I know, I know," Sally said. "I want a tricycle, no, no, I want a bicycle, yeah that's it. I'm too big for a tricycle."

"Yeah, yeah that's it, that's what I want, too, " I said, pushing my paddle faster and faster. "I can just see us riding up and down the hill in the front yard."

"Yeah, we could race, see who could go faster," Sally said. "Oh, what fun we will have, and then I noticed Lena slowly pushing her paddle back and forth, looking so sad. Sally and I looked at each other

"I will buy you something Lena," I said, "What would you like?"

"Yeah, me too what would you like?" Sally asked.

"Oh no, nothing," Lena said.

"Come on now, speak now, or forever hold your peace," I insisted.

Lena laughed. "Well, when you put it that way, I would really like a pair of patent leather shoes."

"Oh, nice," I said, "you got them."

"What else would you like?" Sally insisted.

"Oh let me think, let me think," she said, rubbing her forehead with the back of her sweaty hand. "I got it; I would love to go to Barnum and Bailey circus."

"Oh, yes, yes, me too," I said.

"We could all three of us go," Sally yelled, she was getting so excited; she splashed some of the hot water out of the pot.

"Careful over there girls," Mama yelled.

We kept on planning our future in the cotton planting world, and what all we were going to buy with our money. We didn't have a doubt in the world that we weren't going to be successful.

CHAPTER 8

Lena Little Black Girl

Aunt Ginger and Aunt Hilda were over to our house almost every day. They both only lived about a half mile from us. All the other Aunts and Uncles lived further away.

And miracles of miracles, Aunt Ginger and Aunt Hilda began to take a liking to Lena, especially Aunt Hilda. They started fussing over which one of them was going to do her hair.

Aunt Hilda decided she was going to put a new hem in all of her dresses that were too long, which were all of them..

"She's the sweetest little thing, and not only that, she is really pretty," I heard Aunt Hilda say to Aunt Ginger.

"Darn it, it's a shame she's black, if she wasn't I'd take her home with me and keep her," Aunt Ginger said.

I just shook my head, but I didn't say anything. Just give them a little more time, I thought to myself. They were softening up. Before that, they would never say anything like that. I thought sooner or later they might see the light. They really did like her.

Lena took a liking to Aunt Hilda, and started following her around everywhere she went. Aunt Hilda really liked that. I don't think she ever, had anyone take to her like that before.

They also began teaching Mama a lot about southern cooking. I learned a lot, too.

We had a dinner of beans, candied yams, ham and biscuits with sugar cane syrup. Today they also taught Mama how to make candied yams. My goodness did that taste good.

I felt like a good nap. But dishes had to be washed. When that was all done we did take a nice little nap, before we went back down to the creek and finished up the washing. We brought the clothes back up and hung them out to dry on the clothes line. I loved the smell of clothes, especially pillow cases and sheets that had been dried in the sun.

It was getting late and starting to get dark. John and Lena began packing up their clothes and heading for home.

"John, you might as well let Lena spend the night, since she will be back here early tomorrow.

"Can I stay, Daddy," Lena started jumping up and down.

"Are you sure it's o.k.?"

"Of course," Mama said.

When Aunt Ginger and Aunt Hilda heard that Aunt Katrina and Uncle Jim were coming, they decided they wanted to get home before they got there, but they didn't make it in time.

"Oh shoot, here they are," Aunt Ginger, said.

"Why don't you stay for supper," Mama insisted.

Aunt Hilda and Aunt Ginger looked at each other.

"Might as well," Aunt Ginger said, "We're already here."

Aunt Katrina and Uncle Jim arrived with their kids.

"What's that child doing here," Aunt Katrina said, pointing at Lena. "That's just disgraceful."

"What! You shut your cotton picking mouth, before I cloud up and rain all over you," Aunt Ginger almost bellowed at Aunt Katrina. It was the first time I had ever heard Aunt Ginger raise her voice. My goodness she could win the hog calling contest, I thought.

"You take back those hateful words that came out of your mouth. This precious child happens to be a special friend of mine," Aunt Hilda said as she glared at Aunt Katrina, and she walked over and put her arm around little Lena's thin shoulders.

Not to be shown up, Aunt Ginger joined Aunt Hilda as she put a protective arm around Lena.

"This little girl is also a special friend of mine," Aunt Ginger said, staring down Aunt Katrina.

Little Lena's face lit up like the sun just broke through the clouds; she was beaming from ear to ear. You could tell she really liked and admired Aunt Hilda.

That was the moment I fell in love with my Aunt Hilda, Of course I had already fallen in love with my Aunt Ginger. I had never been so proud of anyone in all my whole life as I was of my Aunts.

"That's right, Katrina," why don't you just keep your mouth shut," Aunt Ginger echoed Aunt Hilda.

Aunt Katrina's round, plump face, turned pale. It was clear she was in shock. Her brown eyes widened, and she looked around, until she found a chair and sat her wide body down in it. Did I mention she was really fat? I would say all of three hundred pounds or so, and she wasn't very tall. About five foot two or so inches. She just sat there and glared at Aunt Ginger and Aunt Hilda.

"Jim, Jim come here right now, your sister just insulted me."

"Katrina, how many times do I have to tell you, you have to fight your own battles? If you stir up a lot of shit. You have to settle it. If you can't run with the big dogs, you stay on the porch." he looked around at everybody with a disgusted look on his face, then he turned and stalked out toward the door.

"Wait a minute Jim, she stuck up for this cotton picking, black picaninny here, what do you think of that?"

"I think this is not your house, now is it?" having said that, he turned back around, and continued on out the door.

"I'm leaving then."

"Go right ahead, Katrina. Like I've told you many a time you are a shit disturber. I came here to visit, not to fight and raise hell. Now if that's what you want to do, go on and get out of here, and when you do, don't let the door hit you in the rear."

She struggled up out of the chair, huffing and puffing. She moved slowly, as she lumbered out into the hallway. When she got to the porch she found a chair, she plopped herself down in it. You could tell she was really mad, by the way she sat, her back straight and her eyes not looking to the right or left, but straight ahead.

"She always causes trouble," Aunt Hilda said, shaking her head.

"I don't know how Jim puts up with it," Aunt Ginger said, "she's not the sharpest knife in the drawer. The only reason they got married, was because they had to, if you know what I mean."

Which I didn't know what she meant, but I didn't think I should ask what she meant right now, but all in good time, I would ask..

I had to giggle at that one. Sally crossed her eyes and looked at me. That cracked me up. I started snickering and I had to leave for a minute. I pretended I had to go to the bathroom, and I went outside.

Outside I took a deep breath of fresh air and I thought about how evil and mean Aunt Katrina was and how nice Aunt Ginger and Aunt Hilda were. When I came back in I looked at Aunt Ginger and Aunt Hilda through new eyes. Funny thing about Aunt Ginger she didn't look old to me anymore. I thought that was strange. I knew she couldn't have changed any, but now when I looked at her, she looked attractive to me, and much younger than she did when I first met her. She even had a pretty smile and really beautiful eyes, bright, blue eyes that twinkled. They actually sparkled. Aunt Hilda even looked younger than she did when I first met her.

"Any day now," Jannelle said, with a tiny smile at the corner of her mouth, and a sparkle in her eye.

"Oh my, oh my," Mama spoke up. She had been quiet during the big argument.

"Time to put supper on the table," Mama said

Aunt Ginger and Aunt Hilda started getting warmed over food out of the oven and putting it on the table.

"We'll take care of this, Leota, while you take care of the baby," Aunt Hilda said. Everyone started shuffling around, moving chairs, and setting the table.

"Zemma would you run outside and tell the boys that supper is ready."

I did as I was told. Sally was right behind me. She wanted to see what Aunt Katrina was up to anyway. I stopped by Aunt Katrina and told her supper was ready.

"That's just fine I'm not a bit hungry," she snorted and glared at me, and Sally.

"Yes ma'am," I said, and went on my way.

We went on, then Sally turned around, went back and stood in front of Aunt Katrina.

"You know, Aunt Katrina, You're just a fat, mean old lady," Sally yelled at her.

"What! Why you little turd, I'll get you for that," she shouted, as she struggled to get out of the cane bottomed chair, she was breathless, she gave up, leaned back, and sat back down out of breath.

Sally ran back toward me, looking back over her shoulder, "Oh my, maybe I shouldn't have done that,"

"Maybe not, but good for you. I just hope she doesn't kill you," I said with a grin.

I went on outside and rounded up Daddy and Uncle Jim.

Aunt Ginger and Aunt Hilda took off their aprons, which meant they were through working, and sat down to eat.

Everyone sat down and started to eat, completely ignoring Aunt Katrina.

A few minutes later, she came in and sullenly pulled up a chair and plopped down in it making as much noise as she could. She looked around at everyone but no one was paying any attention to her, so she made more noise rattling her silverware and plate. She plunked her cup down making more noise. She piled her plate high, clear to the top, with food, and started munching noisily away.

"I think something is mentally wrong with her," I whispered to Sally.

"I'm glad she's only an in-law, then, and not related by blood," Sally whispered back.

"Aunt Ginger brought the lemon pie and Aunt Hilda brought the chocolate cake," Mama announced to everyone. "We need to give credit, where credit is due," Mama continued with a little laugh.

Everyone looked at Aunt Ginger and Aunt Hilda and clapped their hands, "We all kinda knew that," Aunt Mable said.

When we were all finished with supper. Aunt Ginger and Aunt Hilda jumped up, and Aunt Hilda announced, "We'll do the cleanup, so the cooks can get some rest, isn't that right girls," and the two started clearing the table.

"Thank you," Mama said.

"No thank you," Aunt Ginger said.

"That's right," Aunt Hilda said.

And several other ladies joined them, but Aunt Katrina didn't move a muscle, she just sat there with her arms folded and a sour look on her face. Everyone just walked around her.

"We best be heading for home while we still have the light," Aunt Hilda said.

Aunt Hilda and Aunt Ginger grabbed their coats and headed for the door. Mama and I quickly packed up food for them to take so they wouldn't have to cook for a day or two.

They eagerly took their food, thanked us as they went out the door and headed for home.

CHAPTER 9

Evening -Entertainmen- News-Radio

*E*verybody listened to the radio in the evenings like we did. After supper in the evening we would all gather around the tall, dark walnut colored box that sat against the back wall in the living room. That was our radio, and we would listen to the evening news. Mama and Daddy would sit in their favorite, and most comfortable rocking chairs, and we, the kids I mean, would huddle together, sitting on our blankets and pillows on the floor, next to the radio.

The newscaster would always start out with news about the depression and how the people were suffering. No jobs, no homes, nothing to eat. It was bad. Then he would go on to talk about the latest thing President Roosevelt was doing to help the people. They would talk about how he was implementing new work programs to help the people, especially the poor people.

President Roosevelt had created a program called W.P.A. which created jobs for the thousands of jobless people. The jobs included working on and building roads and other jobs he created to give people work.

After listening to all the terrible news of the day. We were always ready to listen to a funny program like Fibber Mcgee and Molly, then another one with a comedian Jack Benny, and another Fred Allen. We also liked Amos and Andy. It was a comedy about two black guys. They were really white guys pretending to be black guys, and they were really funny. I don't know why they didn't have black guys, being black guys. Go figure. And then there was a program called One Man's Family.

Tonight it was different; the announcer broke into the programming with a special news bulletin. He said there was a serial killer on the loose. He was on a rampage, mostly in Jackson. He was torturing and killing people. He had already killed six people, two at a time. The police didn't have any clues about who he was. They didn't know if it was one or two killers, because two kinds of weapons were being used, a gun and a knife.

The newscaster said the killer or killers were unusually blood thirsty, leaving a trail of blood and mayhem behind him or them. The newscaster warned everyone to be extra careful at nighttime, warning them to lock their doors and windows as soon as the sun went down. People just weren't used to locking their doors or windows, it was something people just didn't do. But the newscaster cautioned people, that even if they weren't used to locking things up they had better start now.

We all gasped and looked at each other.

"Thank goodness we live in the country and not in the city," Mama said.

Aunt Katrina squealed, "Oh, my good lord in heaven, may God have mercy on our souls. Jim, we got to get home now, right now I say." She had forgotten all about sulking.

"No, I said no, now forget about it," Uncle Jim was getting mad.

She snorted, turned and went back and plopped down in the chair again, folded her fat arms, and glared at everybody. Sara just looked at her mother with a disgusted look on her face. Poor Sara, I thought, it must be terrible having a mother like her.

I was getting nervous just thinking about the killer, but Mama and Daddy were calm about it.

Sara looked really nervous; she kept looking over her shoulder.

I looked at her and said, "Don't worry Sara, there's so many people here, the killer would be too scared to come in. He would definitely leave us alone. He'd be afraid to tangle with so many big guys, I said patting her on the shoulder.

"Besides, we're going to lock everything up," I said calmly.

She just nodded gratefully for the encouragement.

"He probably won't come out in the country anyway. It would be much easier for him to stay in the city. He would get too much attention out here, in the country. Since he would be a stranger and all, we would all certainly notice him," Daddy said.

"That makes sense," Mama said.

"Yeah, I think you're right," Jim said.

Sally started crying, "I know that killer is gonna get me, I'm gonna hide under my bed."

"It would serve you right, young lady, for having such a big mouth," Aunt Katrina," said glaring at Sally.

"Yeah and I'll tell him where you live, you mean old lady," Sally snorted through her tears.

Junior just sat there; his blue eyes were big and wide. "I hope he's not looking for us, I think I might hide under my bed too," he said nervously rubbing his hands together.

With everyone making so much noise, it woke Jenny up, and she started crying.

"Here, here now, quiet down, he isn't even here and he won't be. Why in the world would a killer be here? No one has anything of any value around here," she said and started rocking Jenny back to sleep.

Daddy and Uncle Oglee sat quite, listening to everything going on.

Then Daddy finally broke his silence, "What the heck, if he did show up we'd just beat the living tar out of him."

"Yeah," Uncle Oglee said, jumping up and started punching the air with both fists and everybody started laughing. That changed the mood and things settled down.

We all started discussing the news about the depression and what we thought was going to happen in the future.

When all the comedy programs were over, it was about eight thirty. It was time for bed, time to get everyone settled into the extra bedrooms.

I grabbed a kerosene lamp, and by now I could light the lamps myself, and I made a mad dash for our small room on the other side of the hallway. Sally was right on my heels with both the Sears and the Montgomery catalogues.

We each bounced on our sides of the bed.

Sara shared our bed with us. I told her she could pick the side of bed she wanted to sleep on. There was room enough for all of us including Lena.

Now we had a new game to play, usually we liked to taunt each other trying to convince the other one that they had been adopted. I usually won. I would wind up thinking I had convinced Sally she had been adopted because of her nose. It was different from everyone else's. It was short and upturned. But sometimes she had me concerned about where I came from, because I was so skinny. I was the thinnest one of the kids. Of course Mama always said she had found us both under a bramble bush in the desert.

Sara said she would read a book, while we played our silly game.

But tonight we had a new game, planning what we were going to buy with all the money we were going to make with our own cotton patch.

Sara dropped her book and became interested in our new game. I kinda felt sorry for Sara. Her mother Katrina treated her like her own personal slave. Aunt Katrina had Sara wait on her hand and foot. Aunt Katrina was so lazy she wouldn't even go, and get herself a glass of water, she would make Sara do it. She would make Sara do everything. It was really sad. She even made Sara take care of all the other kids in the family. I thought about Sara's lot in life and decided I would be nicer to her. It really wasn't fair what Sara had to live through.

"Say I'm gonna ask Daddy if I can have my own cotton patch too. I'll bet he'll say yes. Oh that would be a lot of fun. I can hardly wait until tomorrow to find out."

Fat chance, I thought, no way will they let her do that, but I didn't tell her that, instead I said, "Oh I know he'll let you have your own patch too," I said, "Just tell him that Daddy let us have our own patch."

Sara moved over where she could look at our catalogue, "Oh my goodness, look at all the good stuff. Just look at these beautiful dresses."

"What are you going to do with all the money you get from your crop?" I asked Sally.

"Oh, my, let me think," she said.

I was on my side with the Sears catalogue beside me on the bed, with a pencil and piece of lined paper torn from our school tablet. I was busy turning pages and writing down the things I was going to buy.

Suddenly Sally's paper went flying across the bed; I turned to see what was going on.

"What in the world is wrong with you?" I demanded upset because I had been right in the middle of choosing between blue, or pink bed ruffles. Now I forgot which one I liked the best and why.

Sally had tears running down her sunburned cheeks. I felt bad.

"What's the matter; you can't decide which one you like the best? What?"

"No darn it, I don't have a pencil," she sobbed.

"Is that all, we can find another pencil," I reassured her. I got out of bed and started rummaging through the drawers of the ancient worn out brown chest of drawers.

"Here I found one and it's even better than mine," I said as I handed the pencil to my sister.

Sally's dimple emerged immediately.

I grabbed my catalogue and began flipping the pages until I came to the bedroom accessories.

We all put our heads together and studied the pictures in both of the catalogues.

"What are you going to do with your money, Lena," I asked her because she looked so pensive, almost sad.

"I just love this doll. Isn't she beautiful? Look at her hair and eyes, she's so big, she's almost half as tall as me, when she's standing up. I'm afraid to love her too much, because something might happen and I won't be able to get her."

I felt sorry for her, because I knew how she felt. Your dolls became like people to you. I still loved my doll Betty. All I could tell her, "Nothing will happen, don't worry."

"I just can't make up my mind. They're all so beautiful."

We have to have curtains and a bedspread to match." I said laughing as I looked up at the old thin grey blanket that hung above the window. "Anything would be better than that," I said pointing up at the window, "agreed?" I asked.

"If I had a camera I'd take a picture for our scrapbook when we become famous for something or other." We started giggling and couldn't stop. "That's another thing I'm going to buy, is a camera."

"Oh yeah, that would be nice," Sally agreed, and wrote that down on her list.

"Sara, what are you buying with all your money? " I asked her.

"Oh, lots and lots of beautiful dresses."

"That would really be nice," I agreed.

I got out of bed and checked the window to make sure it was locked. I looked at Lena and Sally, "You just never know, better to be safe than sorry."

Just then the door opened and Junior came in clutching his pillow, and dragging his blanket. "Just thought I'd sleep in here with you guys."

"Sure, hop up at the foot of my bed," I said patting the mattress.

"Be sure and lock the door behind you," I reminded Junior.

We finally fell asleep. I fell asleep dreaming of our beautiful bedroom with a rose patterned covered bed spread, matching curtains, and all pink roses. With our own cotton patch, we would be rich. I could hardly wait for tomorrow to come.

Four o'clock came around pretty early in the morning. Mama was up making breakfast. I could smell the bacon and eggs, even pancakes, cooking.

Sally was shaking me, "We gotta get going on our cotton patch," She said.

It was still dark outside, and the fireflies were still flickering around.

Daddy had a roaring fire going in the fireplace, and two kerosene lamps lit. It smelled and looked like a beautiful picture. The lamp light cast an orange glow over everything. The dark shadows cast reflections on the walls. It was really cozy. For some reason the dark shadows weren't scary, they were comforting.

I just hoped the murderer wasn't lurking around outside, just waiting for us.

After breakfast we each took a lantern with us while we headed toward the barn to do our chores. I kept looking over my shoulder for the murderer.

"Let's stay close together just in case he is out here," I whispered to Junior

"You can count on it," Junior whispered back, his voice was shaking.

"What, what did you say? Sally demanded.

"Nothing," I whispered, "Just stay close," I said.

The three of us took turns doing our chores, feeding the chickens, slopping the pigs and gathering the eggs. By the time we were done, it was beginning to get daylight.

The roosters were crowing and the chickens were cackling. Everything outside was awake and waiting to be fed. Even though it was beautiful, it was still kind of spooky, outside watching our giant shadows from the kerosene lanterns leaping and bouncing against the high, wood barn and chicken coop walls. By the time we were done, it was beginning to get daylight.

CHAPTER 10

Planting Our Cotton Patch

What a beautiful sunrise, orange and red with streaks of yellow, the colors in the sunrise were moving fast leaving the sky with just hints of pink and yellow, and it wasn't long before they were all gone with nothing left, but the bright blue of the sky with sunlight and scattered white clouds covering the entire sky. Afterwards we were ready to head for our cotton patch. But we had to wait for Daddy to show us how to get started.

When Lena came back she had something in a paper sack. She looked at me with a secretive smile, then she sidled up to Mama, looked up at her with her black eyes shining and handed her the sack.

"My Mama had this before she died, and I know she would be happy if you had it, since she can't use it, because she's in heaven now, and she's only allowed to wear white robes," Lena said, her eyes shining with tears. I couldn't figure out what the heck she had. I moved in close so I could see what she had in the sack.

Mama pulled out a huge piece of beautiful bright colored material. I was shocked. It was beautiful. Pink roses on a pale grey background Mama gasped, "Oh my goodness child, you sweet little girl. Thank you. Are you sure you don't want to keep this, it's beautiful.

"No, my Mama can't use it."

Mama looked quickly at John with tears in her eyes, "Are you sure?"

He just smiled and nodded his head.

Daddy bent down and took little Lena's hand. "That was the nicest thing I've ever seen anyone do. Thank you, young lady."

"I'll treasure this." Mama said. "Your mother would be very proud of you."

I could see Mama was crying, as she turned and walked slowly back up the hill to the house.

When we finished the wash we brought it all back up the hill and hung everything out to dry on the line out back of the house.

We stopped for dinner.

"John, you and Lena stay for dinner," Daddy said. Mama had started cooking. earlier, before we had started washing, she had killed the chicken then Sally and I had picked all the feathers off the chicken. I had watched her as she dissected the chicken. She did it all with the efficiency of a doctor, as Daddy had often said, while he watched Mama. Mama was so smart, she knew how to do everything.

"Zemma, when we have more time I will show you how to dress a chicken," she said smiling down at me.

"I'd really like that. But I don't like the part of wringing the poor chicken's neck," I said remembering how the poor chicken squawked and hollered when Mama ran it down, caught it, grabbed it by the neck and twirled her around until it snapped the neck. After it snapped, she dropped it on the ground and the chicken went flopping around, its wings hitting the ground until it finally stopped. When I had protested at the sight, Mama reassured me. "Honey it's not hurting, that's just a reaction of the body after its dead."

"Are you sure?" I asked.

"I'm sure," she said.

The chicken was still warm when I picked it up and started plucking off the feathers. You don't have to worry about the feathers around the head," Mama said, and glanced at Sally, "And later Sally, I'll show you how to dress a chicken."

"I'm not a sissy, it wouldn't bother me none to wring its neck," Sally said, looking at me with a grin.

I didn't care so I let her; I would never ever like that part. I don't think she liked that part either, she was just trying to make me look like a sissy. I didn't care; let them think I was a sissy.

Mama reached over and gave me a little hug, "I know honey, and I hate that part too. But we have to eat; otherwise I would never do it. Not in a million years."

"Run out and pick some green beans girls."

We met Daddy and Junior coming back in with a bucket of corn, already husked."

John and Lena were sitting outside at the outdoor table. I knew they would eat out there and we would eat inside. I didn't know why, but that was just the way it was. When I had asked about it, I was told that was the custom and they didn't know why either. It was just that white folk and black folk didn't eat together. No one really knew why we didn't eat together. I thought it was really stupid, but there was nothing I could do about it.

John and Lena came in filled their plates up and went back outside to eat.

After I filled my plate, mostly with fried chicken, gravy, mashed potatoes and a biscuit or two. I went outside and sat beside Lena. They both looked up surprised.

"I like it better out here, the air's so fresh and sweet smelling," I said as I sat down beside Lena.

Sally wasn't too far behind me. "I think I'll join you," she said as she sat down with her plate.

"These house flies are sure pesky," I said as I swatted them with a paper. "You know Lena that was really nice of you to give Mama that dress material. She loves it."

"I thought she might cotton to the idea," Lena said a shy grin on her dark face. "You know Daddy said he would give me a patch of cotton too, he said, he just couldn't have me off in a corner crying my eyes out."

"Oh that's wonderful." I said looking at John. "Now we can compare notes on our cotton crops just like real farmers."

John just smiled, "Sounded like a good idea to me," he said looking down at Lena sitting beside him, "She's a good girl," he said.

"Don't you have any aunts or cousins that would like to have that material to make a dress?" I asked.

Lena looked down and just shook her head.

Mama came out and sat down. She looked at Lena. "You know you're about Sally's size, A little thinner I would think. If I have enough material left over after I make my dress, I can also make a dress for you out of the material. I really think there's enough for that".

"No, no you don't have to do that Mrs. Carter," Lena said, and her face broke into a shy smile, she looked just like the sun had suddenly appeared from behind a tree.

Mama reached over and measured the length of Lena's arms, and the length of her dress. Then she nodded. "This will be easy."

I continued on with my questions, "You don't have any relatives?"

John said "No, we don't have any living relatives left. Three years ago, scarlet fever took almost everyone. The ones that were left were killed by diphtheria. It got everybody just like the black plague. It was a terrible year. Lena's poor Mama had already gone to God."

John and Mama started talking about the depression and the prices of food.

"You know it's just downright unbelievable how the prices have gone up. The cost of gas went up to ten cents a gallon,' John said shaking his head.

"A loaf of white bread is all the way up to ten cents a loaf, I know we can never afford to buy white sliced bread," Mama said.

"Yeah, can you believe it; they actually have frozen food for sale."

When Daddy sat down, he had today's paper that Uncle John had given him. We couldn't afford the paper, so Uncle John always gave us the paper when he was through with it.

The news was pretty sad today.

"Oh my word, look at this," Daddy said, "Baby Faced Nelson has been shot and killed."

"Well, that's too bad," Mama said, picking up the paper and looking at the black and white photograph of Baby Face Nelson. "But that's what happens when you live that kind of life style. You live by the sword and you die by the sword."

"Yep, that's what the Bible says," Junior said, waving his arms around, as if he had a sword. On the front page was a big article and picture about how Baby Faced Nelson had been shot and killed in a shoot out with the F.B.I. It went on about how he was trapped and killed.

"Well, aren't you the smart one," Daddy said, turning and looking at Junior astonished.

We were all surprised at Junior's comment.

"Well anyway, we'll say a little prayer for Baby Faced Nelson, and remind God about how kind Baby Faced Nelson had been to us," Daddy said. "You know there's good in everybody,"

According to the latest statistics, people were dying like flies from starvation. They're even dying, while they are actually standing in long soup lines, waiting to be fed. Even the soup kitchens are running out of food.

"At least we'll always have beans and potatoes," Daddy said laughing.

"Nothing wrong with beans, potatoes and good old fashioned biscuits and gravy," John said.

"We're pretty lucky we live on a farm and can grow our own food," Mama said.

Suddenly something popped hitting and bouncing off the wooden table with a loud thud, and then it hit the ground. It was followed by still another and another. One right after the other it sounded like a shot gun.

We were pretty jumpy, ever since we had heard about the killer being on the loose.

"Oh my gosh, it's the murderer," Sally screamed. Everyone jumped up from the table and started looking around. Then we looked up into the tree.

It was pinecones coming from above. When I looked up, I could see this grey squirrel deliberately knocking pine cones down, trying to hit us.

"For a minute I thought the killer had found us," I said, breathing a sigh of relief.

"Me too," Sally echoed.

"For just a second I thought about that too," Daddy said. We all laughed. "I think we should name him Ornery," Daddy said. So we did. He was known as Ornery ever after that. That cussed squirrel wouldn't move. We all had to pick up the table and move it under another tree. Coco and Nonie were barking at him, but the squirrel just fussed back at them.

After the commotion settled down, John and Lena went home. Sally, Daddy and I went to the other side of our house and looked at our new piece of land. I was so proud and I hadn't done anything yet. I was anxious; I wanted to get started right now.

"Come here," Daddy said. "Follow me and I'll get the seed for you and you already know how to plant it and do all the rest."

"How does this make you feel?" He asked, his green eyes scanned our faces.

"Like a million bucks," Sally shouted. Her voice carried across the field and into the next county I'm sure.

"I just don't know what to say, I'm so proud Daddy. Thank you," I said hoping I wouldn't cry. That would really be embarrassing.

Little Junior came up. "What about me. I want a cotton patch too, Daddy."

"Well Son you're just a mite too young. Next year will be your coming out year," Daddy said as he reached down and ran his fingers through Junior's sun bleached tow head.

"But I'm a boy, and that should count for something."

"Well not in these modern days, it doesn't," Daddy assured him.

"It just isn't fair," He insisted stubbornly.

I thought about it for a minute, and then I said, "You can have half of mine. We'll be partners."

His round freckled face suddenly crinkled with a unexpected lopsided smile, with of course the two teeth missing. "You won't be sorry, partner," he said, reaching out for my hand and shaking it. He stretched himself up like he had just grown a foot taller. I looked at him, and by golly he really did seem to be a foot taller.

Daddy looked at me, "Now you can't change your mind if you should get mad at him. A deal's a deal. Actually if you guys want to, you can draw up a written contract and sign it, like a real business deal, which it is."

"Why sure, we can do that. That would be fun," I said.

"Daddy, that's not fair, she'll have someone to help her, and I won't have anybody," Sally said.

"Yes, but just think about it, you will get to keep all of the money and she will have to give Jr. half of her money. What do you think about that," Daddy reminded her.

Sally was quiet for a minute, then she smiled, revealing two recently missing front teeth, seemed like everybody was missing teeth but me. "That's right, come payday I'll be rich."

When we got to the barn Daddy rummaged around until he found a sack of cotton seed. There wasn't much left in there, but he poured out what there was. There was about a coffee can full of seed. He divided it up into two equal parts. He gave me one, and one to Sally.

I found another empty can and divided my half into two halves, and I let junior take his pick and I kept the other.

"Be careful and don't spill it, Junior," I cautioned him. He was so little I was afraid he might trip or something and spill it.

"Now I think you should know something about cotton and how to take care of it," Daddy said.

" First you dig little trenches and plant the cotton seed and firmly pack the dirt down all around it, " He said squatting down and picking up a little stick and scratched about an inch deep furrow in the ground, "like so" he said standing back up.

"After it comes up you'll wait about two months, and it will start to have flower buds called squares that will appear on the cotton plants. In about another three weeks the blossoms will open. Their petals will change from creamy white to yellow then pink and finally dark red.

"Then after about three days they will wither and fall, leaving green pods, which are called cotton bolls. Inside the boll which is shaped like a tiny football, moist fibers grow and push out from the newly formed seed. As the boll ripens, it turns brown. The fibers continue to expand under the warm sun.

The fibers finally split the boll open and the fluffy cotton bursts out. It looks just like white, fluffy cotton candy.

Now it's ready for harvesting. You can start picking. The crop was done. You take it to the cotton gin and collect your money. Next you get out your old trusty Sears catalogue and the rest you know," he ended with a big grin.

Afterward, back at the house, Mama had changed and fed Jenny and put her down for a nap. She hoped it would be\ an while, because sometimes Jenny was cranky, restless and colicky and just wouldn't go to sleep.

She had the material spread out across the table. It was a huge piece. Mama was really smart; she didn't need a pattern to make a dress. She could just measure and figure it all out just by looking. Everybody told her she should do that to make money, but Mama said no one she knew had the money to buy hand made clothes. Daddy liked to sit out on the porch and visit with the neighbors that came by. Right now Bob Anderson, the deputy sheriff, stopped by and they were talking about what all the neighbors were doing.

I heard them talking about the serial killer that was running a muck in Jackson. Bob said that there was no chance the killer would come out in the country. That was good news to hear.

Usually I loved to sit and listen to what the grownups were saying, and Mama was always telling me to get outside and get some sun, as if I needed more sun. That was a joke. But tonight I felt restless, I had a date with Sear's Catalogue, and it beckoned to me. That for once, would be more fun than listening to the grownups talk. Sally had already gone to our room, and I knew she was already making plans on how to spend all that money; we were going to get from our crops. She was wearing out the Sears Catalogue before I even had a chance to put my order in.

I called Junior before he went to bed. "Let's make our contract out partner."

He came running with pencil and paper in hand.

We sat down at the dining table and started figuring out how to make out our contract.

Daddy was sitting at the table with a big grin on his face.

Junior and I both looked at Daddy.

"Now Daddy how do we make out our contract?" I asked.

Daddy just smiled at us, "Just say, I Zemma and I Junior agree to be equal partners in our joint cotton crop. We agree to pay equal expense and agree to share equally in the profits from the cotton crop. You both sign and date it, and you both have a copy. That's all there is to it. We did exactly what he said, and were very proud of ourselves as we waved our papers around.

I checked on Mama and Daddy before I went to bed. Mama was cutting out her dress and Daddy was reading. He was reading out loud so that Mama could hear the story too. They both loved Zane Grey. But they also loved to read philosophy. They had told us all about Socrates, Diogenes, Plato and a few others I couldn't remember. They usually read together sitting by the roaring fire in the fire place. They would also take turns reading out loud. I could see Junior.

sitting on the wood floor beside Daddy, his head was leaning against Daddy's legs. His eyes were half closed, but he was still wide awake listening.

We usually sat around and listened too, but not tonight. Sally and I had too many plans to make on how to spend all the money, we were going to make with our cotton crop.

Sally and I drifted off to sleep exhausted from all the mental activity we had just put ourselves through.

CHAPTER 11

The Tornado John Hurt

When morning came, we had a lot of stuff to do. Since it was summer we didn't have any school. We rushed through our chores so we could get busy working our field. I let Junior get all his chores done before, I yelled for him to come help me with the cotton planting.

By the time Junior got there Sally and I had already divided our field up between us.

The phone rang. It was too early for someone to call. It was only four o'clock in the morning. When Mama answered the phone, she gasped. "Are you sure, Aunt Ginger?"

She had hung up the phone just as Daddy came rushing through the kitchen door, slamming the screen door shut behind him. "My God, it's looks terrible outside," he yelled.

"There's a tornado headed our way." Mama yelled back. "What shall we do?"

"Get in the basement," Daddy yelled. Mama grabbed Jenny, her bottle, blanket and diapers and ran outside and down the basement steps into the basement. Daddy grabbed Junior, "Come on kids," he yelled over his shoulder.

Uncle Oglee grabbed Sally by the hand and rushed her into the basement.

"Oh dear, this is just what I was afraid of, tornadoes," I moaned, as I felt myself starting to shake all over.

I was close behind everyone as I grabbed our two dogs, Nonie and Coco. "Hey Sally, come here and take one of the dogs, help me hurry up."

"No, no, you bring them here, I'm already in the basement and I'm not coming out," Sally yelled back.

"Darn you Sally I'll remember this," I literally screamed at her.

"Here I got them," Uncle Oglee came back, reached down and took both dogs from me and headed back down for the cellar door.

"Come on honey," he said motioning for me to stay with him, he reached back with his free hand and took my arm and helped me down the steps

I was so mad at Sally; I could have strangled her with my bare hands. For the life of me I couldn't keep the tears of rage, from running unchecked down my dirt smudged face.

After we were all in, Daddy reached up and pulled the basement door closed just in the nick of time too, just as a large red can of something hit the half open door.

There was a terrible crash above. I was so scared, my teeth just chattered so loud I couldn't talk. I was freezing to death.

This was exactly what I had nightmares about. It had suddenly turned freezing cold. There was so much noise above us. Clanging, banging and bumping noises. It sounded just like it would break right through the top of the cellar door.

This was terrible, what if one of us had been out in the cotton field or down by the creek and we couldn't get to them in time. Thank God everyone was here. My mind kept racing with all the what if's.

I could hear the chickens squawking, and all the animals crying and yelping.

The dank, damp, moldy smell of the cellar almost made me want to throw up. There were all kinds of spiders down here with us, I am sure that included a few black widow spiders with the red dots on their bellies. I was really afraid of black widow spiders, almost as much as tornados. The floor was red dirt, the kind of dirt that would stick to your clothes and was really tough to get out. Of course that was the least of our worries.

We waited for a while, until eventually everyone stopped crying. It finally got quiet. Sally and the baby were still sniffling. I was holding on to Junior trying to be the big brave sister, but I could see and feel the silent tears running down Junior's freckled cheeks and splashing on my bare arm.

Junior was quiet.

"Listen," Daddy said, "We're completely safe here, and nothing can touch us, so settle down and don't worry. This is really why we have a cellar. Just think, it would have been such a waste if it had never been used. Of course we did use it.

We stored everything down here, Irish potatoes, yams and onions. Mama's canned tomatoes, peas, beans and corn. I didn't mention to Daddy that we were just plain lucky to be all be together when the tornado hit. Because I knew he was just trying to calm us down.

I couldn't hear what anyone was saying because of the racket outside. Coco and Nonie were barking, and Jenny was whimpering. It was almost too much.

It was so sad; I could hear the poor chickens crying. The cows Molly, and Josephine, the billy goat Jake, and our two horses old Dan and Mary were all in the barn. If the barn hadn't blow away, they would be safe.

I worried about what we would find when this was all over.

About an hour later, we decided it was all over. Daddy raised the cellar door and the wind was still blowing so hard, it almost pushed and swept us back down into the cellar. Paper, dirt and branches were still flying around.

A small limb whacked me in the face as I crawled out of the cellar on my hands and knees. It didn't hurt much, but it scared the heck out of me. I looked up and the sky was a mess. Debris, dirt and dust were all floating around making the sky a hazy grey. The sun had disappeared leaving just a faint yellow glow behind the broken, dark grey clouds.

"Are you hurt honey?" Mama asked as she brushed the leaves out of my hair, and used her apron to wipe the blood off my cheek.

"No, no." I said, shaking. I was still trying to be brave as I looked around at all the devastation. This was even worse than my nightmares had been. The chicken shed was flattened clear to the ground, parts of it everywhere. There was blood all over the ground. Dead chickens were scattered everywhere, even on top of the sheds. There were a couple of crying, squawking chickens caught up in trees, flapping their wings.

But the good news was the barn was still standing. Molly, Josephine, Mary, Dan and Jake our goat were all still standing although a little discombobulated as Daddy would say.

As I looked at the house I noticed some of the shingles had flown off the roof to only God knows where. Some windows were broken. There was glass all over the floor, junk everywhere.

"Let's go see if our Sears Catalogue is still there," I yelled at Sally.

Daddy turned the radio on.

"I got it," Sally said with a grin as she pulled out both of the catalogues, from under her worn out blue sweater.

"Oh sure Sally, you would save paper catalogues, but not your poor, little, live pet animals. Wouldn't you know it; she had taken the catalogues to the cellar with her. Sure she could bring the catalogues, but she couldn't help me with the dogs.

"Oh I knew you would save them," she said, with what looked like a smirk on her face.

Oh, well that was just Sally, she just couldn't help herself. I just had to shake my head, bless her heart.

Daddy turned on the radio; it was still in one piece only because Daddy had thought to bring it to the cellar with him when the tornado started.

"There's a lot of devastation along the Sepsi Creek run. Several families were hurt and lost everything," the male announcer on the radio said, "so far we have heard of several deaths," he went on.

"Isn't that where John lives," Oglee asked, looking worried.

"Oh my goodness I hope it isn't anyone we know." Mama said, clutching her hands together.

"That would be kind of hard since we know everybody," Daddy said.

That was true I thought. We did know everyone. I was afraid to find out who had been killed. I really hoped it wasn't John.

I heard someone crying, I turned and looked out the door. There stood little Lena with blood all over her. Her dress was almost torn off. Her bare legs were scratched and bloody. Her arms and face was covered in blood.

"My Daddy, my Daddy's hurt please come help."

Mama ran to her, picked her up and carried her to the kitchen.

"Just sit still honey while I clean up your wounds," Mama whispered hugging her, as she reached under the sink for a clean wash cloth. "Zemma bring me a towel and a pan of water."

Daddy took off on a long run out the door and down the path to John's house.

"Don't worry Lena; my Daddy has gone to look after your Daddy," I told her. "He'll take care of him. He can fix anything."

Lena looked at me, her eyes brimming with tears. "I think it's too late," she said in the middle of a fresh burst of tears. She was standing there, her thin body was shaking from head to toe. My heart sank. That would be terrible, I thought.

She doesn't have any one else, no family, no one, what would she do. They would probably ship her off to an orphanage for black kids. I couldn't stand the thought.

We were all waiting for Daddy to come back home with the news of what had happened at John's place. Sally ran out back to see if the tornado had harmed our cotton patch, which I tried to tell her the tornado wouldn't hurt flat land without anything on it. She came back grinning from ear from ear, and I knew for sure nothing was wrong.

Aunt Ginger came rushing up the steps and into the kitchen, "Is everyone o.k.?" she gasped out of breath.

"We're all fine," Mama said, "and how is your family?"

"We made it through o.k. Sam's a little upset. It kind of wrecked the project he was working on. He was almost finished. He was making an oak wood set of table and chairs for a customer. Now it's scattered in pieces all over creation and the countryside."

"That's a darn shame Aunt Ginger, he does such beautiful work," Mama said sympathetically.

"I tried to call, but of course the phone was out of order," Aunt Ginger continued. "Like I told Sam, the important thing is that everyone was safe. We got the kids into the cellar. Thank goodness they were both home, when the tornado hit."

CHAPTER 12

The Dress

When I checked Mama and Daddy's room to see if there had been any damage done in there, I saw Lena's dress all finished, spread out flat on the bed. It was beautiful. It had a white bow at the neckline which was just the touch it needed. I was so proud of Mama, the miracle worker. I didn't know how she did it but she had finished Lena's dress last night. She must have stayed up all night long.

After Mama had patched Lena up with bandages, peroxide and iodine, she sat Lena in a chair. She ran to her bedroom and quickly came back holding Lena's dress in her hands.

Lena gasped. Her black eyes looked like huge saucers. "Oh dear lord look at that, is that mine?" she whispered looking at Mama.

Mama just nodded and smiled.

"But where's your dress?" Lena asked

"It coming in its own good time. Come over here little girl, and lets try this on and see if I need to alter it a bit here and there."

Mama slipped Lena's old dress off over her head, and then slipped the new dress back over her head and pulled it down over her thin hips.

Everyone gasped. "It's beautiful," I said, "It fits perfect. Mama how did you do that? How did you know what size to make it?" I asked.

"Mama you are a genus," Sally said.

"You mean genius," Mama said.

Sally looked taken a back, and a little sullen. "I mean a really smart lady."

"That will work, thank you honey," Mama said, and Sally looked happy again.

Daddy opened the door and came in; we hadn't even heard him coming. He looked surprised when he saw Lena. "You look pretty as punch in that dress."

Lena was standing against the kitchen wall, her arms wrapped around herself. "Thank you, Mr. Carter. How's my Daddy?" Lena asked, looking anxiously up at Daddy.

Daddy went over to her, bent down and gave her a hug. "Your Daddy is pretty sick right now, but he's going to be alright. Frank and George helped me get him out from under those beams that had fallen on top of him. They are on their way to the hospital right now. We called Dr. Roberts and he got there as fast as he could. He was there in time to save his life. That man's a saint."

"You'll take care of my Daddy won't you?" Lena begged, her big black eyes looked up at my Daddy, her tears were making pathways down both of her dirt smudged cheeks. Her eyes were glazed with fear. Her lips were trembling as she searched for more words.

"My poor Daddy, I want to be with my Daddy." She pleaded. "He'll be all by his self. He will be so scared."

"No, your Daddy won't be alone. Besides he's really brave. He'll be with all the nurses and Doctors at the hospital. He's going to be just fine after they get through working on him,"

Lena slid down, with her back against the wall until she sat on the floor. "What about me, can't I go too?" She leaned forward and put her head in her hands and cried softly "I don't have anybody. Where can I go? I guess I'll have to go to the colored orphanage."

Mama went over to her, sat down in one of the cane bottom chairs and pulled her up off the floor and into her lap. "No, don't be silly, you won't have to go to an orphanage."

But Lena thought she knew better and kept sobbing quietly.

"You'll stay right here with us until your Daddy get's back home. He has just got a couple of broken bones and a cut on his leg, outside of that he's perfectly alright."

"Mama, maybe you can give her an aspirin, so she can go to sleep?" Daddy said looking anxious.

"Let's make a bed for her, over here by the fireplace so she'll be warm all night. He had no sooner said that, when we had all gotten together and made a bed for her out of four orange crates tied together. Daddy went to the back room and brought out a single bed mattress for Lena to sleep on. We usually used that for a pallet for any babies that came to visit. Then they brought out a pillow and several blankets to put over her.

"I'll sleep with her so she won't be scared," Sally said.

CHAPTER 13

Our Guest Lena

*M*ama and Daddy went into the next room to talk privately. That was a signal for Sally and me to sneak around the corner, into the next room, when no one was looking. We could put our ear to the thin wall and listen to what they were saying.

"What are we going to do with the poor little thing?" Daddy asked.

"Well we sure can't let them haul her off to an orphanage. Those places are hell holes, " Mama said.

"What happened?" Mama asked.

"Poor John was trapped under some timbers. Thank God, George and Frank were already there. We were all trying to get him from under the timbers without hurting him. He was bleeding like a stuck pig, the blood was gushing from the arterial artery in his thigh, but I managed to tie it off and stop the bleeding. But all John could think about was Lena. He made me promise I would take care of her. He told me to go over where there was still part of a room left."

I went over where there was a butcher block table with a drawer in it. It was turned over on the ground. He said to get all the papers out of there and bring them over to him, which I did.

He had me write that I would take care of Lena until she grew up in case he didn't make it. Die, that is. He insisted that I write the word adopt." Daddy stopped and looked at Mama.

"What else could I do? I thought he was a dying man, so I would have signed anything he wanted."

"It's going to be okay, John isn't going to die like he thought," Daddy added.

"Adopting, that would have been pretty difficult anyway. I don't even know if they would let white people adopt a black child," Mama said.

"I think we could find a way to adopt her if we really had to," Daddy said.

"Don't worry; it won't come to that because John's going to be alright."

"Yeah, after we signed everything, we told him he wouldn't have to worry about anything, because we had managed to stop the bleeding. He was relieved, he sighed, closed his eyes and I could tell he was praying."

I was peeking through a little crack in the door frame and I could see Daddy run his hand over his eyes.

"Oh God, it was terrible. He was bleeding so bad I thought he was a goner. He looked deader than a door nail. My Lord things can sure happen in a hurry."

"George and Frank took John on into town to the hospital, which was only about ten miles. It was probably so rough in that old truck, that it seemed like a hundred and fifty miles to John," Daddy finished, wrapping up his tale of what happened.

Sally and I rushed back into the living room without getting caught. Mama and Daddy sauntered back in. We were all busy looking at different things that the tornado had torn up. Lena was still sound asleep.

"You know Mama, our bed is big enough for all three of us to sleep in. Sally, Lena and I," I said

"You're right," she said.

"When I went to John's house, it was torn up completely; it lay flat on the ground flatter than a pancake. I found him under a six by six timber." Daddy was telling every one. Of course we already knew about everything because we had spied on them.

The door opened and Uncle Jim and Aunt Katrina and all six kids came rushing through the door, slamming it behind them. I knew Mama must be thrilled. We had all lived together at one point in time back in Texas, and I think that's when the hostility started.

CHAPTER 14

The Birds and The Bees

And as I mentioned before I didn't think much of Sara either. She was just a little older than I was, about fourteen I thought, but she was a terrible tattle tale and trouble maker. Not only that but she was so unpleasant, always whining about something or other. I had to admit she seemed to know a little bit about everything, boys especially. Stuff like that. She hung out with boys all the time. I had to say, she had tons of hair raising stories to tell me. I couldn't resist listening to her. I enjoyed hearing about all her escapades with the boys.

She told me about the time when she first started getting boobs, she went behind the barn and showed all the boys that were around, her new boobs. I could not believe my ears. She was pretty plump, so her boobs were very big.

Of course I didn't have any boobs yet, but I certainly would not show them to anyone, if I did have boobs.

"See," she said suddenly raising her shirt. Oh yes, she certainly had boobs all right.

"Put your shirt back down," I said, "quick before someone sees you."

"I don't care if they do see me, I have something to show them," she said laughing, "you're just jealous.

"I'm not either, that's just disgraceful," I shouted. Even though I was just a little jealous, I would never in a million years admit it.

She's the one who told me about the birds and the bees. I mean she told me how babies were born and I was so shocked, I thought I was going to faint from pure horror. Of course I didn't believe her for a minute. I had always heard that the stork brought babies and I was positive that was the way it was.

I wert directly to Mama. I'll never forget the look on her face. I would say it was a look between surprise and dismay. Her blue eyes got a little bigger and she kept looking up toward the ceiling, as she mumbled," Hmmm."

"Honey come over here sit down with me and I will explain it all to you," she said as she pulled a chair out for me to sit down.

A terrible feeling of fear shot through me, a horrible thought came to me. What if it's true? Oh dear lord I hope not, I thought. Oh no, this terrible feeling of dread came over me.

We sat down; she was quiet for a minute as she thoughtfully ran her fingers along the flowered tablecloth. Then she started her story about how love was beautiful, and when a man and woman fall in love and get married they would come together in a special way so they could have a baby, and start their own family. She went on to explain why men and women were built different so they could make the coming together work. It was basically what Sara had told me, but totally different.

Still, after that every thing was a blur as she went on to explain a little more in detail. Then she explained that menstruation was a woman's body's way of preparing for the wonderful act of creation. She went on to explain that would happen to me soon. She said when it happened to me, I would feel a little uncomfortable. I would bleed a little down there, you know where you go pee, for several days, and then when it was over I would feel fine again.

"When does this happen?"

"Every month."

"Every month! Oh lord that's terrible," I felt sick. I thought I was going to throw up.

"No, no, don't think of it that way honey. Remember every woman goes through this."

"But that's not fair, what happens to the boy when all this is happening to a girl?"

"Well actually nothing, but he doesn't get to feel the joy of motherhood. He misses out on all those beautiful feelings. God made us special. He put us in charge of carrying on the human race. What a wonderful responsibility we have been given and trusted us with, don't you think?"

I just nodded. I was sitting there in a state of shock. It didn't sound too special to me. I had heard my aunt Alice screaming her head off when little Earl came into the world. Now I understood it all. They had told us that Aunt Alice had accidentally spilled a pot of hot boiling water on her stomach when she was lifting it off the stove, just before the stork delivered the baby Earl. It all hit me like a bolt of lightning. Now, I also understood why grownup women would say their visitor had come, and that was why they felt terrible.

After that conversation, I would never be the same again. I got up and stumbled off toward my bed. I just wanted to go to bed, pull the sheet up over my head and go to sleep, and never wake up again. I could feel my mother's sympathetic eyes on my back following me as I stumbled away.

Thinking about how this all started, I thought about my cousin's story. So she was right, not completely right, but right enough about the important parts.

I remembered how it had all started. We were arguing with my cousin Sara, and about all the things she had told us.

But to be fair, my sister Sally and I weren't angels either. We would tease her. One time, (we were in the same class at school) she accidentally wet her pants and we teased her so bad. The poor thing went home crying, then I did feel bad.

We also teased her when the teacher spanked her. We told her the teacher beat all the silk out of her new dress. We were actually jealous because she had a store bought dress, made out of what we thought was silk. We thought that was funny, but it really wasn't, after I thought about it. I was sorry and ashamed of myself later.

But when she told Aunt Katrina and Mama about it, I was even sorrier. The lecture I got still makes my ears burn. Aunt Katrina thought I needed a good slap up side the head. I would much rather have had a slap, instead of the talking to that I got. I really felt like a worm after that. Any way I didn't think much of Aunt Katrina or Sara.

CHAPTER 15

Prejudice

When Aunt Katrina saw Lena on the floor pallet with the rest of us, I thought she was going to get a hatchet and chop us all up into little pieces. She covered the lower half of her face with her hands, and gasped.

I watched her grab Mama by the arm and pull her into the next room.

"You're crazier than a hoot owl," She yelled. You people haven't got a lick of sense, letting your girls sleep with that little black girl? No telling what she has and they will catch it.

"You just shut up and mind your own business, you know you're meaner than a crooked snake," Mama said, stopping her in her tracks and turning to her. "If you don't like it, you can just pack up your brood and leave this house right now."

I was ready to rush to Mama's side to help her, but to my surprise, she didn't need any help from me or anybody for that matter.

Was I proud of her? Anyway Aunt Katrina rushed off to tell Uncle Jim all about it, but I don't think it did her any good because Uncle Jim was definitely the boss in that family.

I soon realized danger loomed ahead when Oglee walked in. He kept running his long tapered fingers through his black windblown hair, trying to make it lay down without combing it. He looked like a handsome dangerous pirate. That was when I saw Sara staring at him. She was obviously smitten. She glanced at him, with what was supposed to be a come hither look as she casually, lightly brushed her hair away from her face with her bright red colored fingernails.

I thought I was going to throw up again. It seemed like I had been feeling like throwing up a lot since Sara arrived. I rushed over to Oglee's side, determined to put a stop to whatever Sara had planned to do. I grabbed Oglee by his shirt pocket and led him, more like yanked him into the hallway. "What the heck?" he gasped.

"Stay away from her," I whispered, glaring back at Sara, "She's no good."

He glanced at her quickly, then back at me, "Oh heck that's easy, she's just a little kid, not even my type."

"Thank goodness, you know she's really only fourteen, even though she dresses and acts a lot older," I whispered.

He just laughed that wicked laugh, and his black eyes twinkled, "You silly thing I've got better things to do than waste my time on little kids. I've gold hunting to do."

I was relieved. Thank goodness, I had warned him just in the nick of time. She hadn't impressed him at all; he knew how old she really was.

I moved casually away to the other side of the room and continued to watch for further developments.

Sure enough, Sara sashayed back over to Uncle Oglee as he came back into the living room.

She reached over and grabbed him by the arm, looked up and actually batted her eyes and said something. I couldn't hear what she was saying, but I could certainly tell she was flirting. I wanted to throttle her. I could feel my face getting hot. If I could only get my hands on her, I would strangle her; I mean really kill her if I thought I could get away with it. Well not really cause I wouldn't want to go to hell, but I would sure like to.

He smiled, and gently disengaged her hand from his arm, and said something I couldn't hear, and moved around her.

Sara looked stunned, then I could see her eyes searching for me. Somehow, she knew I had something to do with this. I quickly averted my face, turned and moved toward the outside door.

"What did you tell him?" I heard this angry voice behind me, definitely Sara's voice.

A tremor of fear ran up my spine. How far would she go?

"Whatever do you mean?" I asked, completely innocent, making sure my green eyes were wide open and innocent looking, as I turned and stared at her.

"You bitch," she said.

I was shocked. No one had ever called me a bitch before. I had to get a breath of fresh air, after being called a bitch. I looked for the door and made a beeline for it. I stalked off because I simply couldn't think of anything to say that was as wicked as what she had called me.

I bumped into Oglee outside.

"Was she pissed, I mean mad?" he asked with a chuckle, after he saw the look on my face.

"I should say so, she called me a bitch," I said, still smarting under the insult.

Oglee started laughing. "I wish I could have been a fly on the wall."

We continued to clean up the mess after the Tornado. Everything began to settle down.

Everyone was tired and hungry, and of course we had a huge dinner of fried chicken, mashed potatoes, gravy and corn.

Little Lena was staying with us until her Daddy was well, and of course after that Uncle Jim and aunt Katrina went home sooner than they had planned.

And I thought, what's gonna happen next.

CHAPTER 16

Visit to Hospital

The next morning the sun was shining and everything had settled down until almost normal.

We were all eating breakfast and Lena kept looking at Daddy and clearing her throat, as if she was trying to say something.

"Mr. Carter, do you think I could go see my Daddy sometime," she finally got it out.

"Sure honey, maybe even this afternoon when we get through with all our chores," he said smiling at her, he reached over and patted her hand.

"Where is the County hospital, is it very far?" Lena asked.

"It's not very far, I'd say about twenty miles or so, about half as far as it is to Jackson."

"Oh thank you so much, Mr. Carter," Lena said, as she looked up with tears in her eyes.

"Oh, can I go too?" I asked.

"Sure," he said.

"I think I'll run to the library and check out some gold hunting books," Uncle Oglee said.

Daddy filled an empty bucket with water just in case the radiator ran dry on the way to town. "I've been having radiator problems, so I don't want to take a chance it will run dry," he said as he put the bucket of water in the truck.

It seemed like a short trip. We were there before we knew it.

When we got to the hospital, and went in, I was truly shocked. The place stunk to high heaven. I really did feel like I was going to get sick. How could these people work, smelling this all day?

When Daddy told the fat, blond lady behind the desk fanning herself with a newspaper, who we were, and who we were there to visit, she told us we had to go around back, to the black section of the hospital. Each time she would wave the newspaper, the flies that had settled on a piece of white cake on the desk would scatter, flying everywhere until one settled on my arm. I shook it off, thinking, oh my gosh, I wonder where he's been. I didn't know they ever allowed flies in a hospital.

The nurse shook her head angrily, and pointed at Lena, "She's black, and she can't be in this part of the hospital.

"You can't make her do that, it's not right," I said, my voice was shaking because I was so mad.

The nurse jumped up from her chair, pointed her forefinger toward the front door and said in such a loud voice, you could hear her all the way down the street. "You get to the back, all of you, now get."

I looked at Daddy. I was so mad I could spit.

"Zemma, let's go to the back. It's a rule, I know it's a rotten rule, but it's a rule."

So around to the back we went. I glanced at Lena and tears were running down her little cheeks.

Uncle Oglee glared at the nurse, turned, reached down and picked Lena up and carried her in his arms out the door.

"You should be ashamed of yourself," he yelled back over his shoulder.

She slammed the newspaper on the desk and yelled, "Get,"

So, around to the back and on to the other side of the building we went. I was still muttering to myself.

"Daddy why do they have rules like that," I asked.

"I don't know honey, just ignorance. When people grow up being taught one way they just don't know any better. I was taught the same way. I used to think the same way, when I was young. I didn't know any better until I left and lived among people that thought different. That's when I realized it was wrong to think that way. Someday these people will know better, I hope. Or maybe not, maybe they'll always be ignorant. Like I say, most of them are good people; they just don't know any better"

I mulled that over for a while. I looked over at Lena. She really looked cute in the new dress Mama had made for her. It had a wide white collar with a big bow in the front at the neck.

When we walked into the small, grey room where Jim was, he had his eyes closed. He looked like he was sleeping. He jerked when we made a noise, and his eyes opened wide with surprise. Lena ran into the room and threw her arms around his neck and started crying.

It even smelled worse here, than it did in the front. And the flies were everywhere.

The walls were bad. They were grey color, with ugly blackish spots all over them, as if somebody had tried to clean some dirty spots and it had only made it worse.

"My what a pretty dress, where did you get it?" Jim asked Lena.

"Mrs. Carter made it for me out of the material that I gave her. Remember right before the tornado."

"Yeah, yeah, but I thought she was going to make herself a dress."

"I know, but she made one for me first, and she said she would make one for herself after she was finished with mine. She said there was plenty of material for both.

"That was right nice of her," Jim said.

"Who did your hair honey? It's mighty pretty, too."

"Mrs. Carter did," Lena said smiling shyly, looking down at her feet.

Mama had gotten Aunt Matilda's housekeeper, Lula Bell, who was black, to teach her how to fix Lena's hair. It turned out pretty. She had put red ribbons in the braids. When she got through, she looked like a little doll.

Jim nodded his head in approval. He looked like a mummy with bandages everywhere.

He had a cast on his right arm and leg, and a white bandage across his forehead and all the way around the top of his head.

"Jim, I wanted to tell you not to worry about your crop, everyone is pitching in and working the fields for you."

"Really, naw, you're fooling me."

"Nope, everyone, even people from thirty, forty miles away."

Jim lowered his head, but not before we could see tears roll down his weath-ered cheeks.

"Bless their hearts, who would have thought it. Tell um thanks for me. They can count on me to repay them as best I can."

"They don't expect anything like that from you. They just want you to hurry up and get well. The doctor said it won't be long and you will be out of here," Daddy said.

I looked around; the window could stand a good cleaning. The scenery outside was pretty depressing. Garbage cans lying on their sides, with gar-bage spilled out all around, like raccoons had paid a visit during the night before. Dead weeds and grass knee high. You could tell no one had ever cut the weeds.

There were two other patients in the same room with Jim. Both of them looked pretty sick. One looked like he was in a coma or something. He didn't move. Flies were sitting all over his face and hands. I moved over and started shooing them away from him, but it didn't do any good. They would come right back and settle at the corners of his mouth. So I finally pulled the sheet up over his face. At least that would keep them out of his mouth. He didn't move. He didn't even look like he was breathing. The other one was trying to get a nurse. He kept coughing and struggling to breathe.

He kept pushing the call button, but no one came. The skinny little old man was white headed with a white beard. He even had a grey tint to his black skin. You could call him a grey man.

Uncle Oglee couldn't stand it any longer. He went over to the poor man and asked him if he wanted help in getting a nurse.

The man nodded his head with a weak smile on his thin, wrinkled face. Uncle Oglee rang the bell and waited, and waited and waited some more.

"This thing must be broken," Uncle Oglee said, and he tromped out the door and down the hall.

"Hey somebody," he yelled down the hall, "We need some help down here,"

Finally Daddy got out of his chair, went out the door, down the hall, and disappeared around the corner. We could hear some loud talking then Daddy coming back followed by a huge black guy.

"Now what's the matter here, Jackson?" The huge black giant of a man demanded as he stomped up and stopped at the foot of the bed. He stood with both hands on his hips glaring down at the little old grey man.

"I had an accident," the little, grey man whispered fearfully, we could barely hear him.

"Oh hell no, Jackson, yo didn't, when all you gotta do is ring that dammed bell there, you hear. Whatcha think that's there, fer? Ring that bell," the big black man yelled again as he picked up the ringer and swatted the frail, little man with it.

"Now who do yu think's gonna change your ass."

"I rang and rang that bell, but nobody came," he whispered.

"Don't be mean to him," I yelled.

"You wanna change him," he yelled as he turned and glared at me.

"You behave or I'm turning you in," Daddy's voice suddenly rang out.

"I'm sorry sir, but he does this on purpose"

Daddy snorted in disgust, turned and went back down the hall.

We heard more loud talking down the hall, then feet tromping down the hall.

A huge black lady appeared at the door with Daddy right behind her.

The big guy instantly started changing the grey man.

"Jefferson, you lazy scamp. You better start doing your job right or you'll find yourself walking down the road with your lunchbox, you hear. You lazy no good bum." She stomped over to the other side of the bed, put her hands on her hips, and began to watch him.

Jefferson changed his attitude. He quickly changed the sheets and redressed the little old man.

The two walked back down the hall and she was still bending his ear.

She looked back over her shoulder and yelled, "Thank you sir for letting me know what's going on."

It was a big relief getting out of there. It was so depressing, it was awful. Now it even smelled worse since they had changed the little old man. The building itself was depressing to look at. The paint was coming off in big patches everywhere. Underneath the patches of no paint the wooden boards were rotten in some places, and was greenish moldy looking in other places. The building was depressing and terrible to look at. The blinds on the windows were torn in some places and hanging loose in other places. I couldn't go fast enough to get out of there. I felt like I couldn't breathe, I was choking. I needed fresh air.

We got home without having to use the bucket of water for the truck.

A few days went by and we got our cotton planted.

Uncle Oglee was still planning his first lost gold search. I have to admit I could hardly wait to go after the gold myself. With Uncle Oglee, of course. I had to hurry things along with all my chores because I wanted to get started.

"Speaking of gold, today would be a good day to head for the library. We also have that appointment to visit old Dr. Bradley. He knows everything about everything," I said, starting to hound Uncle Oglee.

"There's a bus that runs about three miles from here. I've got a bus schedule, wait a minute and I'll go get it," I said, and jumped from the chair, almost turning it over, as I ran to our bedroom to get it.

"I don't want to go, Sally said. I'd rather stay here and look through the catalogue with Lena."

"But I want to go," Junior said, "I could help."

"Not today, it's not because you're too little, it's just because I think you need to stay here and keep an eye on the birds that might try to scratch up the cotton seed we planted."

"Yeah, that's right I could stay here and make a scarecrow to keep those rascals out of our patch. Yep, that's a good idea and that's what I'll do."

I just loved Junior, he was always so agreeable. Now if that had been Sally, she would still be yelling and complaining that she didn't want to do it.

I'll have to bring him back something, I thought, bless hislittle heart.

"Sure, that'll be fun," I assured him.

Daddy had walked in and was standing by the stove. He reached over, lifted the round lid from one of the burners with a metal lid turner and looked inside to see if the stove needed more wood. It was okay, so he laid the lid back down.

"Oglee, do you think you could drive the truck into town?" he asked with a smile on his sunburned face.

"Sure can, Sir. Do you mean you're letting me drive your truck?" Uncle Oglee gasped.

Daddy nodded.

"I just don't know how to thank you, Sir," Uncle was beaming from one ear to the other.

"Just drive careful, because you don't have a license yet."

Everyone was shocked, even Mama, she actually dropped her dishcloth, but she had the biggest smile on her face.

"Well Son, you've been the greatest help around here, I just feel like I would like to do something for you."

"Oh thank you Sir but you've already done so much for me. I can never pay you back," Uncle Oglee looked so grateful, and happy, it was almost sad.

"Just be careful." Daddy said patting him on the back. And if you want you could get your license while you're in Jackson."

"What a great idea, getting a license," Uncle Oglee said.

To get to a library, we had to go to Jackson, which was only about forty miles from where we lived. As we drove down the country road with the windows down, the sweet scent of jasmine floated through the air making me feel almost as if I were in another world. The scent was intoxicating. We didn't have anything like this when we lived in Texas, although we did have beautiful flowers. I couldn't remember anything that smelled like this.

I looked over at Uncle Oglee's smiling face. He looked as happy as a little bird suddenly released from his cage.

He was driving free, along the thick, tree lined wooded area of the road, with the window down and a light Jasmine scented breeze ruffling through his black hair as it floated through the car. We were on our way to find gold at the end of the rainbow and who knows what else.

CHAPTER 17

Jannele Library-Lost Gold

The building ahead was grey and somber looking from the outside, even more so when we got inside.

But the librarian was young and pretty, about eighteen, I would say. I was surprised; usually they were much older and sour looking. I could tell Oglee was impressed. He kept looking at her and asking her unnecessary questions, like how long have you worked here, but she didn't seem to mind. He never acted this way with any of the other girls he had met, like Constance for instance. They would make a cute couple I thought. There I go match making again, I was just a romantic, just couldn't help myself.

She was blond, little and just a little taller than I was, which made her about five foot two. More important, she was very pleasant, even charming I might say.

"You're looking for lost gold?" she asked, with a smile. "You know that's very strange, you're the third person this week that's been in here looking for information about lost gold," she said her brow was furrowed. "I wonder why, I can't ever remember anyone, asking about that before. By the way, my name is Jannelle Finley," she said smiling, she stretched her hand out first to me, which really shocked and impressed me, then she turned to Oglee.

"Really? Nice to meet you, my name is Oglee Baxter, and this here is my niece Zemma Carter."

"Nice to meet you," I said, stretching out my hand.

"Likewise," she said, shaking my hand, and smiling.

"Well maybe it's because there was an article in the paper a couple of weeks ago, about lost gold bullion during the civil war, which must have generated a lot of interest," Oglee said openly interested.

"Oh, I know my Uncle owns the newspaper and I wrote the article. My Uncle loves stuff like that, and so do I, so he let me write the article. We own the Mississippi Herald Weekly. It's a local weekly newspaper.

Uncle Oglee looked shocked. His mouth dropped open and his eyes widened. He stared at the young lady for a second, and absently scratched the dark stubble that had begun to appear on his chin.

"Really, you wrote that. Well I'll be switched, you must be pretty smart."

"That was really good, and I mean that, it was a well written piece. Very interesting. It certainly captured my interest." He suddenly grinned that captivating grin of his and said, "And I'm not saying that just because you're pretty as punch," he continued with that wicked grin, the one that made the ladies swoon, I thought.

She actually looked stunned, "What did you say, well I never," she stuttered. Then she laughed a cute tinkly laugh, "You certainly are quite the ladies man," she retorted regaining her composure. She looked up at him with renewed interest, her blue eyes shining. Anyone could tell that she was definitely interested.

He laughed, "No sir, I have never told anyone that in my whole life," He said emphatically, he stopped and his face turned serious, "Do you write other stuff for the paper?" he asked.

"Why yes as a matter of fact I do, actually I even write a small column called "Social Events of the Week". It's nothing really, but I enjoy it. Someday I plan to be an investigative reporter. I have my application in all over the country at major newspapers.

I know this is a bad time to look for a job like that, well it's a bad time to look for any kind of job right now." She paused, looked off into the distance, but you just never know, it could happen.

I could see Uncle Oglee's face light up. He had the greatest respect for anyone that was smart; he had such a thirst for knowledge himself. "You must be pretty smart to be able to do that," Uncle Oglee said with an admiring but wicked grin, "Could I be your assistant?"

The pretty blond girl started to giggle, "Sure," then she quickly recovered, and turned toward the closest shelves of books.

"Well, let's see," she said as she quickly moved toward other shelves, reached up and carefully chose several books. She brought them over to the table where we were sitting. "Here's one of the books the last two guys was reading. It was titled, Lost Southern Treasure.

She and Oglee had their heads close together scanning through the pages. There were torn pieces of blank paper marking some of the pages.

"Oh my gosh, here, here's our place on the map," I said.

Jannelle's excitement was building as her small, slender fingers ran across the map. "Look, it says there were two soldiers that holed up there with the gold. Then they disappeared. No one ever saw them after that," I whispered. I was so excited, I could hardly sit still.

"What did these two critters look like?" Oglee asked. "I'm sorry, what's your name?"

" Jannelle Finley and what's your name?" she asked. "Im sorry, I know you told me, but it slipped right by me," She said smiling sweetly, her blue eyes were shining. "This is so exciting."

"Would you like to join us with our gold hunting excursion?'

She stood still, her face a blank with surprise. She thought for a minute, and then she grinned. "Why not, I know a lot about the area, and I know what books and maps to look for. And again, I say, why not. That sounds like fun, besides who knows we might hit it rich."

"That's great," Oglee said, unable to control his enthusiasm. "I guarantee you will not regret it. He held up the two books he had in his hand. "And I want to check these two out."

"Wait, here's another one that's good," she said and rushed over to another aisle, picked another book from the shelf. and added it to his collection.

"If we discover anything," I said, "We will split it three ways, what do you think?"

"Oh thank you," Janelle said, "I think that's wonderful."

"Absolutely," Uncle Oglee agreed nodding his head vigorously.

Jannelle gave us a library card and the books, "I'm going to check one of these books out for myself," she said.

"When and where shall we meet?" Oglee asked Jannelle as he watched her with intense black eyes.

"How about the little restaurant across the street?"

Jannelle thought for a minute, biting her under lip. "Everyone would know what we were doing. How about my house or your house."

"Sure you're right; I think people are pretty nosey around here. They would guess what we were up to," Oglee said. "How about our house, we're out in the country. Will you have transportation; we live about three miles out of town."

"Of course," Jannelle said, brushing back a long blond hair that had fallen into her eyes when she leaned forward to take a closer look at one of the documents shown in the text book.

"Look at this, it shows that most of the activity was in Georgia. It says in May 24, 1865, two wagon loads filled with gold were robbed at the Chennault Crossroads in Lincoln County. It goes on to say that the gold was supposed to be loaded onto a ship in Savannah, Georgia.

"Oh isn't this exciting?" I whispered.

"You two are new in town, right? Jannelle asked, "I haven't seen you around," her blue eyes scanned Oglee from the top of his head to the bottom of his feet. She paused, "You look a little like a gypsy," she stopped suddenly when she saw the shocked look on Oglee's face, "Oh, I mean that as a compliment, you know a romantic Gypsy," she continued to stumble over her words, obviously embarrassed.

"I've been called worse, "Oglee laughed. "It must be the red plaid shirt I'm wearing."

She reached over and gently touched his arm, "Please forgive me, and you know what I mean."

"But the answer to your question, is I'm really new in town, but my niece, here has been here longer than I have. Her Daddy was born here, and has just returned to do some farming on the old homestead. And he's married to my older sister.

"Of course I know who you are," she said looking at me. "Well I'm new too, I'm really from California. My parents were killed in an accident and I had no one else except my Aunt and Uncle Finley. They're really nice, and offered to take me in. I plan to finish college here. My folks left me enough money to do that."

"That's great, what are you majoring in."

"Gold hunting," she said grinning.

"Oh, so you're one of those smart alecks," Oglee said chuckling, "I've met that type before."

I watched the giant library door swing open and let a short plump woman in her fifties walk quietly into the library. She sat down in one of the chairs behind the long, worn, oak table.

"Good afternoon Mrs. Regemy, can I help you with anything."

"Yes Janelle, if you could, could you find a copy of "Of Mice and Men "by John Steinbeck for me, I would be ever so grateful."

"Why yes, actually I have two copies in the library right now. My goodness are you sure you want to read that? You know there was a question, at one time, about whether it was a decent piece of literature or not. That is, if we would even be allowed to get a copy of "Mice and Men," Jannelle said surprised.

"Shame on them, I'll read anything. I want to read this. After all, this is a free country. Who are they to tell me what I can read and what I can't read. I'll read anything I feel like reading," Mrs. Regemy began to rant; her blue eyes were glittering like twin fireflies.

That's when I decided I liked her.

I moved in closer and said in a low voice, "Good for you, I'm going to read it myself, first chance I get.

Jannelle smiled, "You're absolutely right, I have read the book myself."

"Well, what did you think?"

"Pretty spicy, I liked it," Jannelle said laughing.

Oglee and I walked toward the library door.

"I'll see you at our place tomorrow, and we'll map out a plan," Oglee said.

I felt like teasing him but I wasn't sure how far I could go. I knew I really liked her, and I hoped they liked each other, cause I thought they made a cute couple.

"Pretty nice girl wouldn't you say?" I asked Uncle Oglee, glancing at him out of the corner of my eye. I couldn't stop myself from giving away how I felt about the situation.

He looked down at me, batted his long black eyelashes, and said, "I should say so, mighty nice, mighty nice," his face was glowing. Ah yes the plot thickens, I thought. "Like an angel I would venture to say, and smart too."

We walked out into the empty street.

He stopped, turned and looked at me, "You know what! Can you keep a secret?" he asked with a big smile all over his face.

"Why of course, I can," I said, oh goodie I thought, a secret, he would actually trust me with a secret. "You bet I can keep a secret, what is it, pray tell?"

"She's the one. That's the girl I'm gonna marry," he said, his black eyes were shining.

"What? I say What? Really, that's for sure? You really mean it?" I asked, I couldn't keep my mouth closed. It kept dropping open. "But how do you know?"

"I just know. How do I know that the sun will set tonight, How do I know the sun will rise tomorrow? I just know."

"Yep, absolutely."

"But how do you know? What if she said no," I said, trying to figure him out, how could he know for sure?

"I just know, and she won't say no," he said just beaming. "I just know," he repeated.

When we got there, we hadn't realized it, but the town was really small. There was only one brick, country, general store that carried everything from dresses to food. It had all kinds of bright colored, tempting knick knacks displayed on a shelf in a big glass window.

A big feed store was further down the street, with bales of hay sitting out in front of the store. In between the store fronts there were small houses where people lived. They were called the city folk. Further on down at the end of street there was a cotton gin, where everyone took all of their cotton to be milled. This was also the place to take your corn to grind your corn into cornmeal, but I hadn't seen that yet. Oh yes, I almost forgot, there was a Bank of America, which was the same bank that Baby Faced Nelson had robbed. It was the most important place in town.

Since it was a depression, everyone was having a hard time, so they depended on the bank to lend them money to get through the winter until they got paid for their cotton crops.

They were all scared the bank would close like a lot of banks had already done. "We would all be up a creek without a paddle," the farmers were fond of saying.

The wooden sidewalk was hard on my bare feet, since I would only wear shoes in the wintertime when school started.

I thought about Jannelle for a minute then I said, "I'll have to agree with you, she's pretty nice, I like her."

" But, I'm surprised that she took the gold hunting seriously," he said shaking his head.

When we got home every one was waiting for us.

"Tell us about your day of gold hunting," Daddy said chuckling.

"I couldn't help myself, I was bubbling over with all the knowledge we had gathered at the library. I could hardly contain myself when I started telling them about Jannelle and all the information she was able to gather.

"Wait a minute, leave something for me to tell," Uncle Oglee said, trying to put a stop to my monologue.

"Okay, okay," I said laughing, and I finally stopped to take a breath. I shouldn't hog the conversation. I realized I had become pretty long winded.

"Well, she's right, all of a sudden there's a big stir over the lost gold bullion. It all started after the article was written in the Mississippi Herald.

Suddenly out of nowhere there were two new city guys in town asking a lot of questions about the lost gold and a lot of other things. In the article there was a mention of the old Grayson Manson.

John Grayson said there were a couple of men out there asking his Daddy a lot of questions. He didn't like it one bit, because he said his Daddy didn't know anything about anything.

"Oh that's a shame," Mama said, "Bothering poor old Mr. Grayson."

"Well they'll get tired and move on to other things, maybe on into Georgia." Daddy said.

"That's right," I said as I slapped the mosquito that had been buzzing around me. It finally settled on my arm and bit me, nasty little critter that he was, but I got him, "anyway that's the last place the gold had been seen. That's probably where we should be looking right now."

"Wait a minute, you had better take things slow and easy, sometimes when there's a lot of money involved there are a lot of very bad people also involved. They're after the same thing you are, and they're not too nice about how they go about getting it. Even killing people," Daddy cautioned us.

"We know Daddy; there are even new people in town asking about the gold bullion."

"George said there were two new guys at the feed store this morning asking questions abut the history of the town. He said they looked like the New York criminal types, maybe Mafia not just your usual crooks, whatever that means," Oglee said, shifting from one foot to the other. He acted as if he was ready to take off on the run after them. I couldn't help but laugh.

Oglee wouldn't know what to do with one if he came face to face with a tough wise guy. I had read about them.

When we sat down to supper, it was a relief to have Aunt Katrina and Uncle Jim and their brood gone. As usual supper consisted of left over's, red beans seasoned with ham, fried chicken, corn bread and molasses was pretty tasty.

In Texas we ate a lot of corn tortillas, enchiladas, tacos, hamburger meat made into different casseroles. But here we ate beans, ham, eggs, lots of eggs and more beans of some sort. Fried chicken was a favorite in both states.

"Things are sure different here than they were back in Texas," Oglee said.

"How so," Daddy asked.

"Well for one thing, the food we eat."

Daddy nodded, "That's right; we usually eat what's in season, corn, beans, yams, ham and chicken of course are always in season. We always eat good."

"You know what I heard," I said, feeling important that I could contribute something interesting to the conversation.

"No what," Mama asked. She seemed to be the only one that wanted to know what I had to say.

"Since it's only July I haven't started school yet, but I heard that all the kids bring stuff to school, you know food that they grew at home. And the cooks at school would cook it for the kids at lunch time; you know food that they grew at home.

Some people would bring corn, beans, tomatoes, others bring, chicken. No one ever goes hungry. Everyone eats the same thing."

"They do that here?" Oglee asked, looking at me in amazement, "That's really nice. I don't know of any place that they do that."

"Me either," I said, nodding agreement.

"We do that in our school too," Lena said proudly. Lena had settled into the family as if she had always been with us. It was nice having her here.

"I wish I could go to school too," Junior said sadly.

"Well after you start, you will wish you were right back here," Sally piped up.

"It must be a southern custom then, not just because this is a depression, because they were doing that when I went to school," Daddy said.

"I'll really be glad when I start to school, I said. Just think of all the new friends we'll make Sally."

"Oh Bah Humbug," Sally said, " I don't need any new friends."

"Oh Sally you say that just because I said I wanted new friends, I'm on to you," I said, staring at her trying to make her think I knew more about her than she knew.

I was pleased, I think it worked.

She looked down at her plate and started nervously moving her silverware around.

"You think you're so smart, you know nothing," she said clenching her teeth and sticking her chin out.

I didn't know anything, but I wished I did, but she didn't know that.

"Oh hear, hear, hear now girls lets be nice," Mama said.

We both shut up, rather than look like a shit disturber, as I had heard one of my uncles say. We especially cared what Daddy thought. Certainly neither one of us wanted him to be ashamed of us. In fact, I had rather get three spankings from Mama, than to get one lecture from Daddy. Daddy never, ever spanked anyone. He would only lecture. It was Mama's job to do all the spankings. When Daddy said he was disappointed in me, it made me feel really awful, so guilty and ashamed of myself.

CHAPTER 18

Strangers in the Night

We hadn't heard much about the killer that was still on the loose.

The days passed uneventfully into weeks, until one day the black storm clouds suddenly starting gathering. The wind had started to blow up a storm, it was whistling around the corners. It became really spooky.

That night it started to rain, and rain some more. Thunder and lightning dazzled the night sky. It was beautiful but chilly. So this was the beginning of fall. It was loud, noisy and wet. All the red, yellow and orange tree leaves started flying, wildly, blowing in the wind. The sky was filled with all kinds of debris, sticks, leaves and limbs, the smaller limbs went flying into the air, leaving the bigger tree branches, then falling onto the wet, red dirt.

I looked out through the curtainless windows, across the outside hall and into the dining room window. The limbs on the mulberry tree were weaving back and forth so hard I was afraid the tree would tear apart and come flying through the window, so I made sure I moved myself to the other side of the room.

"With the storm starting, we'll just leave the dirty dishes for tomorrow," Mama said hastily gathering everyone up and moving them across the hallway to where the large library room with another fireplace was. It was warm in there too, because Daddy and Junior also had the wood stove going.

We gathered around the stove with blankets for everyone, and listened to the racket outside. It had begun to rain. Little drops at first then the drops grew into a giant hailstorm. The hail was pounding on the windows like storm meteorites from mars.

Daddy was sitting with a woolen blanket draped around his shoulders.

I started laughing, "Daddy you look like um Heap Big Sitting Bull."

Daddy said, "How."

Everyone laughed.

There was a sudden loud knock at the door and I almost climbed the wall, "What was that, a tree limb, a rock, or was it actually a knock on the door," I squeaked.

"It was a knock on the door," Daddy said, knocking over a kitchen chair as he jumped up with Oglee right behind him.

We looked out the window but couldn't see anyone. I thought I saw a man outside, but it would be hard to see anyone, through all the rain, hail and stuff flying around.

"I peeked out the side window, and I could see the shadowy forms of two men standing almost flat against the door. That was a little scary.

"Wait Daddy, they look funny, they are right against the door. Something doesn't look right."

"Who is it?" Daddy yelled out to them.

"No one you would know, just let us in out of the storm."

"Can't do that, we don't know you. But you can wait out the storm in the barn." Daddy yelled back.

"That's not very neighborly," they shouted back.

"Who are you looking for?" Daddy asked.

"We are looking for the old Randolf place.

"Oh, that place burned down years ago; I think you're looking for the Henderson place. Just go straight down the road about five miles and you will see it. Good luck," Daddy said with a note of finality.

"We really don't appreciate your attitude," one man growled, his voice was raspy. He had a strange accent, a different way of talking. I didn't recognize it. It was short, choppy and fast.

"Listen here fellows I have a shotgun here that says keep on going your way," Daddy said, now he was getting mad.

"You'll regret this fellow," the angry stranger continued, mimicking Daddy's use of fellow.

By that time I was standing behind Daddy with the other shotgun, not that I knew how to use it, but if worse came to worse I would scare them to death. Uncle Oglee came up behind me, reached down, smiled and gently took the shotgun away from me.

"Be careful with that, you might shoot a toe off," he whispered, looked at my big barefoot toe and grinned.

Through the window, I watched the two guys slowly trudge on, inching their way on through the wind, rain, mud and slop, as they slowly made their way down the wet driveway and onto the road.

The wind was blowing so hard the man with the hat had to hold it down with both hands, while his friend blindly followed close behind him. They both had long, black overcoats on, that ballooned out around them, almost like wings spreading out, and getting ready to take off in flight. They looked like something on the hard cover of a mystery book.

Daddy was so mad the frown lines doubled between his eyes. "We haven't heard the last of those two. They are certainly not from around here," he added in a worried tone of voice.

"Leota, get on the phone and call Charles Henderson and let him know that those two are on their way to see him."

"We can't be fooled," Mama said, "they'll be back, If for no other reason than to scare us to death."

We all went around making sure that all the doors and windows were locked, which wasn't an easy task, because the locks on almost everything were broken. No one in this county locked their doors at night, that is not until recently, since the killer was known to be on the rampage. So Daddy put nails into the windows bolting them down for the night.

"I think those guys stirred up a hornets nest," Sally said.

"They sure scared me," Lena said.

"Well I'll tell you, they better not mess with Daddy and Uncle Oglee," Junior piped up.

"That's right little Buddy," Uncle Oglee said, reaching down and pretended to punch him in a make believe fight.

Mama called the Henderson's.

"We'll certainly be on the lookout for those two" Helen said," Charlie is getting his shotgun out as we speak. I think I'll call the Sherriff just for the heck of it."

"They really do sound like trouble," Helen said hanging up the phone.

"Anyway it won't hurt anything if we do let the sheriff know what's going on," Mama said.

I spent most of the night with my nose glued to the window, as I drifted off to sleep.

When I woke up the next morning, the sun was shining after the storm, everyone was fine, except the place was a mess.

I had a crick in my neck from sleeping against the window sill all night. The gate had blown open and the hogs were roaming around, uprooting anything they could find. They had already found the yams.

After breakfast, the three of us, Junior, Sally and I ran outside, we didn't have to be told what we should be doing. We knew, already we should be out rounding up the hogs and what was left of the chickens and hustling them back to their pens. While we were at it we gathered up the eggs that were miraculously left untouched in their nests. You might say we killed two birds with one stone.

After all the excitement died down, I didn't know what to concentrate on, my cotton planting or gold hunting. I was torn between the two loves..

"Oh my goodness, I thought of the cotton. I hope our cotton is alright. I flew out the door slamming the screen door behind me as I ran out to our cotton patch. I breathed a sigh of relief when I looked at it. It was okay, a little beat and battered, just a hair worse for the wear.

I looked closely, oh my goodness the little cotton flowers were ready to bloom. Good thing they hadn't bloomed yet. If it had the storm would have torn up all the flowers.

I could hear Mama singing in the kitchen, "I've got the world on a string," then she went into, "It don't mean a thing if you ain't got that swing," both songs were Cab Callaway songs.

We all liked him. I came into the house, and went into the kitchen, where I found Uncle Oglee sitting at the worn, oak, kitchen table. He was staring down at his tattered gold map spread out on the table.

Uncle Oglee watched hungrily as Mama cooked breakfast. The scent of bacon, ham, hot biscuits and eggs filled the large warm kitchen, and made me hungry too. Although the food was better here, I really did miss my friends in Texas especially my best friend Mary Jane. We wrote letters back and forth, but it wasn't the same. And then there was Sam, the boy I liked when I lived in Texas. He didn't even know I was alive or that I liked him, only Mary Jane and I knew that little secret. Sometimes I suspected he liked me, but I wasn't sure. But I do digress, back to now.

I sat down beside Uncle Oglee, leaned over and peeked at his gold map. At first I couldn't make heads or tails out of it, and then I spotted our house on the map. Oglee had marked it with a red pencil.

"Wow, there we are," I said looking up at Oglee.

"Yep," he said, a smile brightened his whole face. "Where shall we start," he paused, looked over at Mama, turned back to me and winked, "I guess we could start right here in the kitchen, first start pulling up the floor boards about here," he said pointing toward the fireplace.

"What," Mama said her blue eyes wide, a startled look on her face," I don't think so, not in my lifetime," she stopped as she realized she was being teased.

Uncle Oglee grinned. You could tell he was struggling to keep a straight face, but he just couldn't do it.

"You little Rugrat," she said, a smile slowly emerging on her pretty face, and she swatted him with the dishcloth she was holding. She shook her head, turned around again, reached over and swatted him again.

"That first one wasn't good enough," she said, then she went back to the stove, picked up a platter of steaming bacon and placed it firmly on the table. "I do declare, you don't deserve this, but I must admit you almost had me there," she said mimicking a southerner.

Oglee chuckled and reached for the bacon. Everyone sat down for breakfast.

"Leota, one thing I can say about you, you're a darned good cook and you can sing too," Daddy said.

"Amen," to that, we all echoed.

Daddy cleared his throat, looked at Oglee with a serious look on his face and said,

"Son, I think a good place to start looking would be on the left side, outside of the house. There used to be a very large kitchen on that side and it wasn't rebuilt after it was burned down. You could get one of those thing of ma jigs that detect metal and you could use that to search for gold, even go under the house and see what shows up. What do you think?"

Uncle Oglee was ecstatic. "Wow! What a great idea. Thanks a lot Claude. I wonder where I could get one of those things."

Daddy sat thinking for a minute as he munched on his bacon. He stopped suddenly, holding his fork in midair.

"By Golly I know someone that had a thingamajigs he used to search for money on the beach when he went to New Orleans one summer. I bet he still has it because he never throws anything away. I think we should call him. Zemma get the phone book and look up Charles Henderson. We called him the other night. He's one of our third cousins or something like that, if I remember right. He's a heck of a nice guy. If he still has it, I know he would be happy to lend it to you. If he does, I'll call him, if not we'll have to make a trip to Philadelphia Mississippi that is."

Oglee jumped up "I'll get it," he yelled, he was so excited he couldn't sit still, and I must admit so was I.

"Where is it?" he asked.

"Here it is," I already had it; I had beaten him to it since I knew where it was, in the bookshelf on the second shelf. It was one that hadn't gathered any dust.

I was ruffling through the pages, Oglee was beside me jumping from one foot to the next, "Hurry, hurry."

"Here it is," I yelped as I handed the book to Daddy.

"Good, good, now let's hope he still has it," Daddy said as he got up slowly and moved to the phone on the kitchen wall.

"Back, you two, you're breathing down my neck. You're so close I can't see the number.

"Sorry, sorry Claude," Uncle Oglee said as he backed up just a hair.

The phone rang and rang, and on it'd ninth ring Daddy was getting ready to hang up when Charlie finally picked up.

"Howdy," He said panting, all out of breath. "By God this better be important or I'm gonna be mighty pissed, I was way out back fixing the gate."

"I'm mighty sorry Charlie; I didn't mean to cause you a heart attack. I was just wondering if you still had that thing that you used to hunt coins with on the beach. Remember it was a few years back."

It was quiet for the longest time, and then he finally spoke. "You mean you had me running my butt off, just for that. Have you lost your mind Claude? Yeah I think it's around here somewhere. It's in the barn I think. I haven't got time to look for it now. But if you want, you can look for it yourself. You're welcome to do that. You know I wouldn't do this for any one else."

"Thanks Charlie, I really appreciate it, you know that."

"Halleluiah, let's get going," Uncle Oglee yelled.

"Wait, after we get the chores done, okay," I said.

"Oh sure, sure just point me in the right direction."

"Be careful, and don't step in any cow plops," I said.

"I know," Oglee said, "Remember I was raised on a farm, and you just don't forget things like that.

CHAPTER 19

Metal Detector

It was four in the morning. Outside, darkness and the freezing cold wrapped itself around us. We moved toward the barn to feed the chickens, slop the hogs, and last but not least feed and milk our two cows, Molly and Josephine.

Oglee knew how to milk cows because we had cows in Texas. He took Molly and I took Josephine. While we were working, we kept looking over our shoulder for those two strangers to suddenly come creeping out of the darkness and into the orange light of the lanterns. As my head was bent over the milk pail I fully expected, at any moment, to feel giant hands reach out and grab me from behind.

"I wonder if those two strangers went on to the Henderson's," I asked Uncle Oglee, as I kept dodging the cow's tail as it suddenly started switching back and forth, just barely missing my head by an inch. This activity almost knocked over my half filled pail of warm milk.

While I waited for an answer, I could hear Daddy singing, "In a shanty in old shanty town."

It gave me a nice secure feeling when I heard him singing.

"Hopefully the sheriff scared them off. Some one should call the Henderson's and see if those two men showed up there."

"I'll ask Mama when we get back in."

"Well, I guess this is it," Oglee said hopefully, as he stood up and we started trudging back to the house with full buckets of milk. It was just beginning to get light. The sky was turning yellow orange, quickly leaving the dark purple behind.

Roosters were crowing, in the chicken house, and the hens, not to be out-done by the roosters were noisily announcing their egg deliveries.

The stillness of the night was gone and the loud noises of the day had begun as everything was moving about.

Even the dogs started barking, which was unusual this early in the morning. That made me a little uneasy.

"I wonder why they're barking. Could be there's a stranger lurking about the barn," I whispered.

"What," Oglee said suddenly alarmed, as he turned quickly and looked behind him.

Our steps moved faster as we hurried toward the house.

"Hey there," a gruff voice yelled out in the semi darkness. It came from behind a tree just next to me.

I threw my pail of milk into the darkness in the direction of the voice. I started running in my bare feet, toward the house like I had wings.

Uncle Oglee hung onto his pail of milk but he was just two steps ahead of me.

"Oh, my good God in heaven, we're goners," I screamed.

"Oh hell yes," Oglee's terrified voice floated back over his shoulder toward me.

"Wait just a minute you two," the voice from the darkness continued, "I got to thinking about it, curiosity got the best of me, so I went out to the barn and found the metal detector, so you wouldn't have to come over and look for it. Besides I wanted to hear more about the great gold hunting escapade."

Our feet slowly stumbled to a halt. We turned and looked at Mr. Henderson, who was standing beneath the giant oak tree that overshadowed the chicken house. He was bent over laughing.

"I've never seen anything quite like it. It was so funny. I'm truly sorry about the spilt milk, though," he said, as he stopped laughing.

"I'm just glad you're not who we thought you were," I stammered with a sheepish grin on my hot face, feeling both relieved and embarrassed.

After Uncle Oglee caught his breath, he started laughing," I've never been so scared in my life."

"Well here I brought over this what-cha- ma call it metal detector," he said, and handed Oglee a long pole with a funny gadget on the end of it.

"I guess you're Charlie Henderson, thank the lord," Uncle Oglee said, laughing good naturedly, after he finally regained his composure.

"Yep, that would be me," he said.

Mr. Henderson was a clean shaven man. He was short, heavyset, about five foot eight or so. He was fairly good looking; he had blond hair and blue eyes and a cheerful looking face. I would guess he was about forty something.

"Well, thanks a lot; we were going to head over to your place, as soon as we were done here. Come on in and have some coffee," Oglee said, " I'm right behind you as soon as I scrape some of this crud off my boots," he continued as he scrapped the cow manure off his feet onto the wooden steps.

We went on into the house, with me trailing close behind, listening to every word. I was smart enough to not step in any cow manure. I had to smile to myself as I watched Uncle Oglee continue to scrape the crud off the sides of his boots.

"Yeah, we're really interested in finding the gold bouillon," Uncle Oglee said as he reached down and patted me on the head, "Me and my little Buddy here."

Mr. Henderson nodded his head, "You know what, if I were a young man I would be right there with you."

Mama and Daddy looked surprised when they saw Mr. Henderson come in with us.

"Well I'll be darned; it's good seeing you Charlie. To what do we owe this visit?" Daddy asked.

"Well I brought this here metal detector over for the kids," he said as he briskly rubbed his hands together, because it was still cold outside. "Nice and warm in here," he continued.

"About those strangers, did they come to your place?" Daddy asked.

"No siree, they didn't show up, but someone sure did. The dogs were rais-ing holy hell, somebody was out there, but we could never see who it was. Somebody was snooping around out there. This morning I checked all around, but as far as I could tell nothing was taken. I could see fresh footprints in the garden area. I just don't know why anyone would be messing around out there."

"It was probably them," Mama spoke up, "From what we could see through the window they looked mean and hard. They certainly weren't pleasant looking. They even threatened us."

"I'll be darned, I wonder what they wanted," Charlie said.

"I think they're looking for the gold," Sally spoke up.

Up until then the kids had all been quiet and just listened, which is what we were taught. We were never to interfere when grownups were talking.

"I think she could be right, there has been a lot of interest lately in the lost confederate gold," Uncle Oglee said.

"Please sit down Charlie and have some coffee," Mama said as she sat a hot steaming cup of coffee on the table before him.

"Well, thank you Leota, by George I believe I could stand a nice cup of coffee, thank you much."

"You know, I would just let you have the detector. I wouldn't even want it back, but I'm saving it for my youngest son Jeff. He's interested in all kinds of things. I think he's gonna be a collector like his old man. "

"That's right, you are a collector. If I remember right you have quite a gun collection. "

"That's right. So far I have fourteen guns in my collection," he said proudly. "I'll probably leave them all to Jeff. He's quite a marksman. He loves to hunt. He always wants to tag along whenever I go hunting. My other two boys don't give a hoot about guns or hunting. Neither my wife Margie nor my two girls Annie and Janie care for any of my hobbies. So thank goodness for Jeff," he said laughing.

"I wanted to ask you something, "Daddy said.

"Ask away," Charlie said.

"Did you sell your mineral rights?"

"No, but by golly Harry Belton keeps pestering me to sell. He's just like a pesky fly. I've told him no a dozen times."

"Yeah, he asked me too, and I told him no," Daddy said

"He's a strange character. You know I was on the jury when he sued the county hospital and the Doctor. We could see him sueing the hospital, but not the Doctor. But he had them combined into one case, and we couldn't see that the Doctor did anything wrong. He did the damage to his leg himself. I had to vote no."

"Is that right?" Daddy said.

"My God was he mad. He said he'd kill us, and see us all in hell if it was the last thing he ever did," Charlie related the story.

"Good grief, he sounds crazy," Daddy said.

"Yeah, sure glad he got over that," Charlie said with relief.

"I guess so," Daddy agreed.

"Well anyway, when he gets going on something he's a big pest," Charlie said as he hitched up his pants with his thumbs. He wasn't wearing the usual farmer overalls.

They continued to talk about things I didn't have any interest in. So I went to my room to get a coat and my winter shoes on, so I would be ready to go gold hunting with Uncle Oglee. Sally wasn't interested in gold hunting, thank goodness, and I told Junior I would share anything I got with him. I told him to be sure and water our cotton patch if I got tied up with gold hunting. He was tickled with the responsibility.

I talked to Sally and she agreed that we would share our cotton profits with Lena.

CHAPTER 20

The Gold search Starts

I went back in the kitchen when Mr. Henderson left. Oglee was sitting at the kitchen table with his map, making notes about the spots that the gold could be.

I pulled up a chair and sat down beside him. He reached over and ruffled up my hair. I swatted at his hand.

"Darn you, now I'll have to comb it again."

"What about the graveyard, Uncle Oglee. How are we going to find out if there is any gold buried there?"

"O, ooo, that will be your job, I'll keep the evil spirits away, while you dig up the grave," he said with a scary evil cackle.

"No really," I said laughing. I ran my hand over my head trying to smooth down the hair that was sticking straight up.

"Well little Zemma, we'll definitely leave that part of the investigations, for the last."

"I totally agree," I said.

"Today we will pick up Jannelle and head for Connehatti and check a couple of places there. There's a good library there too, Jannelle had said. There's also a spot next to a tree in the Connehatti graveyard. Looking at this map, I think we can find the spot pretty easy."

"How're you getting to Connehatti?" Daddy asked.

"Well I thought we would ride the two horses Dan and Jane." Uncle said, glancing over at me.

"That's a good idea, but I have a better one."

"Really," I said wondering what the heck it could be."

"I thought maybe I would take you two into town, it's not all that far. I thought maybe I would pick up some new vegetable seed and other supplies for the farm."

"Wow you'd really do that for us?" Oglee asked. "And I thought I would pick up Jannelle and take her with us. She's really interested in looking for the gold too."

"Is that a fact," Daddy said as a slow grin began to start at the corners of his mouth and spread. "It wouldn't have anything to do with how cute she is, now would it?"

Oglee's face turned red, he grinned, nodded and said, "You got me."

Daddy liked Oglee. He treated him like he was one of his own.

"That's really nice of you Claude," Oglee said, nervously shifting from one foot to the other.

"Would you like to drive the truck? You know how to drive don't you?"

"Oh sure, sure, I drove Daddy's old truck all over the ranch and took it to town whenever Daddy needed something."

"I just can't believe you'd let me drive your truck again."

For that matter neither could I, I didn't realize my mouth had been hanging open, and dry until I closed it. Maybe Daddy would even get interested in our gold hunt.

We hopped in the truck and waved goodbye to everybody. They looked happy when Daddy promised to bring back candy for everyone.

We stopped and picked up Jannelle. She was dressed so cute in a pretty yellow, flower print dress with a little bonnet that matched it. She looked like a little doll from Sears and Roebuck. I heard Uncle Oglee gasp when he saw her.

Daddy chuckled at Oglee's reaction. Daddy and I looked at each other, and I grinned, and Daddy winked.

When we picked up Janelle, they decided that Janelle and Oglee would sit up front in the cab, and Daddy and I would sit in the camper.

It was fun riding along in the truck; I was sitting in the camper looking out of the window at all the scenery.

Everybody said it was the prettiest time of the year. The Magnolia and Honeysuckle, and Crepe Myrtle were all in bloom. The wonderful honeysuckle scent just filled the air and a light breeze floated the smell through the air. I loved all the flowers, foliage, pine trees, hickory nuts and pecan trees. The beautiful brick houses were well groomed. A little too well groomed. I liked places that were just a little wilder, with a more carefree rustic look about them. But, there were some that were a little too wild. These were so over grown; to the point you wondered if anyone even, lived there.

As we continued on our way, we could hear Oglee and Jannelle chatting away.

We had to be careful and watch out for the wild animals. They would jump out, and run across the road, in front of us, when we least expected it.

Daddy and I would chat about the cotton patch. This was the season for all the things we grew. We even had a patch of sugar cane. Corn, string beans, butter beans, lettuce, cabbage, tomatoes, yams and last, but not least, sugar cane. We even had a mill to make the sugar cane into syrup. My that syrup was the tastiest stuff I have ever eaten, especially when you poured it hot, on pancakes and waffles. All the time we were talking we were keeping an eye on Oglee and Jannelle in the front. They were talking so low we couldn't hear what they were saying. Oh, we would catch a word or two every now and then, but just enough to get the drift of their conversation.

We were in Connehatti before we knew it.

"Where should I park?" Oglee asked as he turned and looked back over his shoulder at us.

"Anywhere is fine son. You go ahead and find the library or wherever you want to stop and I'll walk to where I want to go, then I'll come back and find you."

"There's the library," Jannelle said as she pointed to tall, reddish looking brick building.

"That sounds fine." Daddy said.

Daddy got out and walked on down the brick street. I watched him as he walked away. He walked with that special shuffle; he called it the Carter walk. It's like he's leaning forward, headfirst, bracing, and pushing forward against the wind. He walked slowly, as if he had all the time in the world. After he told me this, I started noticing that they all walked that way. Very strange, I thought.

I wonder if that's the way I will wind up walking. I really hoped not. It didn't look too lady like.

The three of us drove on down the street to the library. Conehatti, the town was bigger than Sebastopol, but not as big as Jackson. All the houses along the street were two or three stories tall, with beautifully groomed yards, framed with beautiful flower gardens.

"Just beautiful, beautiful," I murmured to myself.

When we went into the library, Oglee and I followed Jannelle since she seemed to know what she was doing. We each found a book about gold mining and took it back to a table to read.

The librarian was tall, slender, white haired, really pleasant, ancient looking lady. She looked like she was glad to see us since the library was completely empty.

She and Jannelle knew each other instantly, so they smiled and exchanged a few. pleasantries.

"Look at this book, someone's been reading it. Here's a page that's dog-eared,"

Jannelle said, "I'm just outraged," she said in her slow southern accent. She got up and took the book to the librarian.

"Doesn't she sound cute when she's mad," Oglee leaned over and whispered. I looked at him. He looked absolutely smitten. His eyes were wide and dreamy looking. He had a silly goose smile on his face. I just couldn't help myself, I had to giggle. I placed my finger to my lips, and strained my ears to hear everything they said, Oglee nodded and listened too.

"Would you just look at this Hanna, somebody dog-eared this book in several pages. That's just a disgrace."

"It surely is Jannelle, and I know who it was," she said nodding her head vigorously. "It was those two strangers; I had never seen them before. They both were dark. They looked like gangsters, like the Mafia, I would say."

"You don't say?" Jannelle said.

"Yes and they were here a long time yesterday looking through a number of books that had something to do with gold hunting."

"Could you please come over here and see if these other books were the ones they were looking at."

"I'd be so very happy too, honey," Hanna said, as they walked arm in arm back to our table.

"Everybody, this is a very dear friend of mine, and I would like for you to meet her. She's so kind to help sort all this out for us."

"So nice to meet you" Oglee said as we both got up. Oglee held out his hand and she reached over daintily and shook his hand.

I just nodded and said, "me too."

We looked at our books and Oglee found a dog eared page in his, but mine was clean, so I knew they weren't interested in mine.

"You know what, they checked out one, and now that I think about it I have another one just like it. Would you like for me to get it for you."

"Oh yes indeed, I surely would if you don't mind," Uncle Oglee said.

"I would be delighted, I'll go get it right now."

"What a break this is for us," Oglee said reaching over and giving Janelle a little hug.

She was surprised, her face turned pink, she smiled up at him and she didn't move away. That was a good sign, I thought.

Hanna came back with the book. "This is it and if I remember correctly, they had a small piece of paper in between pages 215 and 216."

"My goodness, I'm I so glad you have such a good memory, thank you Hanna," Jannelle said, giving her friend a little hug.

We left the place with a good feeling and an armload of books. All of a sudden the good feeling went away and I felt like someone was watching us. I looked all around us, but I couldn't see anyone suspicious.

There was a man and woman sitting on a bench talking. There were some people coming out of a grocery store with a load of groceries.

A woman was walking across the street with two little kids in tow.

I continued to look, and then I spotted two men in the ice cream store. It was them. I knew it instantly. One was tall and heavy set, dark with a mustache. The other man was much shorter and fat, and also dark. They were definitely watching us. I knew they had seen us come out of the library with our books. They were most definitely interested in us. I reached over and nudged Oglee.

"Don't look now, but there are our two bad boys in the ice cream store."

"Oglee and Janelle were really clever about the way they handled the situation. They didn't look right away, Oglee said loud enough for them to hear him.

"Oh Jannelle, there's an ice cream store. Would you like an ice cream cone?"

"Yes indeedy I would. Make it a double scoop of chocolate please, pretty please."

We were suddenly there, turning and walking into the store. We didn't look at the two men as we passed them. We walked up to the counter.

"What would you like Zemma?" Uncle Oglee asked.

"I'd really like a double scoop of chocolate ice cream cone. Then I thought maybe Uncle Oglee didn't have enough money for two scoops, "No, make it one scoop," I said.

Uncle Oglee said, "Make it a double all around," as he waved his hand in the air.

After we got our cones we sat down at a little table in the corner. We laid our books down on the table. The tall man in the black suit sidled over to our table and casually picked up one of the books and looked it over as he turned it around.

"Doing a little gold mining, young man?" He asked Oglee in a cold voice.

"Nope, but I am writing a book about lost gold mines." Oglee said as he looked up at the man unafraid. "Do you know anything about gold mining? If you do, please share it with me, because I want all points of views, so the book will be interesting," Oglee continued looking him straight in the eye.

CHAPTER 21

Uncle Oglee and Jannelle

The man looked over at Jannelle, "And I suppose you are here to help him write this book of his."

"Why yes I am," Jannelle stammered, "But I don't see that it's any business of yours," Her blue eyes had turned to blue steel as she continued to look up at him. He stared back, and then moved back to where he was standing with his buddy, who stood leaning nonchalantly against the counter. They continued to stare at us. The tall one moved his jacket back so we that could see his shoulder holster with a gun.

Daddy suddenly opened the door and walked in, apparently he had sized up the situation. He stood in the doorway for a second, then to my horror he walked over to the two guys in black and said, "You two wouldn't be the guys who tried to break down my door the other night would you?"

"They both looked shocked, "No, what the hell you talking about," the tall guy asked, and if you would move aside we would like to go."

"Well, if you're sure you're not those guys," He said his voice hard and cold. He slowly stepped aside and they brushed past him in a hurry.

The lady behind the counter said, "You know they had guns under their jackets, they looked dangerous."

"I know, they're nothing but bullies. They like to intimidate people. They're very sneaky and dangerous at night when no one can see them. The kind that would shoot you in the back when you least expect it."

"Daddy," I said as I ran up and threw my arms around him. "I was so scared; I thought they were going to shoot you."

"Me too," Uncle Oglee said, "How about an ice cream cone."

"Yeah," he said, and chuckled. "I wouldn't mind one, I think that would cure everything. "

"Did you two get everything you were looking for?"

"Yup, we just have to make one more stop. There's an old abandoned house, with a well on it. I would like to investigate that place on the way home. Do you know the place Jannelle; it's called the old Johnson's place?"

"I surely do. The owner passed away a few years back, but I think he has a son that lives in California or some place like that."

In one of the books it mentioned wells were good places to hide things like gold buillon, and another place it mentioned that confederate solders would seek refuge in the Johnson place. I just thought the Johnson place must have a well, "Oglee said thoughtfully. "Claude, would you mind if we took some time today and checked the old place out?"

"Of course not," Daddy said

"I know exactly where it is, this is exciting," Jannelle said as she moved forward in her seat. "Keep watching to the right, there should be a little dirt road about two miles down the road, turn there, and about five miles down the road is a huge old abandoned house. At one time it was a beautiful house that looked like a castle, now it just looks like an old haunted house."

About an hour later we came up to it. It was all so overgrown with weeds, tall brush, hedges and huge gnarly trees.

"Wow, is this some place," Daddy said. Even he was impressed. "Are we going to have some stories to tell Mama and the kids tonight?"

"We had better hurry because it will be dark pretty soon, and I don't think I want to be here when it gets dark," Jannelle said.

We started walking down an old ivory colored flagstone walk that had thin green blades of grass growing up through the cracks. The walk led us to a wooden porch with several missing planks. It circled the whole house. Honey suckle vines had grown up over the windows and into the tall walnut trees. The yard was filled with wild oak, hickory nut and English gum trees. It looked ghostly but smelled wonderful with all the wild flowers and unattended rose bushes.

As we got closer a little tickle of fear ran down my spine. I wondered if we were doing the right thing. The massive double oak doors hung slightly ajar. Someone had already been there before us. We snuck in quietly, tiptoeing down the hallway. All the paintings that used to hang on the walls were gone and left lighter spots on the faded wallpaper, marking the space where they had been.

"This is exciting," I said shivering in anticipation as I began moving forward a little bit at a time.

Oglee turned and smiled as he looked down at me. He placed a finger to his lips, which meant for me to shut up.

"Oops," I whispered. I was getting careless, I thought. No matter how careful I was the floor creaked. Of course, we sounded like a herd of elephants tromping through the house.

Janelle spoke up. We hadn't heard anything from her for quite a while.

"It's fun to look around inside the house, but I don't think there's any gold inside the house, do you?" she whispered, grinning, making fun of Oglee's intense expression. She looked up at Oglee, as she struggled to keep a serious face.

"You're right, I really doubt it, but it's fun to look around," Oglee whispered back.

The house was still magnificent inside. There were long rows of windows, with remnants of velvet drapes that hung loosely from the rusty rods; their tie backs had long been gone. The furniture that was there was covered with layers of dust. In a way it was still kind of beautiful. Dark mahogany tables, tall buffets with cut glass windows. Jannelle lingered over the intricately carved chairs as she rubbed her slender fingers over the carvings. As we moved into the kitchen, we marveled at how huge the room was with two large pantries off to the sides. Against the far wall there were several wood cook stove with giant ovens.

We reluctantly left the kitchen area and moved up the winding staircase to the bedrooms, how many we couldn't guess.

"Uh-oh. Look at this," Oglee said, "Fingerprints and hand print in the dust, on the railings"

"Someone has been here recently, and they might still be here," I whispered, and pointed.

We slowly crept up the squeaky stairs, trying to be quiet was pretty hopeless, I made sure I was the last one up, not that I was chicken or anything like that. It was just I could get out of their way a lot faster since I was younger, and could move faster, I figured.

A sudden flapping noise rushed above, and swished by our heads, I turned and started running back down the stairs.

"Stop it, Zemma, it's only a bunch of bats that were holed up in the top floor. Good thing it's daytime or you'd be in Georgia by the time we stopped you."

"Oh shut up," I said, and sheepishly crept back up the stairs from whence I came. "Well, I guess we've scared off any dangerous people by now, if there were any," I said feeling disgusted with myself.

Daddy just laughed, I was so glad he was with us.

"Well who, did you say?" Uncle Oglee said laughing.

I remained silent the rest of the climb up. We finally reached the top of the second floor. We started checking each room. Lordy, lordy were these people rich or what. I didn't know there were such people. I just couldn't believe it.

The bedspreads and curtains were unbelievable. Sears catalogue had nothing this pretty. Just wait until I tell Sally and Lena about these bedrooms. Each bedroom was as big as our house. I just knew she wouldn't believe me.

"You know if I were rich, I would buy this and fix it up, to where it was back like it once was, and live in it," I said, overwhelmed with its potential beauty.

We moved on up to the third floor. Everything was old but still beautiful. I fell in love with everything; this made me want to be a decorator when I grew up, and rich of course. Things changed when we got to the attic. Funny, we had debated whether we would even continue on up into the attic or not, finally decided that it was a go.

Talk about cobwebs, Lordy, I'd never seen such cobwebs in my whole life. The webs were actually strong and tough to tear through them, not like the usual wispy spider webs.

"Hey, this is strange there's a pathway where there aren't any spider webs. What do you think that means?"

"It means someone else has been up here before us," Daddy said, and I do think he was right.

We managed to work our way through a bunch of upturned furniture, and opened boxes packed full of stuff. You could see someone had rummaged through the boxes, leaving things scattered everywhere. It looked like our dogs Coco and Nonie had a field day playing in the boxes. Any way, as we moved on, we could see someone had been living there, and they weren't too neat either. There was a cane bottomed rocking chair and beside it was a small brown oak table with a radio sitting on it. There were candles that had been used on the table.

"Look at these candle, guys. They could have burned this beautiful house to the ground."

"Good grief," Jannelle said, shaking her head in dismay. (Dismay, new word I had learned.)

There was a single iron bed with a blue and white checkered patchwork quilt and a feather pillow thrown on top of the unmade bed. The bed was just like the one we had in one of our extra bedrooms. There was a bay window with a window seat, so you would have a good view outside. I walked over to the window, and looked down. You could see everything, especially someone coming up the driveway. Outside of that it would be a beautiful view if the window wasn't so dirty.

"Someone's living here for sure," Oglee announced in a whisper.

The four of us stood still as if we'd been hypnotized. We recovered and started looking around, moving much faster than we had been moving before.

"Oh look, this door goes to their bathroom," I said as I hurried moving to the next room. We decided we had seen enough upstairs and started making our way back downstairs. This must be their kitchen. It was huge.

"Oh my goodness look at this giant wood cook stove," I went on, "And look, at this huge wood box next to the stove." A tea kettle was sitting on the still warm stove.

"We've got to get out of here. The stove is still warm. I'll bet they're still here," I muttered. "Oh gee gosh almighty, let's get out of here before we are confronted by someone or something," I said, in a low voice. "Time to go everybody," I whispered.

"Yeah, you're right. They probably went through a secret door and are hiding somewhere and watching us right now. "

"Oh, no, no, no," Jannelle whispered, "I want out of here. I'm leaving now, as fast as I can get out of here."

"Me too," I echoed her plan of action. The only one that lingered behind was Daddy.

We heard a car drive up and park. I ran to the window and looked out. Someone had just driven up and parked beside our car. I felt weak in the knees. I thought I was going to faint. I looked at Daddy.

We heard a car door slam and steps entering the house through the front door.

"Oh what to do, what to do" I whispered

"Oh hell fire and damnation, if this isn't a godawful predicament. We'll have to find an empty room and hide in it," Uncle Oglee said.

"Follow me," Daddy said as we quickly, quietly moved on down the hall behind Daddy, he stopped and turned. Talk about spooky. Leaping shadows were dancing up and down the hall walls. I was so nervous, my bare feet were beginning to tingle.

"Let me think a minute," Daddy said, wiping the sweat from his forehead.

"I've got it. I know what to do. Oglee, you pretend you're a real estate salesman, and you're trying to sell Jannelle the mansion. We'll pretend we don't even know this guy is here. Now Oglee, start talking like a Dutch uncle to Jannelle. Then he said, "Follow me." He turned and started down the stairs. It was already getting dark outside, so it was really dark inside.

"Look a here, Miss Jannelle, isn't this a wonderful old mansion. You could make just a few adjustments and it would be a prize home again"

Oglee went on talking in a loud voice, "Just look at this fine wood, the wonderful design of the place. "

"You're right, Mr. Carter. This could be a showplace," Jannelle said.

I was so proud of them. I couldn't believe my ears. They played their parts like they had been actors all their lives.

It was quiet; the stranger hadn't made a sound. We had made it down the stairs and were on the first floor.

"Well what do you think, can I take it off the market Jannelle?" Uncle Oglee said.

I looked at Uncle Oglee and whispered, "Sold I'll buy it, " and I crossed my eyes and stuck my tongue out. I thought Uncle Oglee was going to lose it.

His mouth dropped open, he crossed his eyes and rolled his head around. I almost giggled as we started through the front door.

We all walked out the front door, Oglee and Jannelle still making noises that sounded like talking.

When we got outside, we acted like we were surprised to see another car parked beside ours.

"Wonder who that is," Oglee said pointing to the car, "I hope it's not another Real Estate Agent."

"I didn't see anyone," Daddy said.

I was sweating like a hound dog chasing a rabbit, but the important thing was we had made it. We got out of there, lickity split. A hail of red dust followed us, as we sped off, bouncing down the crooked red clay road as we left the old mansion.

When I looked back I couldn't see any one following us, thank the lord.

As we flew down the road, I yelled at Uncle Oglee, "Slow down Uncle, we don't want to hurt Daddy's car."

"Oops," He slowed down immediately, and looked over at Daddy who was looking straight ahead with his poker face on.

Daddy didn't say anything, but he had a little twinkle in his eye.

"That was so smart, Mr. Carter. How did you ever think of that?" Jannelle asked

"I don't know honey; I guess that desperation will make you think of a lot of things.

"You know what, we forgot to look for the well," Uncle Oglee said.

"Well, there'll be another time," Daddy said.

When we dropped Jannelle off, Uncle Oglee lingered on the porch steps. He hadn't kissed her yet, but I knew he must be thinking about it, when the front door suddenly opened up.

"Good evening, Mrs. Finley," Uncle said. That put an end to any lingering thoughts along that line, that Uncle Oglee had been treasuring.

I couldn't help but giggle. I knew it was bad, but I just couldn't help myself. She went in and the door closed. That was the end of that.

A very sad Uncle Oglee trudged back to the car and got in. He didn't say anything. I knew it was better I kept quiet, or I might get an earful.

When we got home it was pitch black. No moon and no stars, which meant it was overcast and was going to rain.

Daddy looked solemn when we came into the kitchen.

"I'm so sorry we're late," Daddy said looking at Mama.

"I know you must have been worried, but we were trapped. While we were investigating this old colonial house that was on the gold map, guess what happened?"

And Daddy started telling her all about the things that had happened to us. Everyone was all ears. Whenever Daddy would stop to take a breath. Sally, Junior and Lena would stare at him, with their mouths open waiting to hear more.

They would say in unison, "Then what happened?"

"Oh, I wish I had been there," Sally complained.

"What, what happened then?" Junior repeated, urging him on.

Lena was quiet, her dark eyes were big, her mouth open in anticipation waiting to hear more.

"Well, that sure was good thinking. That could have turned into a nasty situation. Thank goodness, none of you were hurt," Mama said, breathing a deep sigh of relief.

"Don't worry, tomorrow I'll wash the truck, and get rid of all the red dust," Oglee said.

"Wasn't even thinking about that." Mama said.

Mama left to put Jenny to sleep then came back. "Thank heavens you're home safe and sound. I was really worried about all you rag muffins."

"Sorry, Mama," I said.

"Now its bedtime," she reminded us.

I'd forgotten that here we went to bed with the chickens, and woke up when the roosters crowed, mainly because we got up so early. Here we didn't have any electricity like we did in Texas.

I couldn't tell if she was mad or not, I looked at her, searching her face for telltale signs of anger, but there weren't any.

Mom and Dad never argued about anything, that we knew about anyway.

I know they must argue sometimes, because they were only human, but I just never knew when. I know the friends we had in Texas would tell us how their parents would argue all the time. They couldn't believe our parents didn't argue.

"You must be hungry, I'll warm up some supper for you," Mama said.

Uncle Oglee and I both, protested.

We sat down to warmed up fried chicken, mashed potatoes, and gravy (as only Mama could make.) and corn on the cob.

Oh, my, was it good. Even now, my stomach growls just thinking about it.

Uncle Oglee reached into his pocket to get his little dictionary and thesaurus which he always carried with him.

"I need to find a word that would describe today's happenings better than we have," he said opening his thesaurus. I have to mention here that Uncle Oglee was determined to become the most self educated man that ever existed. He loved words, and he loved to read. He wanted to know and use ever word in the dictionary. He was an exceptional person. He used words that I had never heard of, sometimes he would use the wrong word for the wrong situation, but never the less he would use a big word anyway. I do believe that someday he will be the most educated man in the world. Maybe, go down in history as a genius.

Mama had always admired her little brother for his dedication and desire to become educated.

"I don't know where it comes from. This driving desire to be smart. Even when he was little he wanted to know how everything was spelled. To hear him talk, you would think he was a college graduate," Mama said. She laughed, "I sure didn't fall from the same tree."

"I didn't either, spelling was one of my weak spots among many other spots," I said, as I reached over and took the dictionary from his hands and started ruffling through the worn pages As I glanced through the pages some of the words were underlined and the pages were dog eared. I looked up at him and grinned. "I know what Santa Claus should bring you for Christmas. A brand new dictionary. That will be the first thing I'll buy with my cotton money."

"I'd sure like that, that is if I believed in that old rascal," he joked.

"What! You don't believe in Santa?" Junior asked, his blue eyes as wide as saucers.

"Oh, no, just joking, of course I believe in him," Oglee hastily reassured him.

"Well, what's your next plan?" Dad asked, pushing himself away from the supper table.

"You know, I think we should start checking around here first. The gold could be a lot closer than we think," I ventured to put forth my ideas.

"Oh, I forgot to tell you Aunt Katrina and Uncle Jim and their brood will be here tomorrow for the night," Mama said.

I started giggling, "You better run for the hills, Uncle Oglee," I said.

"Oh shoot, I'll put on my armor."

"You're right, tomorrow after all the work is done we'll start checking all the area on the left side of the house, with that metal detector thing."

"You know there are a couple of old wells here that have been covered up. They've been here long before my time," Daddy said. "That's a good spot to look."

Next day. We were all out bright and early, running around, doing our chores fast, so we could get to our gold digging.

Oops, I almost forgot my cotton crop.

"Zemma, I'll go ahead and get going on the gold digging. I've got the metal detector," Uncle Oglee Said.

"Okay," I said as I headed for my cotton patch. I felt terrible because I was going to miss out on all the excitement of using the metal detector for the first time. Darn it! Anyway first things first. Junior and I finished chopping the little cotton plants. When we finished, we made sure we watered the planted rows really good.

CHAPTER 22

Spoils of Gold Digging

I rushed back to the side yard, to see how far Uncle Oglee had gotten with the detector without me.

"See," he said laughing as he pointed to about a foot high pile of metal things. Several square nails, a dish pan, a tin cup a tool of some sort; a piece of a pitchfork, the list goes on and on

"So honey, you haven't missed a thing."

I looked around and giggled when I saw all the holes and mounds of dirt piled up.

"Looks like the ground squirrels and gophers had a field day, and a party," I said walking around surveying the grounds turbulence.

"Just shut your mouth, smarty pants, grab a spade and go to work," he said with a sideways grin on his face. I had never seen a smile like his on anybody else's face. One corner of his face would go up in a normal smile; the other side would go up just halfway. It was really cute.

I walked around searching the yard for a handful of sticks. When I was done, I picked up the metal detector and started going over the area that Uncle Oglee hadn't reached yet. Whenever I heard the detector make a racket I would place a stick on that spot. One spot I got a huge racket, so that's the spot I started at.

I started digging, digging and digging. "I think this thing must be in china," I said leaning against my spade handle, my tongue hanging out, and sweat running like a river down my face, my shirt and on into my overalls. My shirt was sopping wet.

Uncle Oglee was sitting on the ground, his back leaning against the trunk of the mulberry tree. He was laughing and shaking his head.

I rested for about a minute, and then I jumped back in my hole and started digging again. I was so mad.

Suddenly my shovel hit something; there was a loud clink as it scraped across something. I almost went into shock. I was so surprised. I reached down and started scraping away the dirt. It was bright shiny gold.

"Oh my God," I breathed.

"It's gold," I screamed.

Uncle was there in a second, almost in the hole with me.

I reached down and picked it up. It was a bright, shiny gold buckle.

"Oh my goodness," Uncle Oglee said "Look at that. That's gotta be worth a lot of money." It had been wrapped in a leather bag of some sort and the spade had raked the bag off the buckle.

"Here I've been digging hole after hole and nothing. But you, you little rascal come along and first hole you dug, look what you get."

I looked up at him and grinned, "But it's half yours, we're partners, remember."

"Oh no, Pumpkin, it's all yours. I wouldn't think of claiming any part of it,"

"That's not the way it works."

"Let's go show Mom and Dad what we found," I said, grabbing him by the hand and dragging him toward the front door.

"My goodness," Daddy said turning the buckle over and over in his rough work, worn hands. "It's a confederate officer's belt buckle. What a find."

"Little Zemma found it. She was halfway to China when she dug it up." Uncle Oglee said, his face beaming.

"Almost," I said.

"Follow me," I said as I ran outside to show them where I'd found the buckle. I was so excited, I almost fell down.

"Watch your step, the hole's pretty big," I said, laughing at myself.

"Wow, you really did dig a big hole," Mama said

The blue jays were already hopping around in the hole, grabbing earth worms and pulling them up. They were having a feast. When we arrived, they angrily flew up into the mulberry tree, and waited for us to leave.

I picked up the metal detector, and started poking around in the hole. A huge metallic racket went off.

"What the heck," Daddy said, "There's more stuff down there." He picked up the shovel, jumped into the hole and started digging.

None of us could believe it. I was holding my breath, the shovel pulled up some kind of oiled cloth. Dad dropped the shovel, picked up the bundle and brushed the red dirt off.

We watched and waited breathlessly, as he unwrapped the package. A grey, wrinkled, confederate officer's uniform became visible. We watched in awe as a grey confederate cap fell from the bundle.

Dad shook his head and smiled, "It just gets better and better," he said as he handed the bundle out to me, and he started digging again.

The shovel hit something metal. Daddy threw the shovel down and started digging with his bare hands.

He found a bundle wrapped in what looked like cow hide. When he pulled it out and unwrapped it. It was a confederate, colt revolver still loaded with shells.

"Careful, Claude," Mama said, "It could go off any time."

"I know," he said, turning it over. He leaned in closer trying to read the manufactures name. He rubbed the handle to read the engraving.

"It says it's a Colt Root model 5 revolver 1886. The handle has checkered Ivory grips. This is quite a find," Daddy said. He handed the gun to Oglee.

"Boy, would Henderson love to get his hands on this," Daddy said "Just look at the condition that it's in."

Oglee was in shock. "You just bet your bottom dollar he would. This is a beauty. Wow, I'll bet this is worth a lot of money," He said, smoothly running his hands up and down the barrel.

"Careful with that thing," Mama said pushing it away from her.

I picked up the detector and started poking around in the hole.

"There's more stuff in there," I said as the detector kept making noises.

Oglee handed the revolver back to Daddy, then grabbed the spade and started digging. Nothing came up, but there were still noises.

He stood up shifted his shoulders back and forth several times, then wiped the sweat from his face and went back to digging.

"I just don't know, we might wind up in China, like Zemma said after all," he said laughing. "I can hardly stand this excitement," he went on. He crawled out and handed the spade back to Daddy.

The more Daddy dug, the louder the detector sounded. "Good grief how far down is this thing,"

"Hey, you wanna try this for a while," Daddy said and handed the spade back to Uncle Oglee.

"Keep on going, hurry, it might be gold," I said, jumping from one foot to the other.

Sally came running from the front of the house, "Uncle Oglee, your friend Jannelle is here, and she wants to see you."

He stopped, dropped his spade and started crawling out of the hole. By the time he got out and dusted himself off, Jannelle was coming around the corner.

"Oh my goodness, I see you've found something," she said, looking toward the gun lying on the ground. She picked up her speed and started running toward us.

Uncle Oglee eagerly started explaining all the happenings that had been going on.

"Oh my goodness, this is just too much, I can't believe it all. And there's more," she said looking down into the hole.

"Yep," Oglee said as he jumped back into the hole.

"Well sir, you know what, we're all so tired now, we should wait until tomorrow to continue."

"No, no," I screamed, horrified at the very notion that we should stop. Then I realized he was pulling my leg.

"Let me take a shot at that," Jannelle said, reaching down to pull Oglee out.

"That's a great idea," Uncle said as he reached for her hand and pulled himself out.

Jannelle jumped in, grabbed the shovel, started digging and throwing dirt out over her shoulder. I was impressed, so was everyone else I think. What a worker.

After a few minutes Uncle Oglee said, "Here, let me spell you for a while,"

"Nope I'm fine," just then her shovel made a clink. "Oh hear that, hear that," she hollered.

Everyone was hovering over her in the hole. By this time we had quite a hole dug in the red dirt. Uncle jumped in beside her.

"Here, let me help you," he said, digging in the dirt with his bare hands.

Their hands touched something and Jannelle squealed.

"It's really long, "Jannelle said, "I think it's a sword."

By the time they got it out and unrolled the oiled leather that was wrapped around it, they could see it was a long beautiful shiny metal sword. The handle was ornate gold with mother of pearl designs inlaid in the handle. Jannelle and Uncle came out of the hole with their treasure. I had never seen anything like it.

Daddy took it and looked it over good, "It's a confederate Calvary sword."

"I'll write down all the inscriptions and look them up at the library," Jannelle said, "I can hardly wait until it opens up

"Let's go in the house and see if we can figure out what all this means, and for heavens sake, don't say anything to anyone about this."

"Heavens no, that's all we need is for those two strangers to find out about this."

I looked at Lena, "Remember Lena, not a word to anyone, not even your Dad because someone might be listening. The less he knows the better off he is. You just never know. If they think he knows something, they just might torture him until he tells them everything he knows."

"Oh no," Lena said.

"Zemma girl, I think you've been reading too many mysteries,"Uncle Oglee said, laughing as he rubbed his dirty hand across his forehead to wipe the sweat away.

"Wait a minute, Zemma, don't let your imagination run away with you. That's pretty far fetched," Mom said, with a smile on her face.

Lena looked relieved, and I tried to defend my position. "Well, you know it could happen. It happens all the time in detective stories."

"But that's stories honey, they're supposed to be exciting, or you wouldn't read them," Mama said.

I looked around and everyone, but Lena had a smile on their face. Maybe I had gotten a little carried away.

"Let's cover everything up so if those guys do come around again, which I'm sure they will, they won't notice we've been digging, "Daddy said.

"Oh no! We're not done for now are we? It's early, it's only five o'clock," I protested.

"Yeah, let me dig a little," Junior protested.

"You can have a turn at digging after supper, I promise," Daddy assured Junior.

"That's good, we'll come back out here after supper, and we better keep our eyes open and peeled out for the bad guys."

"Listen, listen, there's more stuff right here," Uncle Oglee yelled. He had only moved a few feet closer to the house.

"Sh-h-h-h," Mama said, "Not so loud."

"Let's hurry up and have supper and get back out here," I whispered.

We all gathered around in the kitchen and started watching Daddy polish the Confederate gun.

Uncle Oglee picked up the sword and started swishing it around.

"Stop that little brother. If you want to do something, you could polish it up," Mom said as she playfully snapped the dishtowel at him.

"Oh, so you want to duel," he said pointing the sword at her.

"No, and you stop it," she said laughing and backing away.

"Okay, I'll polish it up," he said rubbing his fingers along the side of the blade, "I wonder how many men this blade has killed?" He said.

"Oh no, don't, I can't even think about that," Jannelle said scrunching up her face and closing her eyes.

I agreed with Jannelle. That was a pretty horrible thought.

"It's almost time for supper," Mama said, "Ham, molasses lima beans, okra, biscuits and gravy.

"Would you like to stay for supper, Jannelle," Mom asked.

"I would be honored Mrs.Carter," Jannelle said, her face lighting up like she had just discovered gold.

Everyone sat down to eat.

"I brought information, which I thought was interesting," Jannelle said.

"Well, way back when, after the Civil war was over, the confederacy wanted to return the gold bouillon that France had given them to fight the war. To do this they had to bring the gold from Richmond, Virginia, to Anderson, South Carolina by train and from there by wagon. They were hoping to get the gold to Savannah, Georgia. From there they planned to load it on a waiting ship to France. Then all heck broke loose and the two wagon train loads of gold was robbed at the Chennault cross roads in Lincoln County.

That was when the Chennault Plantation became known as the Golden farm. For many years people would search in that area for gold coins. From time to time they would find a few coins in the ditches that the winter floods had washed up from somewhere.

To this day the legend persists that treasure was hastily buried on the original grounds of Chennault Plantation and remains there.

"Oh my goodness," Mama said.

"I think we're really onto something," Oglee said.

Dad decided he would find a good hiding place for our treasures.

CHAPTER 23

Again Strangers in the Night

We usually went to bed about eight o'clock, but tonight we were all wound up, nervous and excited about our discoveries.

"I'll want to go out and dig some more," I said.

"No, not now, it's too late," Mama said.

"I think I'll go out for a while," Uncle Oglee said.

"I think I'll go out, too and dig a little more," Daddy said.

"Poor junior, look at him, sound asleep. I know I promised him, but he's already asleep. I'll let him dig until his little heart's content tomorrow.

Junior was sound asleep, with his head leaning against a pillow at the foot of Daddy's chair. Daddy tiptoed over and gently picked him up, his head fell back against Daddy's shoulder. Daddy quietly carried him off to bed.

"Please Mama can I dig just a little more," I begged.

"Aw alright, just for a few minutes," Mama said.

"Hallelujah, thanks Mama," I yelped, and I skipped toward the door.

No one else wanted to go.

I don't know why, but I started walking on my tiptoes and all three of us weren't saying anything as we snuck out the back door.

We were walking quietly to our digging site by the big Mulberry tree, when suddenly we stopped dead in our tracks. I stood still and couldn't breathe.

Just ahead of us under the Mulberry tree, the moon was shining on two dark shadowy figures. Two dark shadowy human forms were moving about our diggings. it seemed like the sound of cricket's, katydids and croaking frogs was deafening, and I don't know what it feels like to faint, but I think that was what I became feeling. The full moon was out and we could see clearly. I was shaking so bad, my teeth were chattering so loud I knew they must be able to hear me, and it wasn't because of the cold.

Daddy held his finger to his lips, meaning silence until we were almost within six feet from them, then Daddy shouted in his loudest gruffest, big bad wolf voice, "What the hell are you sorry jackasses doing out here?" he was so loud I knew he must have shaken the mulberry tree.

The shorter man leaped straight up in the air, and the other one tripped and fell in the hole. They both screamed. It would have been funny, if it hadn't been so serious.

When out of the blue, the sudden hoot of an owl on the limb just above my head, rang out making me almost lose my pajamas. I stood like a statue clutching my pants. I bit my lip when I clenched my teeth together, trying to stop shivering.

"Nothing, nothing just walking by," The tallest man croaked as Daddy was shining the flashlight directly into his eyes.

"Those aren't even the same guys," I whispered, completely surprised.

I was confused; these weren't the two men we had seen in town. I had never seen these guys before. This was even scarier; it meant there were more people after the gold than we thought.

The shorter man had recovered a little bit, and now he was becoming belligerent.

"It aint against the law to be just walking along the countryside," He snorted, standing up straighter, taking an arrogant stance, in an apparent effort to look taller.

"Zemma run in the house and get the shotgun, I guess I'll have to show him how against the law it really is to trespass on someone's property," Daddy said. He was really mad now and it showed in his voice.

"Wait a minute mister we didn't mean any harm, we're sorry. We just made an honest mistake," The taller man said, from where he was still standing in the damp hole in the ground.

"We'll be moving right along about now." The shorter man said. He had red hair, and beady brown eyes, and he had lost his smart alecky attitude. You could see his eyes clearly, when the flashlight hit his eyes. The other man had blue eyes, a blond mustache and long thin, blond hair. Both men's clothes were shabby, their shoes were noticeably worn and scuffed, as they walked around.

"Why don't you help your buddy up out of the hole there," Daddy suggested in a cold hard voice, I had never heard Daddy use before..

"Oh sure, sure," he said, reaching down and helping his buddy up.

When I got back with the shot gun I was clean out of breath, because I had run every step of the way. Now was no time to tarry.

Daddy took the gun from my hands and nodded his thanks. He turned and pointed the gun at them and, "Now get."

"Don't worry, we're getting," the tall one said.

"Now I'm calling the sheriff when I get back in the house and I don't want to see your sorry hides around here again."

"You won't see us again, "the short one muttered.

As I stood barefooted under the mulberry tree waiting to see what was going to happen next, I became aware of the cold, ripe mulberry's juice squishing up between my toes. Eeek! I could hardly stand it, but I stood still as I watched Daddy raise the shotgun up above the stranger' s heads and shoot into the mulberry tree.

The blast almost deafened me. Showers of mulberry's, limbs and leaves came crashing down, raining mulberries all over the heads of the two guys. They looked up, blue red mulberry juice streaming down all over their faces. They screamed louder than before, threw their hands up in the air and ran for their lives.

"Don't you ever put your foot on this property again, or you'll get a shot in the seat of your pants," Daddy yelled after them.

"I guess they'll never show their faces around here again," Uncle Oglee said.

"Not necessarily," Daddy said, "The lure of gold is mighty powerful."

We all hustled back into the house, each one of us voicing our opinion about the two strangers and what they might do next.

Then we went on to discuss the future of our gold hunting operation. It was truly exciting. Suddenly I had so many things to think about. I didn't know which one to think about first. Our gold hunting, the fortune we were going to make on our cotton crop. The new romance that had suddenly blossomed between Uncle Oglee and Jannelle. Lena, I had to think about what was going to happen to Lena. Also, I wasn't sure we would stay here and not go back to Texas. Then there was starting a new school. When summer was over we would start in our new school. I had to admit I was just a little bit scared. I didn't know anybody in that school.

As I snuggled down under the covers I kept an eye on the window. I could see clearly because of the full moon. The mulberry tree looked like a shadowy giant, its arms spread out across the sky. I kept watching for shadowy figures to reappear under the tree. It was a comfort to know that Daddy and Uncle Oglee were also watching for the strangers to come back.

The next morning at breakfast, while everyone else was talking about the two strangers, Daddy was headed over to his brother Jim's to get help with the well problem.

Oglee was hot to trot. As soon as breakfast was over, he was out under the mulberry tree and started digging as fast as he could.

I hurried up with all my chores, so I could join him. A few old tin cans, bottles, snuff and tobacco tins later, we decided to give up for a while. I took Junior and went to the cotton patch to chop cotton. He was a good worker which surprised me because he was so little. He was really smart for being only six.

"Look at this Zemma, the plants are already four inches high. Look how fast they've growing."

"I know we're gonna have cotton before we know it. You know, it really feels different when it's our own cotton patch."

"Yeah, I hope we get some rain soon. It'd be awful if our plants dried up," Junior said, looking up at the bright sunshiny sky. Not a cloud in sight.

"Thanks a lot Junior, I hadn't thought of that. Now I got something else to worry about." Egads that would be disastrous, I thought.

I looked back at the house and I saw Jannelle's horse. She was already here, ready to look for gold and of course see Uncle Oglee. I smiled to myself.

I suddenly felt something tickle my bare foot. I looked down as I jerked my foot up. It was a little brown lizard that had run across my foot and was now well on his journey to somewhere else. Lizards didn't bother me, but snakes; now that was a different story.

"Junior, let's take a break and go to the house for some water."

"Naw, I think I'll chop a mite longer," He continued chopping not missing a beat.

I just looked at him. He will probably grow up to be the president.

I hurried along the path back to the house. I didn't want to miss anything.

When I got there, Uncle Oglee and Janelle were sitting on the porch swing deep in an intense conversation.

Uncle Oglee was leaning forward, holding Jannelle's hand. He was in the middle of telling Jannelle about last night. She was looking up at him, her blue eyes shining with excitement.

"Oh my goodness I wish I could have been here," Janelle said, "What did they look like? Were they the two men we saw in town? "

"They were ugly, but they were different fellows, not the ones we saw."

"What next?" I asked looking around at everyone.

"Maybe a trip to Georgia to the Chennault plantation," Uncle Oglee said, his black eyes shining with excitement.

"Me too, me too," I said, jumping up and down.

"Wait a minute here, that's a long ways off," Mom said.

"Mama's right, we have to think this thing through. What are you going to do after you get there?" Daddy interrupted.

I thought about that. What would we do after we got there?

"You know what?" little Junior piped up, "I don wanna hunt for gold, I jes wanna be a cotton farmer, " he said proudly, hooking his thumbs into his overall straps, and taking a stance, like he'd seen grown men do.

Daddy laughed, looked at him, reached down and ran his long fingers through and ruffling Junior's tow headed hair. "And a good farmer you'd make, son."

Junior looked up at Daddy and smiled proudly.

I was surprised he didn't want anything to do with gold hunting. Sally wasn't interested either. As for Lena, she just listened and said nothing one way or another.

Since I had my own cotton, things were different, the cotton planting and chopping had become fun instead of a chore. We, also had to go over to Lena's house and chop her cotton.

CHAPTER 24

Watching Cotton Grow

*I*t was a thrill watching the first slender, tender green cotton sprouts break through the surface of the plush, rich fertilized surface of the ground, and then unfold into a slender sprout with leaves. It broke my heart when I had to thin the plants out by chopping and killing perfectly good plants.

When I complained to Daddy about killing good plants, he said, "If you don't thin them out, your plants will be too crowded to be healthy and productive. They will wilt and die.

That made sense I decided, so that helped me get going again, thinning out the little plants.

I continued working but my mind wandered off thinking about the gold mining. I knew it was a long shot, but what if we actually did discover gold. The possibilities were endless, almost more than my little pea brain could handle. We could buy a new house, a new car, and new clothes all around. I could buy art materials to paint with. Even buy a piano and lessons to learn how to play it. That was just about all there was. I ran out of things to buy.

Lena said she wanted to buy a piano. She could use one too, because she had a very pretty voice.

When the day was over, we lit the coal oil lamps and had supper.

Daddy came in the house looking tired, sad and angry.

"What's the matter, Claude," Mama asked when she saw the expression on Daddy's face.

"That blasted cotton picking well is going to dry up, I think."

"No," Mama said. "How could that be? They've never had any problems with it before have they?"

"No, not when someone else owned it. I swear I think we're jinxed."

"What can we do?

"We'll either have to dig it deeper or start a brand new well," Daddy's voice sounded tired. "I'll have to get my brothers to help me dig a new well."

"In the morning first light, I'll go get Jim and see what he thinks,"

"Well, let's have supper now," Mama said.

"This sure throws a monkey wrench into things," Uncle Oglee said, "We'll just have to get busy and dig a new well."

"Things will look better tomorrow, so let's just sit down and eat supper," Mama said.

This was still the best time of the day, I thought. We could still hear the crickets, katydids and frogs sing their songs. After supper we could all sit around the large, wooden kitchen table with our special projects. Me with my drawing, Sally working on her Sears's catalogue list. Mama and Daddy reading a Zane Grey book aloud so we could all hear the story about the cowboys in the Wild West. Junior was lying on the floor, on a woolen blanket, beside Daddy's feet with his chin resting in his hands, listening. His eyes were glued to the reader's face which at the moment was Daddy.

My sister had control of the Sears catalogue. She was deeply engrossed in making numerous shopping lists. I was content to listen while I drew a picture of Mama reading. Uncle Oglee was almost sound asleep on the floor by the fire. He had wrapped himself in a blanket with his bare feet as close to the fire as he could safely get. Jannelle was sitting next to Uncle Oglee leaning her back against him. Lena sat close to me, while she listened and watched me draw the picture.

"You know what Zemma, it looks like your Mama, your picture does," Lena said smiling up at me.

"Oh thank you Lena, I know it doesn't but thank you for being so nice," I said feeling grateful for the praise.

"Let me see, let me see," Sally said, dropping her list, getting up and coming over, she bent down and looked over my shoulder. "Ha, no it doesn't, lt looks more like Coco, she said whooping and hollering, as she went back, and sat down with her catalogue list, satisfied that she had done her worst.

I knew that's exactly what she would do. "Next time, I won't let you see. So there, smarty pants," I said, I knew I shouldn't let it bother me, but it did hurt my feelings.

Jannelle said, "Let me see," and she leaned over to see the page.

I turned the page, so she could see.

"Oh, very, very nice," she said, nodding her head, and smiling up at me, which made me instantly feel better. "It does look like your Mom."

"Thank you," I said, surprised.

"This is all so wonderful and comfortable, and I do hate to leave, but I had best be getting home, or my Aunt and Uncle will have the hound dogs out looking for me." Jannelle said laughing, and jumping up from where she had been sitting. She straightened her skirt and reached for her plaid jacket that was hanging on a chair. She had been sitting next to Uncle Oglee.

Uncle Oglee almost fell into the fireplace when he scrambled to a sitting position.

"Oh, I'm so sorry I plumb forgot, it seemed so natural that you should be here. Claude could I borrow the truck to take Janelle home," He asked as he yanked on his socks and put on his shoes.

"Sure."

"Why don't you come back tomorrow?" Mama asked.

"Could I? And I could continue to help look for the gold."

"Of course," Mama said.

I glanced at Uncle Oglee and his face was pure happiness. I looked at Daddy and he turned his head to hide a smile.

Uncle Oglee was back home in less than an hour. I wanted to ask him all kind of questions, but I didn't dare.

CHAPTER 25

Tonsillitis

I woke up during the night with a terrible sore throat. I was coughing so hard I thought I was going to die. It just hurt so bad I could hardly breathe. I knew what it was. This had happened to me before. It was tonsillitis. I had been having tonsillitis off and on for about three years, and it was getting worse. The last time I had it the Doctor told Mama and Daddy I would have to have my tonsils taken out. If I didn't have them out, the side effects would be bad, I would have lasting damage to my body. I had a temperature of 103, and even with aspirin, they had trouble bringing the temperature down.

I could hear them talking to the Doctor in low voices. That really scared me. I didn't want them operating on me. I sure didn't want to go to the hospital.

"What an operation, no," I complained, " I don't want anybody cutting on me," I said, voicing my extreme dismay. (dismay, a new word for me.)

"We'll talk about it later," Mama said in a worried voice, as she patted the top of my head smoothing down my ruffled hair. The doctor left a bottle of pink medicine for me to take and several days later I felt better.

Soon I was back out taking care of my cotton patch.

"Thank goodness," Junior said, teasing me. "I have just been working my little butt off," he said laughing.

Junior and I liked to tease each other, back and forth. "Now you're going to have to work twice as hard to make up for lost time," Junior continued.

"Sure," I said, "I could have died, and all you cared about is how much work I caused you," and I gave him a playful little push.

"Mom, Mom she's hitting me," he yelped. He scrunched up his face and made some squealing noises, pretending to cry.

"Shut up or I'll give you something to cry about," I said laughing, and gave him another little push. "If you don't hush the old devil's gonna get you for lying," I threatened him.

For some reason, being around my little brother made me feel good, like he looked up to me or something.

Mama was used to what she called nonsense, and didn't pay any attention to us.

Daddy suddenly appeared out of the blue at the back door, and yelled out to us, "I'm going to town today. Do you want to ride into town with me, Zemma?"

"Why sure," I stammered, really surprised. Was he really asking me to go with him to town? Wow! How lucky could I get?

"I need someone to help me do the shopping."

Junior didn't say anything, he just looked down, and went back to chopping.

"Yeah sure, anything to get out of working," he yelled after me, as I dropped my hoe and took off in a long lope, and was out of there lickety split. I looked back over my shoulder and saw him just standing there, leaning on his hoe handle with a big grin on his sunburned face.

"Hey Buddy, you better get your hat on or you're going to be sorry. You're already getting a red face," I yelled at him.

"Oh' ok," he said, dropping his hoe and heading toward us.

I kept waiting for every one to start kicking up a fuss, because I was getting to go to town with Daddy, but they weren't. Everyone was quiet, no one said anything. I thought that's really strange. Maybe everybody had something better to do, something I didn't know anything about. I didn't care, I wasn't going to question my good fortune. What could be better than going to town with Daddy?

I hurried, running around, getting ready. I was holding my breath, waiting any moment for Sally to start complaining about her not being able to go to town. That would surely throw a monkey wrench in my plans to go with Daddy.

After I washed up, I put on my white Sunday dress, with the red bow at the neck, Of course I put on the only shoes I had. They were a little tight already. Oh my goodness, I hope I get a new pair of shoes by the time I go to school.

As we drove down the red, dirt country road, on our way to Forrest, I was really happy.

"Do you think we could get some ice cream when we get to town. "

"You betcha, honey."

Everything along the road was green and in bloom. The crepe myrtle trees were all in bloom, beautiful reds, purples and pinks. Honeysuckle vines climbed and hung from the pine, oak and nut trees. All the yellow, blue, orange and red wild flowers were growing along the red dirt banks and in between all the green underbrush and trees. The scent was really a mood changer. It smelled and looked like I was in a strange and beautiful kind of fairy land. Oh, if I were only a painter, I could commit all this beauty to a canvas.

Daddy and I seldom had a chance to talk like this. I was so happy. We chatted about our cotton crops, about all the things we would like to buy when our crops came in. We talked about education, college and the future. He thought an education was very important. He only went to the tenth grade, but he was very well self educated. Daddy liked to talk about the great philosophers, like Plato, Diogenes', Socrates and others.

Before I knew it we were in Forrest. It was small compared to Jackson but much bigger than Sebastopol. They had plank board sidewalks and all kinds of stores. Almost immediately I spotted an ice cream store. It was a small red brick building with long lengthwise glass windows in front and pink canvas overhangs for the windows. There was a giant sign on top of the building with a cartoon picture of a little boy licking a big ice cream cone. Next door was a furniture store on one side, with beautiful furniture displayed in the window. And on the other side was a hardware store with a small garden tractor displayed in it's window.

We parked on the street next to the store, got out and went inside. It was cool and refreshing to get out of the heat. There were pictures of different colored ice creams displayed on the white walls. There were lists of the prices and names of all the ice creams that they made.

I was literally drooling as I looked at the metal cartons of ice creams displayed behind the counter.

There was a tall, thin, blond lady behind the counter in a pink uniform and a cute pink hat on her head.

"What would you like, sir," the lady asked Daddy. She batted her eyes at him and smiled sweetly as she moved closer to us.

"Thank you, Miss. Just give us a minute here," he said as he turned and looked at me, "What would you like honey,"

I was overwhelmed, I wanted everything. I finally settled on chocolate.

"I'll have chocolate, thank you."

"And what would you like, sir," she said not even looking at me, but continued to look at Daddy.

"I'll take the same, please, maam, thank you."

"Coming right up. You can take a seat right there," she said as she pointed to a little round white table with two chairs,"

I couldn't believe my eyes and ears, I do believe she was flirting with Daddy.

Daddy's face turned a little red, he turned and motioned for me to sit as he sat down in the nearest chair.

She immediately brought the ice cream over, and gave him his ice cream first. I felt invisible.

"Well, it's nice meeting you. Are you new in town?" she asked. She continued to stand there.

"Well no, I was born in Sebastopol, but I left, and now my wife, family and I are back to live here on our farm," he said in a curt voice.

"Is that right," she said. She didn't move.

I thought lady, can't you take a hint.

"Well, I guess we better go," Daddy said getting up. He pushed by her and quickly moved toward the door.

"Oh, do you have to go?" she complained, and smiled up at him.

As we rushed out the door, he looked down at me and grinned.

"Let's get the heck out of dodge," he said grinning, his face was still red.

I laughed, "That was a close one."

"Yeah, that lady was a little crazy," he said as we climbed back into the car and set about finishing our ice cream.

"I have to tell you something." He said. "We really aren't here for shopping."

"No what?" I asked apprehensively.

"We have an appointment with a Doctor named, Will Hawkins We are here to have your tonsils taken out," he said quietly.

"I just knew it. I knew something just wasn't right," I moaned.

I knew it wouldn't do any good to protest.

"I'm sorry," he said, but you know it's for the best. If we didn't, you could get sick and die," he said

"Well let's just do it and get it over with. Will it hurt," I asked fearfully. "What a traitor," I said looking at him.

"Heck no, it won't hurt, they just put you to sleep and you don't feel a thing."

"And I'm supposed to believe a traitor," I said, and I couldn't help but smile at the expression on his face.

He started to say something, and then he saw the expression on my face and realized I was teasing. "No, you just can't trust anyone now days," he said with a grin.

We drove about two blocks and pulled over in front of the only three story building on the street.

"This is it," Daddy said as we got out of the car, walked a few feet down the street and entered the brick three story building. We walked into the big lobby with a big desk against the far wall. It had a deep red carpet and the walls were lined with doors with different signs on them. On the right there was an elevator. I didn't know for sure, because I had never actually seen an elevator.

"We're not going to a hospital," I asked.

"No," Daddy said, "This is much better. He does the surgery right here in a surgical room. After the surgery you spend the night right here in a recovery room with a nurse. I stay here also, in a room next to your room. Then we go home tomorrow. That way you're not exposed to all the germs at the hospital."

We entered the elevator, Daddy pushed a button and swoosh, up we went taking my stomach with it.

"Good grief, was that an experience," I gasped.

We got out, I was a little dizzy, and we went down a carpeted hallway and stopped at a door with the Doctor's name on it. We went into a brightly lit white room. There was a short, dark haired lady in a white uniform and white nurse's cap, sitting behind a glassed in reception office.

"Good morning," she greeted us, "you must be Zemma," she said smiling at me.

"Yes," I said, and began to shake. I was suddenly scared to death when reality grabbed me.

"Come with me," she said coming from behind the cage.

"I'll see you in a couple of hours, or do you want me to come with you?" Daddy asked, bending down and giving me a good hug. It made me feel a little bit better.

"I'll come with you," he said taking me by the hand and walking with me behind the nurse, which made me feel a little better.

"Thank goodness," I said looking up at him.

We all went into a little room and the nurse took me behind a screen and helped me change into a thin white gown. She brought me back out and helped me up onto a cot with sheets on it.

"The Doctor will be right in," she said as she left, closing the door right after her.

Daddy came over and took my hand.

"Now honey, don't worry about a thing, this will be over before you know it, and we'll go back and get some more ice cream," he said, and suddenly grinned, " and at a different store."

At that I had to giggle, "That's for sure," I said, "or she just might kidnap you," I added with a grin.

The door suddenly opened and in came the Doctor. He seemed nice. He shook hands with Daddy. Then he turned to me. He was short, and a little on the heavy side with grey hair and a full round face. He was very pleasant looking when he smiled. I thought to myself, he looks a little like Santa Clause.

"Hello young lady," he said with a big smile. " Now don't you worry about a thing, this will be over before you know it, and you'll feel so much better. No more sore throats."

The nurse came back with a tray with something on it. I looked at Daddy and before you know it, the nurse had given me a shot of some kind. I felt really dizzy.

"Ouch! That really hurt, why didn't you tell me you were going to do that?" I yelped in surprise.

O dear me, I thought, she just gave me a shot with a needle, and she hadn't warned me at all. After that I didn't trust her at all.. I watched her like a hawk, who knows what she would try next. Although, I thought it was a good thing she hadn't warned me, I would have been sick with worry, and I just might have put up a fuss.

She and the Doctor laid me down on my back on the cot, and wheeled me out through the door down the hallway and into another room where the ceiling lights were really bright and the room was filled with all kinds of shiny metal medical equipment.

They put a mask on my face that had an evil smell. It smelled so bad I thought I was going to choke to death. Then as my Dad would say, that's all she wrote.

When I woke up I was so sick. My stomach hurt so bad. I sat up and the nurse was right there with a white basin for me to throw up in.

I sure didn't feel like ice cream. What a joke that was. Just like the trick to get me there. I still wasn't sure how I felt about that. I guess it made sense. If they had told me I was going to have surgery, I would have been a wreck. I might have been so worried I wouldn't have been in any condition to have surgery.

Anyway, the nurse left and Daddy rushed in with a big smile on his worried face. "Guess you don't feel much like ice cream," He said with a faint smile.

I just shook my head, no. "You did it again, you fooled me," I tried to growl, but I could only whisper.

The Doctor came in with a big smile. Daddy was right there beside him.

"Well, well young lady it's all over and you did just fine during he surgery. It's a good thing you got them out because they were very, badly infected. They were just pouring poison into your system. Even the adenoids were bad, and they had to come out too."

Adenoids, what the heck were adenoids, I wondered. Well, what ever they were, I didn't have them anymore.

The Doctor turned to Daddy and said, "Like I said Mr. Carter, everything worked out fine. Just keep her in bed a day or so. No romping around or rough housing. It's a good thing you got her in here when you did."

I don't remember much about the ride home. I slept most of the way.

When we got home, the first thing Sally said with a big grin on her face was, "How do you like the way we tricked you?"

"Aw, shut up, any way, you know I had ice cream, " I could barely whisper.

CHAPTER 26

School Starts

It was September. And it was fall already. What had happened to the summer? It was gone and now it was time for school to start.

I really had mixed feelings about that. I was just a wreck thinking about it. One minute I would be excited and wanted to go, and then again when I thought about how I didn't know anybody in school, I would get scared and try to think of ways to get out of going.

Of course, the night before school started, it started to rain, and rain some more. Thunder and lightning dazzled the night sky. The lightening would streak across the sky, lighting up the sky until you could see everything for a second as if it were daytime. When it disappeared, it would be followed by the earth and house shaking blast of thunder that would nearly knock your pajamas off. It was beautiful but scary, chilly and wet. So this was the beginning of fall. It was loud, noisy and wet. All the red, yellow and orange tree leaves started flying, blowing wildly in the wind. The sky was filled with all kinds of debris, sticks, leaves and flying limbs which were tossed up into the air. Tree limbs were yanked from their mother trees, and left the bigger tree branches behind, still attached while they flew into the air, then they would fall back down, hitting the ground and sinking beyond sight, deep into the wet, red, clay dirt.

School starts tomorrow, I kept thinking. I was so excited I didn't think I would be able to sleep even a wink tonight.

The next morning the rain was over and the sun was shining, bright and innocent as if nothing had happened the night before.

For the first day of school, Sally and I were getting to wear the new dresses that Mama had made for us. They were beautiful, actually, she made them out of fertilizer bags like Aunt Ginger had taught Mama how to do this neat, new trick. She showed her how to make clothes out of fertilizer bags. First, she ripped the fertilizer bag seams out of the empty bags, next she bleached the bags with a mixture of soap, Clorox bleach and water. When she got through with it, the material was a thick, bright beautiful white. You would never guess they were made out of fertilizer bags. The dresses turned out to be beautiful and expensive looking.

"My goodness, it looks just like white linen material," Mama exclaimed.

Aunt Ginger nodded wisely, with a proud look on her wrinkled face. You know linen is very pretty and very expensive," she told me.

"You're so smart, Aunt Ginger. You know we have tons of empty fertilizer bags around here. When we finished planting all our crops. You know, the crops of cotton, corn, tomatoes and all the other vegetables. The lists go on and on," I said.

"Don't forget planting hay to feed the cows."

"That's right," Mama said, "that too."

"If anybody asks about the dresses, I'll tell them that the dresses were made out of linen, "I said.

"Good idea, "Mama said, "You're right, if they have the nerve to ask, then that's the answer they deserve," Mama said with a conspiratorial smile on her tired face.

Mama packed school lunches for us. She made ham sandwiches out of left over breakfast biscuits. She also put peaches from our own peach tree, and added a boiled egg. For desert, she added two sugar cookies each, that were left over from last night.

We waved goodby to everybody and headed down the driveway to the public dirt road, which Daddy said was about a mile long. So we would have only one mile to walk.

When we got to the end of our road, we waited on the side of the big public dirt road for about thirty minutes. There was an old worn out wooden bench beside the side of the road, that somebody had made long ago.

Then we saw it. The giant orange school bus rumbling and winding it's way down the crooked, red dirt road. It left a trail of red dirt and dust that bounced and floated up, around and behind it.

Sally and I looked at each other. I was so excited I could hardly stand it.

"I'm scared," I said, gripping her arm.

"Ouch! You must really be scared, you're hurting my arm," Sally said.

"Not me," Sally boasted, as she pulled her arm away and started rubbing it with her other hand.

"Oh, sure you are, you just won't admit it," I said grinning at her.

She suddenly grinned back, "Well maybe, just a little."

"You know, we can look at it this way, we'll make new friends," I said cheerfully.

"Yeah, you know what, that should be easy, practically everyone is related to us."

"That's right. And at least, if all else fails, we have each other," I said, throwing my arm up and around her shoulders. "We'll make sure we sit together." For the first time I gained comfort from that thought. "Good idea," she agreed.

I could hear all the noise the kids were making, talking, yelling and laughing even before the bus reached us. The bus rumbled up to us and came to a stop.

The kids on the bus didn't seem to notice that we were alive. That made me feel invisible, but I felt better. I got on first, looked down the aisle of the bus, I couldn't see two empty seats together. Oh shoot, I thought, what am I going to do. I looked back at my sister and shook my head. I saw her look around and then she sat down next to a little girl about our age.

I kept looking around and started to sit down next to a girl with long black hair. She shook her head no, "I'm saving this seat for my friend," she said putting her hand down on the empty seat, and turned her head away from me and looked out the window. She made it plain that she was ignoring me.

I was so embarrassed. I looked past her to the next seat behind her.

The little girl behind her, looked up, smiled and patted the seat next to her.

"Here, you can sit here," she said and continued to smile. She was shorter than me, and she was pretty with a round face, blue eyes, and long blond hair, that was tied back in a pony tail with a blue ribbon.

I abruptly sat down. "Thank you," I whispered gratefully.

"Don't mind her," she whispered loud enough for the girl to hear her, as she motioned her head toward the mean girl and added, "She's just a little snot,"

I smiled, nodding my head, that I agreed.

The black haired girl just looked away angrily, and tossed back her head.

"My name's Amy, what's your's? "She asked.

"My name's Zemma," I said gratefully, and so a long friendship was started.

"It looks like they even have high school kids on the bus,"

"Yeah," Amy said, "My oldest brother is on it too, and he's a freshman in high school."

"I'm in seventh grade," I said.

"Well, me too," she said eagerly, "that's great, we'll be in the same room."

I explained to her that I had a sister that was in the same grade as I was. Even though she was fifteen months younger than I was. It all started when she started school at five instead of six. The reason was because my parents didn't want us going to school by our selves, all alone "

"Having a sister so close in age must really be a lot of fun."

I agreed that it was.

"I'm really nervous, because this is the first day in this school," I admitted to Amy.

"Don't be," Amy said, "You just go to Mrs. Smith's office, she's the principal, you know and she will sign you up and tell you where to go."

"Gee thanks, I'm so glad I met you Amy, I'll see you later in class," I said. I got off the bus and found Sally.

She was waiting for me by the front steps of the school. We proceeded into the school through the wide front door, down the giant oak floored hallway, that was empty of any decorations, and found Mrs. Smith's office.

There was a short line into her office. But we didn't wait long before we were seated in Mrs. Smith's office. Mrs. Smith was short, heavyset and old, with white hair rolled into a bun at the nap of the neck. She was very stern looking with thin lips, and penetrating blue eyes behind wire rimmed glasses. She had deep frown wrinkles and a double chin She never smiled once, the whole time we were sitting stiff in our chair, facing her behind her huge blond oak desk. She seemed like she hated her job, by the way she slapped her paperwork and pencils around. She even slammed a book down so hard on her desk, and I almost jumped right out of my skin. Eventually we got all signed up and headed for our assigned classroom. Classroom 2B.

Sure enough, when we got to our assigned classroom, there was Amy. When she saw us she beckoned us over to her desk. She motioned for us to sit down in the two empty desks next to her desk, one in front of her, and one behind her. I sat in the empty desk in front of her and Sally sat in the one behind her. Now we were settled for the duration.

The classroom door opened. A young, pretty, redheaded, woman, somewhere in her early twenties, I would guess, walked into the room and stood behind the large, dark, wood desk.

The room suddenly became quiet.

"My name is Miss Hunt, and please, would the class come to order," she said tapping the desk with a small, silver, metal gavel.

It took a couple of minutes for the rowdy boys to settle down when they realized the teacher was present.

Miss. Hunt was smiling patiently.

"Hello everyone, I'll tell you a little bit about myself. I'm strict, but I'm fair, and we'll get along just fine if you do what I tell you, treat me with respect and do your homework. You look like smart girls and boys. If you have any problems, don't be afraid to ask for help. And so the seventh grade in Sebastopol began.

The name of the girl that sat in the desk in front of me was Jane.

She looked back at me and said, "My name is Jane," she said smiling. She was a pretty girl with long black hair and green eyes. She was about the same height as I was, but she was a little heavier than I was, but so was everybody in the world, I thought.

"Hi," I said, "My name is Zemma," I said feeling really happy, like I had made a new friend.

She smiled, and turned back around facing the front of the room.

School was good and I liked it. I looked over at Sally and she was grinning from ear to ear. She looked at me, and nodded her head in the direction of the girl behind her, and mouthed *new friend,* I got her message, she had made a new friend too.

Sally got up to go sharpen the pencil that they had given her with the new tablet, and other books. As she went by she leaned over and whispered in my ear. "That girl said my dress was very pretty, and I told her that it was made out of real linen, and she was really surprised."

I said, "Oh no, you didn't." Sally had more guts than anybody I knew.

At the end of the school day, it was back on the orange school bus, and on the road home.

CHAPTER 27

Planning Trip to Georgia

"When can we go to the next place on the map?" I asked.

"Maybe later, when we've finished looking everywhere here. We have a lot of looking to do here, before we go to Georgia and look around the old plantation where the gold was last seen," Uncle Oglee said, looking thoughtful, his brow furrowed.

"I'll bet there were a lot of men killed over that gold," I said feeling excitement travel up my back.

"That's not good, nothing worth that," Junior said.

"Oh, my," Lena said.

"Oh I don't know, if they were bad guys and they were trying to take my gold, I'd kill them," Sally said.

"Yeah, I'll bet you would, especially if they tried to take your Sears catalogue away from you," I joked, giggling.

"Ah, shut up smarty pants," she said scowling at me.

I just giggled.

"Did Uncle Oglee tell you about our well problem," I asked Jannelle.

"Indeed he did, but that won't be such a big problem. Everyone will get together and help dig a new well," she said cheerfully.

"That's really good to know," Uncle Oglee said.

"Yes, that's what's nice about these people, they have their faults, but when push comes to shove, they're right there to help you when you need it most."

"We have a lot to do here before we travel somewhere else looking for gold," Oglee said, shaking his head. "That trip would take several days." He stopped and looked at her, his black eyes searching her face. "Would your folks let you go on a big trip like that? Maybe we could go in a couple of months."

Her heart shaped face looked serious. She looked down at the ground, scraping her foot back and forth in the tall Johnson grass. She was obviously thinking. "I know, I can take my little brother, Jackson and you can take Zemma as chaperones," she said. looking at me with a conspiratorial (new word, for me) smile. My Uncle would definitely want to go with me.

Uncle Oglee laughed, "That might work."

I was delighted, to put it mildly. Her little brother was fourteen and I might say, very cute. I grinned to myself, I might need a guardian. My little heart actually skipped a beat, silly girl.

"I'll have to talk to them like a Dutch uncle," she said with an impish grin, "but I think I can make it work."

I was thrilled and excited beyond words at the very prospect of our new adventure. I knew Mama would let me go with Uncle Oglee.

Mama appeared on the front porch. "Dinner's ready. Zemma run down to your cotton patch and bring Junior back with you. If we left him be, he would chop cotton until dark."

We laughed, and I ran lickety split to get him, I wanted to hurry back, and not miss anything.

We all sat down to dinner and the conversation got hot and heavy. Sally, Lena and Junior all wanted to go. It was tough explaining to them all the reasons they couldn't go.

We talked about which way was the best way to go. Jannelle said she could get maps at the library.

"You know, I have relatives in Georgia, they would put us up while we were there," Jannelle said, excitement building in her voice.

"We need to travel light," Uncle Oglee said.

"That's easy for me," I said, and laughed "I don't have any clothes anyway."

Sally was pouting, "I hope your cotton sprouts dry up and blow away."

Junior jumped up turning his chair over, "No, no don't you worry Zemma; I'll take good care of our plants."

"Take it easy there son," Daddy said.

"I know you will," I said smiling and patting Junior on the back. "It looks like good weather, maybe you can get started early day after tomorrow," Daddy said.

Mama was quiet. I could tell she wasn't too hot on the idea.

"I just don't know about this," Mama said, slowly shaking her head.

"I think they will be alright. Especially since Jannelle has relatives there.

"Wel, we wouldn't go for at least a couple of months anyway," Uncle Oglee said.

"I'll take Jannelle home, then come back and get caught up on some work around here.

After they left, Lena sidled up next to me and sat down on the bed. I held the Sears catalogue out to her, so she could pick her favorite things to get when we made our fortune.

"I sure wish I could go with you," she whispered, she didn't want to say it too loud because she didn't want Sally to get all upset again.

"That's alright; I'll tell you all about it when we get back. I promise I won't leave out anything. And of course when we hit the pot of gold, you will get your share too."

"Really, really for real," she said with a gasp.

"You can bet your bottom drawers on it," I reassured her. It made me happy just watching the look on her face.

CHAPTER 28

Talk About the Depression

I could hear Daddy turn on the radio. He always turned it on at six o'clock for the news. After that we would listen to Amos and Andy. Then we listened to George Burns and Gracie Allen, and Jack Benny. We all rushed to the living room to hear what the news was for the day. The news was always bad, more about the depression. President Roosevelt was going to save us all. He was putting in programs to help people get jobs. It was bad, the newscaster said. Men were jumping out of high story windows because losing all their money was just too much for them. I guess you would feel like that if you had a lot of money to lose, and suddenly lost it all. It wouldn't hurt us because we didn't have any to lose.

We needed to hear the weather report, because if it rained it would hurt our new, tender cotton sprouts. As I rushed into the living room, and sat down on the floor beside the radio, I was praying. Please don't let it rain yet.

The radio was a big brown wooden box that was about the size of a bale of hay that sat up on its end. It was pretty. It had carvings all the way across the front beside the knobs. Uncle Jim and Aunt Katrina had given it to us, when we first got here. They said someone gave it to them, and someone else had given them another one. They said it was our coming home present. That was nice of them. That was about the only nice thing they did for us. When I said that Mama would frown and shake her head.

The weather man said there would be no rain for a few days.

"Hallelujah," I shouted.

"That's great," Daddy said.

But all the other news was bad. The news reporter said there was a story of a poor woman who had to give up her baby because she was too poor to feed it.

There was another story about three people who were standing in the soup line waiting to be fed when they dropped dead right there on the streets of Chicago. The news was all bad.

I heard sniffling behind me. I turned around to see Mama crying.

"That's too terrible, that poor mother having to give up her little baby because she was too poor to feed it," she whispered.

"At least we have food," Uncle Oglee said.

"Let's change the subject and talk about the gold we are going to find," Uncle Oglee said as he stood up, reached down and dusted off his knees, where he had been bending down on his knees.

"And don't forget our cotton crop. That will be good news when we harvest our crop." Junior said.

"Let's go out and dig some more under the mulberry tree," Sally said.

"Let's get all our chores done before supper time and then we can dig for gold," Daddy said.

We all rushed around doing our chores. The usual chickens, horses, cows or should I say two cows.

Everyone was talking about the two strangers and wondering if they would return tonight.

"I told Sheriff Dan about them and he said he would keep an eye out for them," Daddy said as he bent over and dumped a bale of hay into the pen for the horses.

As I listened to them, I felt shivers run up and down my spine. I thought of all the mystery shows we listened to on the radio. The "Shadow Knows" and The Mystery Show, to mention two of my favorites." When it got dark we had all the same effects. The crickets, the hoot owls, and the wind whispering and moving the leaves in the shadowy trees. The squeals and squawks of unknown, unseen animals and insects. My imagination would take off, when it got dark and the full moon would come out and the dark shadows would start leaping as the wind rustled about in the trees.

We didn't have enough money for curtains yet to cover the windows but we did have sheets that worked just as well, no one could see through them, so if the bad guys did sneak up they couldn't see in.

The dogs, Coco and Nonie were barking, jumping up and down gnashing their teeth. They were pulling on their lines that were tied to the clothes line to keep them from escaping and getting lost in the woods, or being eaten by a wild cat. They did love to wonder out of the yard and into the freedom of the bushes and trees. The raccoons and other wild animals were to be reckoned with, and would hurt them if they went into the woods alone. We wouldn't let them stay outside during the night.

"Listen to those dogs. Those guys are back, I tell you," I whispered into Lena's ear. Lena's eyes were big as saucers and the corners of her mouth were turned down as she reached out and grabbed my arm.

"No, they wouldn't dare, your Daddy has the shot gun," she insisted.

Junior had been listening. He reached out and yanked my overall strap. It scared me half to death when he started pulling me back. I thought the boogie man had got me.

"Darn it Junior, you scared me half to death. I'm on pins and needles as it is."

"But what if they have a bigger gun and there are two of them, maybe they both have guns. They could mow us down."

"Oh no," Lena started to sniffle.

"Never happen," I snorted and pulled back the white sheet that covered the largest window in the living room.

"Nothing to be afraid of," Sally said, sounding brave.

I knew how brave she was, she would be the first one to get the heck out of Dodge, as one of the cowboys in Zane Grey's books would say.

"Supper is served," Mama announced, as she put a hot bowl of white gravy and biscuits on the red and white checkered table cloth.

"Mama, that smells wonderful," I said as I leaned forward to get a good strong whiff of the delicious gravy.

Mom had set the table with all the leftovers from dinner, except for new hot buttermilk biscuits. Delicious fried chicken, gravy, mashed potatoes, and green beans with bacon were just as good as it had been at dinnertime. Mighty tasty I would say.

She finished feeding Jenny and started wiping Jenny's chin before she put her in the new oak playpen Daddy had built for her before we even got her.

"Mrs. Carter, I must say you're a much better cook than my Daddy. About my Daddy, how was he today?" Lena asked as she turned and looked at Daddy.

"He was so much better this morning. The Doctors all say he's strong as an ox, and is mending much faster than they expected. He should be ready to come home in a couple of weeks."

"Too bad, he won't have a home to come to," Lena said, her face was sad as she looked down at her plate.

"Oh, didn't I tell you, all our relatives and neighbors got together and started building you a new house. Of course Oglee and I are leading the pack," Daddy said with a smile, "So don't say a word, we want him to be surprised."

"Oh, you're just wonderful," Lena said, wiping away the tears that had started rippling like a dark river, leaving pathways down her checks.

As I watched her, I felt tears running down my own face. This feeling was new for me. For the first time I thought I was going to burst, I was so surprised and proud at the kindness of my relatives.

CHAPTER 29

Our Mineral Rights

*I*t was late for someone to come driving down the driveway to our house but here they were.

It was Harry Belton, a distant relative of ours of some kind. He stopped by from time to time to chat with Daddy. He would bring Daddy up to date on all the local gossip. It seemed like he always knew everything, even almost before they happened. He slowly got out of his Model A Ford. He hadn't been the same since he injured his right leg cutting down a huge pine tree when he was logging last summer. The leg had never healed right since the accident.

He was still angry because he blamed the hospital and doctor for botching up his case.

He was so mad he took the hospital and the Doctor who did the surgery to court, but poor Harry lost his case. When he lost he was really mad. He added the people on the jury to his hate list. He said he would get even with every last one of them. But after the court case ended, the people on the jury said it was Harry's own fault that his leg didn't heal right. They said there was evidence that Harry didn't take care of his leg like he was supposed to, after he got home from the hospital. They said that he got mad and cut his leg cast off, a month before the cast was supposed to come off. He was supposed to wait and let the Doctor take the cast off a whole month later.

He probably had good reason to be mad at the hospital for the poor care he got, but they weren't responsible for his bad leg, sounds like he was.

I had heard all kinds of horror stories about the county hospital. Aunt Helen said that a friend of hers had lost his leg when he went in to have a boil lanced on his right leg and they actually cut off his left leg and it wasn't even the sore leg. Another story was a little girl went in to simply have her tonsils out and she left the hospital feet first. She had bled to death. Another time was a boy went in, just to have a wart taken off his hand. He had the wart taken off alright, but he died from a blood infection three days later. The stories went on and on. It makes me shiver just thinking about it.

Daddy said he had rather go to the veterinary than to go the hospital.

Anyway, Harry Beltran said that some company called "Jackson Mineral Right's Company," was buying up all the mineral rights to everyone's property. He didn't know who was behind it but he suspected that it was someone we all knew well, but he just couldn't imagine who. It was someone who had reason to believe there was either oil or gold in the valley.

"He's paying a good price to the land owners for the mineral rights. I think they said two dollars an acre. That's so tempting I think I will sell my mineral rights," Harry went on, "and you should too," he said.

"Sounds good alright, but I think I'll just hang on to mine," Daddy said.

"Thank goodness," I breathed, "That would be terrible to sell our rights then strike gold."

"The chances of striking oil or gold are next to nothing," Harry said, "Might better think it over Claude."

"Claude, that was a very wise decision. I think we will find gold," Uncle Oglee said, beaming from ear to ear.

They started talking about the weather. I got bored and went to see what Sally and Lena were doing. Of course, they were lying on the bed looking through the Sears catalogue again.

CHAPTER 30

Peeping Tom

J joined them, but I was nervous about the open spaces in the sheet hanging over the window. I got off the bed and tried to adjust the sheet over the window, but it just wasn't big enough to cover the window completely. I finally gave up and got back on the bed. "I'll sure be glad when we get our new curtains."

"Yeah," they both agreed but didn't seem to be too concerned about the window.

Just as I got settled back on the bed, I heard the bushes rustle outside. I was up like lightning, and back at the window. As I looked out I saw a dark figure running through the shrubbery, and down the driveway.

"There he is, somebody get him," I heard myself screeching to the top of my lungs. The three of us almost got tangled up in the bed clothes, as we rushed to the living room where Mama and Daddy were seated at the dining room table talking quietly.

"What in the blazes," Daddy said.

They both jumped up, Oglee came from the bedroom across the hallway.

"I saw him, I saw one of those men out the window," I said out of breath.

"Which way did he go?" Uncle Oglee yelled.

"Down the driveway," I said.

"All of you stay inside," Daddy said, as he grabbed his shotgun, and he and Oglee went outside.

We stayed inside and watched from the window. Junior came in, slowly rubbing his eyes.

"What happened?" he asked.

"We just had an uninvited visitor and Daddy and Uncle Oglee went out to get him," I said.

"Oh did they take the gun? He asked as his eyes searched the room for the shotgun. "Good," he said when he saw that it was missing.

We heard a loud gunshot.

"Oh Dear, I hope they didn't have to shoot him."

"They got him," Junior said.

We watched breathlessly as the three figures walk up the driveway.

"Well, all three were walking, so I guess he didn't get shot," I said.

"He's smaller than our guys," Sally said.

They dusted off their feet as they came up onto the porch.

I ran and opened the door so they could escort the trespasser into the living room.

He was a very sad and sorry looking young man. He didn't look up when he came in. He kept his head down. He didn't look like any of the guys we had seen before. He looked much younger. Maybe late teens or early twenties, a college kid even. He was small and slender, clean shaven, short brown hair and brown eyes. He was fairly nice looking and scared looking.

He was mumbling how sorry he was, that he didn't mean any harm.

"I'm so sorry. I was downtown when I heard people talking about this place and how you people were gold hunters. I was just curious. Didn't mean any harm. Just used poor judgment. He looked like he was going to cry. He reached in his back pocket; his fingers were shaking as he fumbled with some papers, almost dropping them, as he sorted them out.

"Here's my I. D. I'm not a criminal. I'm a student at Mississippi State. Just here for a vacation, doing a little fishing. He could hardly look up at Daddy as he handed him his papers.

I could see a smile tugging at the corners of Daddy's lips as he looked over the papers.

"Son, you should never go peeping into people's windows. You can get into a heap of trouble. Could even get shot. You know there is a killer, still on the loose that they haven't caught yet, so I'd be mighty careful about where you go at night time, or you could just be mistaken for the killer and get shot."

"I know, I know. Can't tell you how sorry I am."

Daddy sat the shot gun down against the wall. And the guy looked up at Daddy with a look of relief on his face.

"Well, James Harrison< I was going to turn you over to the sheriff, but you seem to be pretty above board. Just not too smart. I'm going to turn you lose, just don't ever come around here again."

"Thank you sir. I really appreciate it. Didn't mean any harm, I swear. And believe me I will never ever show up here again." He reached for the door, opened it and almost ran down the hallway.

I started to giggle, and couldn't stop. When I finally stopped. "Daddy, that was really nice of you," I said.

"Yes it was," Mama said.

"I wouldn't have been that easy on him," Oglee said with a grin, "I think I would have made him suffer a little more."

"Me too," Junior said "after all he was peeking through a strangers windows."

"Well thank goodness he wasn't a bad guy," Sally said.

"I agree with Sally," Lena said.

"That's enough excitement for tonight. Let's go to bed.

CHAPTER 31

A Bloody Murder

*E*arly that morning as soon as it got daylight, I could see the dust of a car coming down the road.

"Somebody coming," I yelled as I watched them drive into the yard.

"Who is it honey?" Mama yelled back from the kitchen. "Its Sheriff Dan and deputy Bob," I answered.

Mama came to the screen door, as the two got out of the car and started to walk slowly up the pathway, they stopped and talked for a few minutes then continued on to the house.

Sally and I were behind the door, behind Mama, so we could hear everything that was said.

"Howdy Leota," Dan said, "Is Claude around?"

"Sure Dan, you come on in and I'll get him."

Daddy appeared from the back. "Hi fellows, what's going on?"

"Well sir, we just had our first real crime in Scot county?" Bob said. "And it's a nasty one."

"Really, do tell, what happened?" Daddy asked, surprised.

"Well sir, you just won't believe it but you know Charlie, Helen and Jeffery Henderson, in fact I think they're related to you. Well sir, I'm so sorry to tell you that all three of them have been murdered. As you know Jeff was only twelve. So you know by that, whoever did this was pretty bad. The murderers used a gun and a knife. Looks like there were two of them, one used a knife and the other used a gun, we're just guessing, of course, we'll have to do more investigating to know for sure. So far, we have an all points bulletin out, to be on the lookout for two strangers. We are asking anybody and every body for any information at all about these two. It was pretty brutal. The sadistic son of bitches tortured them, apparently trying to get more information, from them about anything, they may have hidden. And of course they took all of Jack's gun collection. I've already contacted all the gun dealers in Forrest and Jackson and where ever else I can think of. It's terrible that this should happen to such a nice family, or anybody's family for that matter. Thank goodness the two girls were away at their cousins, for the night."

"Oh my god, that's terrible," Daddy said.

"Oh my goodness," Mama gasped.

"Well now that you mention it. We had some trouble the other night. There were two unsavory characters that showed up here the other night. They sure acted like they were looking for trouble. I had to get the shot gun out, and run them off. "

"That sure sounds like that could have been them."

"What did they look like?" Dan asked.

Daddy scratched his head and then proceeded to describe them.

"I'll say you're mighty lucky they went on their way."

"I would keep a lookout for them if I were you. You just might be next on their list." Dan said.

"Yeah, they might want to get even," Bob said.

"Tell you what I will do; either Dan or I will make frequent runs out to your place here, to discourage them from coming back."

Mama brought out two cups of coffee and a freshly baked pie from yesterday.

"Please sit down and have a piece of apple pie," Mama said pointing to the table.

"Oh, my goodness how nice of you Leota. I don't mind if I do," Dan exclaimed

"Me too. Thanks a lot," Bob said.

Sally and I kept out of sight because we knew they would run us off, and not let us hear anything about this. We kept our ears glued to the door.

"What do you think happened?" Daddy asked.

"Well they tore up the place pretty bad. Looking for anything it looks like," Dan said. "They even slashed the couch cushions looking for hidden money, I guess. The bed mattresses and pillows were also slashed."

"They even tortured Jeff, the little boy, probably to make the parents give them information about where they had their valuables and money hidden. They tortured all three of them by pulling their fingernails and toenails out. They cut them all over, slashing their arms, legs, stomach and across their chests, with some kind of hunting knife," Dan continued.

"Oh yeah, they also cut off three of little Jeff's fingers on his right hand, then they strangled him to death. They finally slashed Helen and Jack's throat when they got through with them," Bob added.

"It was just horrible," Dan said, "They even shot all three of them in the head, just to make sure they were good and dead. It was the bloodiest scene I have ever come across," Dan said.

"They raped and sodomized poor Helen."

"Yeah, it's enough to give you nightmares for the rest of your life."

"Oh my God," Mama gasped. "This just makes me sick, poor, poor Helen. Poor little Jeff. The man or men would have to be insane to be that bad." Tears started running down Mama's face and she left the room.

"That's hard to believe," Daddy said horrified.

"What kind of people would do that?" Daddy went on.

"Well, they are not really people. They're animals," Bob said.

"Well, one good thing, we got good fingerprints. They were really crazy. They left evidence everywhere," Dan said.

Sally and I were really scared.

"What do you think? Do you think they will come here?" Sally asked.

"I don't know, I hope not," I answered. "What's sodomized?"

"Don't know," Sally said. "But it must be something bad."

"Now we really have something to worry about," I said looking at Sally and shaking my head as I saw Junior coming around the corner and into the room.

"Hey Junior, there's some really bad murderers on the loose." Sally said.

"Oh I know, I heard it on the radio," he answered.

"No, no there's more. They just murdered the Henderson family, even Jeff."

"What! Really, that's bad, are we next?"

I went rushing into the kitchen where Mama and Daddy were. They were sitting at the kitchen table, looking like they were still in shock.

"I wonder if it were the two guys that were here," I said, I just knew it must be them, that was just too much of a coincidence.

Mama looked at me. "Did you hear about the murders?"

"Yeah, Sally and I were behind the door listening to everything the sheriff and the deputy had to say. It was awful."

"That's too bad," Mama said.

"I know, we're going to have to be careful and stay together at all times,'' Daddy said.

Just then Oglee came into the kitchen, "What's a late sleeper?"

"You are, little brother," Mama said.

"I know, I'm so tired, I just don't know why, because it's just so quiet here at night time," he said grinning and rubbing his eyes. He looked like a little boy with his black hair, sticking straight up in the air, all tusseled, as usual, when he woke up from a nap.

"What's all the fuss about?" little Lena asked. as she came into the kitchen.

"There's been more murders, and they're here, where we live."

"Oh no, no, are they gonna get us," Lena began to cry.

"Oh no, Lena, we have Daddy, Uncle Oglee and me to protect you," Junior said, as he came over and put his arm around her.

"Oh that's right, that's good" she said smiling down at him through her tears.

"Well let's get on with our day," Daddy said.

"I thought maybe the killer had moved on to another county or something, because we hadn't heard anything about him or them in a while," I said looking up at Daddy.

"Yeah, I kind a think everyone was thinking like that," Daddy said.

CHAPTER 32

Too Poor to Buy Salt

"We're going to have to run into town again. I forgot to get salt, when we were there, "Daddy said.

"Can I go with you?" Uncle Oglee asked, "And maybe we could swing by and pick up Jannelle."

"Of course," Daddy said with a big grin that reached his green eyes.

"I might as well go along too," I said, hopping in before they could tell me no.

"We need to stop at the general store and get some table salt for the food," Daddy said.

We stopped and picked up Jannelle and of course Uncle Oglee was as happy as a Jaybird.

When we got to town, Daddy went inside the store while we waited outside. I sat on the wooden bench and watched the people walking down the wooden sidewalk. I loved to watch people and try to imagine what they were doing, where they were going and what their life was like.

When Daddy came out, I could tell he was angry. His face was red and his green eyes were glittering, flashing like fire.

"What's the matter Daddy?"

I suddenly felt scared. I've never seen Daddy like that.

"That bastard wouldn't sell me a nickel box of salt, sorry kids. I didn't mean to use that kind of language. Anyway I didn't have a nickel on me, so I asked if I could charge it. He said no, he wasn't in the banking business."

"I can't believe it," I gasped.

"Harrison has known me all my life, and he wouldn't let me charge a nickel worth of salt."

"He treated me like I was a bum."

Daddy was standing there like he was in shock. Gerald Albertson came up and stood in front of Daddy, and put his hand on his shoulder. Apparently he had been in the store when this happened.

"That's alright," Gerald said, "He's a mean son of a bitch. Let's go on over to the drug store, I know they have salt there."

"Naw, that's okay Gerald thanks, but we can get along without it."

"I insist, in fact you'll hurt my feelings if you don't. You'd do the same for me."

Daddy finally gave in and we all followed Gerald to the drugstore.

They couldn't say enough bad things about Harrison.

Daddy's face was red, I could tell he was embarrassed, but he tried to cover it up by making a joke. "Old Harrison must have got up on the wrong side of the bed."

"I don't think he even goes to bed, he's so evil I think he sleeps in a coffin," Gerald said.

"You mean like a vampire," I said laughing.

"Yep," Gerald said. "That's exactly what I mean."

We decided it was time to head for home, Daddy thanked Gerald again for getting us the salt, and we were on our way.

The truck had been acting funny. It grunted and groaned as we drove off.

We had gone about five miles and started up a long red clay hill. It finally made it to the top of the hill, groaned and came to a stop. Daddy pulled up the hood and started fooling with the innards of the engine. Nothing happened. Uncle Oglee tried his hand at fooling with the engine. Nothing happened "I'd try my hand at it, but I know I couldn't fix it, "Jannelle said.

"That does it. We're going to have to walk home. Or pray for someone to pick us up and give us a ride home," Daddy said.

We had been walking along quietly for a while thinking our own thoughts. It must have been almost an hour when Daddy broke the spell.

"Let's play this little game. Look around you and burn this moment into your brain, impress everything you see in your memory. Look at everyone, and burn it in your memory, remember how everyone looks and commit it to your memory, remember everything you see. I guarantee that you will always remember this moment as long as you live."

I looked around and committed everything I saw, heard, or smelled to my memory. I could smell the fresh, wet, red, clay dirt that had been stirred up by a tractor, along the sides of the road. It smelled good almost like dirt that a fresh rain had dampened. There were beautiful blue and yellow wild flowers that smelled fragrant, growing alongside of the bank. The tall pine trees cast shadows across the road. The beautiful green of the English Gum trees. The hickory nut trees with green moss growing on the northern sides of the trees. Tall underbrush grew in the gaps between the trees. There were a few bushes with orange red berries on them. The colors were great. Again I wished I was an artist and could capture the beauty of the nature all around us.

It was true, to this day, I have never forgotten that moment in the forest I was looking up at the blue sky with the soft billowy grey, white clouds that were forming above and along the horizon. The clouds were moving fast as they tumbled across the sky. They were turning dark as they began bunching together. I became alarmed. It was getting dark.

"By golly, it's going to rain," Uncle Oglee said as he grabbed Jannelle by the hand and ran to get under the trees."

"You're right there's going to be a storm," Daddy said, as he grabbed me by the hand and ran, pulling me toward a clump of trees. A grey squirrel ran across the road just ahead of us. The race was on, us or the squirrel. The squirrel beat us and ran up the same tree we were aiming for.

We all started laughing as the rain came down in a torrent, soaking us to the bone. We were soaking wet in the matter of minutes.

We huddled together under the biggest tree we could find. The loud thunder bellowed all around us and the lightning struck a tree in the distance.

"This reminds me when I was about ten when my friend Joe and I got caught in the terrible storm. Luckily we found this cave and stayed there until it was over. It turned out to be fun. We started exploring the cave and found smalL treasures. An old gold buckle with a belt. A confederate hat. And a couple other things."

"Oh my goodness, do you remember where it was, the cave I mean," I asked.

"Yeah, let me think a minute, It was about five miles from the house. Funny we never went back. We must have gotten busy or something more interesting came along.

"That could be where the gold was hidden," Uncle Oglee said. His black eyes shining with anticipation.

Jannelle clapped her hands in glee, "Yes, yes it really could be."

When we get home you'll have to show us where it is and we can start digging," I said.

CHAPTER 33

Another Murder

The rain slowed up a drizzle.

We heard the sound of a car coming down the road behind us, we stopped and waited anxiously. Who, friend or foe, would come around the bend.

"I don't recognize him," Oglee said, squinting his eyes. As we watched a marked car appeared in the mist.

"Oh I do," Jannelle said. "I know him. It's Bob Anderson," she said, sounding pleased.

He drove up and stopped beside us. "Fellows would you like a ride home," he said with a big grin on his clean shaven face. He kept looking at Jannelle with a happy look on his face. I could tell, it was obvious he liked her. Drat! Too bad for Oglee. It looks like he has some unexpected competition. Bob was tall, slender and clean cut looking with short, wavy, brown hair. He was wearing his tan sheriff's uniform and a silver badge. He was nice looking, but not nearly as good looking as Uncle Oglee.

"You bet we would like a ride. Mighty happy you came along," Daddy said, and we watched him come to a complete stop. Uncle Oglee helped me into the back seat of the police vehicle.

"Hey Janelle, please sit up here with me," Bob said, a big smile on his face. As he patted the seat beside him.

"Why thanks Bob, don't mind if I do," Jannelle said with a smile.

Bob jumped out ran around to her side of the car, opened the door and helped her onto the seat.

I snuck a peek at Uncle Oglee's face. He had no expression on his face at all; it was a still, cold, stone-faced look. I had never ever seen him look like that before.

Daddy and Uncle Oglee exchanged looks and jumped in.

"Mighty nice that you came along, Bob," Uncle Oglee said pleasantly, "Sure saved us a lot of shoe leather."

"Well thanks Oglee. Hey, Claude have you given any more thought to selling your mineral rights?" Bob asked, scratching his chin as if he were deep in thought.

I was surprised Bob remembered Uncle Oglee's name, since he had met him only once.

"No sir Bob, I've thought about it, and I've decided I had better not sell them, thank you anyway for the offer," Daddy said.

"You know three hundred is a good price for just taking a chance. That's what it amounts to, it's just a bet. You know what I bet we could get the company to go up to three hundred and fifty dollars.

"That's another thing Bob, who does actually own that company, who's behind it. No one seems to know."

"I just don't know, Claude, but Harry Belton seems to be involved somehow."

Suddenly a man ran out into the middle of the road waving his arms up in the air. He was wearing the usual farmer uniform, striped blue shirt with sleeves rolled up. and overalls. He was tall and stocky, sun bleached blond, blue eyed and a mustache.

"Woe, guess I'd better stop," Bob said slowing the car down to a stop.

"Help, there's been a murder! Come quick, follow me, it's back here, down this path way," he said, screaming at the top of his lungs with a high pitched voice.

Bob jumped out and started following the man up the red clay embankment and on down the green grass covered path.

"You guys stay here until I get back," he yelled back over his shoulder.

Of course we didn't, Daddy and Oglee looked at me and I shook my head no. No way was I going to stay behind alone, and wait for a murderer to get me. Nope, not me, I'm not stupid.

We trudged along behind this guy, making our way through the weeds, grass and bramble bushes. We must have gone about a mile. From time to time, I could hear some furry little animal scurrying about. As we passed through the underbrush, startled blackbirds and sparrows kept jumping up and, flying out of the bushes, and into the rainy sky. It was still drizzling rain a little bit.

I could hear the guy talking over his shoulder.

"This here property belongs to the Kincaid's, and my house and farm is over yonder hill," he said pointing to the left. "I always take a shortcut across his property to get to the McDaniel place."

Suddenly I could smell this terrible odor, and I clenched my nose shut with my fingers.

"Oh my God in heaven, what's that smell," Uncle Oglee said.

"That's it, that's what I found. Poor dead Mr. Kincaid," the man said.

We walked into an opening in the brush, and trees and into a clearing where a small wooden cabin stood. As we got closer the buzzards flew up, from where they had been sitting next to the front door of the cabin.

"Shoo-shoo," the guy yelled, "get out of here."

More buzzards flew up, and settled in the tops of the closest pine trees.

"Oh crap," Bob said, I know John Kincaid. I went to school with him."

Bob opened the door and they all went in, holding their noses. I followed and wished I hadn't. This poor man was all tied up, sitting, leaning in a corner with dried blood all over him. His face was so beat up and bloody, you couldn't even tell who he was.

"Yep, whoever did this used a knife and a gun. See here, they shot him clean through the head," Bob said pointing to his head. I groaned, and I didn't mean to.

"Oh my God," get the kid out of here, and you too Jannelle, you shouldn't be in here either," Bob yelled.

He turned and shooed everybody out. He reached over and took Jannelle by the hand, and said, "Honey, you shouldn't see any of this."

Uncle Oglee moved in like lighting, put his arm around Jannelle's waist, "got this Bob," and moved with Jannelle back down the path.

"I'll call for backup," Bob said, reaching for his phone, in the meantime he said, "What's your name, sir."

"It's Jack Thorton," he paused, "and Jim Kinkade and I were good friends."

"Mr. Carter and Jannelle, I'll have a car here to take you home," he said, glaring at, and purposely ignoring Uncle Oglee.

Daddy looked down and took me by the hand, "Honey, try to forget what you just saw. Come on; let's get the heck out of here."

We started moving back through the underbrush and bushes. Soon we were back to the road.

"We'll wait here for the car to pick us up."

I felt like I was in a daze, like things weren't real. I was just so tired. How could someone do that to another person? They would have to be a monster. I felt kind of dizzy.

The car did arrive eventually. It was another younger deputy, named George. He was average looking, brown hair, brown eyes a pimply face and he was short and a little stocky.

It was still raining some when we got home.

"If it doesn't stop soon, it's going to ruin our crops. The plants aren't strong enough yet to stand up to this kind of rain."

"I wonder if Bob knows who really owns The Mineral Rights Co.?" Daddy said. "It's sure strange that no one seems to know who owns it, why are they keeping it such a secret."

"Yeah, that's peculiar," I muttered.

I stopped thinking about the gold and started worrying about my cotton crop.

When we got home, we were cold and wet. Daddy and Uncle Oglee built a big roaring fire in the living room fireplace. Mama had supper on the table. We had chicken and dumplings and biscuits, which I love almost more than anything.

Sally, Junior, and Lena weren't too happy because we were gone too long. We explained we were trapped in the rain and had to walk a long way and didn't have any fun at all. Uncle Oglee and Daddy discussed how they were going to bring the truck home, and how they were going to fix it tomorrow.

It was almost dark when it stopped raining. Daddy and I went out to see what damage the rain had done to our cotton plants. Some of them were flattened to the ground. Daddy said they were savable. He said that if it didn't rain anymore, and the sun came out tomorrow, then they would be alright. I was so relieved; I said a prayer of thanks.

Daddy had gotten his brother Dave to help him with the well. He knew Dave had put in a new well a couple of years ago. His brother said he could get a couple of neighbors to help. They were going to start digging Monday morning, bright and early.

Sunday dinner was coming up. Every Sunday a big dinner was at one of Daddy's sister's or brother's house. These were always fun. Tomorrow was Sunday dinner and it would be at Mary Jane and Uncle Franklin's house. They had a really nice house, and Uncle Franklin was the minister at the Baptist church. They were very particular about everything.

I always felt a little nervous and uncomfortable around them. I noticed when I overheard the ladies talk. Aunt Mary Jane always criticized the other ladies about something, when they weren't there. I grew to really dislike her. She was a tall plump lady, always dressed nice. She very seldom smiled, and never looked directly at you, and never in the eye.

All the rest of the family had a great sense of humor. They were always joking and laughing at the dinner table most of the time. All the Aunts except Mary Jane would tease and make fun of each other. Mary Jane would say something hateful about someone, and then say bless her heart.

For instance today I heard her say as she shook her head," Jo Anna, bless her heart, always looks so tacky, you notice how, right now her slip is showing about a mile longer than her dress. She thought just by saying, bless her heart made everything she said, all right.

She just made me want to throw up. I watched the reaction of the other ladies. They didn't pay any attention to her; they just went right on talking.

I got a kick out of the things the other aunts would say to each other. Aunt Hilda told Aunt Mable, "You know you're uglier than a spider sandwich."

Aunt Mable just looked at her and answered her back, "Now you're just plain making me sad looking at you, since you're you're uglier than a mud fence, that's been dabbed with tadpoles."

Aunt Hilda laughed and said, "Ouch, that just plain hurt, not only that, but did anyone ever tell you, you're so slow, you couldn't fall out a tree in a hurry?"

Aunt Ginger got into the fray by telling Aunt Alberta, "If you can't run with the big dogs, you have to stay on the porch, with the cats."

This would go on throughout the whole dinner, each one seeing who could say the meanest thing, and tell the biggest joke, and get the biggest laugh. The men were just as bad, only they waited and took their jokes outside. Only their jokes were a little rowdier and not meant for the ladies tender ears. That's why they waited and took their jokes out on the porch.

I was tempted to get a notebook and write these things down, but I was afraid I would get caught.

When dinner was over, I would always be so full I was miserable.

I noticed they were beginning to accept my mother.

CHAPTER 34

Junior

A new day and the sun was shining, and our crop was saved. When we started doing our chores, one of the things Sally and I always did was take our horse Dan for a walk in the pasture. Every day Junior put up a plea to take Dan for a walk, but he was always told he was a little too young.

"You know son, you're just a little too young to take the horse out yet," Daddy said.

"But he's so tame, he wouldn't hurt a fly. "

"I know, but what if an accident happened, "Daddy insisted.

Mama said, "Absolutely Not."

"Why not, I do everything else around here that everyone else does," he insisted.

Mama looked at him and shook her head "You should grow up to be a lawyer" she said.

"Aw-w Mama we should let him go just this once and lead the horse," Daddy said.

"Oh alright, I give up, I still don't feel right about it," Mama said.

"Oh happy days are here again," Junior yelped, jumping up and down.

"Okay, but you girls go with him,"

Junior took the reins and marched ahead of Dan.

We walked as far as we usually went then turned and started walking on our way back. I was looking at a black crow that had landed on a fence post, when I heard a scream next to me. I turned and looked. Junior was lying face up on the ground, and Dan was standing over him.

"Oh my god," I screamed. I dropped to my knees and reached under Dan and started pulling Junior from under Dan.

"Sally, quick go get Mama and Daddy, hurry," I screamed.

As I pulled Junior out from under Dan, Dan just stood there. I realized what had happened. Junior had tripped on a little pine tree that had started to grow in the path, and when Junior fell, Dan kept on walking and stepped right in the middle of Junior's stomach. When Dan stepped on him, he had put all his weight on his stomach, which flattened Junior's stomach to the ground. Poor little Junior just moaned, and cried softly.

"It hurts, it hurts so bad."

When Mama and Daddy got there I was holding him best I could in my lap. I couldn't stop crying. I felt guilty. I felt I should have seen what was going to happen.

Mama started crying. Daddy reached down, picked him up and started running to the house with him. Mama was running after him. When we got to the house Daddy realized we didn't have a car, the truck was stuck on the road.

"Who can we call?" Mama said.

"I'll call Jannelle," Uncle Oglee ran to the phone, picked it up and apparently someone was on the phone.

"Please let us use the phone, this is an emergency, it's a matter of life and death.

Little Junior has been stepped on by a horse. We have to get him to a hospital before he dies," Uncle Oglee was shouting on the phone. They must have gotten the message, because he started talking to the operator.

I could hear him talking to Jannelle. "You and your Dad are coming in your car. Please hurry, thank you."

"Please don't take him to the county hospital," Mama was pleading.

"I know you have to have cash to go to the Forrest General Hospital," I could overhear Jannelle say. "We would let you have it, but we don't have any money now, oh God I wish we did." she went on to say.

"Where are we going to get the money?"

Mama said wringing her hands around a dishtowel.

Daddy got on the phone and started calling everyone he knew, no one had any money "If he goes to the county he'll never come out alive," Mama said, holding her head in her hands.

Jannelle and her father got there in just a few minutes, and they left immediately while we stayed home by the phone and waited to hear from them.

When Daddy called he told us that they refused to take Junior no matter what he promised to give them. They had to go to the County hospital and he said it was horrible. It was dirty and they didn't take Junior right away.

Uncle Oglee grabbed the phone, "Claude, why not sell the mineral rights to Mr. Belton. Get as much as you can, call the Forrest General hospital and see if they will let Junior in for three hundred dollars."

"That's a great idea, I'll do it."

We waited and waited to see what would happen.

About an hour later, Daddy called and said everything was fixed and Junior would be moved to Forrest Hospital. That of course, didn't mean Junior would be saved but he would have a much better chance.

Mama went through the motions of cooking dinner with all of us helping.

We didn't do anything but sit around, cry and wait.

Daddy called again. He said the doctors said, he had peritonitis and it was almost a death sentence. There was no medicine that would cure it. The only thing they could do was surgery, and hope for the best. Daddy said that someone would come and pick Mom up and take her to the hospital. After she left, we all sat down and cried some more. I knew this meant she was needed there because she might not ever see him alive again.

Not that it mattered any more, but the idea of gold hunting wasn't possible, because we had sold our mineral rights. That wasn't important now any more. Only Junior was important. We sat through the night waiting, waiting. People started phoning, asking what they could do to help. That was really nice. In the morning all the relatives and friends and even people we didn't know started bringing food and drinks. I was really surprised at the kindness of everyone.

Daddy called and said a surgeon from Jackson was coming out to Forrest to do the complicated surgery on Junior. He would be there in about two hours. I couldn't eat or sleep. I wished I could just go to sleep and wake up and everything would be back the way it was before.

The first night finally passed, and another day had started. I must have fallen asleep sometime during the night on the living room couch. The Doctor did the surgery as soon as he got there. We waited and cried, and cried and waited some more. I could hardly stand it. It was like a dream or like a bad nightmare. My chest hurt, like my heart actually hurt.

Poor Mama and Daddy. I don't know how they stood it. Mama could hardly stand up. She would get up and lean against the wall for a minute, turn around, come back and sit down, then she would get back up again and lean against the wall, then she would sit down next to Daddy, and Daddy would hold Mama in in his arms for a while, then he would get up and walk down the hall back and forth.

They would keep asking the nurse if the surgery was over yet. They would say, "No not yet."

Now we just had to wait and pray.

Finally Doctor Gray came out and told us he had survived the surgery. It had taken six hours to do the surgery. Now again, we just had to wait and pray. The Doctors were hopeful he would make it.. They let Mama and Daddy go in his room and sit with him.

Sally, Oglee, Lena, and I were sitting in the waiting room until he recovered from the anesthesia. I must have gone to sleep on one of the benches until a nurse came out and said we could go into his room and see him. One of the nurses had covered me with a blanket while I slept. The blanket fell to the floor as I got up. The nurse came over and picked it up as she took me by the hand and led Sally and me to Junior's room.

He looked so little in the big white hospital bed with the railings on the sides of the bed pulled up.

His face was thin and almost as white as the hospital sheets.

He smiled just a little smile.

I sidled up to his bed, leaned over and whispered, " How you feel,?" which was a stupid question, but I couldn't think of anything else to say.

"It hurts badly," he said. "Right here," he whispered, as he put his hand over his stomach.

"I know," I said, "it must be terrible." I felt tears coming in my eyes.

Daddy would call back to the house from time to time to let everyone know how Junior was doing.

Three of our aunts and uncles had come to the house to stay with us. They cooked and took care of the house. Our uncles took over the care of the cotton crops, except mine, Sally's and juniors. We knew how to do our own crops. The days turned into three days.

Sally and I went home for a while.

Later the third day, the dreaded phone call came. It was Daddy and he was crying. He said Junior had died, and was in heaven now. He said they would be home soon with him. It was awful.

They were home in about two hours. Junior was brought home in a long black car. Two men in white uniforms got out, opened the car door and carried Junior out. They brought him into the living room and laid his little body on the couch and covered him with a sheet. Then they went into one of the bedrooms and brought one of the beds out and moved it into the living room, then closed the door. They picked Junior up and gently placed Junior into the bed. The two men went back to the black car and brought some strange kind of equipment with long tubes and different shaped pans attached to it. They also brought buckets, sheets and rubber looking bed covers and left that in the living room. They asked everyone to leave the room and shut the door.

The grownups took us kids out of the house and over to Aunt Ginger's and Uncle Sam's house. I don't know where Mama and Daddy went. We stayed there for the rest of the day.

I felt like I was in a walking nightmare. I just couldn't believe any of this.

I cried so much, I didn't think I had any tears left, but I did. Each time I would stop, a new batch of tears would start. I just couldn't stop.

Sally kept crying and beating the pillow she was clutching.

Aunt Ginger kept crying and holding Sally and I. She was holding me so tight I could hardly breathe.

"Why did God let this happen? I just don't understand this. Why?" I asked Aunt Ginger.

"I don't know why these things happen, child," She sobbed.

"I just hate God," I cried, my voice cracked and raspy.

"No, no honey, don't say that. God had a reason for this. We are just not meant to know why. But he has a reason for everything."

"There's just no reason for this," I insisted.

"No," Sally said, "there isn't any reason for this."

Aunt Ginger finally gave up.

I fell asleep holding my pillow.

I woke up with Aunt Ginger shaking me.

"We'll take you girls home now. Your Mom and Dad will want to see you."

When we got back home it was just getting dark. The black car was gone, but all the relatives were still there. The women were cooking supper. There wasn't much for them to do because people had brought tons of food already cooked.

Mama and Daddy were just quietly sitting at the dinner table, looking off into space, not saying anything. Their eyes were red and swollen almost shut, from crying.

We ran to Mama and Daddy and threw our arms around first one, and then the other and started crying all over again.

We both kept saying how sorry we were.

"It wasn't your fault girls. It just couldn't be helped. It just happened. He's in heaven now," Mama said, as she kept rubbing our backs.

Daddy couldn't say anything; he just kept crying and holding us. He kept saying over and over again, "I should never have let him go.

I wanted to see Junior. I just felt if I could see and talk to him. He would somehow wake up.

"Can I see him please?"

Aunt Ginger looked at Mama, and she nodded, so Aunt Ginger led me to the living room door, opened it let me in and quickly shut the door behind me. Suddenly I realized I was all alone in the semi dark room.

The smell was overwhelming; I was shocked at the smell. It was so powerful I thought I might pass out. It was a strong chemical smell. I later found out it was formaldehyde.

There was a kerosene lamp sitting on the bedside table by the bed. The lamp cast an orange glow across the bed where Junior's small figure lay covered with a pretty patchwork blanket that I had never seen before. One of the relatives must have given it to him.

I slowly moved toward the bed. He looked very much alive, like he was just sleeping. I leaned over and touched him.

"Wake up, you have to stop this, you hear me," I whispered. Junior had always minded me. He had always done everything I told him to do. I just couldn't believe he wouldn't open his eyes. I shook him and told him again to wake up. When I touched him I realized his hands were cold, ice cold. I started crying.

"Junior, you just have to wake up. You can't be dead," but he didn't wake up. He didn't move a muscle, that's when I really knew he was gone forever. Really gone forever. I was truly broken hearted. Nothing could ever bring him back. Nothing.

When I left the room, I just felt broken, felt really broken into pieces. I would never be the same again. I guess I hadn't known before that he was really gone. All I wanted to do was go hide somewhere, go to sleep and never wake up.

I stumbled out of the room back into the dining room where everyone was and continued walking to my bedroom. I got into bed, pulled the covers over my head and went to sleep.

It was dark when I woke up. I looked at the clock on the dresser. It was midnight. I looked around and saw Sally in bed asleep.

It was like we were in a walking nightmare.

That morning we got ready for the funeral. He would be buried in the Damascus graveyard I heard someone say. The family went in a long black car and Junior was taken in front of us in a long black hearse. We all drove slowly up this winding red, dirt road, until we got to this graveyard where only Carters or Carter relatives were buried. This was the first-time I had ever seen a graveyard. The graveyard was surrounded by tall pine trees with a few hickory and English Gum trees mixed in the forest. It was cold and spooky. Overhead, rain clouds were gathering. The sun disappeared as the clouds moved over the sun.

The preacher, a short heavy set man, dressed in a black suit, with a short black beard stood by an open hole in the ground and said a few words which I couldn't understand.

I felt sick when I watched them lower Junior's casket into the hole in the ground. I covered my face because I just couldn't watch them put him in the ground. He'd be all by himself under the dirt.

I couldn't even remember the drive home.

When we got home, again I went to bed and went to sleep under the covers.

When I got up for dinner. The food was placed on the table, and every one was quiet as they sat down to eat. One of my uncles, the one that was a preacher said a prayer called a blessing for dinner. Mama wasn't there.

"Where's Mama, "I asked Sally.

"She's in the bedroom, crying, Sally said.

I pulled Aunt Ginger aside and asked her about the awful smell that was in the living room when Junior was in there.

She stood there for a minute, wet her lips, looked away for a minute looked back at me and said, "Well honey, you see the mortician has to prepare the body for the funeral and to do that, they have to use this chemical. The chemical is called formaldehyde and they inject it into the body to preserve it. It's too bad it smells so bad.

"Why," I asked.

"Well honey, that's really all I know," she said looking down at the floor.

"Thank you, Aunt Ginger," I said suddenly feeling sorry for her. I could see it was hard on her. She looked tired and the rolled up bun at the nap of her neck had begun to come unraveled and long gray strands of hair was hanging down in front of and behind her ears.

My aunts and cousins were really good. They stayed about a week and took care of things, the chores outside and inside.

The worse thing, it started to rain on Junior and he was out there all alone, all by himself, under the ground, with the rain pouring down on him.

"Sally, it's raining on him," I said crying,

"I know," Sally said, "but just remember he's not really there. He's in heaven sitting beside Jesus.

I thought about it and she was right, so I stopped and sent a little prayer up to Junior and Jesus.

Things slowly got back to semi normal. They would never again be normal, not ever, never be normal again.

Sometimes, when I would set the table, I would forget and set a place for Junior. Even worse I would forget and start calling him when dinner was ready. I was beginning to think I would never accept the fact that he was gone.

I went back to working my cotton patch, but not with the same enthusiasm as before. I missed Junior so bad. I missed his constant questions about everything.

Every night when I said my prayers I always talked to Junior and told him about all the day's events, told him how our cotton patch was doing. Told him how much we missed him. I would always talk to him and still do.

CHAPTER 35

Jannelle's Old Boyfriend

Last night, on the evening news, there was a news bulletin about this gang of criminals from New Jersey that was operating in the south. They were criminal con artists stealing people's life savings They were telling people they could save, and even make more money by investing their savings, in fake scams to make them rich. They would take the people's money and skip the country.

But the Jackson District Attorney set a trap and caught the criminals. They got most of the money back for the people. They had their pictures in the newspaper. And by golly two of them turned out to be, the strangers in the night that came to our place. The other two were the ones we saw downtown.

"Isn't that amazing?" I asked Uncle Oglee, but, Uncle Oglee had other problems on his mind.

Poor Uncle Oglee had his own problems. It seems Jannelle had an exboyfriend that wanted Uncle Oglee out of the picture.

One day there was a knock on the door, and when I answered it, a big tall guy was standing there. He asked for Uncle Oglee. He was mean and angry looking, although if it wasn't for that he would have been good looking. Blond, blue eyed about a foot taller than Uncle Oglee. I was dying of curiosity, what in the world could he want with Uncle Oglee. Everyone liked my Uncle, except apparently, for this guy.

"What do you want with Uncle Oglee," I asked

"Never you mind little girl, you just go get him, I'm gonna give him the ass kicking of his life," He growled.

"Say what, I don't think so," I growled back. As I turned and ran to go find Uncle Oglee.

I found him, told him what the guy said, and said, not to go see him. "I'll just tell him you're not here."

Well that didn't work, so I followed him back to the door.

"Yeah, what can I do for you," Uncle Oglee said as he walked down the steps to face this guy.

The guy took a swing and hit Uncle Oglee upside the head with a fist. Uncle Oglee's head wobbled as he stepped back, and almost fell down.

"Jesus Christ, what the hell" Uncle Oglee yelled.

"That's for messing with my girl," the stranger said.

"Say what," Uncle Oglee yelled and literally came unglued, he tore into that guy like there was no tomorrow. He had that guy on his back and was tearing the daylights out of him.

"Your girl, you mean Jannelle, man that's my girl," Uncle Oglee was yelling. That's when Daddy came up.

"Hey now, what's going on here," Daddy said, surprise in his voice.

"This here Bo hunk came up and cold cocked me upside the head. No way in hell's he getting away with that."

The stranger looked up from where he lay and started whining, "He went and stole my girl."

Oglee was sitting astraddle the guy, he turned, looked up and screamed, "My girl."

"That'll be enough," Daddy said. He reached down and helped Uncle Oglee up off the guy.

The guy sat up crawled around to a sitting position and got up. He started brushing the dirt off his white pants, and glared at Uncle Oglee..

"Daddy, he started it, he hit Uncle Oglee without any warning," I said.

"You mean he cold cocked him," Daddy asked.

"Yeah, that's it, If that's what it means," I said.

"That wasn't nice or fair play," Daddy said, looking at the guy.

The guy turned and starting walking away. He looked back over his shoulder and yelled, "I'll get even with you, if it's the last thing I do. I'll be waiting for you, you just wait."

"Yeah, bring it on Buddy, you and who's army. Sure, that'll be when hell freezes over," Uncle Oglee said laughing, with his hands behind his ears and waving his fingers back and forth.

I was so mad I went right to the phone and called Jannelle, and told her everything that happened.

She was horrified, and asked if Oglee was hurt.

I was tempted to tell her that Uncle Oglee was hurt and bleeding all over the place, but I was too mad.

"Heck no, He beat the socks off of that other guy," I said.

"Oh good, you mean George."

"I don't know, but he said you were his girl."

"He's a jerk, I used to date him long, long time ago, and I don't know why I ever did. Tell Oglee I'm coming right over, there's something I have to talk to him about, anyway."

I wondered what that could be about, but she didn't offer to tell me, and my curiosity was killing me.

Jannelle was there in about an hour and a half.

She rushed over to Uncle Oglee and gave him a big hug and a kiss. She examined his jaw which was red and swollen where George had hit him. Uncle Oglee looked over Jannelle's shoulder grinned wickedly and winked at me, which tickled the pants off me.

They both sat down on the porch swing and she started talking.

"You know Oglee, my Uncle looked into the mineral rights thing and he found out that unless both Mr. and Mrs. Carter signed the papers, it isn't legal for the guy who supposedly bought the mineral rights to keep the rights. He said that Mr. Carter could give the money back and tear the papers up and you could have the rights back and we could still search for gold."

"But there's just one thing wrong with that theory, and that is we don't have the money to buy the rights back."

"Ah, yes but here's the good part, Daddy said that he could loan Mr. Carter the three hundred dollars and he could pay him back whenever he could, or until we discover the gold, or if he wanted to he could become a partner and not have to ever worry about paying him back." Jannelle was getting more excited by the minute, her voice kept getting higher.

"You have got to be kidding me, he would do that? I like the last idea best where he becomes a partner." Uncle Oglee said. If Claude say's its okay, we'll do that." Uncle Oglee laughed and grabbed Jannelle around the waist and hugged her, and swung her around.

"Does your Dad realize that he hasn't got a chance in hell of ever getting his money back?"

Jannelle laughed, "I think he realizes that."

I stood there with my mouth hanging open; I could hardly believe my ears. Could that be true, I knew Mama hadn't signed the papers.

When Oglee told Daddy what Jannelle had said, Daddy was shocked.

"Are you sure this is true? Daddy asked. "But I wouldn't want to borrow the money from your Dad, Jannelle, I wouldn't know when I could pay him back."

"I'll pay him back," Uncle Oglee said

"You know Oglee I, m so sorry I had to sell the mineral rights, I know you had your heart set on finding gold.

"No, don't even think like that Claude. Little Junior was more important than all the gold in the world. You know we probably would have never found gold anyway. It was more a game than anything else."

"It wouldn't have made any difference anyway," Daddy said, with tears in his eyes.

"That's right," I said.

"There's no question that was the only thing you could do. You did the right thing."

"Wait a minute," Jannelle said, "Remember you won't have to pay him back if you make him a partner."

"That's great, it's a done deal." Daddy said.

"Daddy, Daddy, something is wrong with the cotton bolls." Sally came running into the house yelling.

"What," Daddy said, surprise in his voice.

He dropped whatever he was doing and followed us back outside.

"It can't be boll weevils, I've been watching very carefully," he yelled as he ran out to the cotton patch in question.

When Daddy got out there he bent over the cotton plants as he examined them.

"Oh my God, you're right," He yanked his sweaty cap off, shook it and put it back on.

"We've got to start getting rid of the bad bolls right now. Go in the house and get some gunny sack bags and we'll start pulling off all the bad ones and burn them, before they spread to all the plants.

When they got back with the bags, Mama, Sally and Lena followed them out. Mama put Ginger down on a pallet on the ground at the end of a cotton row.

CHAPTER 36

Dreaded Boll Weevils

"**I** want to help, too," Lena said, her little face screwed up like she was going to cry.

"Sure honey, we'll appreciate any help you can give," Mama said.

Daddy showed us all how to examine the bolls, find the infected ones, pull them off and put them in the sacks. It wasn't as bad as Daddy had thought at first. The weevils had just gotten started. We swept through mine and Sally's cotton patches.

We took the bolls to the back yard, built a bon fire and burnt them to a crisp. I was just sick to my stomach. I had heard so much how bad the boll weevils were. How people had lost their entire crops because of them.

When we were done we went to the big crops, Daddy's crops and started checking his plants. They had just started on one end of a row. We double checked again. So far, so good. When we were finished Daddy went into the barn and got the spray out. He gave us each a spray can and we started going up and down each row spraying the plants. It started getting dark and Daddy decided to quit for the night and would continue the spraying tomorrow.

I was so tired; I could hardly eat supper. I fell asleep with my head on the table. Daddy shook me, told me to go crawl into bed.

"We'll wash dishes in the morning," Mama said. That was a first; Mama never left the dishes till the morning.

Sally and I didn't even glance at the Sears Catalogue.

The next morning, after our chores were done we attacked the boll weevils.

Uncle Oglee had missed all the trouble the night before. He had been visiting Jannelle. When he got home we were all asleep.

He jumped in and helped us spray the weevils.

We were all finished by noon.

Daddy brought us all together. "Let's all give a great big thanks to Sally, here. Sally, bless your heart, you caught the evil boll weevil just in the nick of time."

Sally was surprised. She actually started to blush with all the praise.

"Yep, Sally, you saved us. Just think if you hadn't caught the boll weevils, we might as well have just thrown the Sears catalogue away," I said, giving her a little pat on the back.

"We'll have to keep a close watch to make sure they don't start up again."

Uncle Oglee and Jannelle had started talking about gold hunting again because Jannelle's Uncle was going to help with getting the mineral rights back. He had a lot of pull in the community.

No one knew who owned the Mineral Right's Co. There was a lot of guessing going on, but that's all it was, just guessing. We thought maybe, the same company was now trying to buy all the land up in Scott County. Some of the people that couldn't hang on to their land any longer, because of the depression, had to sell their land. The speculation was that it was someone with lots of money, to be able to afford to buy up the land, but no one knew who.

Apparently everyone didn't know we had sold our rights because they were still messing around our place during the night.

Lena had settled in with us like she was really one of us kids. She was even beginning to stick up for herself when there was an argument. Sally could be pretty bossy sometimes, and now Lena would fuss back at her like a real sister. I got a big kick out of it all, even when she fussed with me.

It was really going to be hard on us all when it came time for her to leave. I began to try to think of things and ways to keep her here with us, cause it seemed that this was where she belonged. Just thinking about it made me sad.

Her Daddy would still be too ill when he came home, for her to come back home.

There was talk of a hail storm coming our way. If that happened, it would be disastrous for our cotton plants. I prayed at night. Please don't let a hail storm hit our cotton, please, please. After that I watched the sky like a hawk.

Every Sunday we had a gathering at one of my aunt's houses. Usually it was either Aunt Ginger, Aunt Mable, Aunt Hilda or Aunt Irene. More often than not it was Aunt Ginger or Aunt Hilda. They lived the closest to us.

We could even walk if we wanted to. Aunt Ginger took charge most of the time. Aunt Hilda was considered the best cook, but all of them were good cooks.

Aunt Mable was considered the funniest one of the girls. She kept everyone laughing most of the time. I think I like Aunt Ginger though the best, because she would take the time to talk and explain things to me. She felt like a friend.

All of them were furious with us for taking Lena in to live with us.

But when Daddy's sisters finally accepted Lena, things quieted down. Especially Aunt Hilda, she really liked Lena, and was always making her little things, like knitting her socks, or gloves, or scarves. Wherever we went, Lena went with us, so when we went to the big family dinners Lena went with us. There would be so many of us they would set up long wooden benches. The first time we went to Aunt Irene's it was very quiet until everyone finally relaxed and started chattering. The food was so good I couldn't stop eating. Sally and I had to take off our belts and left them on the bench when dinner was over. What a stomach ache I would have. Of course, when it got out that we ate so much we had to take our belts off after dinner, we were a disgrace to the family. Darn it, we were too stupid, why didn't we take the belts with us and not leave them on the bench for everyone to see. What idiots.

The relatives got a good laugh out of it.

"They sure let their eyes overload their bellies," my aunt Mable said laughing.

"Well, at least it's a compliment to your good cooking, Aunt Mable," I said, "So you should be flattered," I added with a grin looking at Aunt Mable.

"Well, listen to her mouth, doesn't she sound like one of us," Aunt Mable said laughing.

I was so embarrassed, I coulda crawled under the table and died. Sally was just plain mad. She actually stuck her tongue out and stalked off.

"Well that's what happens when you're such good cooks, you could kill off the young'uns with such cooking," Uncle Oglee said. "I thought about taking my belt off myself, but it was on so tight I couldn't get it off."

He came around the table to where I stood with a red hot face, and put his arm around my shoulder and gave me a squeeze, "She's a girl after my own heart."

Oh, how I loved my Uncle.

And that's when I realized why I wasn't that crazy about my Aunt Mable. She wasn't so funny after all. She was only funny at someone else's expense. Uncle Oglee revealed Aunt Mable for what she was. Everyone stopped laughing and looked at Aunt Mable. Aunt Mable suddenly looked embarrassed and looked away.

CHAPTER 37

Bought Back our Mineral Rights

Daddy and Mr. Fineley, bought our mineral rights back for us.

We got out our shovels again and started looking for gold. First we started looking at the Finley farm. We didn't have any luck there. Even though we didn't find any gold, Uncle Oglee and Jannelle's romance blossomed. They found time to hold hands and make goo-goo eyes at each other. They were the cutest couple. I was hoping against hope, they would get married and live happily ever after. Her ex-boyfriend kept coming around and causing trouble. He began turning up whenever Jannelle was gone and continued to insult and threaten Uncle Oglee. Uncle Oglee just ignored him and treated him like a pesky fly.

There was also Bob Anderson, who hadn't given up on Jannelle. I thought he was more of a threat to Oglee's happiness than the other guy, because he was a much nicer guy. He continued to contact Jannelle, but Jannelle only had eyes for Uncle Oglee. She was no dummy, she remained loyal to Oglee. No one else in the world had beautiful, long, black eyelashes and black eyes like Uncle Oglee. Any girl would kill to have eyes and eyelashes like his.

It seemed like it rained a little bit almost every afternoon.

"What about the caves Daddy was telling us about?" I asked. "We haven't checked them out yet."

At night, in my prayers I would tell Junior aboutevery thing that happened that day. I told him all about our plans to hunt gold in the cave. I knew he would like that.

Jannelle, Uncle Oglee and I packed up all our gear after we finished hoeing all of the cotton we had planned to hoe that day. We figured it was about five miles to the caves.

When we got there, it was hard to find the entrance to the caves. It was overgrown with weeds, grass and blackberry bushes. We chopped and hacked away for almost an hour before we found the hole. The blackberry bushes scratched our hands, arms and faces. We were dirty, bloody messes by the time we got it all cleared away.

It was pretty exciting when we looked into the dark cave. We could see where animals had been living there. The cave must be really deep. Looking in, we couldn't see the end of the tunnel. Thank goodness, Uncle Oglee had thought to bring a flashlight.

After we got in the cave, it was big enough for us to stand up and walk around in it. It was dark and spooky. I felt goose bumps pop up on my arms, and shivers run up and down my spine. Something brushed by my foot and I yelped and jumped back. I looked down but I couldn't see what it was. It was gone.

"What was it?" Jannelle whispered.

"I don't know," I whispered back, "But it felt furry."

"E-gads" Oglee said "I can't stand unknown, little, furry things."

Already this was turning into quite an adventure.

This cave had become like a tunnel. It looks like it went on and on. We couldn't see an end to it.

"What the heck," Uncle Oglee said, "this must have been like a slave escape tunnel, or maybe pirates hide away."

"It's really getting late; we had better start going back. Tomorrow we can start again earlier than we did today," Jannelle said.

"Well, well, batten down the hatches look at what I found," Uncle Oglee said as he reached down and pulled up a red plaid blanket, that had been lying in the corner of the cave in a heap on the dusty, clay ground.

"You know what. It looks brand new, like it had been bought just for this occasion," Jannelle said.

"Someone's been sleeping here," I said.

"Your right, little Einstein," he said reaching over and ruffling up my short hair, leaving my bangs sticking straight up.

"You don't say," I said jabbing him in the ribs with my forefinger.

"It's almost six o'clock right now. He could be coming back any minute now," Jannelle said.

"Oh Jeeze, you're right, we'd better make tracks out of here," Uncle Oglee said.

"Hurry up," I whispered.

We all turned and almost ran over each other in our rush to get out of there.

"I sure don't want to be caught in here," Uncle Oglee said.

"Did you put the blanket back like you found it?" Jannelle asked.

"Of course, I'm not an idiot," he whispered.

"Thank goodness," I said, as we made it out the front entrance before he got back.

"I breathed a sigh of relief just as a heard the rustling of the bushes down the trail.

"Oh my god he's here, hurry, move away from the trail," Jannelle whispered.

We hid behind a large clump of blackberry bushes. I had to bite my tongue as the stickers stuck me through my clothes. Gee! Did that hurt.

A tall, huge burley man with a black beard and black hair parted the brush and appeared at the entrance of the cave. He paused and looked all around before he stepped into the cave. You could tell he's wondering about all the brush and bushes we had just cut down.

We waited a full five minutes before we dared move. We carefully crept silently down the trail, retracing our steps.

"I'll bet he's really wondering what happened to all the brush we cut away. I'd sure give a nickle to know what's going through his mind right now," I said giggling.

"He's scratching his head over that one, alright," Uncle Oglee said laughing.

"Wow, was that a close call," Jannelle said as we started moving faster, down the trail. Then we broke into a full run toward home.

"You know what, that's funny, how did he get in there. We had to cut our way to get in, so he must have been going in through another entrance. He knows we have been in there. I would sure like to know how he's been getting in there".

"We'll come back earlier tomorrow, but we have a problem, and that is figuring out when he'll be home, that is back in his cave," Uncle Oglee said.

"What a wonderful news story this would make," Jannelle said.

"Hold onto your horses, little girlie. You gotta wait until we have safely solved our case.

Jannelle just giggled, "You think."

It was almost dark when we got home.

Lena and Sally came running out to meet us. "We were getting worried about you; we thought the boogie man got you."

She ran up and grabbed me by the hand and said, "Guess what! My Daddy's coming home tomorrow."

"That's great, that means he's all well," I said.

"Well almost, there's a lady that's gonna stay and take care of him for a while. He still has a plaster bandage on his arm."

"You mean he still has a cast on his arm."

"Yeah, that's it. I hope you don't have to go home right away," I said, feeling bad, thinking about her leaving.

"Oh my, I guess that does mean I have to go home. Oh dear, I don't like that idea, although I do want to take care of my Daddy."

We were all quiet for a while.

"Well, I guess we'll soon find out what's gonna happen when we talk to your Daddy."

"We're gonna see him tomorrow. Maybe I can call him on the phone tonight."

The next day we had to postpone our trip to the cave, because not only did we have to help get John home from the hospital and settle him in his house. But we also had to catch up on our chores.

My cotton had started to have cotton. Beautiful! What a sight to see. If only Junior could see our crop, he'd be so proud. I told him all about it that night. I could almost see his little round face with a big smile and dimples. I knew the news would make him happy.

Every day more cotton was blooming. That's what it seemed like to me, that's what it was doing, blooming. Instead of flowers, it was blooming white cotton. We were all excited.

We brought John home from that horrible, stinky hospital. He told us that the two other guys, that were in his room had passed away, and had gone on to heaven. He was almost back to normal, except he still had a cast on his right leg. He got around pretty good on a crutch.

A couple of his black neighbor ladies took turns coming over and taking care of him. One was called Bessie and the other one was called Mary.

"I 'm sure sorry about your boy Junior," John said.

"Yeah, thanks," Daddy said, looking down at the floor. I could tell he could hardly talk about it.

John looked sad and thoughtful. "You know Claude, he was just too sweet, and good to stay here.. He was already a little angel, that for some reason had to spend just a little here on earth," John said.

That was it, I thought. That answered my question of why, why did he have to leave us.

I began to notice something. There were some sparks flying between Bessie and John. Everyone called her Aunt Bessie. I liked her, she was really nice.

When we were at John's she baked a pan of chocolate cookies, and brought them to John's house. She took really good care of John. I noticed John watching her a lot. She was short and fat and very pleasant.

"Just the way I like them," John said.

Daddy chuckled when he said that, "It looks kinda serious," Daddy said.

Lena kept staring at Bessie when she wasn't looking. She would look back and forth, from John then at Bessie. She looked really serious, as if she couldn't decide whether she liked the arrangement or not.

"I'll be coming back home Daddy," Lena said.

"Of course you will honey," John said.

"I don't think we'll be needing extra help," Lena said looking at Aunt Bessie.

"Oh course we'll need all the help we can get," John said quickly looking at Aunt Bessie.

"Okay, I'll be back home tomorrow," she said turning and walking out the door.

"Hey wait jes a minute little Missie aint you gonna give your old Dad a kiss good bye."

"Sure," she said. She turned and rushed back, throwing her arms around his neck and giving him a kiss, "Bye Daddy."

"Bye Sugar, I love you."

I was sad because Lena was leaving. I was going to miss her. It felt like I was losing a sister. Even my Aunt Ginger and especially, Aunt Hilda had grown to love her. Aunt Hilda made all three of us, Lena, Sally and myself, pretty night gowns. They had turned out to be very nice Aunts.

I still didn't like Aunt Katrina. She never, ever laughed or joked. She wasn't any fun at all. She was just a pain in the neck. I felt sorry for Sara. She treated Sara just like she was a slave. She was always calling her lazy, and no good, when actually Aunt Katrina was the one that was lazy and no good.

CHAPTER 38

Hurricane

It was Saturday. A big announcement alert sounded on the radio. The announcer said there was going to be a big thunder storm coming our way. He warned people that it would be a huge storm. Almost like a hurricane.

I was scared. It wasn't a tornado, but a hurricane could be almost as bad.

Our cotton, what was going to happen to our cotton? I started praying, "God, please don't let it ruin our cotton." We were almost done with our cotton crop.

Aunt Ginger and Aunt Hilda ran to their home, and we gathered everything up and ran to our storm cellar. We had plenty of food and water.

We had to postpone our cave exploring.

It was a terrible storm. It was hailing and raining. The wind was blowing so hard, we could hear things flying all around. Water was seeping into the shelter.

The storm raged on through the whole night. It stopped around five o'clock in the morning. The moon disappeared about seven o'clock and the sun came out just like nothing had happened.

We finally climbed out, all cold and wet. It had actually leaked water in on us. Jenny finally quit crying, and passed out from pure exhaustion. All any of us wanted to do was sleep. But first we had to see how our cotton fared during the storm.

I rushed out to see my cotton patch, and I was instantly sick from shock, when I saw my beautiful cotton. My beautiful white cotton was a mess lying strung out all over the ground. It was red brown covered with mud.

I just dropped to my knees and sank into the mud and started crying. I couldn't believe what had happened. This was worse than any nightmare I had ever had about my cotton.

Sally joined me and she started crying and kicking and stomping the broken cotton stalks into the muddy ground.

"Damn it, damn it, damn it to hell," she screamed."

We both just sat down in the mud and cried.

"It's just not fair," I kept saying. "We might just as well throw away our Sears catalogue."

"I know," Sally muttered angrily. "I just hate this place."

"We're not the only ones, everyone lost their cotton crop," I said thinking about it. "Oh my God, Mama and Daddy lost all their cotton too. What are we going to do? We could starve to death." For the first time, real fear struck me. What were we going to do?

We finally got up and realized we were all muddy from head to toe. We started trudging back to the house.

We looked over and saw Mama, Daddy and Oglee looking out over the wet muddy cotton fields. Mama had her head on Daddy shoulder and was crying. Uncle Oglee was just standing there, defeated, with his arms crossed behind and his head hanging down looking at the ground. He looked like he might be crying too.

I'm glad Junior didn't have to go through this. This would have broken his heart.

When we got back to the house, I noticed most of our chickens were dead, or gone.

When we went into the house the phone was ringing off the hook. When I picked up the phone, Aunt Ginger was on the other end of the line, sobbing. We've lost everything, I just don't know where we're gonna get the money for the next crop. We've already borrowed to the hilt. I just don't know what we're gonna do. I guess your Mama and Daddy are in the same boat. What are we all gonna do. Tell your Mama or Daddy to call me when they get a chance.

Next time the phone rang. I let Daddy answer the phone. It was Aunt Hilda, it was the same story with every one. The phone kept ringing.

"I just don't know what we're going to do," Daddy said. My brother Albert is the only brother that has any money saved up, and I'm sure he won't lend us any money, because everyone will be after him for money. The bank certainly won't loan us any money.

"Mama, you know you were right, we should never have tried coming back here and farming. It's all my fault. If we had stayed in Texas, we never would have lost Junior and we wouldn't have been broke."

"Claude, you can't say that. Losing Junior was meant to be. We would have lost him some other way. God would still have taken him," Mama said.

"We'll just have to pray for help, that's the only thing left to do," Mama said.

"Pray, what good is that going to do? What kind of God would do all this to us? No, there's no God," Daddy said and stomped off.

The radio was blasting away about the disaster, about how many people were affected. The announcer on the radio said that people were getting together and making a plea to the government agencies for help, for money, even about getting government loans for cotton seed and fertilizer for a new crop. There were Mississippi representatives appealing to President Roosevelt for help.

"Daddy, do you think the President will help us?" I asked.

"He just might, he's helped so many poor people already. He's our last hope. Jim and I and a few others are going to Jackson to see what we can get done."

Both Daddy and Uncle Jim were good talkers, and if any body could get our message across, it would be them.

Daddy was rushing around getting ready to go with Uncle Jim.

Mama was helping Daddy get ready. Making him look as neat as she could, although his clothes were pretty worn out, they were clean. And of course his shoes were a disgrace, so he had to borrow a pair of his brother Albert's shoes. Thank goodness, they wore the same size.

It was in all the papers, a group of worried hungry farmers pounced on the administration in Jackson, Mississippi, since it was the capital.

Jannelle went with Daddy and Oglee to cover the story for her newspaper. The article she wrote was certainly powerful. It was definitely slanted toward the farmer's side. She wrote about how hard they worked and sacrificed during the year and how brutal it was for their families, when they lost everything to the torrential rains. She pointed out how they would actually go hungry, if they didn't get any help from the government. She begged the Mississippi representatives to go to the government to get aid for the farmers.

Everyone was so proud of Jannelle, especially Uncle Oglee.

"She's not only the prettiest girl I've ever known, but she's the smartest," he said, his face was glowing with pride. . He was in the house and was talking to everyone within earshot.

Mama and Daddy smiled at each other.

"I think he sort of likes her," Daddy said.

"You think," Mama said.

"Aw, isn't love grand," I said looking at Sally.

Uncle Oglee could care less if we teased him, he just smiled.

It was just unbelievable sad, and Junior was gone. Oh how I missed him, every second of every day. Since he was gone, it just didn't matter that much that our cotton crop was gone. The future already was really bleak. I just couldn't forget that he was all by himself, under the dirt and the mud, buried in a hole in the ground.

I felt so sorry for Mama and Daddy for losing Junior. I overheard Daddy say it was his fault Junior had died, because he let Junior lead the horse, especially when Mama had said she didn't think he was old enough yet.

Mama assured him that it wasn't his fault.

I saw Mama wrap Junior's little teddy bear in a small baby blanket and put the bear under her pillow.

Mama and Daddy were talking about moving back to El Paso, Texas, but they didn't want to leave Junior here, in his grave all by himself.

Aunt Ginger said they would take care of Junior's grave if they did have to leave.

At night, I could still hear Mama and Daddy crying, and talking about leaving.

CHAPTER 39

Scarlet Fever

*J*enny got sick. She was running a temperature of one hundred and three. They called Doctor Brown.

He was in the bedroom for a while examining Jenny.

When he was through, he looked very solemn.

"I have some bad news for you," Old Dr. brown said," I'm afraid she has scarlet fever. I have to tell you that an epidemic has hit Scott County. We don't really know where it started."

"Oh my God, not Jenny too," Mama said, and started crying.

"I'll have to quarantine all of you," he said.

"Now I'll have to line you up and examine all of you. We might as well start with you, young lady, since you're right here," he said and reached over, took me by the arm and pulled me toward the table.

"Open up your mouth," He stuck a tongue blade in my mouth and pushed my tongue down; next he put a thermometer in my mouth. "Uh-oh," he said, "I'm afraid you're infected too."

"I'm not a bit surprised," I growled. I pulled up a chair and sat down. "The way things have been going around here, I knew I didn't feel too good, but I thought it was just the weather and our situation."

Daddy and Lena were the only ones that didn't have Scarlet Fever.

Aunt Ginger and Aunt Hilda came over as soon as they found out we had Scarlet fever. They had been infected with Scarlet Fever when they were children so now they were immune to it. They had lost a little brother from scarlet fever. That really scared me. That meant one of us could die from Scarlet Fever.

Doctor Brown turned to Aunt Ginger. We need to get them into bed as soon as possible; I'll give you the instructions for the medication and you can start this young lady right now on the medication and you need to drink lots of water and other fluids.

"This aunt our first rodeo Doc," Aunt Hilda spoke up.

Doctor Brown looked startled when he looked up and opened his mouth to say something, but Aunt Ginger spoke up.

"Don't never mind her; she's got a big mouth," Aunt Ginger said as she poked Aunt Hilda in the ribs. "She's just mad because you're talking to me like I'm the boss."

Doctor Brown just grinned, and put a large bottle of pink fluid on the dining room table.

Uncle Oglee came rushing in. "Why's the Doctor here."

We all jumped in at once to explain that we had Scarlet Fever.

"Over here, young man, let's get you checked out," the Doctor said.

When Uncle Oglee opened his mouth, the Doctor took one look at his tongue, and said," Yep, I can safely say you're coming down with the bad stuff."

"Oh man, that means I can't see Jannelle," he whined.

The Doctor just looked at him, "This is serious business son. You could die from this."

"I am going to have to post a Quarantine notice on the house. That means everyone that lives here is infected and, can't go in or go out."

"Son, I need you to get ready for bed. You're beginning to spike a temp. Did you know you already have a temp 101 and it will go up? We have to start giving all of you aspirin and the medication I have here.

"If I may make a suggestion, we need to have everyone that's sick all in the same room. That will make it much easier on the caretakers, which I presume will be you Ginger and Hilda." It was obvious he knew them both from many years before.

When Daddy was checked, he was okay. "He had Scarlet Fever when he was a kid, " Aunt Hilda said.

Aunt Mable and Mary Jane said they would come and help Aunt Ginger and Aunt Hilda take care of our family, so they could take a little time off, which was really nice.

That worked out well, so the first two Aunts didn't get too tired;

When two of my Uncles showed up, Aunt Ginger's husband Sam, and Aunt Hilda's husband Jack, they explained that they and their wives, had also had Scarlet Fever when there had been an epidemic when they were children.

"Oh my goodness, I had never been so sick in my whole life. I felt like I had gone to hell and I was burning up."

I vaguely remembered people coming and going. I felt wet cloths on my forehead. I vaguely remembered being bathed with cold water. I've never ever been so thirsty. I hurt all over. I don't remember how long this went on.

When I finally came back to reality, I was so weak I couldn't even walk. They told me I had been sick for four days. They also told me I had a very bad case of Scarlet Fever, not a light case like Jenny and Sally, go figure. They said Uncle Oglee and I both had hard cases for some unknown reason. Everyone was much better.

"That's cause I'm made of pioneer stock, you know, and you Zemma are a big sissy," Sally taunted.

'Says who," I said and laughed and pretended it didn't bother me. I couldn't let her know she got under my skin.

Mama and Daddy had been really scared they would lose another one of their children. There were some families that did lose some of their children during the epidemic. That was really sad. We made sure we went to the funerals. I knew one of the little girls that had died.

I looked at her when she was in the casket and she looked just like she was sleeping. I said a little prayer to her and I told her all the people she left behind really loved and missed her. When I said my prayers that night and talked to Junior, I told him everything, about all the funerals and about the children. I told him about Vivian, the little girl that had died. How the persons she loved and had to leave behind. I asked him to say "Hi" for me and would he take care of her until she knew her way around. Of course, I knew he would.

Since we had lost everything, we were at a loss as to what to do. Daddy scoured all over Scot county looking for a loan. There was just nothing else we could do. Daddy really hated to give up of our farm and all of our equipment. There was just no one else to see, no where to turn. Daddy really didn't want to leave it all behind. The land had been in the family for generations, and he truly loved to farm more than anything else in the world. He also wanted to leave the farm to us kids when he was gone, he said.

While Oglee had been sick Jannelle had been leaving notes for him, and he had been leaving notes for her under a rock beside the mail box. They both wanted to start gold hunting again.

The two of them had made a plan to dig for gold in the caves, which of course included me.

Uncle Oglee was really getting serious about Jannelle. They were always together, holding hands looking soulfully into each other's eyes. I felt kind of left out. It was like I had lost my best friend Uncle Oglee.

CHAPTER 40

Golden Caves

"I really have a good feeling about this," I said.

Oglee grinned, looked at me reached over and tusseled my hair, "You have a good feeling about a lot of things."

We were going to explore the caves. This time, we were going as fast as we could go.

I was still a little weak and shaky from the Scarlet Fever, but I didn't want anyone to know.

I noticed Uncle Oglee wasn't as quick as he was before he got sick, so he wasn't back to his old self either.

We packed a couple of shovels, and a flashlight and Jannelle packed a big picnic lunch and a lemon pie. I giggled when I watched Uncle Oglee when he saw the lemon pie. His black eyes got big and he opened his mouth and was practically drooling.

"Oh my," he murmured, as he watched her move the pie over to the corner of the basket to make room for the paper plates. He finally pulled his gaze away from the pie, looked at Jannelle and said, "When did you say lunch was?" Jannelle looked really pretty in a thin blue dress with flowers on it. The neckline had a dainty lace yoke, with matching lace stitched all around the hem of the skirt. To finish the picture off, she had two blue bows in her braided blond hair that matched her blue eyes.

Uncle Oglee didn't know what to look at, Jannelle or the lemon pie.

"Oh my, oh my," he murmured. He scratched his head pretending, to make a decision.

"Not yet, not yet, Jannelle said, laughing shaking her finger at him.

"Looka hear, here's the same blanket that was here before, only it has been rolled up and placed neatly in the corner, " Jannelle said, reaching over and picking up the corner of the blanket.

"So that means the stranger that was here before is still here," I said, looking around me, and behind me feeling a little nervous and afraid.

"Yep, you got that right, and we better darn well be done and gone by the time he comes home," Uncle Oglee said.

We ran into all kinds of creatures of the animal kingdom, and so far they were small furry little things, rats, ground squirrels, raccoons, even a possum and one animal, we weren't sure what it was, but he was about the size of a large rabbit.

"I hope there aren't any bears holed up in here," Jannelle said fearfully.

"Naw," Uncle Oglee tried to reassure her, "If so, I'll protect you," Uncle said putting his arm around her waist.

"Oh no," I said I hadn't even thought of that.

"Oh sure, that's alright Oglee here will protect us," She said, laughing up at him.

I smiled to myself, he's just saying that so Jannelle won't be scared and want to go home, I thought. Anyway I kept a good look out over my shoulder, so someone couldn't sneak up behind us.

The cave suddenly opened up into a huge opening. There was a spring in the cave somewhere, because there was running water that ran into a large pool of water. It was really something. There was green moss on the huge boulders that jutted out from the walls of the cave. There were two big tunnels that branched out in separate directions. One was quite a bit bigger than the other. You could almost put a whole house in the cave. There were orange and green colored mushrooms growing along the sides of the walls of the cave. There was light streaming in from somewhere, but we couldn't see where it was coming from.

"How long have we been traveling down this tunnel?" Uncle Oglee asked.

No one knew. We just looked at each other.

"Oh cripes sake, what's wrong with me?" Uncle Oglee asked, not expecting anyone to answer, He reached into his front pocket and pulled out his bright, shiny, gold pocket watch.

He grinned mischievously, and said, "The compliments of dear old Daddy, my heritage, only he doesn't know it. He would absolutely kill me if he knew I had his watch and he could get his hands on me. The thing is, he lost it, and I found it out in the yard, but before I could give it back to him, he took a shot at me with his shotgun. So there, goes so much for giving his watch back to him. Serves him right, the old goat."

I giggled; I could just imagine what grandpa would do to him if he knew Uncle Oglee had his prized railroad watch that he'd gotten when he retired as an engineer for the railroad.

"It serves Grandpa right, he shouldn't have shot at you," I said, full of sympathy for Uncle Oglee.

"How long has it been," Jannelle asked, as she was still laughing about the watch.

"It's now three o'clock, good grief, we've been down here four hours, Uncle Oglee," said.

"I can hardly believe that," Jannelle said gasping in surprise.

"Well I can," my bare feet are sore," I said, as I sat down on one of the large rocks surrounding the pool of running water from an underground stream.

I looked around at our surroundings; it was really pretty in a strange sort of way. It was like a story book picture with different kinds of colors. I went to the opening of the larger tunnel. There was some strange kind of rocks along the side walls.

"I do believe it's time for lunch," Uncle Oglee announced with anticipation. Anticipation another big word I had just learned.

Jannelle had made fried chicken with biscuits. She had cut up water melon and put it into a bowl. And of course a whole lemon pie. She even brought lemonade.

She had packed a pretty hand embroidered tablecloth and dinner napkins. She had silverware wrapped in tissue paper. She looked really pretty as she carefully spread the tablecloth out on the floor of the cave and the three of us sat down to eat.

It was drop dead delicious. Thank goodness she had brought plenty, cause Uncle Oglee and I both had seconds.

We had almost finished when I suddenly felt strange. I felt the goose bumps that popped up on my skinny arms. Something was wrong, when I turned sideways and looked over my shoulder.

There he stood. The stranger with the black beard and black eyes.

"Oh my God," I squealed and jumped. "Where in heavens name, did you come from?" I whispered. "Sorry didn't mean to scare you all. I been watching you all eat and I'm mighty hungry and that does look mighty tasty."

Jannelle jumped up, "Would you like something to eat?"

"That would truly be a blessing for a poor, hungry man," he said slowly moving in closer. "That's mighty generous of you. I do appreciate your kindness."

"Sit down, here with us, and I'll dish it up for you," Jannelle said, smiling at him. On closer inspection he didn't look dangerous. He just looked tired, sad and sort of worn out.

When he started eating, he ate like a hungry man that hadn't eaten for a week, which maybe he hadn't.

"With this depression, it's sure been hard on me. I've been getting work where ever I could find it. Been staying here in this cave, cause I got no place else to go. I lost my farm due to the terrible weather. The drought is what got my crops. The work's running out here, so I'm gonna have to be moving along. Go north, I guess, although I hear they're having it tough there too. I hear people standing in the soup lines, are getting so weak they're dropping dead from starvation."

"I know it's terrible," Uncle Oglee said, we're losing our farm and home because we lost our cotton crop because of the storm, and we just can't get the money to buy more seed and fertilizer. It's just a mess," Uncle said continuing, as he ran his hand through his unruly black hair.

"Yeah, Roosevelt is starting all kinds of programs to help the people, but I'm afraid it's gonna be too late for me," the stranger said, looking down at his feet.

"No don't say that. Things have gotta change," Jannelle said, tears began to glisten in her eyes.

"I think we can find some work for you in exchange for food and a place to sleep," Jannelle said walking over to him and putting her hand on his shoulder. "It's just down the road a piece. It's called the Finley farm."

His face lit up with a smile, which changed his whole appearance from one of sorrow to one of pure happiness.

What a shame I thought, his smile would have been nice if his teeth hadn't been so bad.

He seemed like he suddenly remembered his bad teeth, and put his hand up in front of his mouth, and mumbled. "Thank you, miss for your kindness, God bless you," he said taking off his cap and twisting it back and forth it in his rough, work, worn hands.

He started to walk away, and Jannelle called after, "Wait, come back. We want you to take the leftovers here. She started to gather the rest of the food. She finished and handed him the food in a large paper sack.

"Oh my goodness, Miss. I just don't know how to thank you," he said reaching out, taking the food, and then he turned to leave.

"Wait, don't leave, we know this is your spot and we're through for the day. We're leaving right now and you can stay," Uncle Oglee said, with a big smile as he reached out to shake hands with the guy. The guy shook hands with Uncle Oglee and thanked us again.

"Just a minute," Jannelle said, she grabbed her purse, ruffled around in it, brought out paper and a pencil, "Let me give you the name and address of our farm. You give them this paper, and tell them that Jannelle sent you. They will give you work, food and a place to stay

When we watched him walk down to where his sleeping bag was, we noticed he was dragging his left foot.

"Oh, the poor guy's crippled," Jannelle whispered.

"It's too bad people have to live like that. I wonder when, besides today, was the last time he had a decent meal. Poor guy," I said.

Uncle Oglee was quiet as he watched the guy disappear down the tunnel.

"Penny for your thoughts?" Jannelle asked Uncle. She was watching him out of the corner of her eye.

"Oh no," he said, coming to life as he looked up at her. "I was just thinking, if I didn't have a great family to take me in, there but for the grace of God go I."

"I hope he does stop at the house," Jannelle said.

"Well, let's get back to our gold hunting," Uncle said jumping up.

"You know, at first, I thought he might be the killer, but now I know he couldn't be," I said, thoughtfully.

"Yeah, you're right," Uncle Oglee said, at first I was pretty suspicious too, but now I know he couldn't be."

"Why don't we go down, and check out this bigger tunnel," he continued, as he turned and looked down into the depths of the tunnel, "There seems to be a light source of some kind coming from somewhere in the tunnel."

"You know what, we forgot to ask him, was how he got into the tunnel, since we know he came in through another entrance," I said.

"You're right," Uncle Oglee said.

We walked down the tunnel for about thirty minutes according to Uncle Oglee's pocket watch.

"Look at these strange rocks at the top of the tunnel."

Uncle stopped and looked at them closely. "That's funny, their not stalagmites or stalagtites. Sometimes they are found in caves like this in the Carlsbad Caverns.

He took the shovel reached up to the ceiling and started tapping the rocks loose.

Several fell to the floor. More rocks under the first rocks started falling. The new rocks really looked different.

Uncle Oglee dropped to his knees and started examining the new rocks.

He started breathing really hard, and started gasping for breath as if he could hardly breathe.

"What's wrong, Uncle, are you allergic or something,?" I asked him becoming worried.

He stood up holding one of the rocks. His face had turned white. He took the shovel, laid the rock on the floor and whacked the rock with the shovel. It broke off into smaller pieces. He picked the pieces up and looked at them close.

He turned and held a piece of the rock up. "Ladies, what we have here is gold ore."

Jannelle and I both yelped at the same time, "No."

"It can't be, you've lost your mind," I said.

"It doesn't look like gold," Jannelle.

"It's not supposed to, its gold ore. It's buried in the rock. It has to be mined out. We'll find gold nuggets in these walls."

"But the gold we've been looking for is bricks of gold bullion," Jannelle said.

"I know, this is not the gold we've been looking for. This gold is actually on our property and it can and will be mined," Uncle Oglee said.

"I can't believe it, we've struck gold, and we're rich. I'm so glad we didn't sell our Mineral rights, thank you Jannelle for making us buy our mineral rights back. And thank your Uncle for loaning us the money to buy it back," I said, my voice hoarse with excitement.

"We've got to keep this quiet for now," Jannelle said, nervously twisting a lock of her long blond hair.

"Hallelujah," Uncle Oglee yelled, jumping up and down knocking a few more rocks down with his shovel, and kicking the walls with his worn tattered shoes. I watched as the strange rocks bounced around on the cave floor and wound up in the corners. because the floor slanted down.

I picked up a couple of rocks, dipped them in the tiny lake of water on the floor of the tunnel and polished them on my white, cotton shirt until the streaks of gold in the rocks looked like what else, gold. The rocks glittered like golden diamonds. I put them in my overall pants pocket.

We eagerly walked down the larger tunnel for a few minutes. Our footsteps echoing throughout the tunnel. It really felt kind of spooky. All the tunnel walls and the ceiling were covered with the golden ore rocks. Now that I knew what they were I couldn't take my eyes off the golden streaked treasures.

We couldn't figure out where the source of light was coming from.

We went on for a while longer and the thin ray of light got stronger and it was coming from a large hole in the ceiling.

We all looked up and tried to figure out where the hole went to.

"I think it's a dried up well that's been covered over," uncle Oglee said, his voice getting higher with excitement.

"I think you're right," Jannelle said, getting more excited.

"Oh, I know where that is," I said, its right behind the barn. It's a dried up well and its right behind the barn. It's covered up, but one board is missing. That's where the light is coming from.

Uncle Oglee looked at his watch, and said, "Oh, it's already six o'clock And we better get going and tell everyone the good news."

We could hardly wait to get out of there, so we beat it as fast as we could go. We noticed the stranger took his blanket. So we didn't have to worry about him coming back.

We made sure we carefully covered the entrance so no one would discover our cave, and then we beat it home. My poor feet were so sore from traipsing around on the tunnel floor.

When we got home, we were all talking at once. Finally we got through to Mama and Daddy about what we found.

Mama sat down and cried, "I just can't believe it," she said, her hands were shaking as she wiped her eyes.

"We saved supper for you," she said getting up and going to the oven and taking out ham, beans, baked candied yams, and corn bread. She brought it all to the table with Sally's help.

Sally was tickled to death, after she finished helping Mama; she ran immediately to the bedroom and came back with the tattered Sears catalogue.

"Oh boy, oh boy, I'm gonna get everything," she shouted, bouncing up and down. "Wait till I tell Junior," she stopped mid-sentence, when she saw the look on Mama's face, "Oh I'm sorry, I forgot."

Mama nodded, "I know, I do the same thing.

And it was true we all caught ourselves doing the same thing, forgetting and calling him to come to dinner or supper or calling him to help with the chores, or help do something else. It was terrible when we kept realizing he just died, over and over again. It was horrible to have it happen over and over again.

Everyone was quiet for a minute then we resumed talking about what kind of plans we were going to make. We would of course make all of our relatives rich and then there was John and Lena. We could buy the farm for John. Since Jannelle was a partner she would make all the people she had on her list wealthy.

Daddy was still sitting in his chair. He looked stunned and speechless.

Well, the first thing, we have to contact is a good gold mining company. For right now, we shouldn't tell anyone. And Jannelle, be sure and caution your folks about talking to anyone about it just now. Have them come over tomorrow and we'll talk about it. They can help us decide what to do first.

"You have to be careful, because Aunt Ginger and Aunt Hilda are pretty smart. They'll catch on, so you have to be pretty careful what you say.

CHAPTER 41

Chicken Thief

*S*leep. Well sleep was out of the question. Sally and I couldn't sleep if our life depended on it.

Something was outside. I woke Sally up.

"Wake up Sally, someone's outside," I whispered.

"What," she bellowed. A burglar or killer could have heard her in the next county, let alone just outside.

"Oh good grief, could you just be quiet," I whispered, I was beside myself.

I saw the shadow of a bent over figure, running across the yard. I heard chickens squawking.

Daddy and Uncle Oglee were up and outside, with a shotgun.

I heard the shotgun go off.

"Oh no, I hope Daddy didn't kill anybody, he's just stealing a chicken," I said, running to the door. Coco and Nonie were right behind me. A lot of good they were, they were more afraid than I was.

"It would serve him right, teach him a lesson, not to steal someone else's chicken," Sally was chattering behind me. "Hope he did get shot in the butt," Sally said.

We ran, stumbling in the dark, to the front door and peeked around the corner. It was really bright outside, there was a full moon and all the stars were glittering. I could see Daddy and Uncle Oglee standing very still underneath the mulberry tree. We couldn't see anyone else. But there were at least a dozen squawking chickens running all over the place.

"A chicken thief, that's what we have here," I heard Daddy say. I heard Uncle Oglee laugh.

"I'll bet he's halfway to town by now, but if he does have a chicken, at least he has dinner," Uncle Oglee said, and continued to laugh, and then Daddy started to laugh.

"I guess we better round up some chickens," Daddy said.

I watched the two of them chase the chickens, both of them laughing.

Finally they had them all rounded up and in their pen. They came in sweaty, and all out of breath,

"I gotta have a glass of ice tea after that," Uncle Oglee said.

"Good idea," Daddy said, as he sat down in a kitchen chair, still out of breath.

"Poor guy, he must have been hungry," Mama said, as she came out of the bedroom and sat down at the table. "It's almost midnight," she commented.

"The train should be going by about now, he probably was a hiker on the last train," Daddy said.

Sure enough, in the distance, even though it was still about five miles away, you could hear the haunting sound of the train whistle as it went by. The sound was so lonesome, it always made me sad.

We all went to bed and settled in to sleep.

Morning came, bright and sunshiny. Jannelle came over early with her Uncle Mr. Finley. He was really excited and ready to go to the cave and see for himself what kind of gold mine we had.

Just as we were getting ready to go, who should come driving up but Mr Belton.

"Uh, oh, we better drop everything, and pretend we're not going any-where," Daddy said, as he hid his shovel behind a bush, "We sure don't want this guy to know anything we're up to. He's the worst gossip in the county."

"You got that right,"Mr. Finley agreed, with a big grin.

"Coco and Nonie are slow, to go about their job of barking at Mr. Belton, because they had a hard night too, last night," I said, laughing, looking at Uncle Oglee.

"Why, did they tell you all about it, smarty pants," Uncle Oglee said, laughing his head off.

Mr. Belton got out of the car, came over, and shook hands with everybody. We all put on our innocent faces.

"Too bad you bought your mineral rights back. That's just like throwing three hundred and fifty dollars, down the toilet you know," he said with a smirk on his face.

"You just never know, there just might be gold in them, there hills," Daddy said joking.

"Sure, sure," Belton said nodding his head, with a straight face. "I hear you almost caught a chicken thief last night," he said, with a slight smile.

"Yeah, that's right," Daddy said surprised, "but how did you hear about that. I don't remember telling anyone about it."

"Oh, I don't know. Someone told me about it, can't remember who told me. I forgot who it was," he said hastily and dropped the subject.

Daddy looked puzzled, and so was I. I know I hadn't told anybody. I couldn't see how anyone would have time to tell anybody. That sure was strange, I thought.

"You had a chicken thief here last night," Mr. Finley exclaimed.

"Yep, we sure did and almost caught him," Daddy said, and continued to look at Mr. Belton.

"Well, I best be going," Mr. Belton said hastily, turned and started to leave.

"Well sir, what did you have on your mind?"

"Well, nothing important, I'll talk to you later. Gotta be going," he said, and took off leaving a trail of red dust behind him.

"I'll be darned. That's sure strange," Daddy mumbled.

"Well, he's a mighty strange fellow," Mr. Finley said.

Uncle Oglee had been quiet this whole time. He suddenly spoke up with a grin,

"If I didn't know any better, I would think he was the chicken thief."

"It sure sounds like he was," Daddy said, and shook his head, "Well that's enough of this, so onward to the gold hunting."

So off we went, except for Mama and Jenny, to see the gold discovery. She said she would stay at the house with Jenny, do her chores, and wait for us to get back.

Mr. Finley was really excited when he saw the gold ore.

"This looks like the real thing. I'll check with a good mining company, one that we can trust. I'll have them come out on the q.t. and tell us what we have here. How big a vein of gold this is. It really depends on how rich the gold vein is. Prepare yourself for disappointment, just in case it's not as rich as we hope it is."

"Well I'm always prepared for disappointment," Daddy chuckled, but so far this sounds great," Daddy said, pleased.

"I'll go right now and get a hold of these guys I know," Mr. Finley said, after we got back to the house.

"Not a word to anybody," Uncle Oglee said, "All agreed."

We all nodded our heads and said, "Agreed."

"Uncle Jim, I'm gonna stay here for a little while, Jannelle said, looking up at Oglee

"O.k. Sis," he said, and left fast, as if he was in a hurry.

"Is he mad?" Oglee asked looking after her Dad.

"Oh no," Jannelle laughed, he loves to drive fast, my Aunt says it's the kid in him.

"Well, that's good," Oglee breathed a sigh of relief.

"Oh you silly, are you scared of my Uncle?" Jannelle said, tickling Oglee in the ribs.

"I'll say you got that right," Oglee laughed.

"Why my Uncle wouldn't hurt a flea."

"Have you noticed I'm not a flea."

They were so cute together. They would make such cute babies, I thought. Wait a minute, I thought, I'm really getting ahead of myself.

What did it all mean quality of a gold vein? Maybe we weren't as rich as we thought. I guess we would just have to wait and hear what the mining company had to say. That was really quite a come down.

Lena and her Daddy came over. He was almost well, but he still limped a little.

"How you feeling, John," Daddy asked, as he pulled up a cane bottomed chair for Jim to sit in.

"Well sir my body's coming along just fine, but my life is pretty much a mess," Jim said, grunting as he sat down.

"You don't say, what seems to be the problem?" Daddy asked, looking at him expectantly.

"The man, that's the owner of my farm, is selling it right out from under me, to a young man that's gonna work it himself. That means I'm plain out of luck," he said, looking tired and old. He looked down at his feet, and shook his head sadly. And of course I'm just like you people, I, too lost my cotton crop to the hurricane."

"Well that's a dammed shame John, just downright tough luck, I'm sure sorry to hear that," Daddy said, looking genuinely sorry.

"What do you plan to do?" Daddy asked.

Well I got a sister that lives in Georgia. I think maybe, I just might go stay with her for a while. But they don't have any place for Lena to stay; they just don't have any room for any more people."

After John and Lena left, we all talked about how much we were all going to miss Lena.

CHAPTER 42

Caught Murderer

*T*he next morning, after breakfast and after all our chores were done, everyone else, mainly Oglee had gone about their business. But Sally and I were still sitting around the kitchen table, talking about everything in general. About Lena leaving, about the murders, and especially, about all the bad luck we had been having.

Suddenly, there was quite a racket going on outside.

It was a car rattling down the rough, wet road to our house. I ran to the window and peeked outside, then I yelled back over my shoulder, "Hey, it's Sheriff Dan and Deputy Bob, and is he in a hurry," I reported.

"I wonder why," Daddy said, as he walked over to the window, looked over my head, and peeked out the window. He quickly turned, went to the door, opened it and waited for Dan and Bob to arrive.

"He sure is in a hurry," Daddy mused aloud.

Dan arrived, followed by a cloud of red dust, and skidded to a stop in a hail of gravel and dirt.

"My God Dan, what's the big hurry?" Daddy yelled.

"We got him," Dan yelled back, as he jumped out of the car, "We caught the dammed, bastard, that rotten son of a bitch. You know the killer. And you would never, ever, guess in a million years, who it is. Well Bob here, actually trapped, and caught him.

"Nah, you actually got him," Daddy gasped, jumping down the three porch steps all at once.

"Who the hell is it," Daddy yelled back.

About that time, Uncle Oglee appeared behind Daddy. "I'll bet it was the two guys from the city," Uncle Oglee guessed.

"Nope," Dan said shaking his head, and opened his mouth to say something, but Daddy broke in, "Then I'll bet it was someone we've never heard of."

"No, wrong again, I told you, you would never guess."

"I give up, who is it,"

"It's Harry Belton," Dan said, and paused looking at Daddy, "Isn't that a shocker."

"What! Why that's unbelievable. Are you sure you got the right man?" Daddy asked.

"Well I'll be darned; I would never have believed he had the guts or nerve to do that. That's a hoot alright," Uncle Oglee said, shaking his head. "I knew he was strange, but never knew he was that strange. I didn't think he had the guts to do something like that."

"This all happened when I was gone. Bob was in charge when I went to visit relatives. My niece was getting married. So, when all hell broke loose, I wasn't even here. I missed the whole dammed thing."

"Well Bob here, had suspected him for a while now, and by golly, he finally proved it. Bob talked the crew into setting up a trap for him. So they all did just that. He set a trap for him, and by golly, he fell right into it. Harry had constantly been pestering us about how we were doing with the case. He was always asking if we had any suspects. He kept asking if we had any clues, and Bob here, got to thinking. He figured out that all the victims were somehow connected to the court case that Harry had lost. Even the judge that was murdered was the same judge that ruled on his case. He went through all the old files, even took them home with him at nighttime to go through them, on his own time."

"I have to admit, we really didn't think much about it, but Bob here, discovered why the only reason Belton hadn't killed John Peterson, the jury foreman, was because Peterson was out of town most of the time. So the next time Belton began asking Bob more questions, Bob was ready for him. He had created a plan to trap him. He figured that if he told Belton, that John Peterson was helping the police with the case. Bob made up a time and place, when Peterson would be all alone and working on the case files. Bob told Belton all about it, which made it easy for Belton to catch Peterson alone. He told Belton that John was taking some police files home with him, to separate and put the files in a certain order. He told Belton that Peterson's family would be out of town to visit other relatives and Bob would be able to work quietly at home alone. That way he could get the job done a lot faster."

"And he went for it," Daddy said incredulous.

"Yep," Dan said, "Hook line and sinker," he stopped.

"You know Bob, you should be telling this story, it's your story," Dan said.

Dan was much older than Bob. When Bob joined the police force, Dan took him under his wing and treated him like a prodigy.

Bob just shook his head.

While I was gone, Bob got about six of the guys together, and set up at John's place, and waited for Belton to show up, and by golly, here he comes, with his big hunting knife and a thirty eight pistol."

"Of course, John wasn't even there. Bob got a dummy manikin from somewhere," Dan laughed, "from heavens knows where, probably robbed a dress store, kidding of course, Bob set the dummy up in John's favorite chair, with his back to the door. When Harry realized he had been set up, it was really a comical sight to see. When Harry attacked the dummy from the back, the dummy slumped over, and fell to the floor in a crumpled heap. Harry just stood there with his mouth hanging wide open, and his eyes were like two, huge, brown sausages, he stared at the crumpled heap of material lying on the floor. His right hand was clutching the knife up in the air, and the other hand dangled straight up over his head, grappling thin air. He looked so bewildered and shocked, it was hilarious."

Bob started laughing and said, "All he could say was, quote, *"What the hell,"* *And* we had handcuffs on him before he could say another word," Bob said finishing the story.

"They all had it coming," he screamed. "You know, he didn't even try and deny it. Not that it would have done any good."

"Well, it's a good thing he confessed," Uncle Oglee said, "Now, you don't have to go to a lot of trouble gathering evidence against him."

"That's not a problem. We had a lot of evidence against him already. He was really careless," Bob said. "He left a lot of evidence, bloody fingerprints, bloody footprints. And, even at one murder scene, he left one of his caps."

"Yeah, he just didn't seem to care," Dan said, shaking his head. "Just not smart at all."

"When we asked him why he tortured his victims, all he would say was, "They had it coming, they put me through hell, so I put them through a little hell myself, and I enjoyed every second of it," he said gleefully. It was plain he was proud and enjoyed just talking about it.

"The guys crazy, that's all there is to it," Bob said.

"Yeah, I've never met anybody that crazy before," Dan agreed.

"Just thought we'd let you know," Dan said as they turned and got ready to leave.

"Oh yeah, and another thing you know the mineral rights, well Harry was getting a one hundred kick back, for everyone that he talked into selling their mineral rights. He had a deal with a company out of New York that was buying up all the mineral rights in this area.

"Well, who the heck would have thought that? I knew he was really pushing people to sell, and I did wonder why," Daddy said.

I'll be darned, I thought.

"Well, I'm sure glad you stopped by and told us what happened," Daddy said, as we watched them get in the marked car and leave.

We all waved as they left. For the first time Sally had been speechless, which amazed me.

"Well I'm sure glad they caught him," I said looking at Sally. "A little scary though, it being someone I know," I said, as we went back into the house.

Mama and Daddy couldn't stop talking about it. They couldn't get over the fact that it was someone they had known for that long. Imagine that, a serial killer, they kept saying.

"You know what I think, "I said.

"What?" Daddy asked.

"I think that was him night before last night. I think he was the chicken thief," I said.

"You know what, little one, I think you're right. It makes sense to me," Uncle Oglee said.

"I think you're right too, no way. How could he know we had a chicken thief the night before," Daddy said.

"I just know in my heart, it was him. He came here to do more than steal a chicken. I think he came here to kill us, but to his surprise, he ran into a shotgun." I said.

"Zemma, I think you hit the nail on the head," Mama said.

"It just gives me the shivers to think about it." I mumble.

In my mind I kept seeing poor Mr. Kinkade sitting in the corner of that wooden cabin, all cut up and bloody, sitting, slumped over, with his head hanging down. I had to shiver all over when I thought about it.

Sally and I both went back to our room. We didn't even have our catalogue game to keep us company any more, and make us feel better. I just wanted to go to sleep and forget all about everything. But it was way too early to go to bed. And tonight of course I had to tell Junior all about it.

When I thought about it, it was really a close call. I think Belton had really planned to kill us. I don't know why, didn't need a reason, did he. He was so crazy, he could just imagine something. It was scary, when you thought about it, that, there were that kind of people running around.

I heard two people talking, and when I went to the window and looked out, I saw Aunt Ginger and Aunt Hilda walking leisurely up the walkway to the house. I opened the door and went running out to meet them. I could hardly wait to tell them.

When I told them, they both screamed, "Oh my God, is everyone o.k."

"Of course we're fine," I said, "but aren't you surprised about who it is, the murderer that is?"

"Oh my goodness yes, but are they sure?" Aunt Ginger asked.

"Absolutely, he admitted to doing all the murders, and wasn't even a bit sorry for torturing and killing all of the victims. He said they all deserved it," I said, shaking my head.

"He's just plain crazy," Aunt Hilda said.

"I' ll go in and talk to Claude and Leota for a minute and then get home to talk to my kids about this," Aunt Ginger said.

"Me too," Aunt Hilda said.

A few minutes later they took off as if they had wings..

Everybody that came by was all in an uproar about catching the serial killer. The day flew by, and we didn't get much done.

CHAPTER 43

Newspaper Article

When Aunt Ginger and Aunt Hilda came by the next day they were still all in a flutter about it.

"It's great that they solved the murder case," Aunt Ginger kept saying. "I never, ever would have thought it was Harry," she went on, shaking her head thoughtfully. "What a hoot that is."

"Me either," I said agreeing with her. "I thought it was the guys that came to our house, that rainy night."

"Me too," she said. "I wonder what ever happened to them."

"I don't know, he might have gotten them, too," I said, half joking, but maybe half not.

"I heard they were all in a gang from New York. I also heard that, they cheated people out of their money, and since then they had been caught and put in jail," I said remembering what sheriff Dan had said.

"Is it true, Lena's going home to stay with her Daddy?" Aunt Ginger asked sadly. "How's he going to be able to take care of her, being all crippled up like he is?" Aunt Hilda wondered.

"I don't know Aunt Hilda, I've been wondering that myself," I said glumly.

"Did you know that Bob has become an overnight celebrity, since he caught Harry Belton, the serial killer?" Aunt Hilda asked.

Our newspaper put out a special bulletin today, featuring the article about Harry Belton.

"Yeah, His picture has been in all the newspapers," Aunt Ginger said.

"Did you read the article Jannelle wrote about Bob catching Harry. They had a nice picture of Bob in the paper, too. She gave him a lot of high praise and it was well written too," Aunt Ginger said.

"Well, he didn't do it all by himself," Aunt Hilda said.

"In the article she gave him all the credit," Aunt Ginger said.

"Oh, I know why," I said. "Dan was in Georgia on a two week vacation. He was there to visit some of his relatives. Someone was getting married."

"That makes sense," Aunt Hilda said.

"How come you know everything young lady?" Aunt Ginger asked, looking down at me with penetrating blue eyes.

I started to stutter, I was so taken by surprise, "We-uh-ll, I- uh-, I keep quiet, I don't say anything, and people forget I'm even there. That way my friend, I hear everything, see everything and know everything," I said looking up, and looking Aunt Ginger straight in the eye, with a big grin on my freckled face.

"Yep, that girl Jannelle is going places someday," Aunt Hilda said.

And I thought, oh dear, how's Uncle Oglee gonna like that. I couldn't wait to get my hands on the paper to see what she said.

"Do you happen to have a copy of the paper Aunt Ginger?" I asked.

"O.K. smarty pants, I just might have a copy. I'll bring it over for you," Aunt Ginger said.

"I don't think your Uncle is gonna think much of it," Aunt Ginger said watching me out of the corner of her eye.

Aunt Hilda and Aunt Ginger exchanged brief glances, and then looked back at me, they looked like they were waiting for me to say something, but I kept my lip zipped, until I could read the article. By their expressions, I could see they had already discussed it. And I couldn't help but wonder what was said. Oh dear, oh dear, I could hardly wait until I could read it.

"Wait here. I'll go get it right now," Aunt Ginger said.

"Oh no, you don't have to get it right now," I yelled after her, but she was gone like a flash.

"Aunt Hilda was laughing and shaking her head, "That girl," she said.

"How about that Harry Belton, who would ever have thought he could do those horrible murders?" Aunt Hilda said, shaking her white head. She looked really nice today in her new dress, she had made it for herself. It was a light, bright blue background, with a pattern of tiny white flowers all over it. It had a dainty white lace collar at the neckline, and a white lace belt. She really knew how to put a dress together, I thought.

Just a few minutes had passed and Aunt Ginger was back with the newspaper, she already had it folded to the front page.

"I didn't have to go all the way home," she said, "I found one in your mailbox."

"That's great, I thought you were pretty fast," I said, as I snatched the newspaper out of her hand, and started reading. They were both watching me like a hawk, waiting for my reaction.

It was a glowing report about how clever, sharp, and dedicated Bob was in figuring out who did the murders. It also had a nice picture of him, in his uniform beside the article.

Sally came in and was reading over my shoulder. "Wow, Uncle Oglee's not gonna think much of this," she said with a little giggle.

"Well, what do you think," Aunt Ginger asked me.

"It's very well written," I said, "She did a good job," I added.

Darn it! I wasn't gonna say any more; I had my mind made up. I knew Uncle was not gonna like it, and I wouldn't like it either, if I were him.

"How about you two staying for dinner? " Mama asked, smiling at Aunt Ginger and Aunt Hilda.

"Nah, I gotta get home," Aunt Hilda said, as she turned to leave for the front door.

"How about you, Aunt Ginger?" Mama asked.

Aunt Ginger looked like she was trying to make up her mind, "Well," she said. Just then Uncle Oglee came in.

"I believe I will stay for dinner if you folks don't mind," Aunt Ginger said, making her decision to stay and sitting down in the nearest chair, as she watched Uncle Oglee pull up a chair.

"Did I hear somebody say dinner's ready?" he said with a big smile.

"That was really great catching the killer. Really good not having to worry about that guy any more," Uncle Oglee said.

"Yeah, quite an article about it in the newspaper," Sally said, watching Uncle Oglee out of the corner of her eye

"Is that right?" Uncle Oglee asked, "And do we have the newspaper?"

"Yeah and the article was written by your girlfriend," Sally said in a low ominous voice.

"Really, well after dinner I'll have to read it for sure," he said with a pleased tone of voice.

"I'll bet its good, cause she's pretty smart," he said filling his plate up with ham, potatoes, biscuits and yams.

So sure enough after dinner, we watched for what we were waiting for, waiting for Uncle to read the paper.

He opened it up, and there it was on the front page a huge picture of Bob and a lengthy article, all about Bob.

"Wow, it's a very long article isn't it," he said, looking up from the paper, "and quite a nice, large photo too."

Everyone was quiet and not a peep out of anyone while he read.

"Wow, he said, as he finished the article, and laid the paper down on the table.

"That was certainly a lengthy piece, and very well done. Quite complimentary, I must say," he said, with a stiff smile on a frozen face, was the only way I could describe it.

I really hurt for him, and I said, "It was o.k. but it was just a little bit too flowery, almost amateurish," I said, feeling the anger begin to rise up inside of me, I was getting mad. "It really was a little much."

Uncle Oglee looked at me with a grateful look of surprise, the frozen look began to disappear and a pleasant smile spread over his face. I slid out of my chair, grabbed the paper and went to my room.

Everyone started talking all at once as I left the room.

CHAPTER 44

Jannelle and Oglee Fight

nother day, another dollar as Daddy would say. It was Monday morning, bright and early; it was the day after the newspaper article came out.

Coco and Nonie started barking and raising a ruckus.

I looked out the window and to my surprise, there was Jannelle on her horse Dapple and I thought *oh dear, oh dear, oh dear what now*.

Uncle Oglee heard her too as he came around the corner and into the kitchen.

I watched her get off her horse. She was all out of breath and behold, she had a newspaper clutched in her hand. Oh dear, I thought, has this girl lost her mind. She actually had the red flag in her hand to wave at the bull, I looked around for the bull Oglee I expected to see him frothing at the mouth. But he wasn't. He was quite calm and very quiet.

He met her at the kitchen door. "Come on in, Jannelle, I see you have your master piece with you," he said with a half smile. I hardly ever see him with just a half smile. And I just never, ever have seen him mad. I didn't think he got mad.

She came in slowly, looking at him with a puzzled look on her face, "You didn't like it?" She asked surprised.

He looked at her for a long minute, "Not much, I wouldn't say it was your best work," he said curtly.

"Really," I thought it was my best work," she said defensively, and continued to stare at him. Her face turned a bright pink, and her blue eyes began to glitter.

"No really, not your best work, but I would say, you sounded like you liked the guy quite a lot," Uncle Oglee said, and just stared back at her.

I felt cold goose bumps of fear pop up on my bare arms.

"Are you kidding, we're friends. Are you crazy Oglee Samson. I think I did a good job on the piece."

"You said, "*he represented the finest specimen of Mississippi manhood,*" Now I'd say that's going a little too far," Uncle Oglee reminded her.

Jannelle was so angry she could hardly even speak. She started to stutter, "Well it's, it's- tr-,u-u-e true," she said, "he's really a nice guy." Her voice was shaking.

I was beginning to feel sorry for her, I think she really did mean well.

"I think you're just jealous," she retorted, with tears starting to fill her eyes.

She turned and ran back out side, climbed up on Dapple, and off they went in a cloud of red dust, Coco and Nonie thought it was a game, so off they went close behind them for a few feet, creating a bigger cloud of dust.

"There she goes, you might never see her again Uncle Oglee," I said, beginning to worry.

"That's alright," Uncle said angrily, "She likes him better than me, any way."

"Oh no, she doesn't," I said, "I can tell. She really likes you."

"Do you really think so?" He asked doubtfully, looking down the road after her. "So why's she acting this way?" he insisted.

""Well, she could say the same thing about you, why are you acting the way you are," I argued.

"I have a reason to act this way," Uncle Oglee said, defensively.

"No, not the way she thinks, she's only Bob's friend, and she thinks you should know that."

"Really, I don't think so," Uncle said, stubbornly.

"I think you should apologize before it's too late, and hope that she forgives you," I said.

"You gotta be kidding, who me, the one to apologize, I'm the victim here," he complained. He started to act silly, by playing like he was crying; he started rubbing his eyes with his fists.

Good I thought, he's already getting over his temper fit, and is seeing the error of his ways.

"O.k. Mr. Smarty Pants," and I threw the little ball, that I'd been throwing at Coco, at him.

"Yeah, just give her a little time to get over it," I said.

"But you're going to have to make her believe you're sorry."

"Oh no, she's the one to say she's sorry," he stubbornly stuck to his guns.

"I don't think it works that way," I said, shaking my head.

"You're going to push her right into Bob's arms," I grumbled.

"Not till hell freezes over," he said maintaining his position.

He turned and walked away," Not in this lifetime," I heard him mumble.

"Oh dear, this can't happen."

Mama had been quietly listening to us talk. "You know, little brother she just might be right."

Uncle Oglee stopped in his tracks and looked at Mama, "You think so?"

"Could be," she said nodding her head.

I looked at Uncle and I could see the wheels turning, oh good, I thought.

Jenny started crying; Mama turned, and went to pick her up.

Hear, here little one, don't cry, food is coming right up," Mama said picking her up and sitting down at the table with Jenny in her lap. Mama already had a plate of crushed yams, chopped up ham, and crushed up peaches just waiting for her. This session had a dual purpose feeding time and teaching Jenny how to talk.

"Here we go," "say ham," she'd give her a bite of ham, "say ham, "and she'd wait for Jenny to say ham, Jenny would say "am," Mama would say "yams" Jenny would say "ams". Mama would say, "Good enough," Jenny would say "nuff." Mama would laugh and say, "good girl," and Jenny would say "ood earl." That would really crack Mama up, and this went on until the plate was empty.

CHAPTER 45

The Breakup

The news that Jannelle and Uncle Oglee had broken up spread like wildfire. Instantly, the girls started coming around, especially Constance. She showed up on the doorstep.

She was very direct. She asked if Uncle Oglee was there, and I wanted to tell her no, but he was right there in the kitchen.

They went outside and sat in the double swing on the front porch.

I stayed in the kitchen by the window inside by the swing, so I could hear everything they said.

Darn it, Sally caught me. I put my finger against my lips to shush her, and thank goodness, she did, but you never know about Sally, whether she will cooperate or not. This time she did, she came over to listen with me.

"They're having a celebration and dance in honor of Bob Anderson this coming Saturday."

"Really, is that right?" Uncle Oglee asked.

"Yes, and I hear Janelle is going with him as his guest."

"Well, how about that," Uncle Oglee said, his back suddenly getting straight as a board.

"Yep, who'd of thought it," Constance said.

"Since that's the way it's gonna be, you wanna go with me to the dance?"

Uncle looked surprised. He sat there quietly thinking for a minute. He turned and looked at her and said, "Well, why not, do you wanna go to the dance with me?"

"Oh darn it, stupid, stupid men," I whispered to Sally.

"Wow, isn't that the truth," Sally said. "She played him like a fiddle,"

"I thought he was smarter than that," I said just boiling with fury.

"Yeah, she's a smooth operator," Sally said, "And pretty too."

"Not as pretty as Jannelle," I said, "We gotta fix this somehow," I said.

"Oh sure, you just do that," she said laughing.

"Let me think, there's gotta be something," I said racking my brain, but there was nothing. "You better help me think, or you just might wind up with Constance as an Aunt."

I looked back out the window and they were still talking.

I just couldn't stand it any longer. I went to the phone and called Jannelle. I got her Mom on the phone. She said Jannelle wasn't there, but I'll tell her you called. I just knew it. She must be out with Bob.

"What's the matter with her," I told Sally. "Maybe she doesn't deserve Uncle Oglee," I said. I was beginning to feel anger toward her. "Doesn't she realize what a catch Uncle Oglee is," I said. I looked out the window again and I could see Constance was getting ready to leave, and to my horror, I watched her lean upwards on her tip toes and pull Uncle Oglees head down and kiss him. I almost fainted and I heard Sally gasp in shock. I could tell Uncle Oglee was in shock too, as he watched her leave, going down the pathway, in her pretty white dress with the blue trim, looking over her shoulder and waving bye bye. No doubt about it, she was as cute as a button.

All Sally could say was "Uh-oh, uh-oh."

"Well, you're a lot of help," I said in a grouchy voice.

Mama came in about that time, "Did Constance leave?" Mama asked.

"Yep, she came and she went," Sally said, with a grin.

"What's going on," she asked, because she could tell by our attitudes and faces that something was up.

"Constance just kissed Uncle Oglee," Sally blurted out; she couldn't keep a secret if her life depended on it.

"She did what? She kissed Oglee," and she started to laugh, she rushed over to the window and looked out.

He saw her peeking through and he came in.

"Is that true? Did Constance kiss you?"

"Yep, she laid one on me," he said with a big grin.

"Well, well, my little brother the lady killer," Mama said laughing and clapping her hands.

"I think it's more like Constance, man killer," he said, his grin growing wider.

I followed Uncle Oglee into the kitchen.

"Why don't you make up with Janelle," I begged.

"Honey, it's too late, she's already going with Bob," He said sadly.

"No, it's not. It's just one dance. You know you really hurt her feelings, and you didn't even apologize."

"I know it's my fault. I'm going to that dance and I'm gonna knock Bob's block off, I'm gonna beat the tar out of him. He's gonna be sorry he ever heard of me. Steal a guy's girlfriend."

"He didn't steal her, you threw her away," I yelled at him.

"Oh no, I did not," he yelled at that, "I would never throw her away."

"Well what would you call it?" I argued.

"Just a little argument, certainly not bad enough to go, and go out with another guy."

"Can't you see my heart's broken? I'm really hurting here, and you're just rubbing it in."

"No I'm not, I'm just trying to wake you up before it's too late," I said feeling sorry for him. He didn't deserve all this.

Mama had been listening to it all. She came over and gave him a hug, "It's going to be alright little brother, you have plenty of time to make up, and I'm sure you will," she said consoling him.

So I shut up and went to my room to try to think of something to save Uncle Oglee.

About an hour later the phone rang and it was for me. It was Jannelle.

"What's up, Zemma?" she asked.

"I have a question, Are you going to the celebration dance with Bob?"

She paused for a minute, "No," she said, "Where did you hear that?

"Well, actually Constance was just over here, and she told Uncle Oglee that you were going to the dance with Bob, and then she asked him if he would go to the dance with her, and then, and then,(I almost stuttered at this) you won't believe what she did."

"Nothing would surprise me," she said angrily.

"Well, she literally reached up and pulled his head down and she kissed him,"

"She did what, why that little witch. You know, she's always been after him," she said. "That makes me so mad I could spit. I could pull her blond hair out by its brown roots. Did he say yes, he'd go to the dance with her?"

"Why yes, he did, but you can't blame him because he thought you were going to the dance with Bob. I think it's stupid that you two are fighting,"

"Well yes," she said, "But it takes two to tango," she said. She sounded like she was crying. Oh dear, I thought, they've got to make up, or they were going to break my heart.

CHAPTER 46

Lena Stays With Us

Someone was knocking on the door. When I answered it, I was surprised to see John with Lena beside him holding his hand.

"Is your Mom and Dad home, Zemma?" John asked.

I turned to go get them, but Mama was right behind me.

"Why come on in, John. Have a seat. Would you like a cup of coffee?

"Why sure Mrs. Carter, he said as he sat down at the kitchen table. "

"Why hello there, John," Daddy said as he came into the kitchen. He pulled up a chair and sat down.

"What's on your mind, John?" Daddy asked. "I was just wondering, could Lena stay with you folks until I get on my feet?" John started right in. He stopped and looked over at Lena.

"Of course she can stay with us. We were really sorry when she left," Daddy said smiling down at Lena.

I was shocked. What a great surprise that was.

Lena looked surprised herself.

"That would be great," I yelped.

Lena's face broke out in a smile, "Really Daddy that would be fun."

"It's settled then," Daddy said reaching down and giving Lena a hug.

"She's become one of my own anyway."

Daddy told John about our gold discovery. He also told him we would share with him, if it turns out like we plan. We were almost afraid to count our chickens before they hatched.

We ran into where Mama was peeling potatoes.

"Guess what Mama; Lena's going to come live with us, while her Daddy goes to Georgia to live with his sister. While he's there, we get to keep Lena here with us."

Mama was shocked for a minute, and then she said "Why that's wonderful," she gasped, reached over and pulled Lena to her, "We are very happy to have you back with us, you know that."

Lena beamed from ear to ear, "I feel like I'm back home again."

It took several days before the gold mining company came to the house. Daddy and Mr. Finley took them to the cave. The men from the mining company were there several hours. They took samples and chipped away at the walls.

We were all nervous wrecks waiting to see if we were going to be rich or not.

Mama started singing playfully, "What will be, will be."

I was surprised, that was the first time I had heard Mama sing since Junior had died.

Daddy was pacing back and forth, in and out of the kitchen. He stopped and made an announcement. "Time to get back to serious things like digging that well. I don't know but it seems like we should have gotten water by now," he continued with a worried frown. Then he turned and went outside.

Things went along uneventfully, like we were just playing the waiting game.

A young man somewhere in his twenties stopped by the house. He came to the back door and asked if he could have some food. He said he would be happy to work for food. His clothes were tattered and old. and his hair was long. He said he was on his way to California to get a job. He was coming from Tennessee where his folks were having a hard time. He said he wanted to get a job and send money back to his folks.

Mama gave him a good meal of left over's and some food for his knapsack.

"If you want to pay us back for food, I know the men could use a hand digging a well."

"Oh sure, I'd be happy to."

When he was done eating, Mama pointed in the direction where they were digging the well. He took off in a long lope.

I watched him run. It was so sad.

CHAPTER 47

The Dance

The dance hallway was beautifully decorated, with colorful banners, balloons and posters. It also had enlarged pictures of Bob everywhere.

The dance was in honor of Bob Anderson. He was king for a day.

Constance was there to pick Uncle Oglee up for the dance; she was there right on the button, at eight o'clock. She really looked dazzling in a bright purple dress that had bows and ribbons everywhere. It was beautiful. Aunt Hilda made it and she really did herself proud.

We all went to the dance, even Mama and Jenny went. That's the way things were done here, dances were family affairs. They even had food. It was like a smorgasbord or a banquet. Everyone brought a dish of some kind. We brought fried chicken, a potato salad and a peach cobbler.

It was really something to look forward to.

Every one was dressed to the hilt. You couldn't even recognize some of the people, because they were so dressed up. Mama wore the dress she made out of the material that Lena had given her. It was gorgeous, she looked gorgeous. Sally, Lena and I wore our new dresses made out of bleached fertilizer sacks that looked like white linen. We had pretty red bows and red belts to match. We felt gorgeous. Even Jenny looked gorgeous in the newest dress that Mama had made for her, out of a little bit of the left over material from her dress. Mama made Uncle Oglee a pretty blue shirt, out of some material Aunt Ginger had given her. And of course he looked dashing and handsome. Daddy wore his tan clothes and he looked handsome.

Everybody was in a festive mood.

When we got there we saw some of the people we hadn't seen since the first day we got here. It was really fun.

And then we saw Jannelle and she was super gorgeous looking, she was in a frilly red dress with a low neckline. What a sight, she was truly a picture of beauty. I thought Uncle Oglee's eyes were going to fall right out of his head.

I waited and watched breathlessly. She was standing over by one of the buffet tables, holding a glass of ice tea.

Uncle Oglee walked right up to her and said "Hello Jannelle, how have you been?"

"Why Oglee, I've been fine, how are you?" She said surprised and obviously pleased. The sudden abrupt greeting startled her, but she rallied around and regained her composure.

So the ice was broken and they began to chat.

And up walks the man of the hour, Bob Anderson.

Uh-oh, I thought we're going to see some action here, I can just feel it, and my heart started beating faster.

So with me being a little kid, and all, no one would pay any attention if I moved in closer, so I could hear everything, so that's exactly what I did.

"Hey Oglee, I heard through the grapevine, that you thought there was too big a fuss being made about me capturing the killer," Bob said belligerently.

Oh shoot, I thought, so Bob's not such a nice guy after all. Well now that's good, so now, Janelle can see the other side to him, which I hoped was bad.

Uncle Oglee looked surprised, he turned and looked Bob up and down, and said, "Well Bob, now that you put it that way, you're absolutely right, I think you were overly praised, and, what do you think about that."

"I think you're a little wimp, that doesn't know what the hell you're talking about," Bob said, with his chin jutting out. He was really showing an ugly side.

That just tickled the daylights out of me. Oh goodie, more, more let's have some more of this kind of stuff, I thought.

Jannelle just stared at Bob shocked, her eyes big, her mouth open, "Oh my goodness, Bob," she said.

Uncle Oglee just stared at Bob and started laughing, "Well, bless your pointed little head, I do think you feel threatened. Now isn't that a shame, a big fellow like you, threatened by a little old fellow like me."

Bob was actually grinding his teeth, he was so mad. "I'm a good mind to just knock the shit right out of you," he snarled.

Oh wow, now he really did look ugly. Who would have thought he had this side to him, Bob the sweet, nice, quiet, mild mannered Bob, I thought. Things sure went to his head in a hurry.

"If you think you're man enough to do it, go for it," Uncle Oglee said, his black eyes narrowed and he began to intently watch Bob, for any sudden moves.

Bob raised his right arm and took a good hard swing at Uncle. Uncle Oglee dodged, and laughed, Bob swung at empty air.

That just infuriated him, and he took another empty swing, the swing was so hard he almost fell down, which made him look down right comical. He was making a complete fool of himself. He was so enraged by this time that his hand automatically reached for his empty gun holster, thank God it was empty or maybe Uncle would have been long gone.

People that had gathered around, and were watching gasped in shock, when they realized that he had actually reached for his gun, forgetting that he didn't have it on him.

Then he seemed to come to his senses, and realized what he was doing. He shook his head angrily, stomped his foot, like a petulant child turned and left.

Uncle Oglee quit laughing and watched him leave.

Jannelle came over to Uncle Oglee, put her arm around Uncle Oglee, and said, "I'm so sorry Oglee, I had no idea he was that kind of man."

He leaned down and hugged her, "That's alright, the misunderstanding we had, was all my fault, I'm so sorry. But, I do think he could be dangerous."

"You're absolutely right," Jannelle said.

The people in the crowd that had gathered to watch the fight came over to Oglee and complimented him on how he handled the situation. Uncle Oglee was actually glowing. Everything was coming up roses.

Oops, we're in for it now, I thought as I watched Constance come bouncing up.

"Well, what have we got here, "she exclaimed in an above normal voice.

"Well, it is what it looks like," Uncle Oglee said with a big grin, "And you know what's funny. Jannelle didn't come to the dance with Bob, now isn't that strange."

"That is strange; I could have sworn that I heard she was."

"Amazing now isn't it, how things get said that aren't so."

"And what's amazing, I just watched the almost fight, that just happened," she said laughing. They all three laughed.

"Well, I guess I'll go cheer Bob up and keep him company. I imagine he needs some," she said looking up toward the heavens, laughing as she left.

"Be careful," Oglee said, calling after her, "I think he might be dangerous."

The dance was a success and I felt happiness filling my heart as I watched Uncke Oglee and Jannelle dancing.

CHAPTER 48

Gold Mine Fizzles

"Now's a good time to go check out that dried up well and see if that's where the light from the tunnel is coming from. Not that it matters, but just out of curiosity I'd like to know," Daddy said.

Daddy, Uncle Oglee and I went to the back of the barn and by golly we found it. While we were there we put another board over the open spot so someone wouldn't fall through and break a leg or worse.

It was close to supper time when the Gold Mining company people came to the door.

"Sorry folks, we have some really bad news. It was what we were afraid of. But the mine isn't worth a lot. It's a very light vein and it won't produce much gold. You can go ahead and mine it, but you won't make very much."

What a crashing blow that turned out to be. We were all so disappointed. Sally was so mad she threw her Sears catalogue clear across the kitchen.

"Bah Humbug," she screeched, her freckled, sunburned face was all screwed up in anger.

Jenny was standing in her playpen. She looked at Sally and said, "Bug," and smiled.

That cracked Sally up, she laughed and said "Did you hear that, she said bug, for humbug.

"Bah humbug," she said again, and looked expectantly at Jenny

Jenny looked back at Sally and said, "Um bug, and smiled proudly.

"Did you hear that Mama, she's so smart," Sally said She looked at Jenny and said, "Smart girl, smart girl,"

Jenny looked back and said, "art erl,"

"Just listen to that," Sally went on.

"You're going to have to watch what you say, because she will be repeating everything," Mama said.

I have to admit Sally had a way with babies, and especially with Jenny.

"Dadgummit, we just can't win," I said, truly disappointed about the gold mine.

After the mining company got through doing their business, there would be nine thousand, maybe ten thousand dollars left for us, which was much better than what the little boy shot at. It was a far cry from being rich, but it did save us from poverty. It was more money than we'd ever seen in our whole lives. Maybe ten thousand wasn't a lot of money to the mining company but to us it was a lot of money.

We would have enough money to buy cotton seed and fertilizer. A new plow, which we needed desperately. Parts to fix the truck up into running condition. Seed for the garden. And of course new heavy duty boots for Daddy and Uncle Oglee. We could also got shoes for every body. We would have enough money to get curtain material for the windows and material for spreads for our beds. We also had enough for material to make dresses for me, Sally, Lena, Jenny and Mama, and shirts and overalls for Daddy and Uncle Oglee. Mama would also have enough extra material to teach me, Sally, and Lena how to sew. We were going to make skirts and blouses. We had enough money to give Oglee five hundred dollars, just in case he wanted to get Jannelle an engagement ring and a few personal things. We had enough money, so we were all happy, we were rich we thought.

Jannelle said she didn't want any part of the gold profits, because there just wasn't that much.

"When we discovered the real gold that was hidden during the civil war, that's when I'll take my share," she said laughing.

Every day they would dig the well and it didn't seem like we were ever going to hit water.

"I just don't understand it, we should have gotten water at least fifty feet ago if not before," Daddy said, totally disgusted as he wiped the sweat and dirt from his forehead.

"How many feet do you have," Mama asked.

"Almost two thousand and that's unheard of to go that deep around here."

"The well drillers are almost ready to quit. I just don't know what we're going to do," Daddy said, shaking his head, sitting down, with his elbows on the kitchen table, and his head in his hands. He was the picture of despair, I thought. I guess we'll just have to start drilling in a new spot. We'll just have to get someone out here to help us decide on a new and profitable spot. There should be water all around out here. And who knows there might not be any water in a new spot."

"We're just spinning our wheels," Daddy said with a halfhearted grin.

"Well tomorrow, I guess we'll make it our last day of drilling."

Lena was sitting across the table, peeling potatoes and watching Daddy.

"Oh woe is me, what are we going to do?" She said, tears started to run down her sunburned cheeks.

Daddy stopped, looked at her and smiled, "After all, we're pretty well off. We've got that ten thousand in gold ore. "Oh my goodness honey, don't you worry your little head about this. We'll make it through this. This really isn't bad at all. Actually we're better off now, than we have ever been before." Mama started smiling, she reached over and patted Lena's arm, 'We'll be Okay."

Lena looked relieved and started wiping the tears away with her shirt sleeve.

"Daddy asked me if I wanted to go spend a few days with him before he goes to Georgia to visit his sister. Is that alright?" She asked looking up at Mama.

"Why of course honey. We'll be here when you get back," Mama said giving her a little hug.

"We'll miss you but have fun and hurry back," I said, giving her a hug.

CHAPTER 49

Oil Well

*U*ncle Oglee and Jannelle walked into the kitchen holding hands, both of them looked like the cat that ate the canary.

"What?" Mama asked.

"We have an announcement to make," Uncle Oglee said.

Jannelle was blushing and Uncle Oglee's face was also red.

"I'll bet I know what it is," I said jumping out of my chair.

"Yep, that's right, we're getting married, Uncle Oglee said, waving his hand with a flourish.

"I knew it," Sally said as she came through the door from outside.

"Me too," I shouted.

"Congratulations," Mama said.

"Uations, uations," Jenny said, kicking her chubby little legs around in the playpen as she jumped up and down. Daddy turned and looked down at Jenny with a look of amazement, "She's talking," Daddy said laughing, reaching down and picking her up.

"Yeah, she's turned into a little chatter box.

"You're my smart little girl," Daddy said, and then he put her back down and went over to Uncle Oglee and Jannelle, shook hands with Uncle and hugged Jannelle.

"The best of luck to the both of you," he said.

Suddenly there was a rumble, the ground started to shake.

We were all terrified. "What's happening?" I whispered.

"I don't know," both Mama and Daddy said in unison.

"Could the world be coming to an end?" I yelled,

Lena and Sally were both speechless.

"It can't be an earthquake, it's not California, cause we don't have earth quakes in Mississippi. Now if this was California, we could be having an earthquake," Uncle Oglee said, looking alarmed, as he reached over and put a protective arm around Jannelle.

The ground continued to growl and rumble.

We all headed for outside, the floor was moving so bad I was walking sideways and I was trembling so bad I could hardly walk.

"It must be God talking," I said out loud, "I wish I'd been better," I cried and I could feel the tears running down my cheeks. "Oh please, give me another chance, I'll be better," I sobbed looking up at the sky. The white fluffy clouds and the tranquil blue sky were all still there. It was as if nothing was happening. "I just don't understand it," I said still looking up.

Suddenly there was a big explosion and a huge stream of black liquid spewed up out of the ground and into the sky, and rained back down on all our heads. It was coming from the well.

"What is it? It's God ending the world," I screamed, "It must be the Devil coming up from hell, to get us."

"Oh my God, oh my God," Daddy said, "It's oil, black gold. We've discovered oil, we're rich, and I mean really rich."

The well diggers were running around like chickens with their heads cut off. "We got to cap it off."

Soon they capped it off, but not before everyone was covered with black oil.

The head guy came up to talk to Daddy. "Wow, man you're rich. You've gotta get an oil well drilling rig company in here to take over the drilling."

"Do you know of a good one?" Daddy asked.

"By golly, I do, "he said.

The word spread like wildfire. Everyone was talking about it.

People were calling nonstop, asking if it were true. They were also asking what we thought their chances were of striking oil.

Everyone was digging a well in their backyard. The well drilling company had never had so much business in their whole life.

Jannelle's Uncle, Mr. Finley was over as soon as he heard. He knew a good, honest oil well digger from Texas.

"I'll call him today," he said, "and see how soon he can get here."

"Thanks Jim, I sure appreciate it. You know I plan to share my good fortune with you," Daddy said.

"Thank you, Claude, but you don't have to do that. I'm happy to help you out as much as I can. Besides I understand we're going to be shirttail relatives," Mr. Finley said with a grin.

I liked Mr. Finley. He was a pleasant man with a good word for everybody. He was known to be a good family man and he was always kind to the underdog. His wife Alice was a little different. She was quiet and a little snooty everyone said. She looked nice. She was tall, just a little on the heavy side and sort of pretty. But she couldn't be all bad, because Jannelle liked her.

Needless to say the Sears catalogue was back in action again. But I had lost some of my original, excitement because of all the ups and downs we'd had. I really didn't trust the future anymore. I remembered all the bad things that can happen. I was afraid to hope too much. I was afraid something would come along and ruin every thing, all our plans could go down the drain in just an instant.

After supper and after everything had settled down, we were all sitting around talking about our good fortune.

Mama got up from the table and said she didn't feel so good.

Daddy got up, looked at Mama. "You don't feel so good?" he asked looking at her closely, then he went to the phone and called the Doctor. Then I heard him call Aunt Ginger. I thought that was really funny, why is he calling Aunt Ginger. Mama didn't look that sick.

"Zemma, could you come here, take Jenny and put her in her crib for me. Since Mama's not feeling very good, I'll see if I can help her," Daddy said.

Suddenly the door flew open and Aunt Ginger and Aunt Hilda were both here. They looked wild eyed, scattered and disorganized, is the only way I could describe how they looked. Their hair was not in it's usual bun. It was hanging, silver, white, long and loose in a pony tail almost to their waist lines. I was surprised, I didn't know their hair was long.

"What the heck, Aunt Ginger What's wrong?" I asked. What's the matter with them, I wondered.

"We're having cake and ice cream at my house, would you and Sally like to come over to my house and have some?" Aunt Ginger asked, out of breath, she sounded like she had been running.

"Why we sure would, but this is so sudden," I said, and grabbed my coat, before she could change her mind. I looked around for anything else I might need before I could go. I was surprised, but who would question ice cream and cake, I thought.

I looked at Daddy and he nodded yes.

"Don't look a gift horse in the mouth," Sally shouted, "Wait for me," she added.

And out the door we ran, right behind Aunt Ginger

We followed Aunt Ginger to her house. She had a cute house, with all kinds of pretty knick knacks everywhere.. When we went into the kitchen she had a big chocolate cake sitting right in the middle of the light oak dining room table.

Uncle Sam was sitting at the table, with a big smile on his face as he clutched a knife in one hand and a fork in the other hand. He was really funny. We all laughed.

"I'm just waiting for cake and ice cream," he said.

We all sat down and had cake and ice cream. Then she showed us around her house. Everything was very cute. She had pretty curtains and pretty bedspreads in all her four bedrooms. It's funny, but this was the first time we had ever been all the way through Aunt Ginger's house.

"Would you guys like to spend the night, since it's so late? "Aunt Ginger asked.

Sally and I looked at each other. Then Sally said, "Sure I'd like to spend the night."

"Me too," I said. I was a little nervous about spending the night away from home. I had never been away from home before, except for the night I had my tonsils out.

The bedroom was really cute. The curtains and bedspread were made out of the same matching material. It had pink roses on a white background. She had pretty paintings of flowers on the walls.

Aunt Ginger saw me looking at the paintings.

She smiled shyly, and said, "I painted those when I was a young girl, I think I was eighteen or so."

"They are beautiful, Aunt Ginger," I said, shocked, looking at her with new interest. "I must get my interest in painting from you." I never, ever would have thought that she painted.

"Well, thank you honey, I just bet you did," she said smiling at me.

"Why did you quit," I asked.

"Well, I fell in love and got married and had my kids," she said with a grin.

I just looked at her and shook my head.

"But I still dabble a little bit," she said shyly.

"Really, I would love to see," I said. Imagine that, I thought, Aunt Ginger an artist.

"I'll show you sometime," she said, "When we have more time." I continued to look around. I went back and looked at her paintings. They were really good.

When I crawled into bed, I noticed that the bedroom set, looked like what they called an antique. It was some kind of dark wood.

I was so tired, I went sound asleep and didn't wake up till it was morning and the sunshine was streaming in through the bedroom window.

"Up and at them, sleepy heads, breakfast is ready," Aunt Ginger said, when she came into the bedroom. Uncle Sam had already had breakfast and was now outside.

After we had breakfast, we were ready to go home.

"They have a surprise for you when you get home," Aunt Ginger said, with a big smile on her face.

"What?" I asked. "More surprises. I don't know if I can handle more surprises,"

"Can't tell you," she said, unrelenting.

"Please tell us," Sally said.

"Nope," she said, sticking to her guns.

We could hardly wait to get home to see what the surprise was.

We opened the door when we got home, we couldn't see anyone.

"Where is everyone?" I yelled, I was beginning to worry.

"We're in here, in the bedroom," Daddy said.

We rushed into the bedroom, and everyone was in there, including Daddy, Uncle Oglee, and Aunt Hilda.

"What's Mama doing in bed, is she sick?" Sally asked.

"No guess what, you have a new baby brother," Mama said with a big smile as she pulled back the covers, and there he was, a little red faced baby.

Sally and I both screamed as we rushed over to the bed and looked at this new creature.

"He looks like Jenny when she was a baby. He's so little, look at those tiny fingers," I said, reaching over and examining his little hands.

"Oh my goodness, look how small he is. He makes Jenny look like a big kid," Sally said smoothing her hands over his blanket.

"What's his name?" I asked, looking him over. I just couldn't believe my eyes. "I didn't even see the stork," I said and then I remembered there wasn't any stork that brought babies. Oh my, oh my I thought.

"He doesn't have one yet, we were waiting for you two," Daddy said. "We will do this the Democratic way. We will all put our favorite name in the hat and let Uncle Oglee pull a name out of the hat, and that will be his name," Daddy said.

"Really, we get a chance to name him,?" Sally asked.

"You certainly will," Mama said.

" Now go get the scissors, some paper and a couple of pencils," Mama said.

"I'll help you, "Aunt Ginger said, as she went with us, to the kitchen, and found scissors, paper and two pencils in a cupboard drawer. We rushed back into the bedroom.

"Oh my goodness I have to think of my favorite man's name," I said.

"I know what I like," Sally said. "I like Wallace,"

"Oh dear, oh dear, I like so many, I like Bob, I like James, I know I really like Sidney. I had just read a book and the boy's name was Sidney. "Be really careful, girls, what ever we pick, he will be stuck with the rest of his life.

Aunt Ginger cut little slips of paper up, and gave each one of us one piece.

Daddy put his Sunday hat on the bed and waited for us to put the name we had written into the hat.

I thought and thought, then I decided Sidney it was.

We wrote down the names we liked, and after Mama and Daddy put their slips of paper in the hat, then we put our names in.

Daddy shook the hat up really good, then held the hat out for Uncle Oglee to draw a name.

Uncle Oglee closed his eyes reached in and pulled out a slip of paper.

"What is it, what is it,?" we all yelled.

Uncle Oglee spelled it out, L-E-N-O-R-D, Lenord.

"Oh goodie, that's the name I picked," Mama said.

I was disappointed, because I liked Sidney.

"What a surprise that was," Sally said, as we went to our bedroom.

" I think Aunt Hilda is here to help take care of Mama," I told Sally. "That's nice of her.

"You know I miss Lena, but she will be back tomorrow, I think," I said.

I thought of Junior. I could see him now, he would be so happy the new baby was a boy. I could hear him now, taking a stance with his thumbs hooked into his pockets, and he would say something like, "That's great, it's a boy, now it's more even two boys against three girls." I could just see his grin, I thought as a deep sadness made my throat feel tight and I felt the tears well up in my eyes.

"Boy, was I surprised to get a new baby. Too bad Junior isn't here to meet him. He would be so happy it was a boy," Sally said as she played with the new baby's fingers.

"Yeah," I said, "I wonder what name Junior would have given him."

The next morning after breakfast, Jannelle knocked on the door and came into the kitchen, waving a letter she had clutched in her hand. "Guess what,?" Jannelle said, "I just heard back from a job application. I sent one of my stories about gold hunting to a number of newspapers."

"The number one newspaper from Dallas, Texas want me to come in for an interview as a journalist for the paper." Jannelle was so excited she could hardly talk.

Uncle Oglee was clapping for her. He was her number one fan. "She's so smart," he said.

"Is that okay with you?" she asked, as she turned to look at Uncle Oglee. "After we're married, will you be willing to move to Texas and start our new life in Texas."

"Of course honey. I'll just get a job doing something, anywhere we go," he said. "Besides, Texas is my home state. I love Texas. That would be good, I would love to see my Mama. I might even stop in to see my ornery old man.

Everyone was excited and happy. We thought about it. If we moved to Texas we would try and adopt Lena. We knew Jim would be okay with it. If we stayed here, we would still try to adopt Lena, but the chances of them letting us do that were pretty slim. But it really didn't matter that much, because she would always live with us anyway.

The only bad thing about it was, if we left, we didn't want to leave Junior behind. If we decided to stay here and live on the farm. We would have enough money to be o.k. even if we did lose our crops, not that we would, but just in case. We all really loved it here, and all our relatives were here except Grandma Sampson.

"Maybe we could get your Mom to come live with us," Daddy said, and Mama looked up from the list she was making out.

"Oh that would be wonderful," Mama she said, her eyes lighting up.

THE END

About the Author

Arlene Fisher Hann has worked as an artist, art teacher, and psychiatric technician.
She was born in Texas and spent her childhood in Mississippi.
Her historical saga, Barefoot, is inspired by her life story.

Hann lives in the Wine Country of Sonoma Valley, California.
She is a proud wife, mother, grandmother and great-grandmother.

www.ingramcontent.com/pod-product-compliance
Lightning Source LLC
Chambersburg PA
CBHW051245260626
47162CB00002B/611